THE ATTACK OF THE GRIZZLIES, 1967

SPECIAL THANKS TO JOHN HECHTEL

WHILE INSPIRED BY REAL EVENTS AND HISTORICAL CHARACTERS, THIS IS A WORK OF FICTION AND DOES NOT CLAIM TO BE HISTORICALLY ACCURATE OR TO PORTRAY FACTUAL EVENTS OR RELATIONSHIPS. PLEASE KEEP IN MIND THAT REFERENCES TO ACTUAL PERSONS, LIVING OR DEAD, BUSINESS ESTABLISHMENTS, EVENTS, OR LOCALES MAY NOT BE FACTUALLY ACCURATE, BUT RATHER FICTIONALIZED BY THE AUTHOR.

LIBRARY OF CONGRESS CONTROL NUMBER: 2021946907
ISBN 978-1-338-76691-2 (PAPERBACK)
ISBN 978-1-338-76693-6 (HARDCOVER)

10 9 8 7 6 5 4 3 2 1 22 23 24 25 26

PRINTED IN THE U.S.A. 40

FIRST EDITION, APRIL 2022

EDITED BY KATIE WOEHR
LETTERING BY OLGA ANDREYEVA
INKS BY BERAT PEKMEZCI
COLOR BY LEO TRINIDAD
BOOK DESIGN BY KATIE FITCH
CREATIVE DIRECTOR: YAFFA JASKOLL

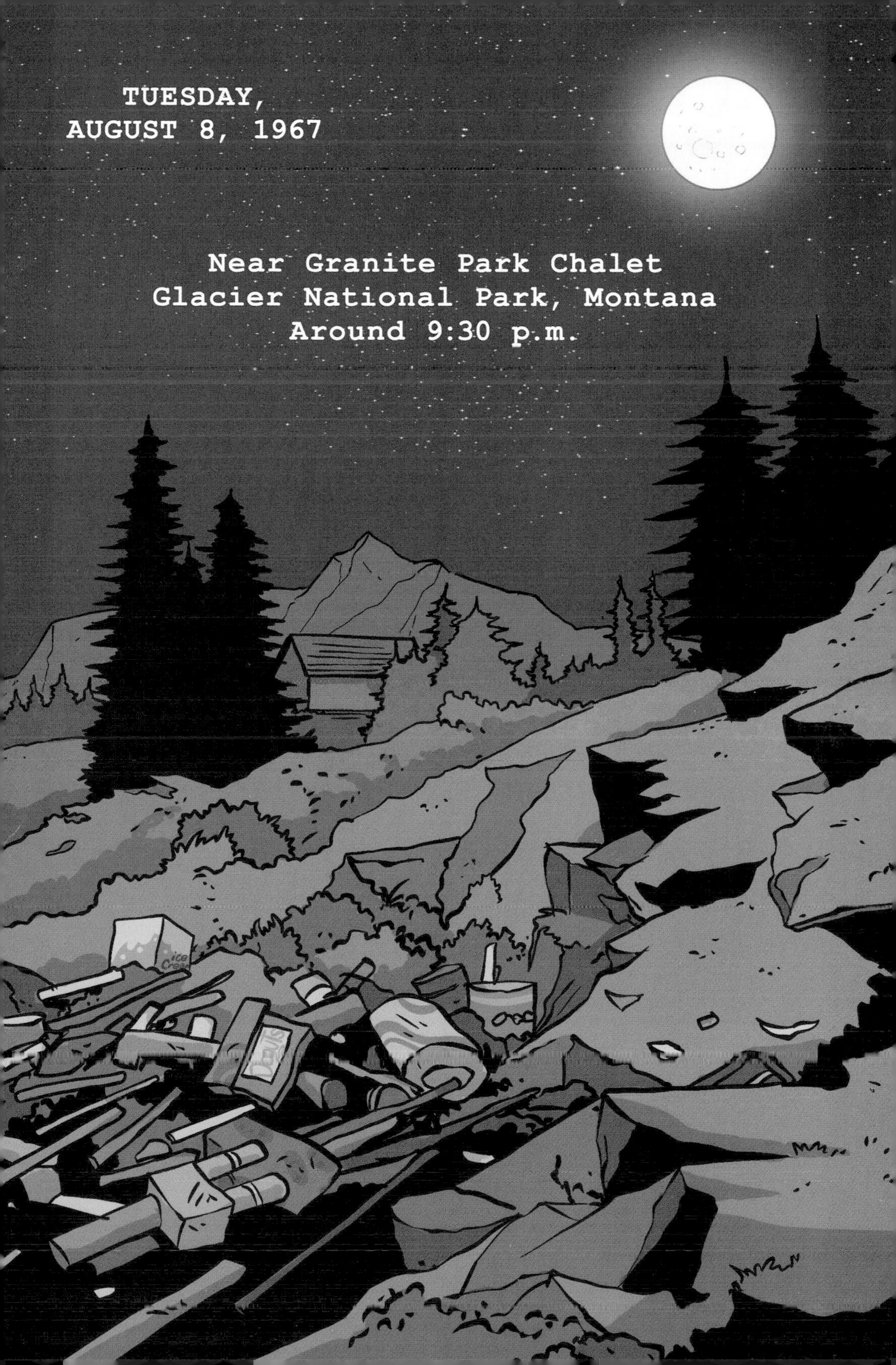
TUESDAY,
AUGUST 8, 1967
Near Granite Park Chalet
Glacier National Park, Montana
Around 9:30 p.m.

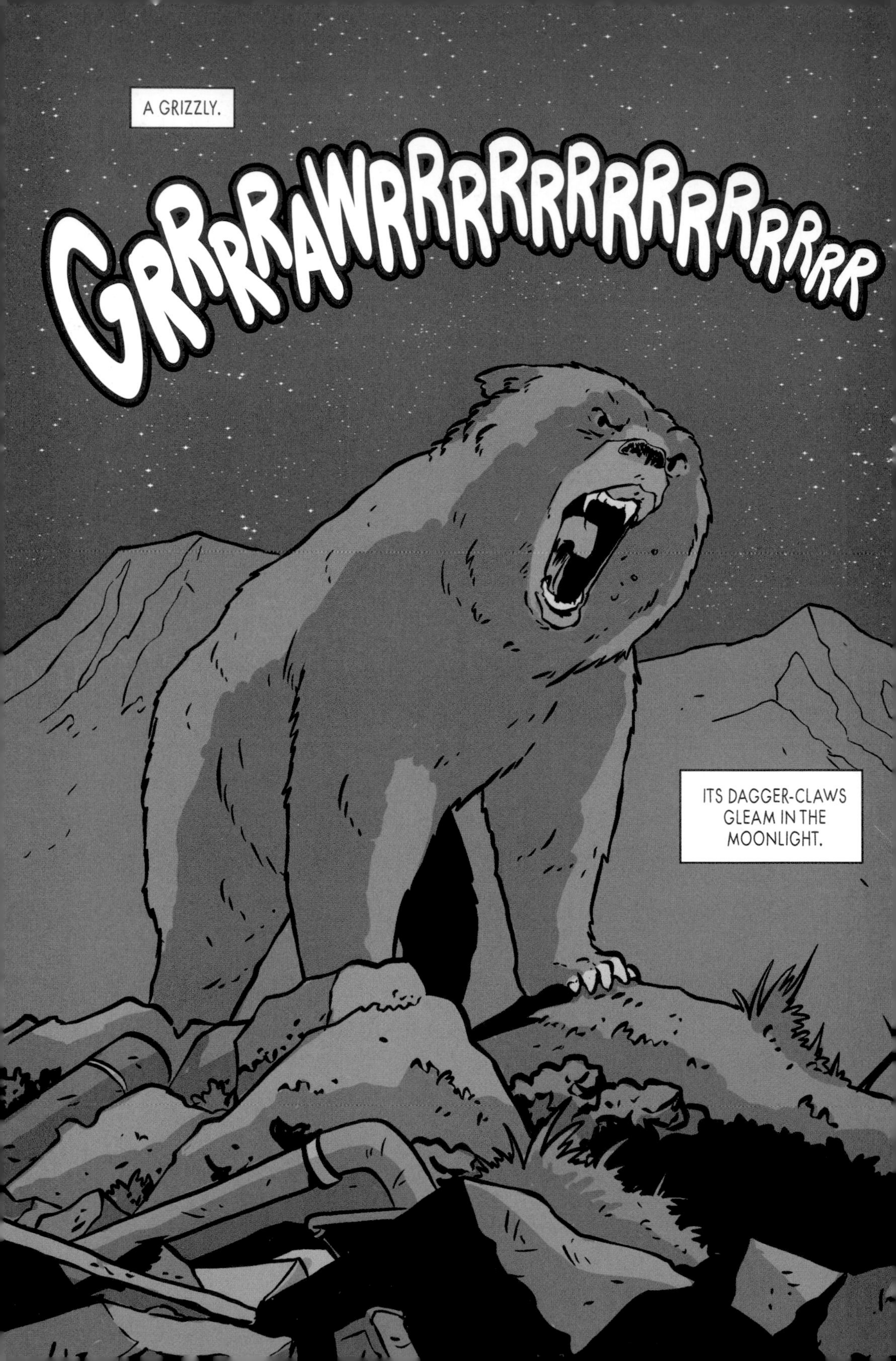
A GRIZZLY.
GRRRRAWRRRRRRRRRRRRRRR
ITS DAGGER-CLAWS GLEAM IN THE MOONLIGHT.

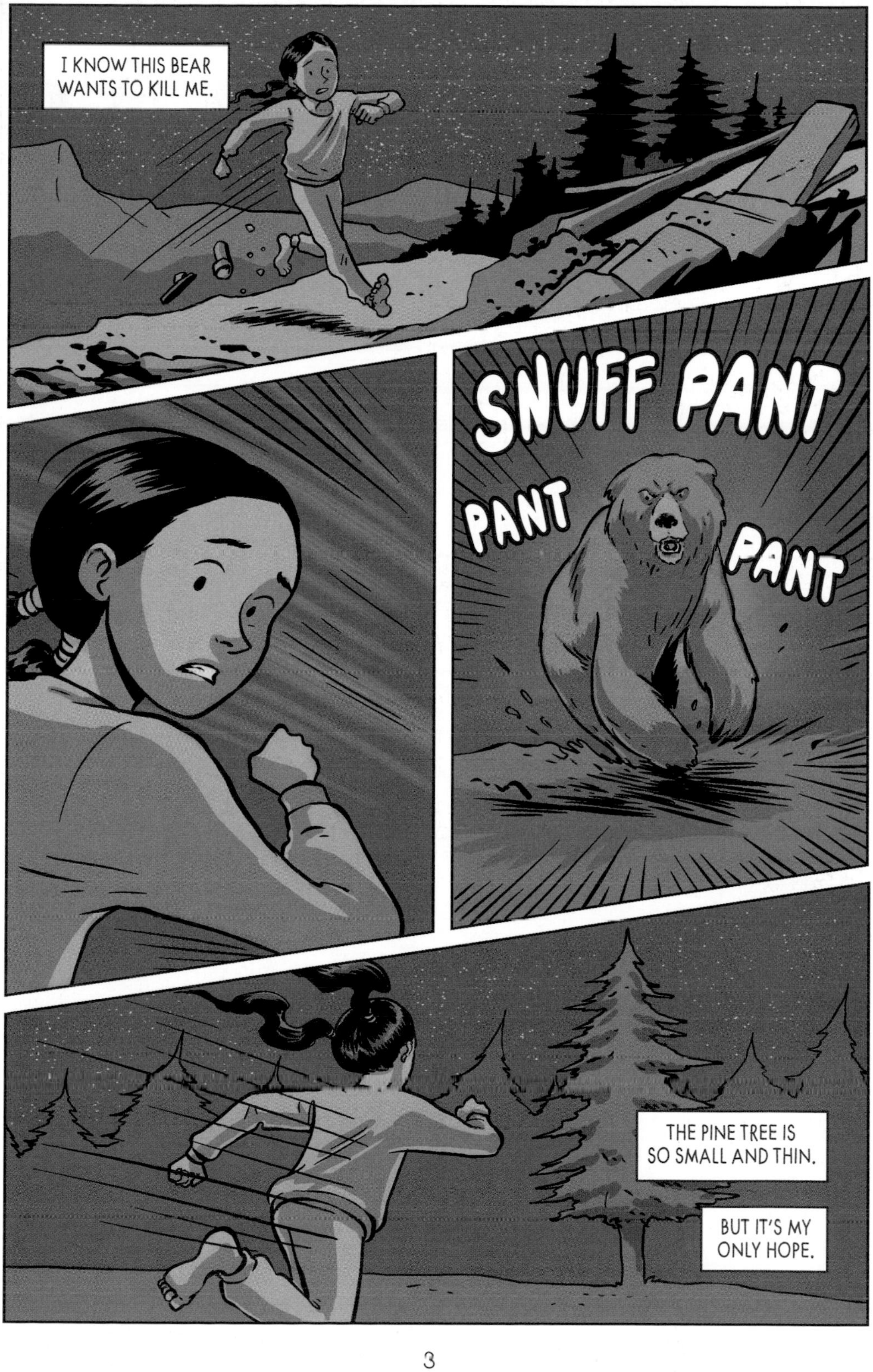
I KNOW THIS BEAR WANTS TO KILL ME.
SNUFF PANT
PANT
PANT
THE PINE TREE IS SO SMALL AND THIN.
BUT IT'S MY ONLY HOPE.

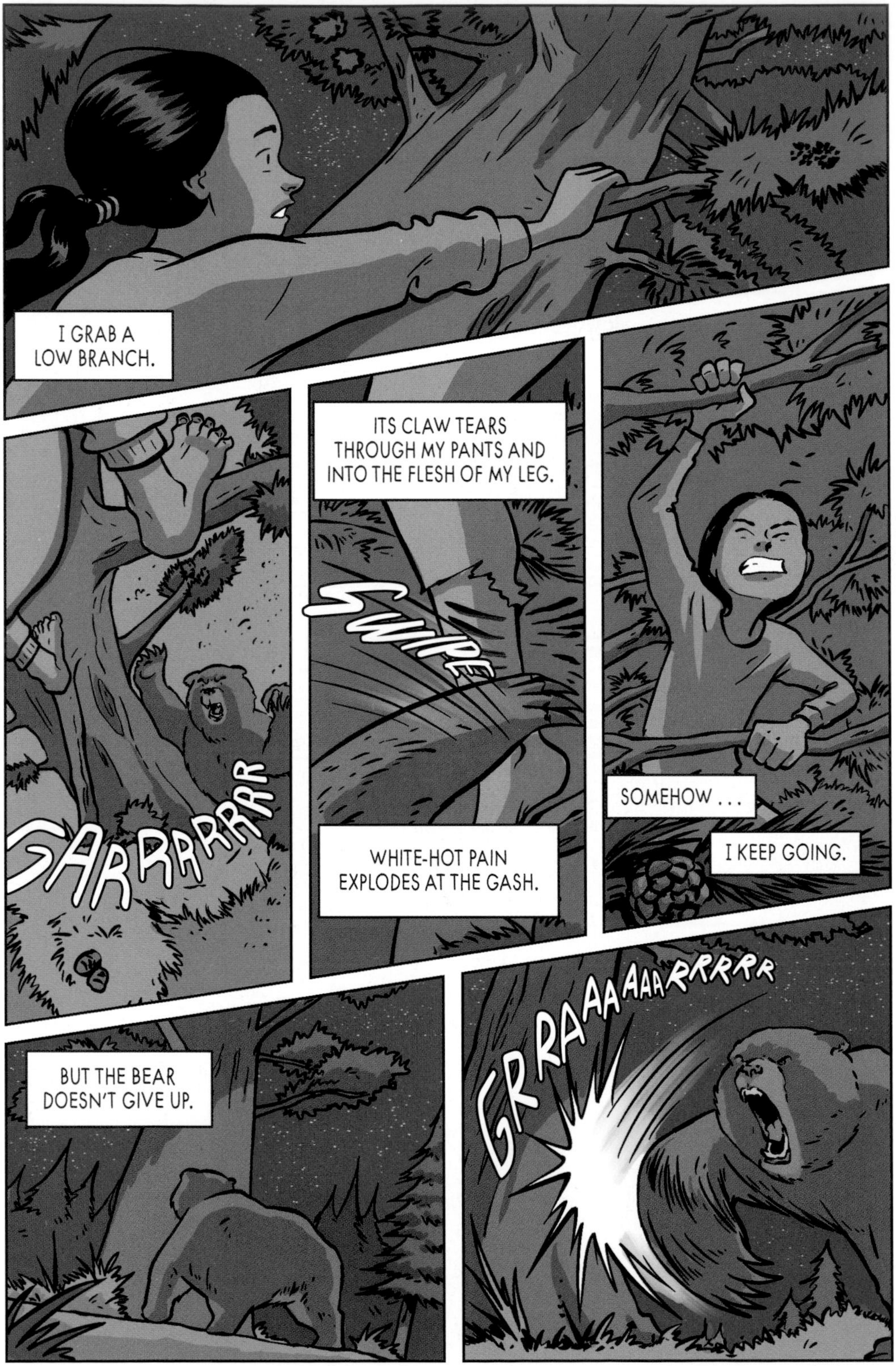
I GRAB A LOW BRANCH.
GARRRRRRR
ITS CLAW TEARS THROUGH MY PANTS AND INTO THE FLESH OF MY LEG.
SWIPE
WHITE-HOT PAIN EXPLODES AT THE GASH.
SOMEHOW . . .
I KEEP GOING.
BUT THE BEAR DOESN'T GIVE UP.
GRRAAAAAARRRRR

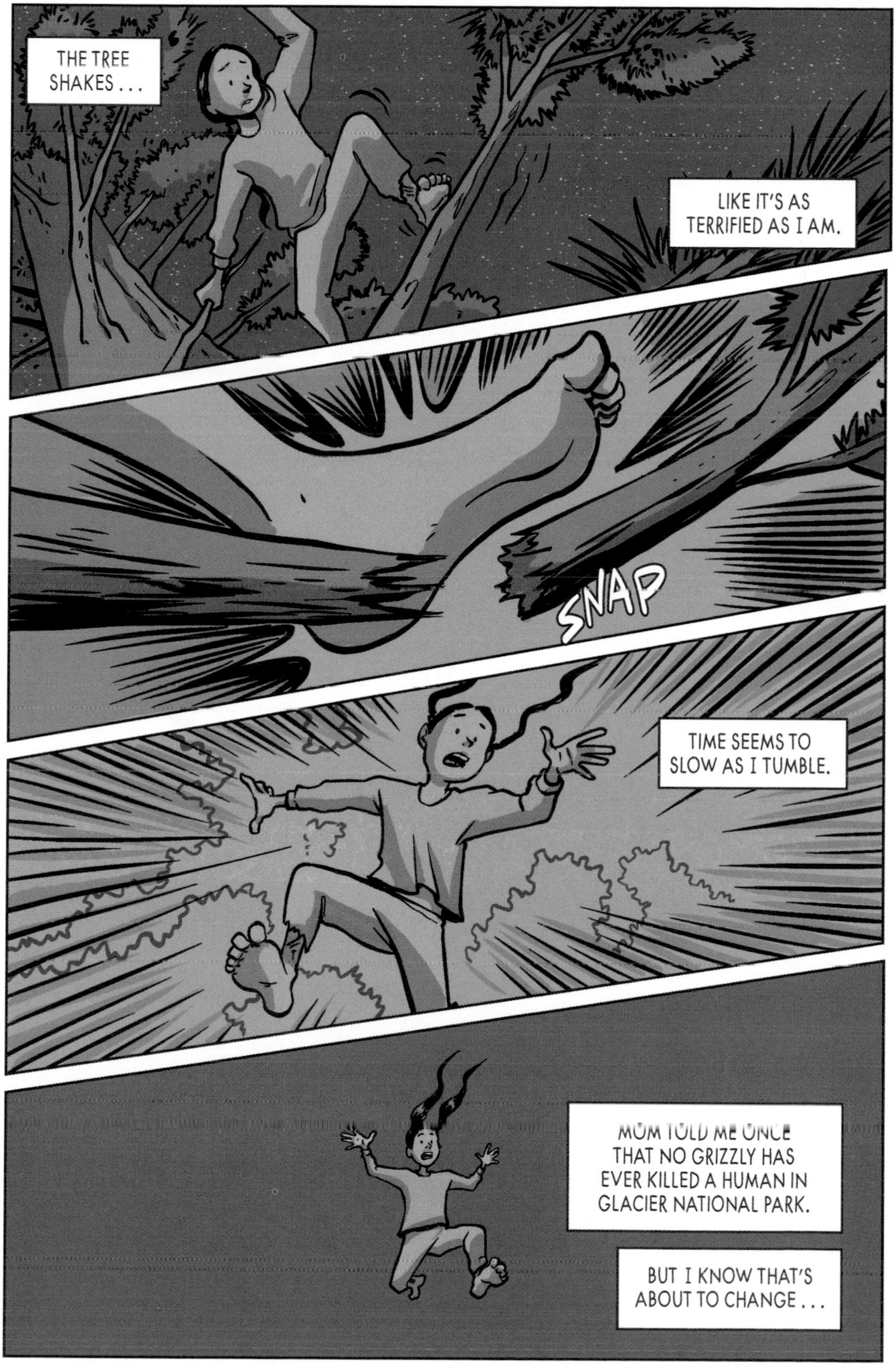
THE TREE SHAKES . . .
LIKE IT'S AS TERRIFIED AS I AM.
SNAP
TIME SEEMS TO SLOW AS I TUMBLE.
MOM TOLD ME ONCE THAT NO GRIZZLY HAS EVER KILLED A HUMAN IN GLACIER NATIONAL PARK.
BUT I KNOW THAT'S ABOUT TO CHANGE . . .

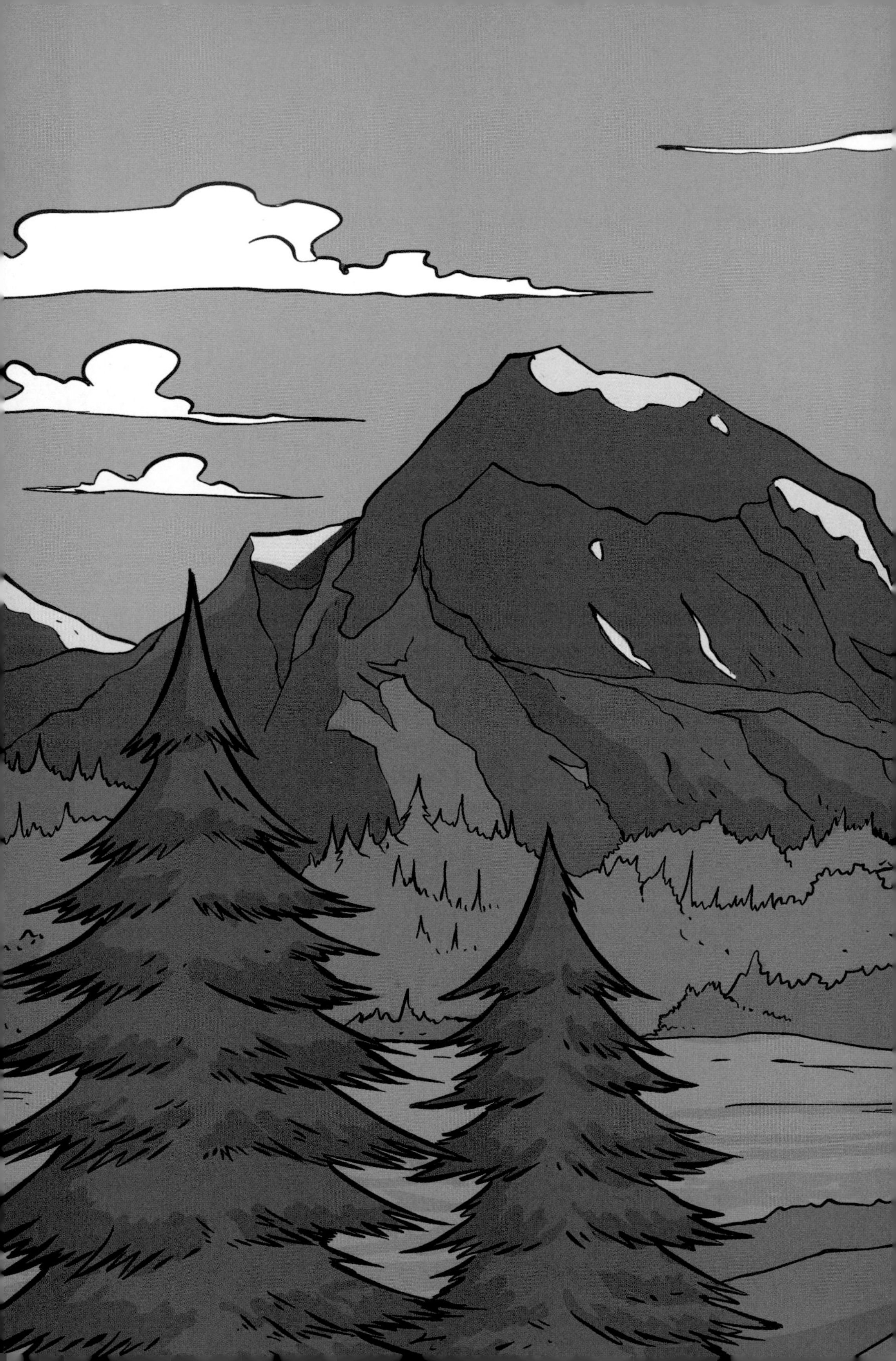

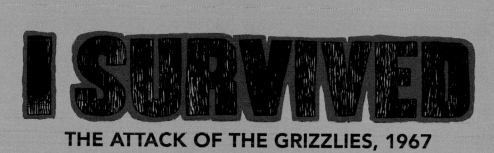

I SURVIVED

THE ATTACK OF THE GRIZZLIES, 1967

BASED ON THE NOVEL IN THE *NEW YORK TIMES*
BESTSELLING SERIES BY LAUREN TARSHIS

ADAPTED BY GEORGIA BALL
WITH ART BY BERAT PEKMEZCI
COLORS BY LEO TRINIDAD

graphix
AN IMPRINT OF
SCHOLASTIC

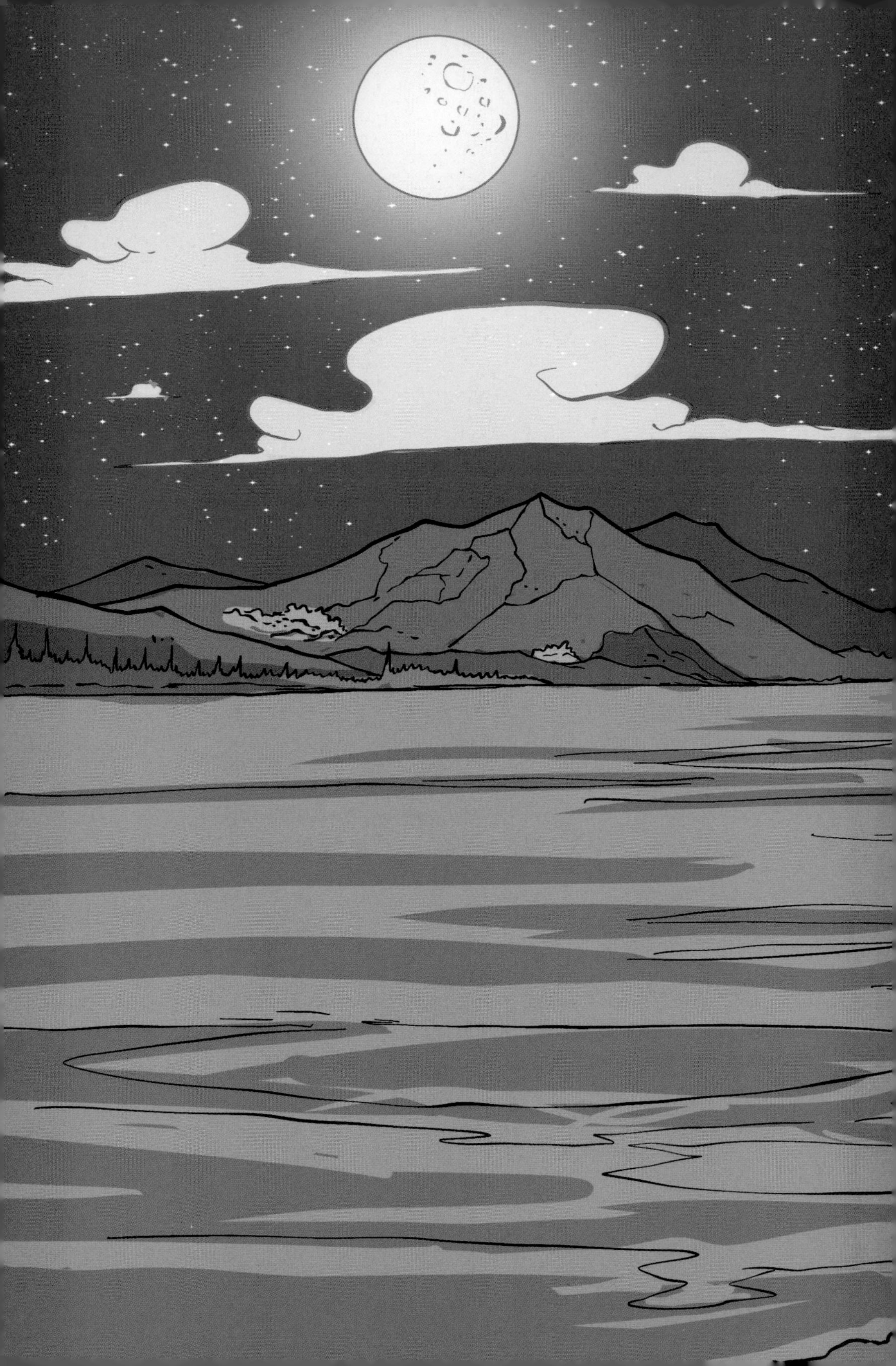

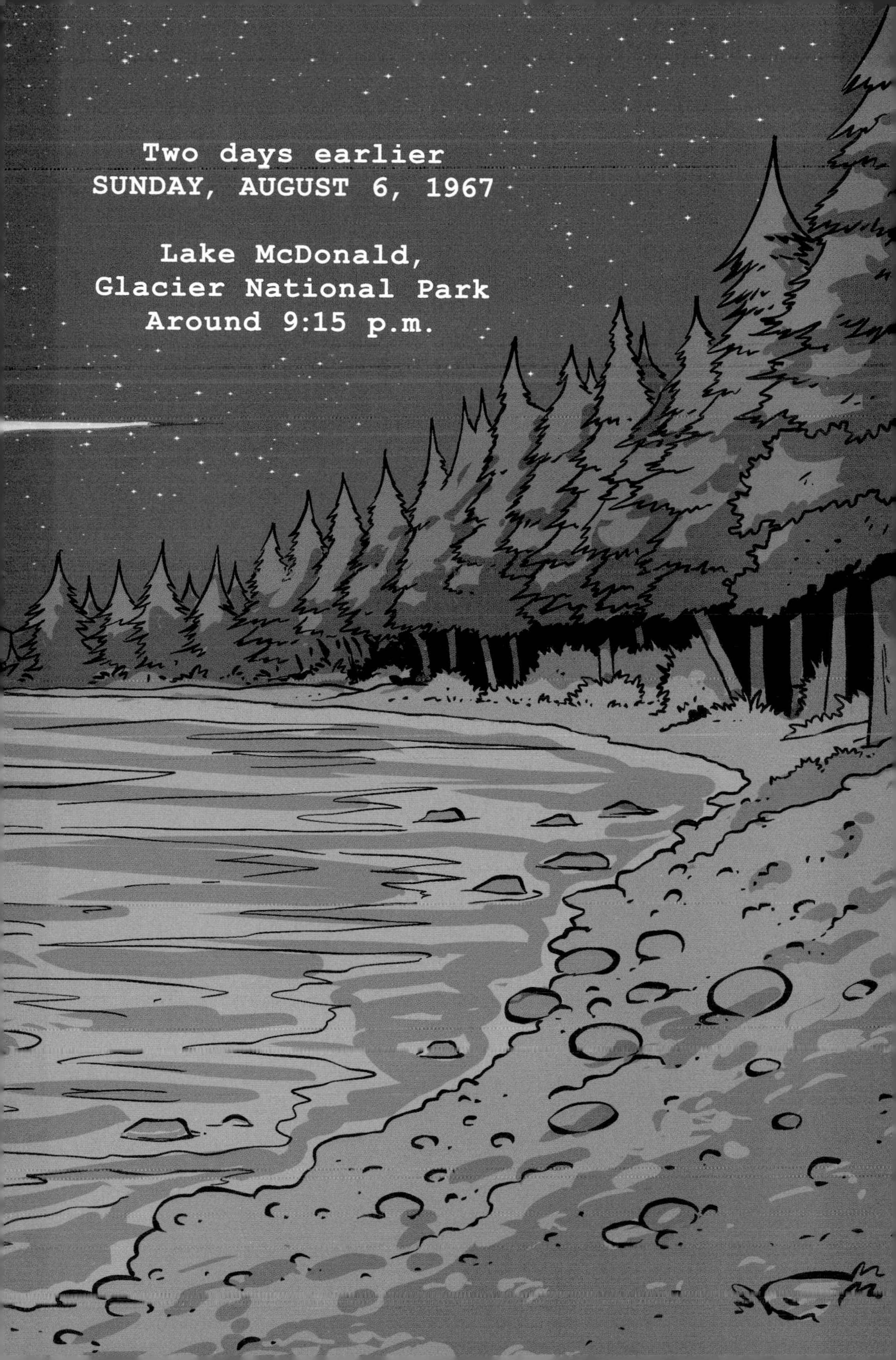
Two days earlier
SUNDAY, AUGUST 6, 1967
Lake McDonald,
Glacier National Park
Around 9:15 p.m.

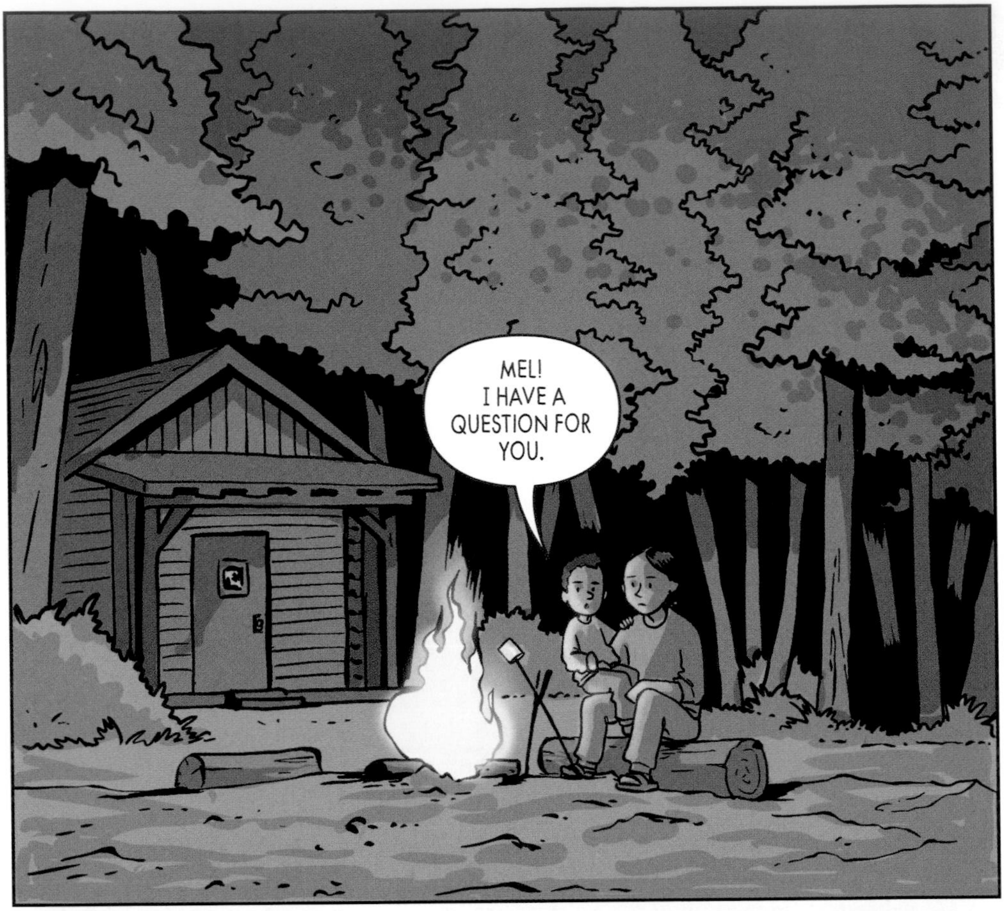
MEL! I HAVE A QUESTION FOR YOU.

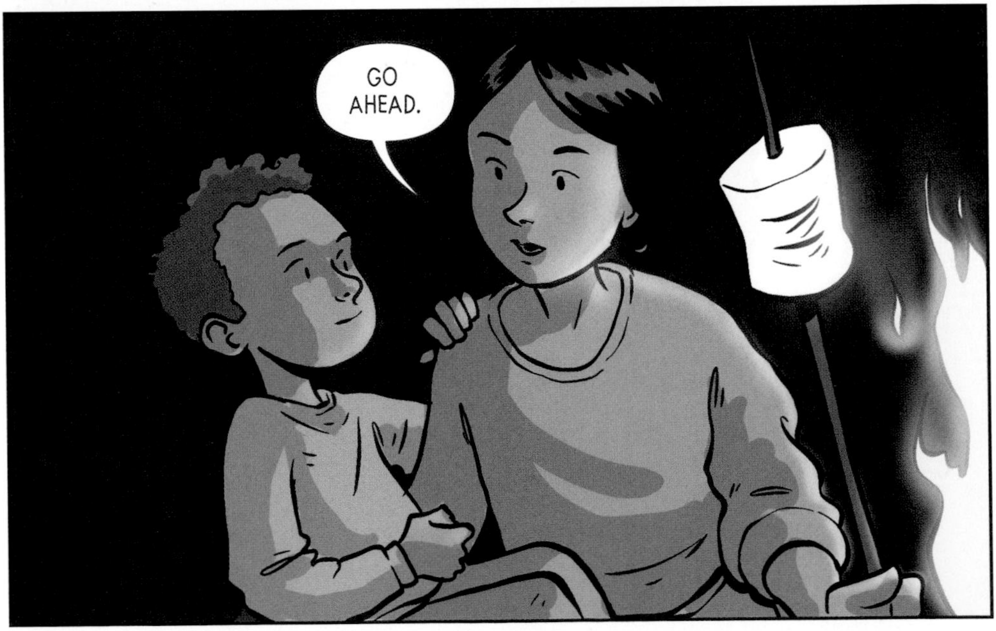
GO AHEAD.

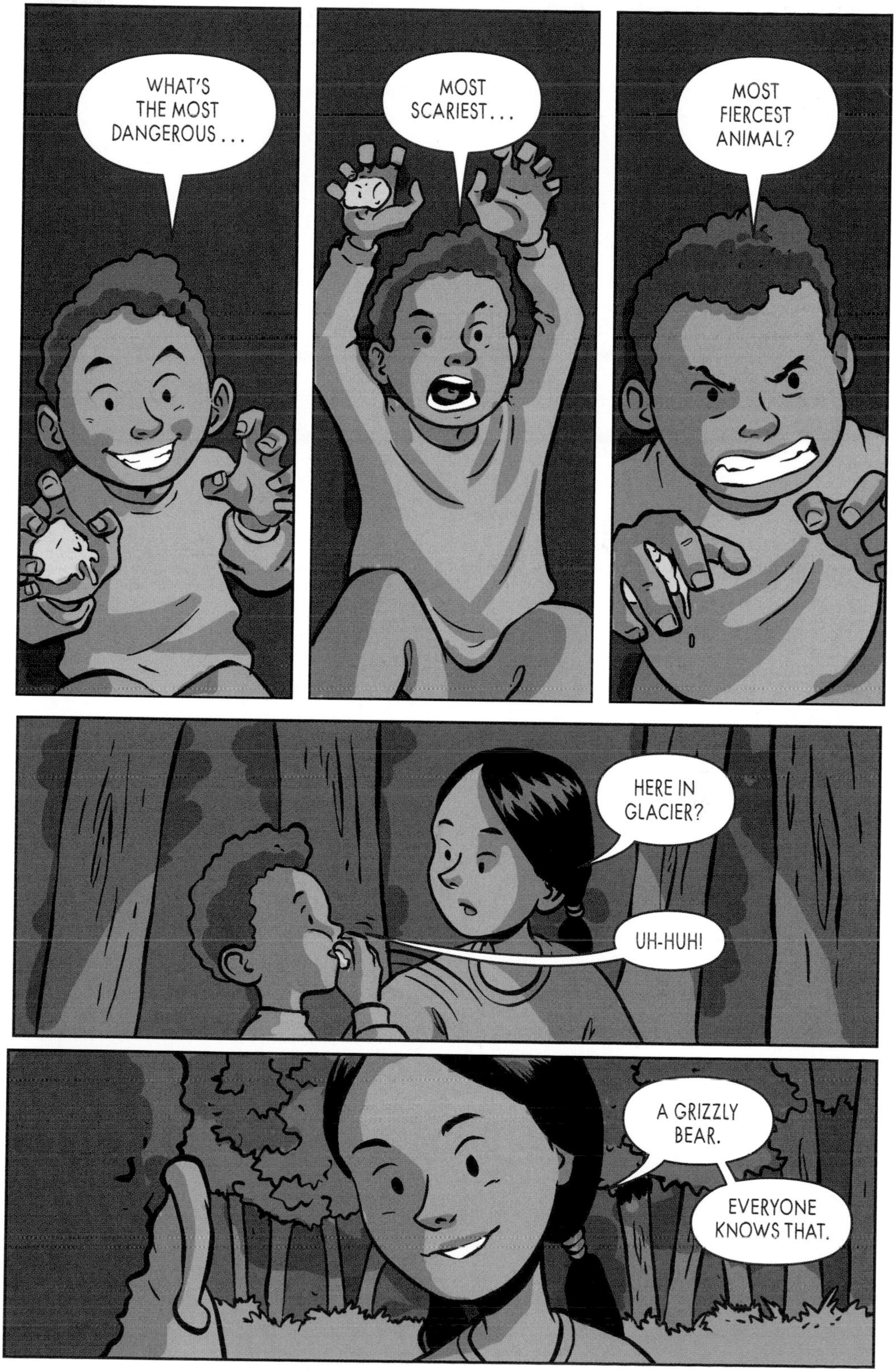
WHAT'S THE MOST DANGEROUS...
MOST SCARIEST...
MOST FIERCEST ANIMAL?
HERE IN GLACIER?
UH-HUH!
A GRIZZLY BEAR.
EVERYONE KNOWS THAT.

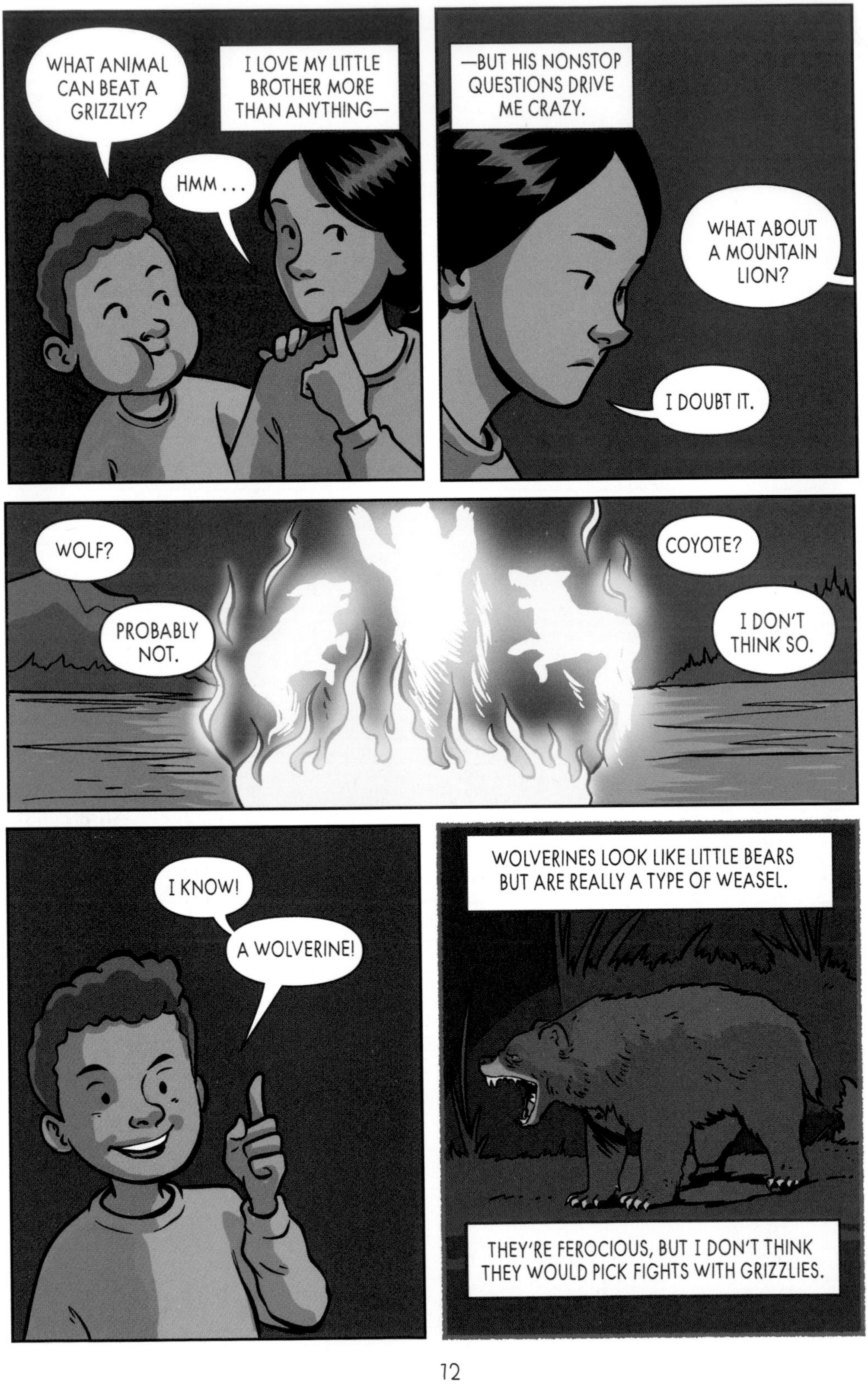
WHAT ANIMAL CAN BEAT A GRIZZLY?
I LOVE MY LITTLE BROTHER MORE THAN ANYTHING—
HMM . . .
—BUT HIS NONSTOP QUESTIONS DRIVE ME CRAZY.
WHAT ABOUT A MOUNTAIN LION?
I DOUBT IT.
WOLF?
PROBABLY NOT.
COYOTE?
I DON'T THINK SO.
I KNOW!
A WOLVERINE!
WOLVERINES LOOK LIKE LITTLE BEARS BUT ARE REALLY A TYPE OF WEASEL.
THEY'RE FEROCIOUS, BUT I DON'T THINK THEY WOULD PICK FIGHTS WITH GRIZZLIES.

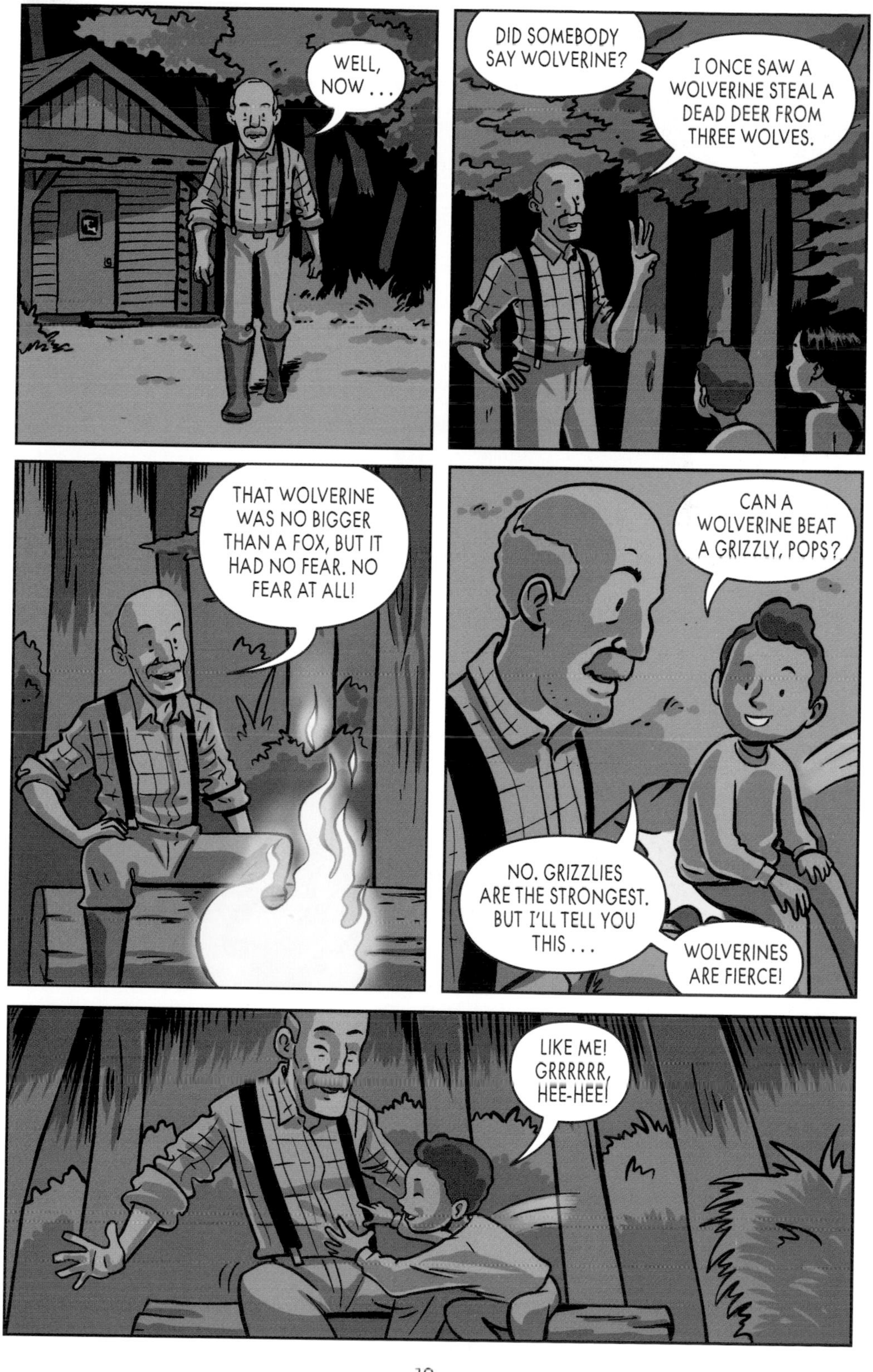
WELL, NOW . . .
DID SOMEBODY SAY WOLVERINE?
I ONCE SAW A WOLVERINE STEAL A DEAD DEER FROM THREE WOLVES.
THAT WOLVERINE WAS NO BIGGER THAN A FOX, BUT IT HAD NO FEAR. NO FEAR AT ALL!
CAN A WOLVERINE BEAT A GRIZZLY, POPS?
NO. GRIZZLIES ARE THE STRONGEST. BUT I'LL TELL YOU THIS . . .
WOLVERINES ARE FIERCE!
LIKE ME! GRRRRRR, HEE-HEE!

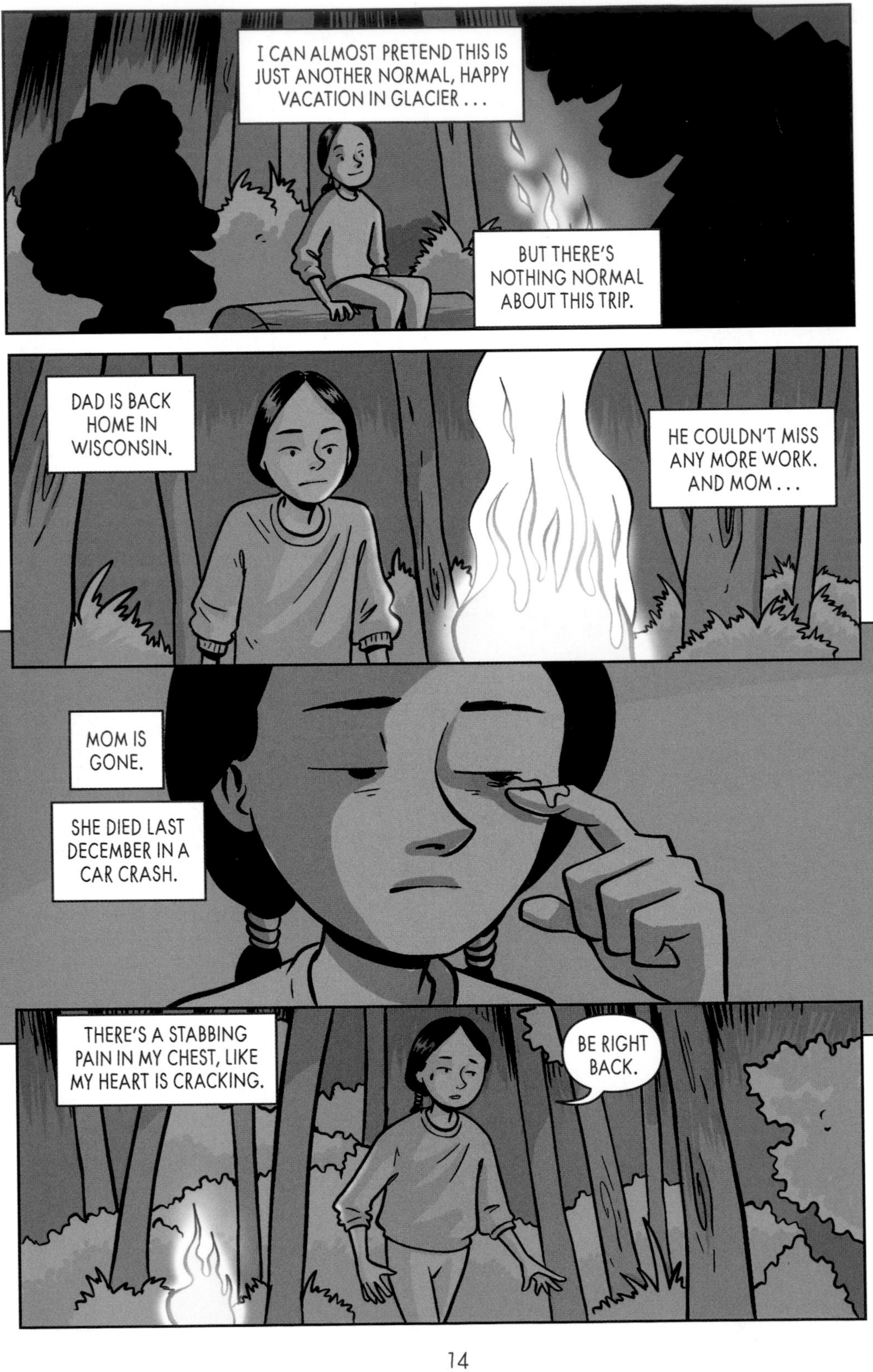
I CAN ALMOST PRETEND THIS IS JUST ANOTHER NORMAL, HAPPY VACATION IN GLACIER . . .
BUT THERE'S NOTHING NORMAL ABOUT THIS TRIP.
DAD IS BACK HOME IN WISCONSIN.
HE COULDN'T MISS ANY MORE WORK. AND MOM . . .
MOM IS GONE.
SHE DIED LAST DECEMBER IN A CAR CRASH.
THERE'S A STABBING PAIN IN MY CHEST, LIKE MY HEART IS CRACKING.
BE RIGHT BACK.

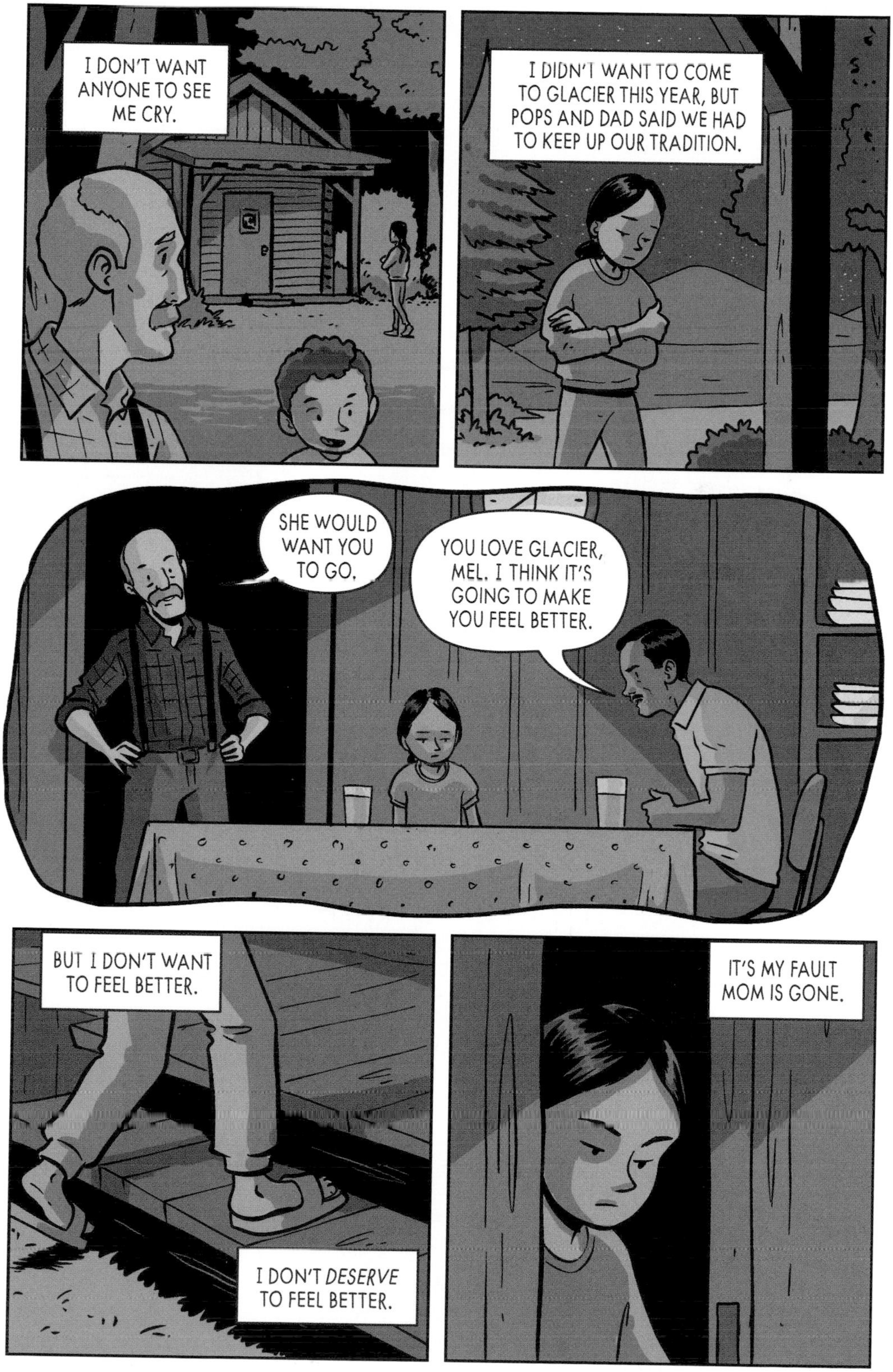
I DON'T WANT ANYONE TO SEE ME CRY.
I DIDN'T WANT TO COME TO GLACIER THIS YEAR, BUT POPS AND DAD SAID WE HAD TO KEEP UP OUR TRADITION.
SHE WOULD WANT YOU TO GO.
YOU LOVE GLACIER, MEL. I THINK IT'S GOING TO MAKE YOU FEEL BETTER.
BUT I DON'T WANT TO FEEL BETTER.
I DON'T *DESERVE* TO FEEL BETTER.
IT'S MY FAULT MOM IS GONE.

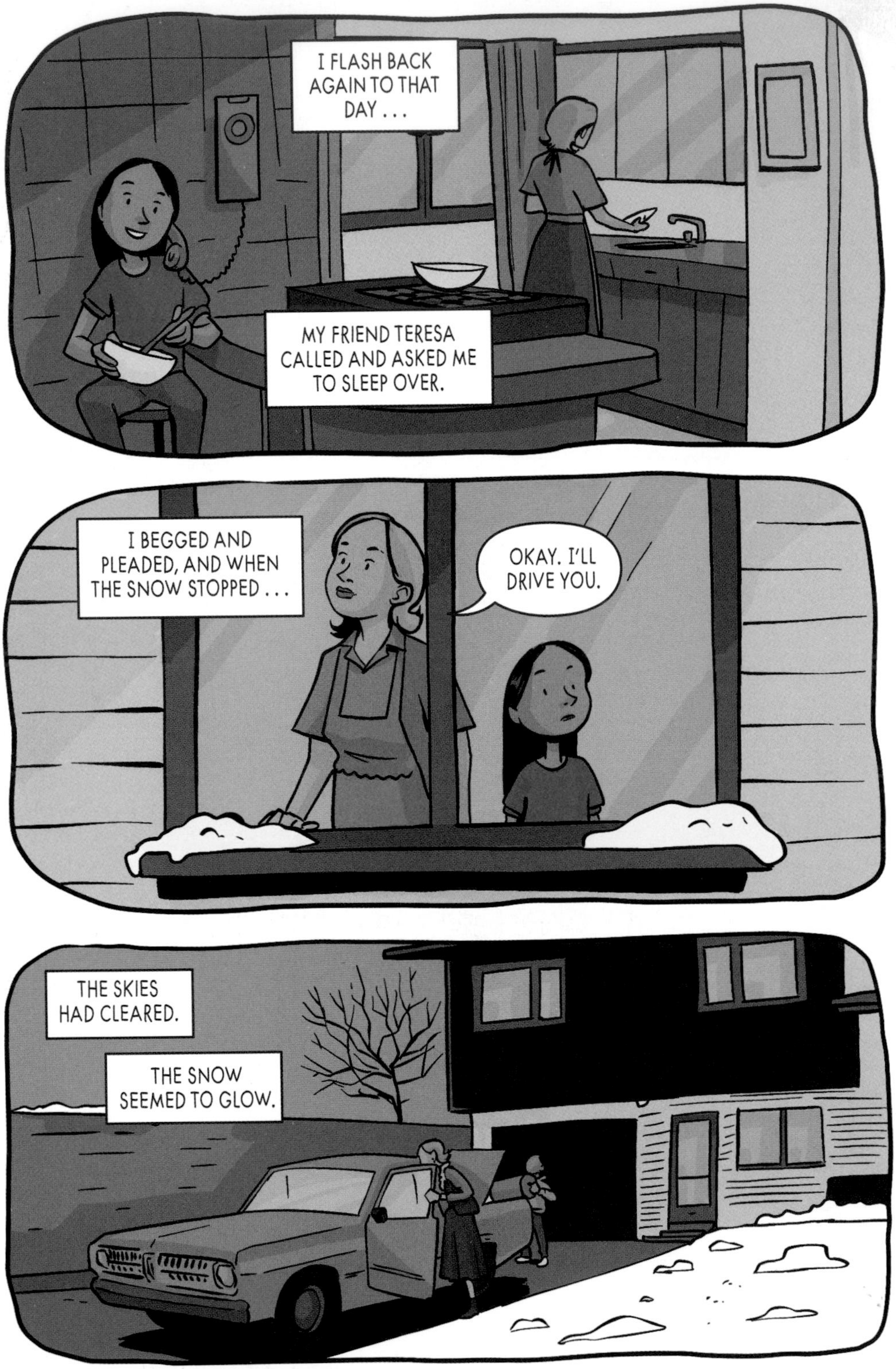
I FLASH BACK AGAIN TO THAT DAY . . .
MY FRIEND TERESA CALLED AND ASKED ME TO SLEEP OVER.
I BEGGED AND PLEADED, AND WHEN THE SNOW STOPPED . . .
OKAY. I'LL DRIVE YOU.
THE SKIES HAD CLEARED.
THE SNOW SEEMED TO GLOW.

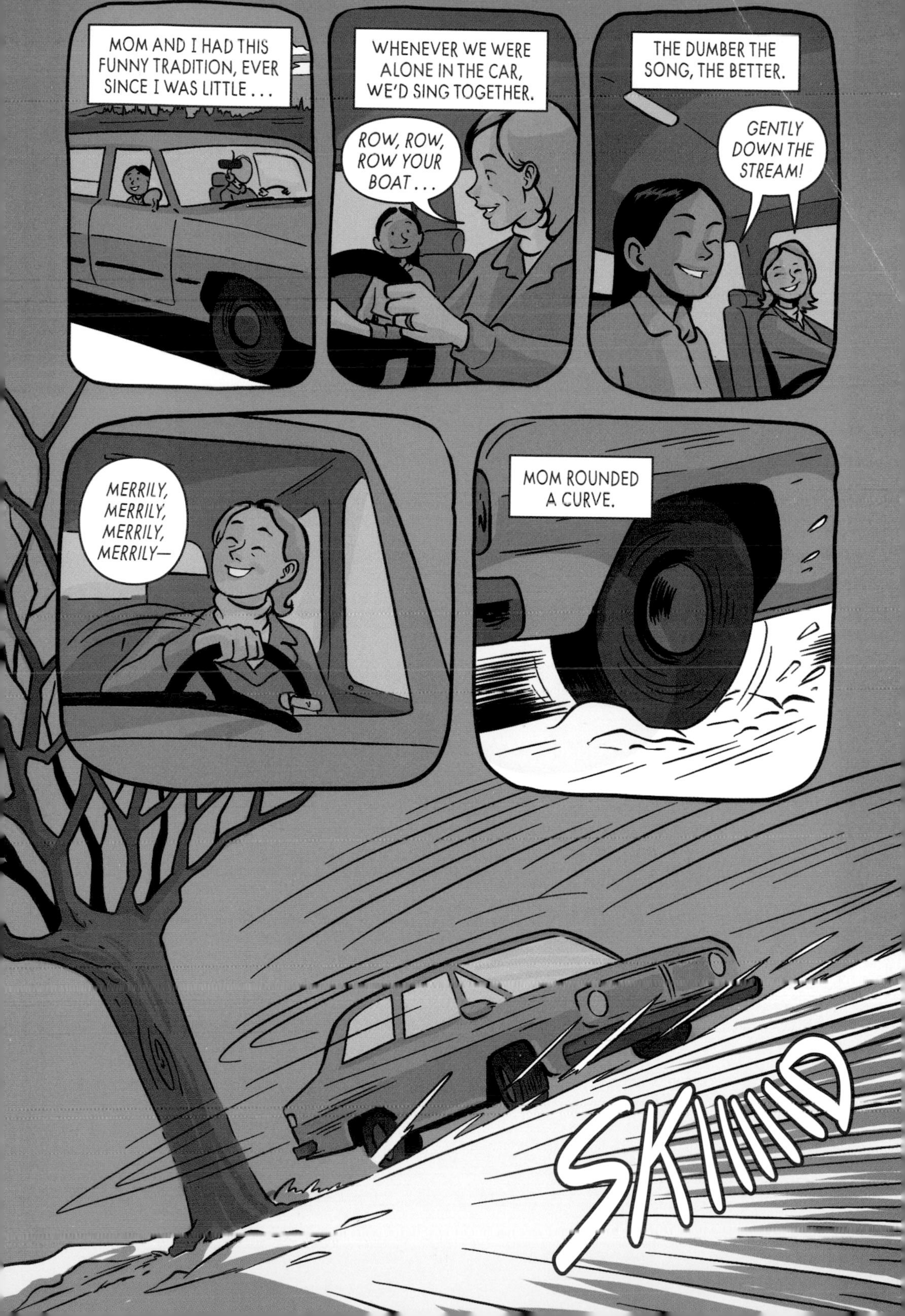
MOM AND I HAD THIS FUNNY TRADITION, EVER SINCE I WAS LITTLE . . .
WHENEVER WE WERE ALONE IN THE CAR, WE'D SING TOGETHER.
ROW, ROW, ROW YOUR BOAT . . .
THE DUMBER THE SONG, THE BETTER.
GENTLY DOWN THE STREAM!
MERRILY, MERRILY, MERRILY, MERRILY—
MOM ROUNDED A CURVE.
SKIIID

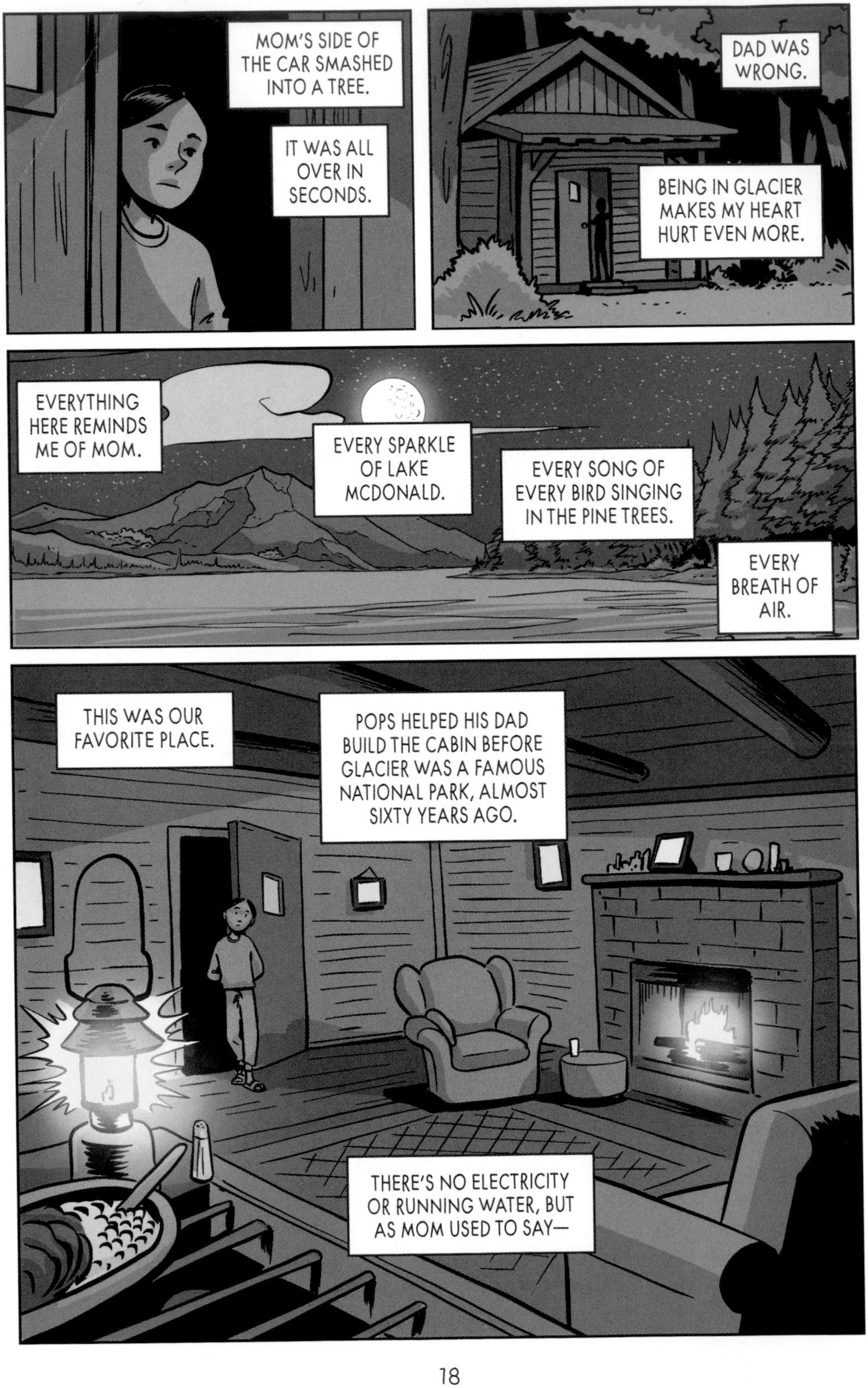

MOM'S SIDE OF THE CAR SMASHED INTO A TREE.
IT WAS ALL OVER IN SECONDS.
DAD WAS WRONG.
BEING IN GLACIER MAKES MY HEART HURT EVEN MORE.
EVERYTHING HERE REMINDS ME OF MOM.
EVERY SPARKLE OF LAKE MCDONALD.
EVERY SONG OF EVERY BIRD SINGING IN THE PINE TREES.
EVERY BREATH OF AIR.
THIS WAS OUR FAVORITE PLACE.
POPS HELPED HIS DAD BUILD THE CABIN BEFORE GLACIER WAS A FAMOUS NATIONAL PARK, ALMOST SIXTY YEARS AGO.
THERE'S NO ELECTRICITY OR RUNNING WATER, BUT AS MOM USED TO SAY—

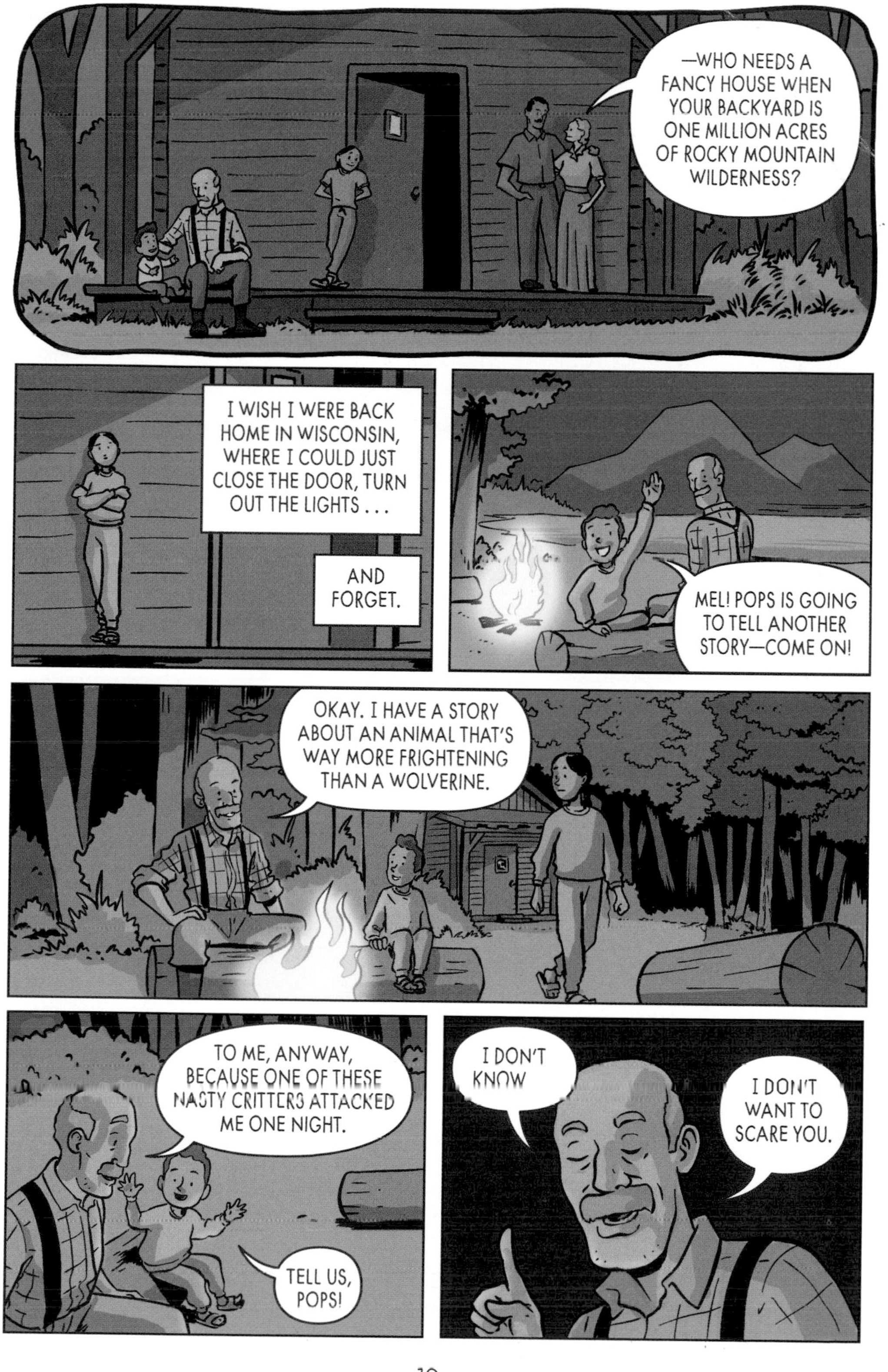
—WHO NEEDS A FANCY HOUSE WHEN YOUR BACKYARD IS ONE MILLION ACRES OF ROCKY MOUNTAIN WILDERNESS?
I WISH I WERE BACK HOME IN WISCONSIN, WHERE I COULD JUST CLOSE THE DOOR, TURN OUT THE LIGHTS . . .
AND FORGET.
MEL! POPS IS GOING TO TELL ANOTHER STORY—COME ON!
OKAY. I HAVE A STORY ABOUT AN ANIMAL THAT'S WAY MORE FRIGHTENING THAN A WOLVERINE.
TO ME, ANYWAY, BECAUSE ONE OF THESE NASTY CRITTERS ATTACKED ME ONE NIGHT.
TELL US, POPS!
I DON'T KNOW
I DON'T WANT TO SCARE YOU.

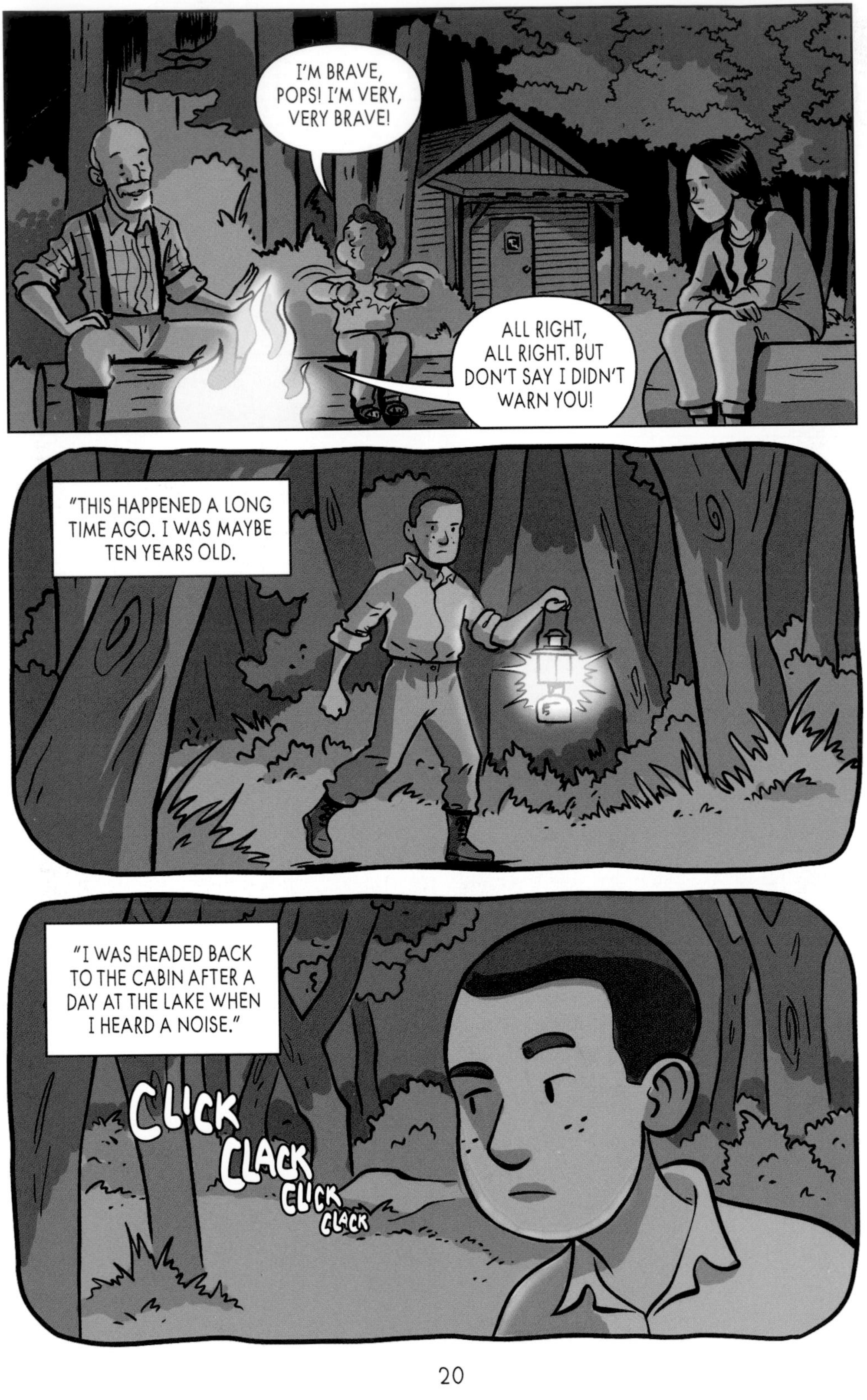
I'M BRAVE, POPS! I'M VERY, VERY BRAVE!
ALL RIGHT, ALL RIGHT. BUT DON'T SAY I DIDN'T WARN YOU!
"THIS HAPPENED A LONG TIME AGO. I WAS MAYBE TEN YEARS OLD.
"I WAS HEADED BACK TO THE CABIN AFTER A DAY AT THE LAKE WHEN I HEARD A NOISE."
CLICK
CLACK
CLICK
CLACK

WAS IT AN ALLIGATOR?

MOST KIDS HAVE TEDDY BEARS. KEVIN SLEEPS WITH A STUFFED ALLIGATOR OUR AUNT CASSIE GAVE HIM.

SHHHH . . .

I SHOULD HAVE STOPPED, OR AT LEAST SLOWED DOWN. MAYBE FOUND A DIFFERENT TRAIL.

BUT I JUST KEPT WALKING ALONG. AND SUDDENLY—

WHAM!

—SOMETHING WHACKED MY CALF.

I NEVER FELT SUCH PAIN IN MY LIFE—NOT BEFORE OR SINCE.

"THE ANIMAL RAN OFF. I NEVER GOT A GOOD LOOK AT IT.

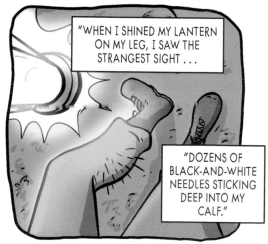

"WHEN I SHINED MY LANTERN ON MY LEG, I SAW THE STRANGEST SIGHT . . .

"DOZENS OF BLACK-AND-WHITE NEEDLES STICKING DEEP INTO MY CALF."

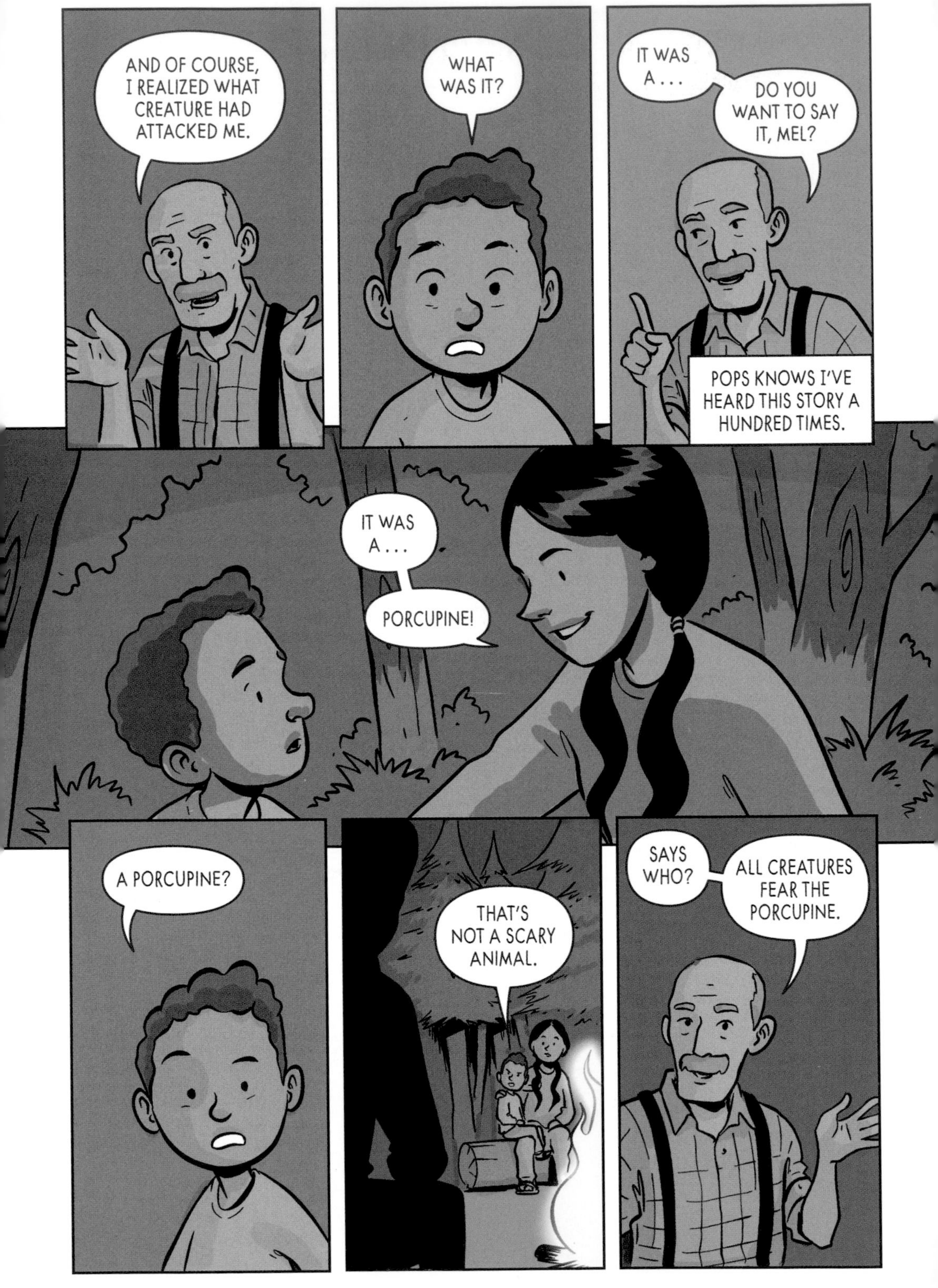
AND OF COURSE, I REALIZED WHAT CREATURE HAD ATTACKED ME.
WHAT WAS IT?
IT WAS A . . .
DO YOU WANT TO SAY IT, MEL?
POPS KNOWS I'VE HEARD THIS STORY A HUNDRED TIMES.
IT WAS A . . .
PORCUPINE!
A PORCUPINE?
THAT'S NOT A SCARY ANIMAL.
SAYS WHO?
ALL CREATURES FEAR THE PORCUPINE.

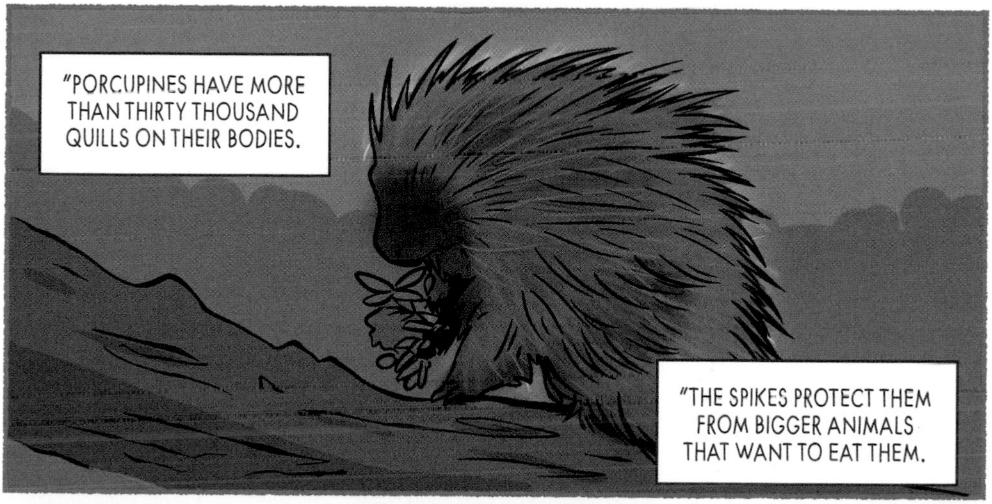
"PORCUPINES HAVE MORE THAN THIRTY THOUSAND QUILLS ON THEIR BODIES.
"THE SPIKES PROTECT THEM FROM BIGGER ANIMALS THAT WANT TO EAT THEM.

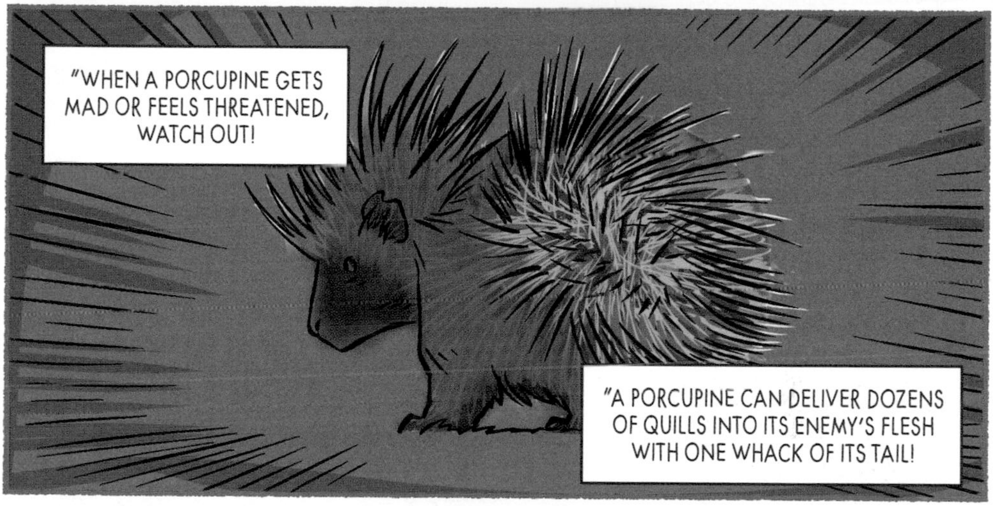
"WHEN A PORCUPINE GETS MAD OR FEELS THREATENED, WATCH OUT!
"A PORCUPINE CAN DELIVER DOZENS OF QUILLS INTO ITS ENEMY'S FLESH WITH ONE WHACK OF ITS TAIL!

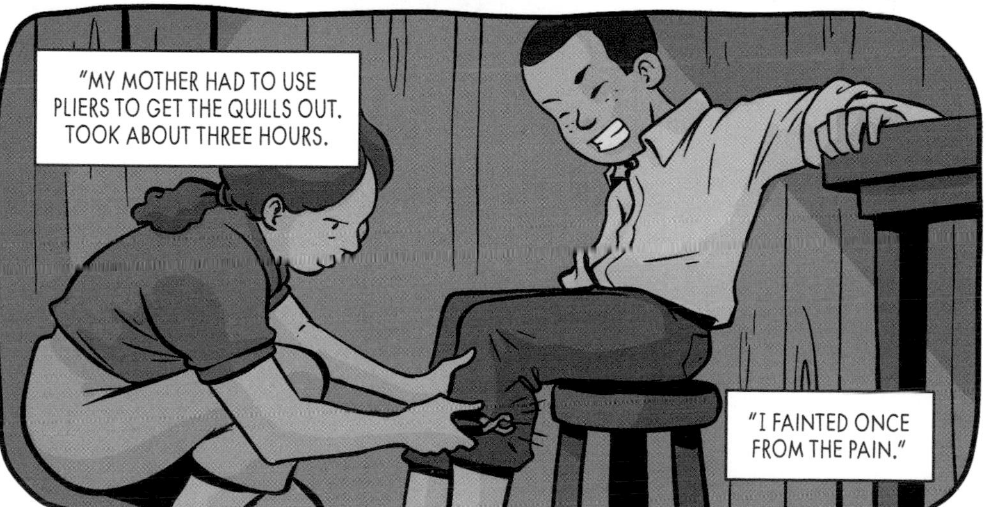
"MY MOTHER HAD TO USE PLIERS TO GET THE QUILLS OUT. TOOK ABOUT THREE HOURS.
"I FAINTED ONCE FROM THE PAIN."

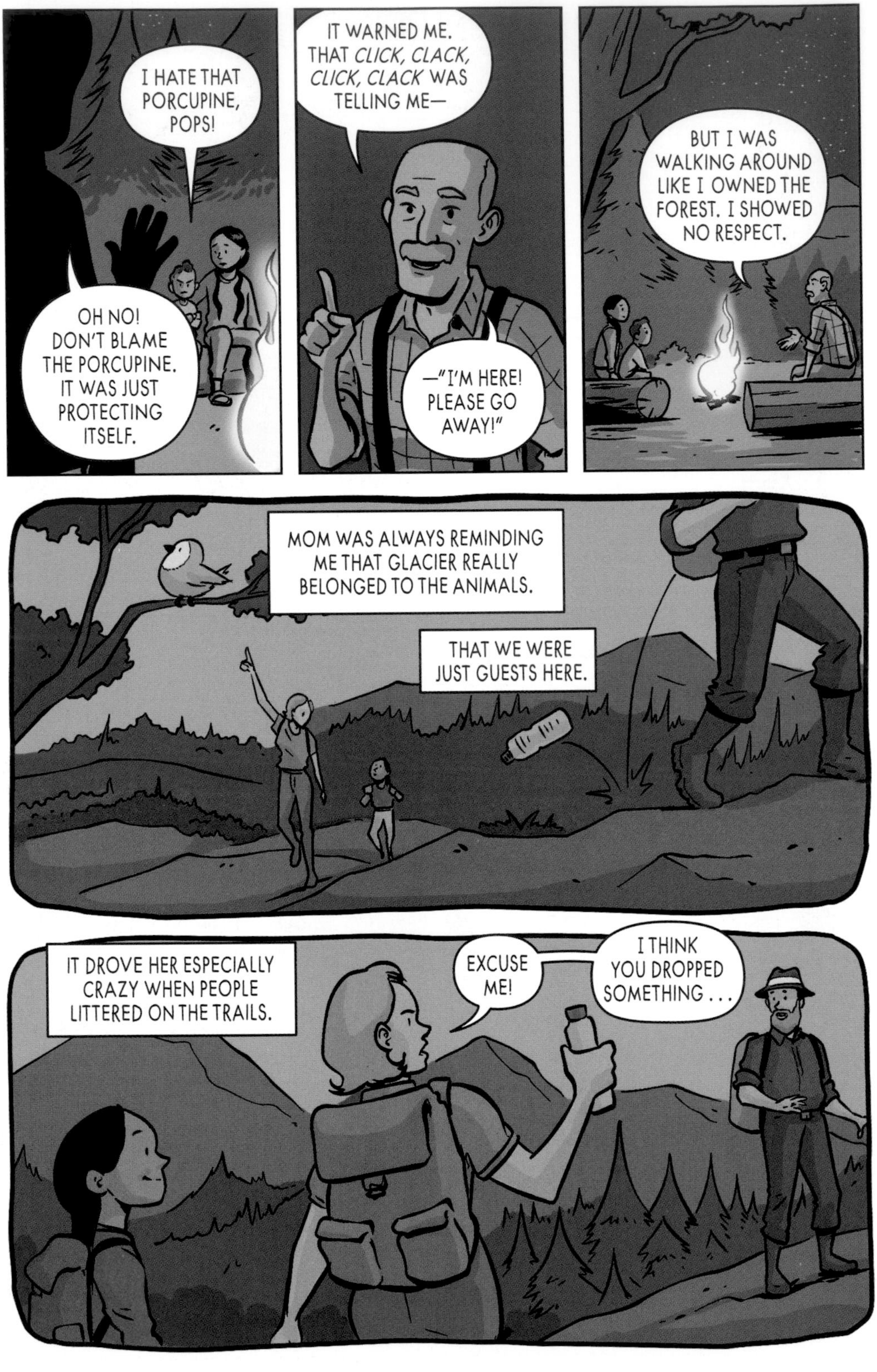
I HATE THAT PORCUPINE, POPS!
OH NO! DON'T BLAME THE PORCUPINE. IT WAS JUST PROTECTING ITSELF.
IT WARNED ME. THAT *CLICK, CLACK, CLICK, CLACK* WAS TELLING ME—
—"I'M HERE! PLEASE GO AWAY!"
BUT I WAS WALKING AROUND LIKE I OWNED THE FOREST. I SHOWED NO RESPECT.
MOM WAS ALWAYS REMINDING ME THAT GLACIER REALLY BELONGED TO THE ANIMALS.
THAT WE WERE JUST GUESTS HERE.
IT DROVE HER ESPECIALLY CRAZY WHEN PEOPLE LITTERED ON THE TRAILS.
EXCUSE ME!
I THINK YOU DROPPED SOMETHING . . .

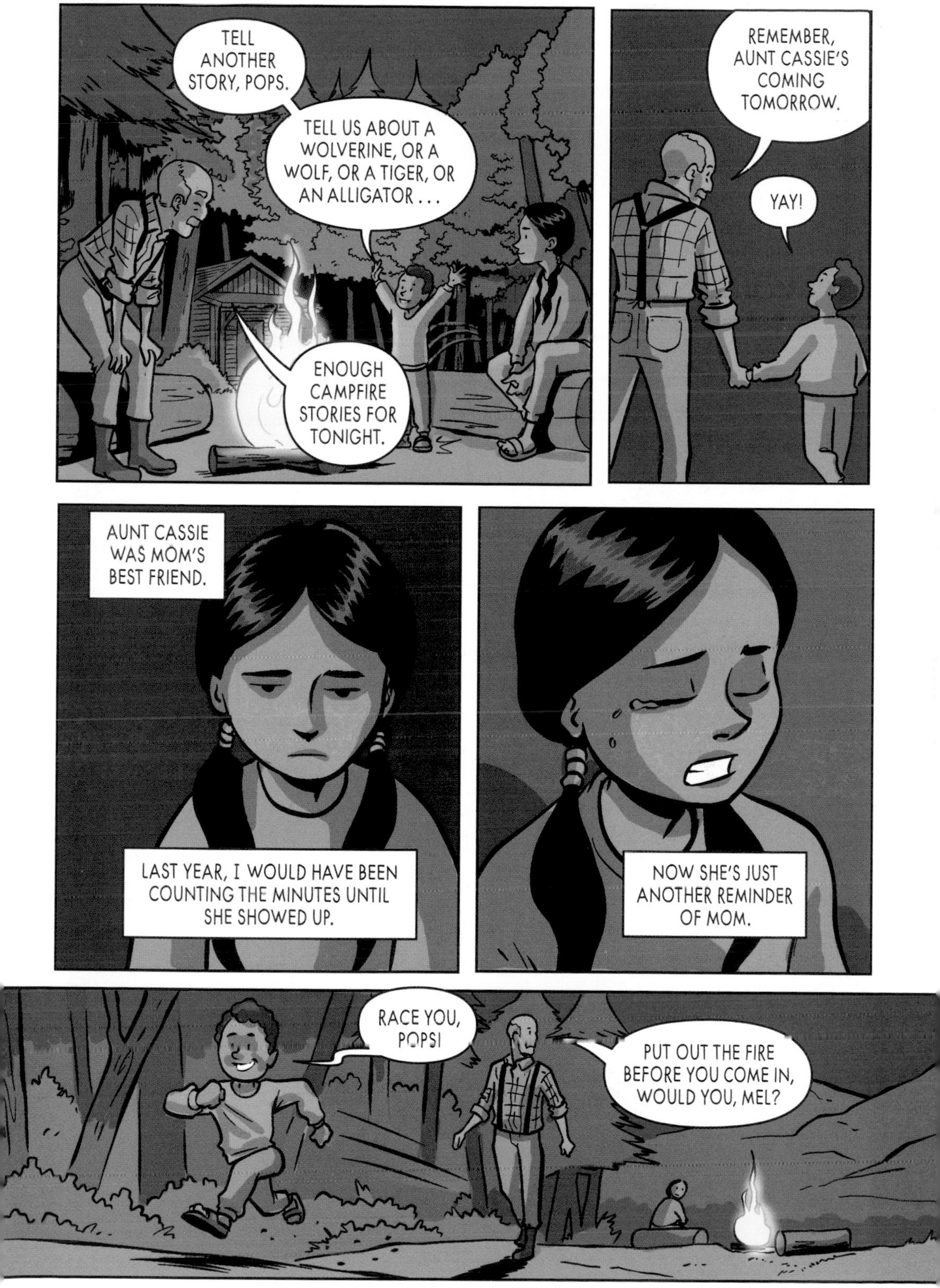
TELL ANOTHER STORY, POPS.
TELL US ABOUT A WOLVERINE, OR A WOLF, OR A TIGER, OR AN ALLIGATOR . . .
ENOUGH CAMPFIRE STORIES FOR TONIGHT.
REMEMBER, AUNT CASSIE'S COMING TOMORROW.
YAY!
AUNT CASSIE WAS MOM'S BEST FRIEND.
LAST YEAR, I WOULD HAVE BEEN COUNTING THE MINUTES UNTIL SHE SHOWED UP.
NOW SHE'S JUST ANOTHER REMINDER OF MOM.
RACE YOU, POPS!
PUT OUT THE FIRE BEFORE YOU COME IN, WOULD YOU, MEL?

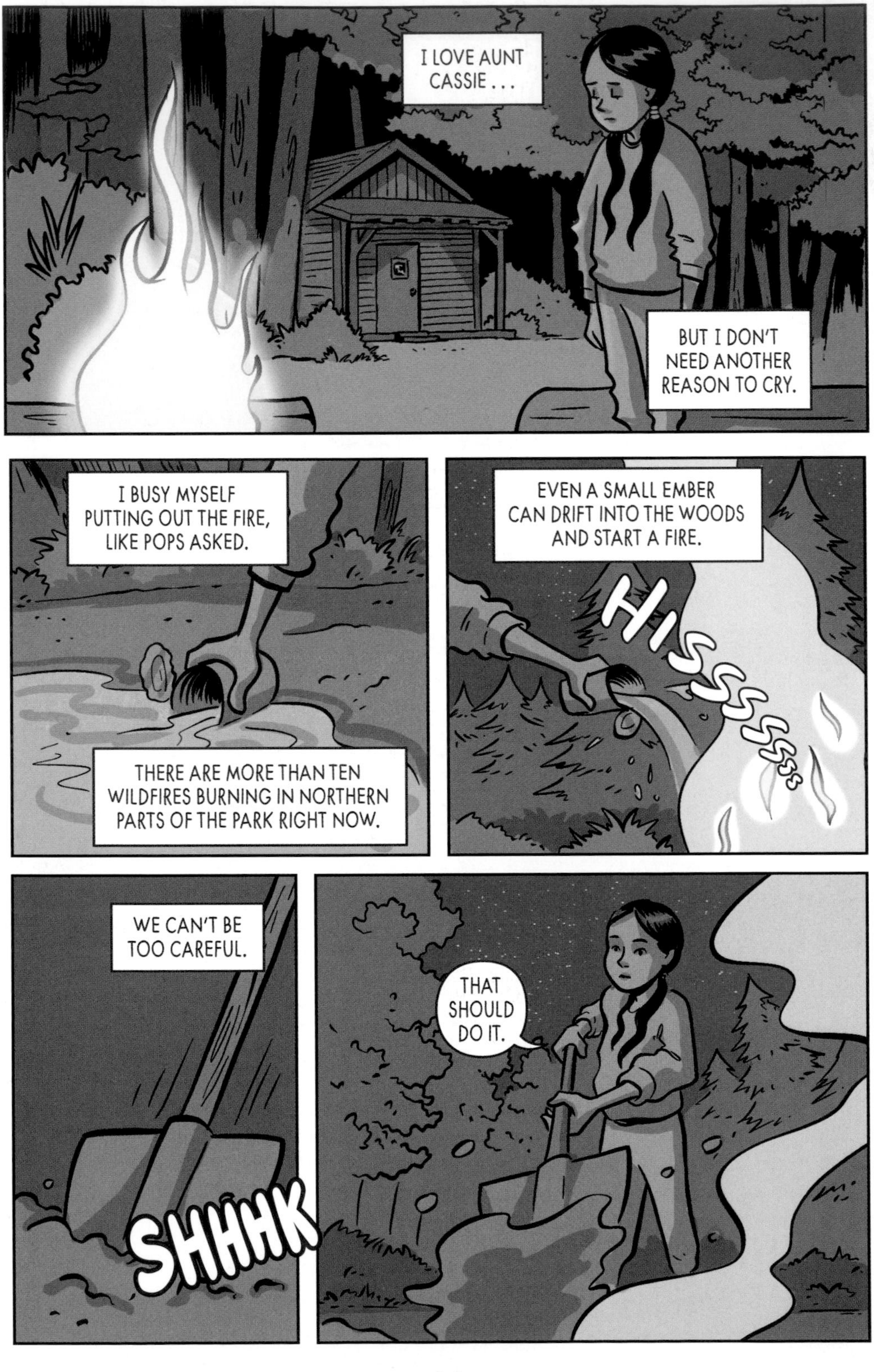
I LOVE AUNT CASSIE . . .
BUT I DON'T NEED ANOTHER REASON TO CRY.
I BUSY MYSELF PUTTING OUT THE FIRE, LIKE POPS ASKED.
THERE ARE MORE THAN TEN WILDFIRES BURNING IN NORTHERN PARTS OF THE PARK RIGHT NOW.
EVEN A SMALL EMBER CAN DRIFT INTO THE WOODS AND START A FIRE.
HISSSSSSss
WE CAN'T BE TOO CAREFUL.
SHHHK
THAT SHOULD DO IT.

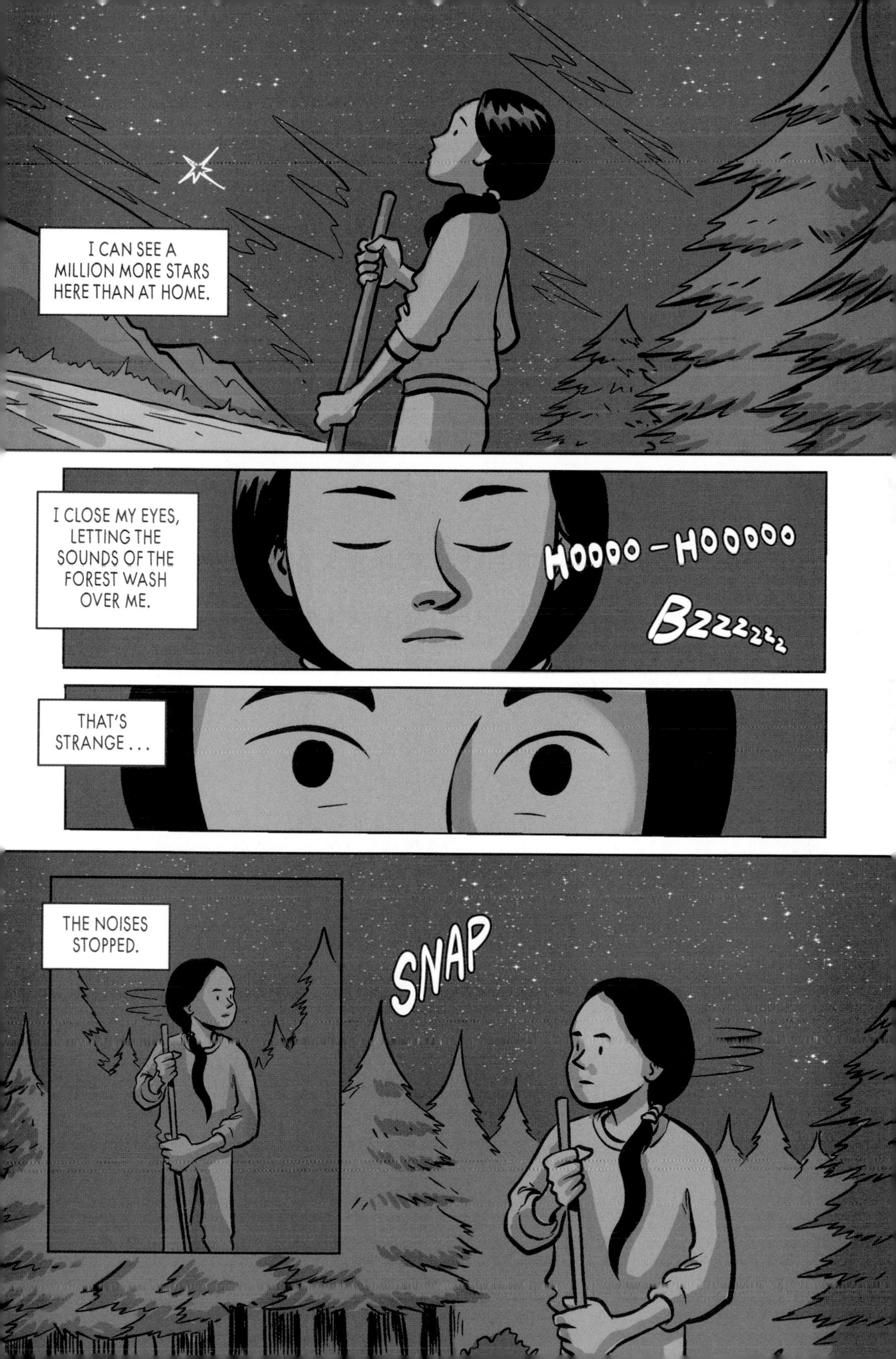

I CAN SEE A MILLION MORE STARS HERE THAN AT HOME.
I CLOSE MY EYES, LETTING THE SOUNDS OF THE FOREST WASH OVER ME.
HOOOO-HOOOOO
BZZZZZZ
THAT'S STRANGE . . .
THE NOISES STOPPED.
SNAP

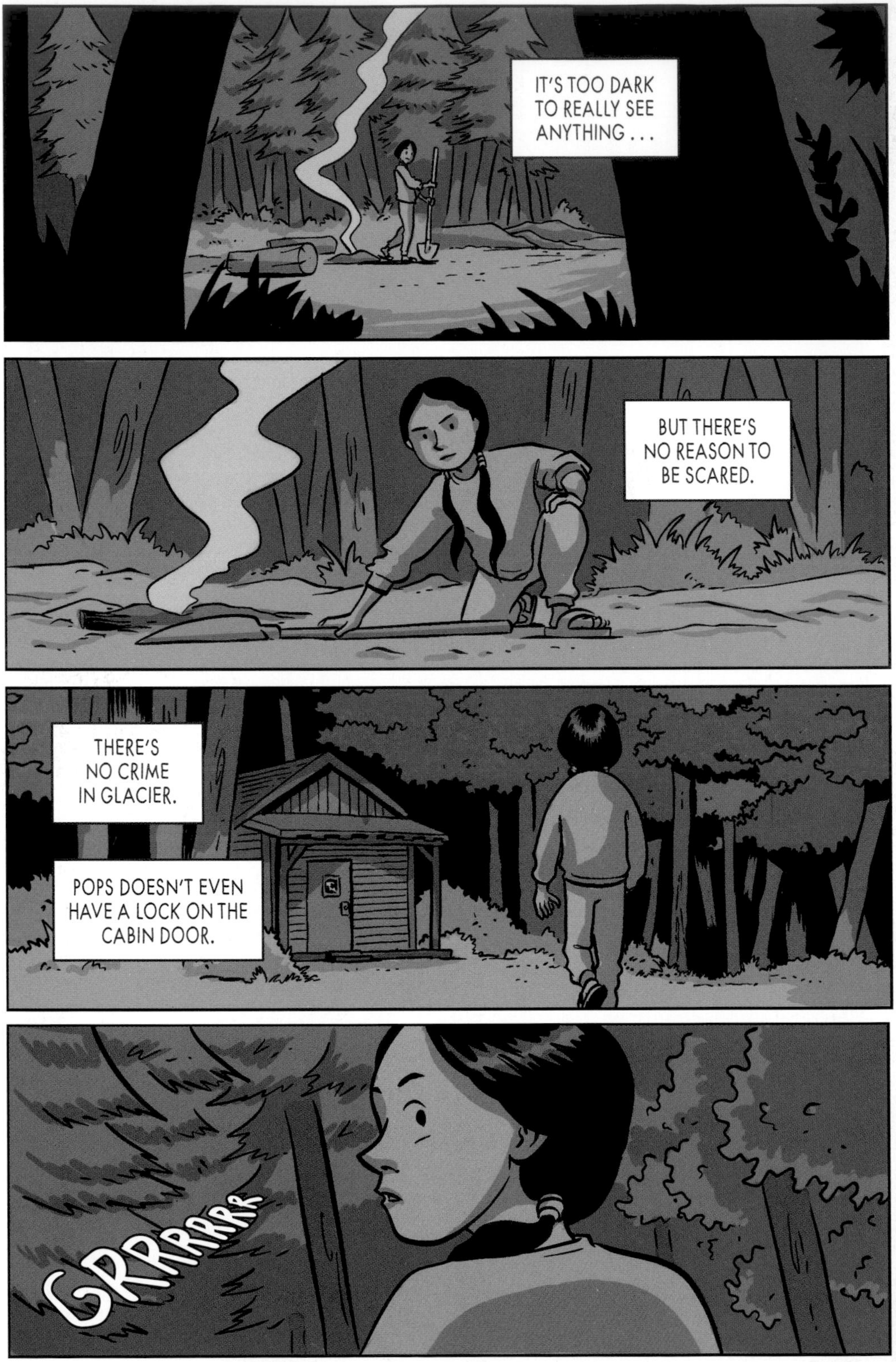
IT'S TOO DARK TO REALLY SEE ANYTHING . . .
BUT THERE'S NO REASON TO BE SCARED.
THERE'S NO CRIME IN GLACIER.
POPS DOESN'T EVEN HAVE A LOCK ON THE CABIN DOOR.
GRRRRRR

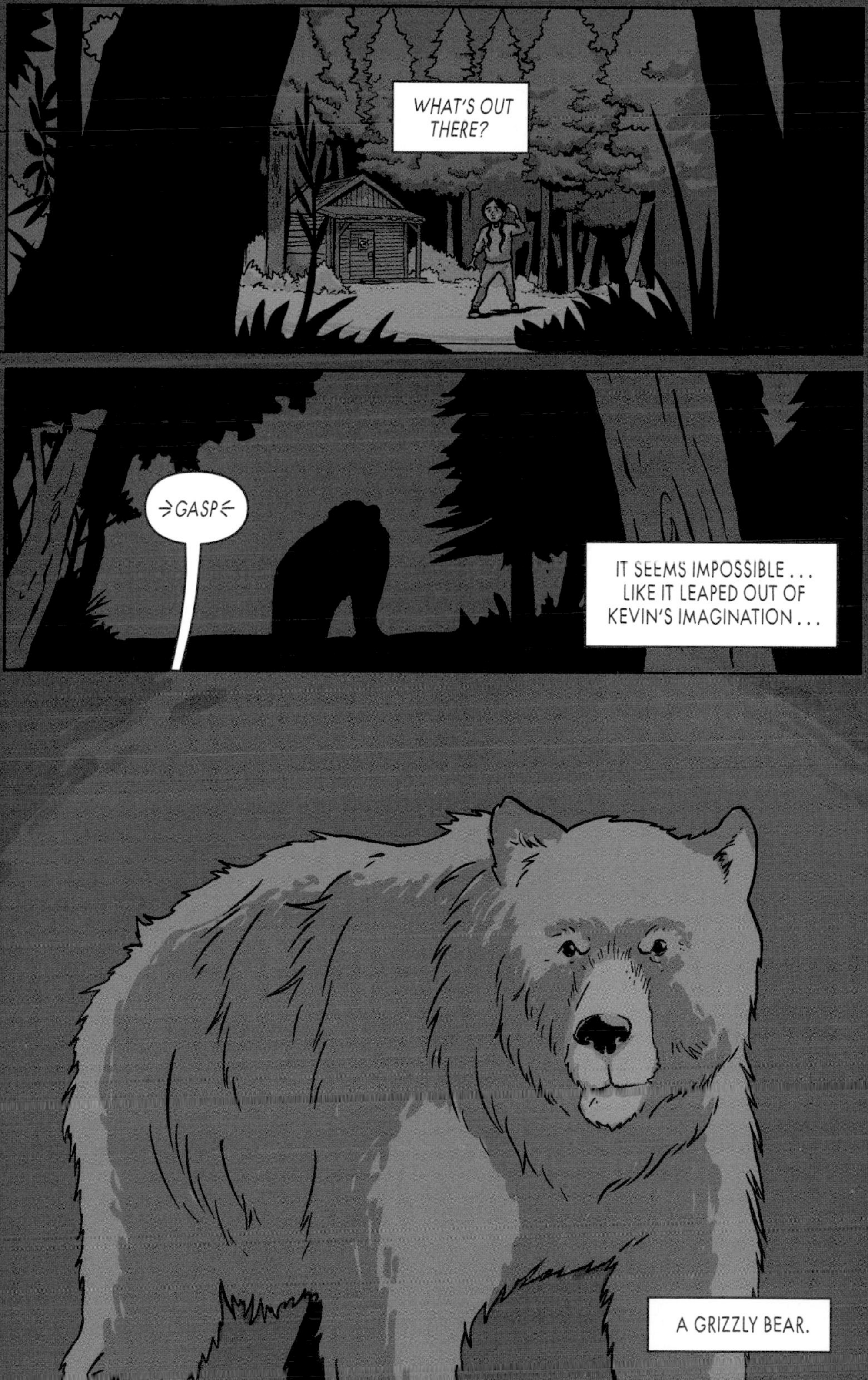
WHAT'S OUT THERE?
GASP
IT SEEMS IMPOSSIBLE . . . LIKE IT LEAPED OUT OF KEVIN'S IMAGINATION . . .
A GRIZZLY BEAR.

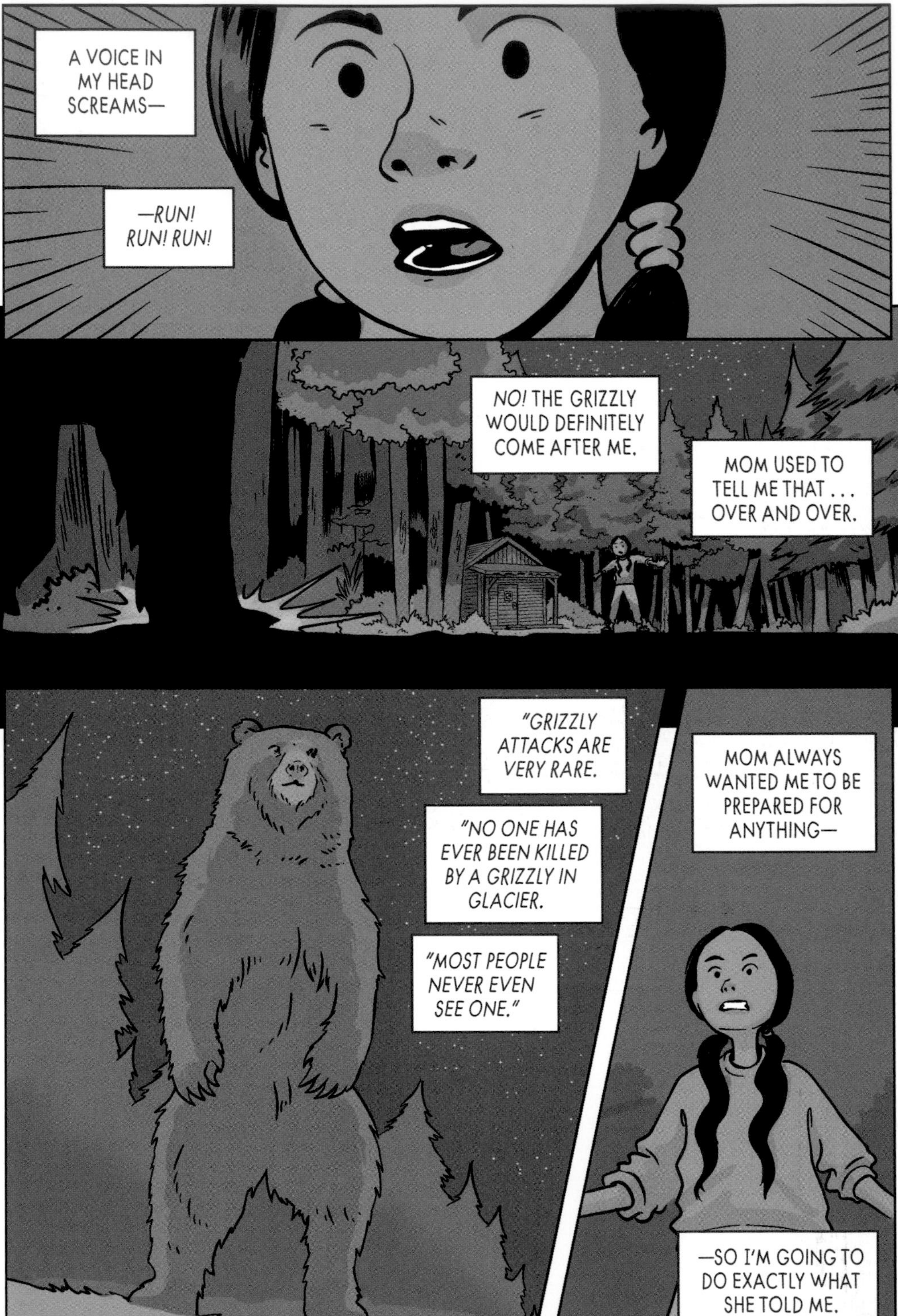
A VOICE IN MY HEAD SCREAMS—
—RUN! RUN! RUN!
NO! THE GRIZZLY WOULD DEFINITELY COME AFTER ME.
MOM USED TO TELL ME THAT . . . OVER AND OVER.
"GRIZZLY ATTACKS ARE VERY RARE.
"NO ONE HAS EVER BEEN KILLED BY A GRIZZLY IN GLACIER.
"MOST PEOPLE NEVER EVEN SEE ONE."
MOM ALWAYS WANTED ME TO BE PREPARED FOR ANYTHING—
—SO I'M GOING TO DO EXACTLY WHAT SHE TOLD ME.

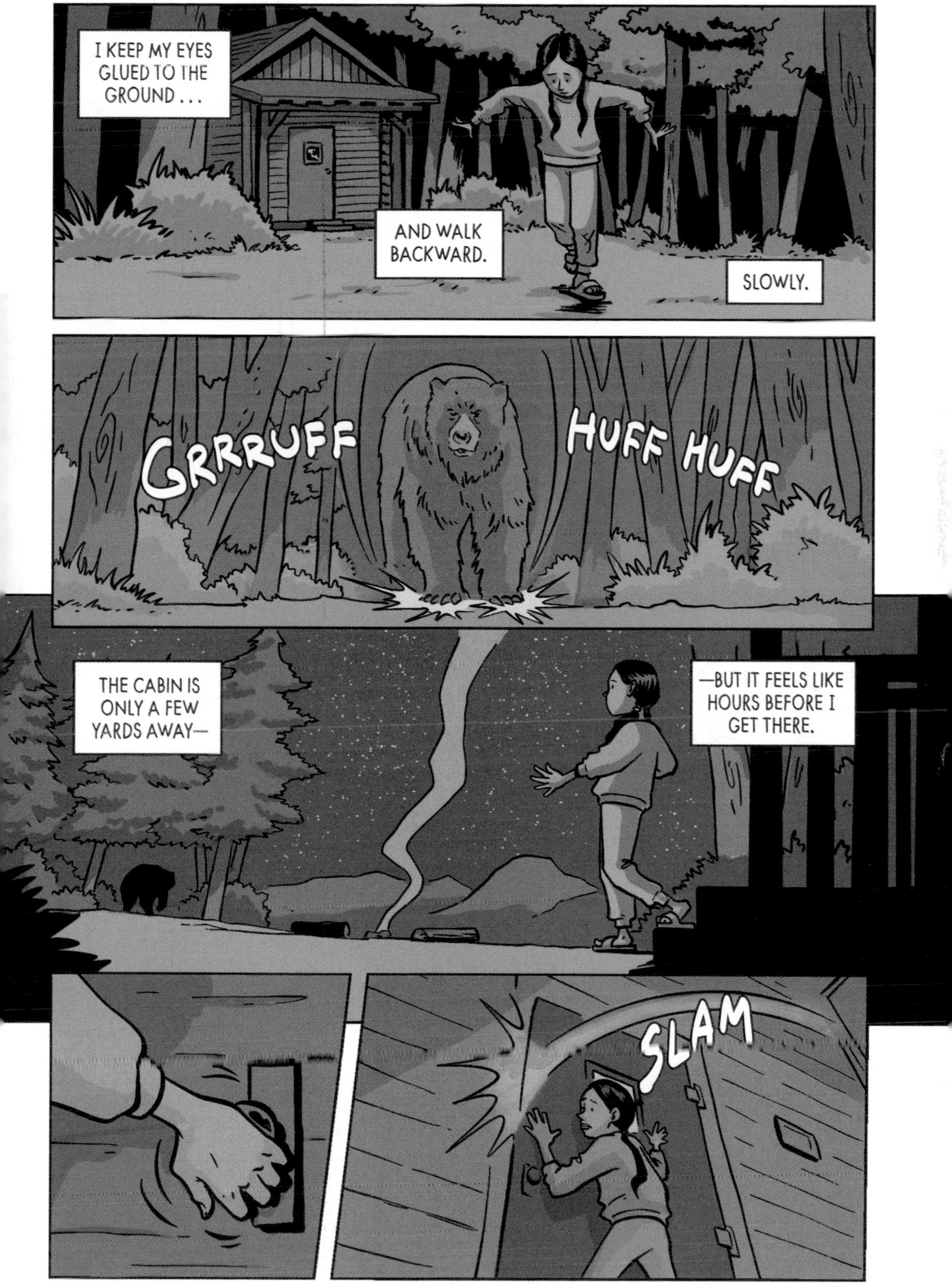
I KEEP MY EYES GLUED TO THE GROUND . . .
AND WALK BACKWARD.
SLOWLY.
GRRRUFF
HUFF HUFF
THE CABIN IS ONLY A FEW YARDS AWAY—
—BUT IT FEELS LIKE HOURS BEFORE I GET THERE.
SLAM

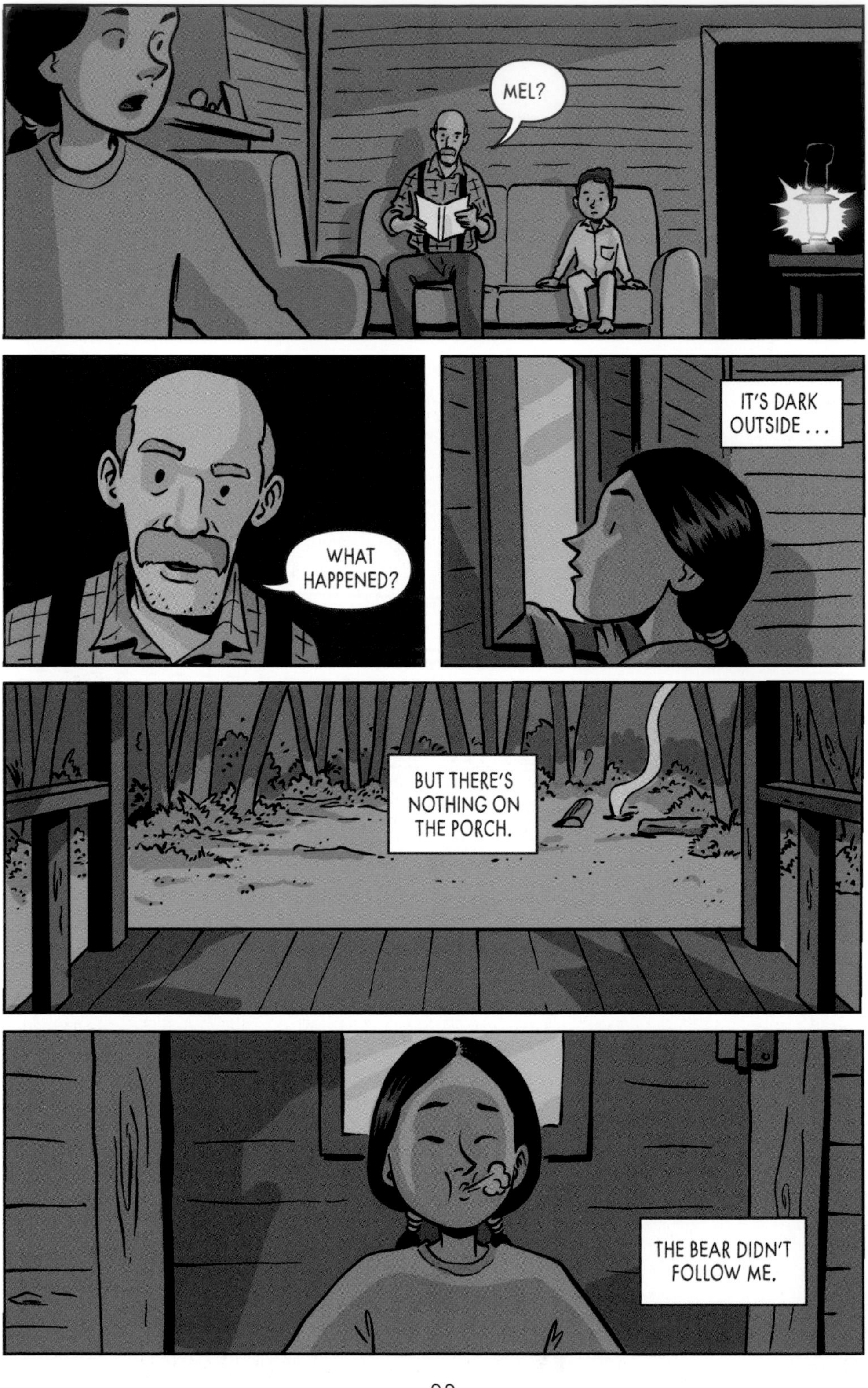
MEL?
WHAT HAPPENED?
IT'S DARK OUTSIDE . . .
BUT THERE'S NOTHING ON THE PORCH.
THE BEAR DIDN'T FOLLOW ME.

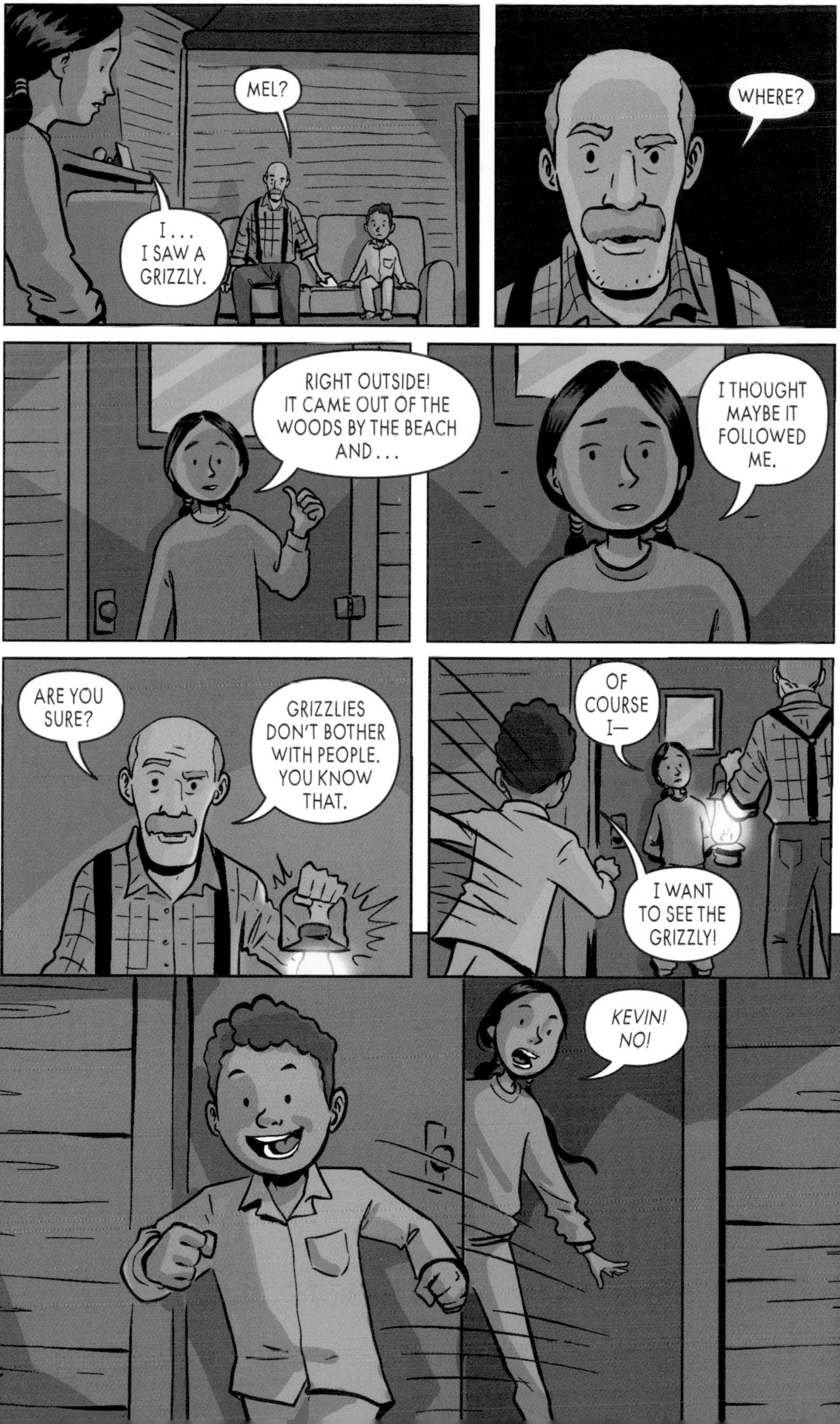
MEL?
I... I SAW A GRIZZLY.
WHERE?
RIGHT OUTSIDE! IT CAME OUT OF THE WOODS BY THE BEACH AND...
I THOUGHT MAYBE IT FOLLOWED ME.
ARE YOU SURE?
GRIZZLIES DON'T BOTHER WITH PEOPLE. YOU KNOW THAT.
OF COURSE I—
I WANT TO SEE THE GRIZZLY!
KEVIN! NO!

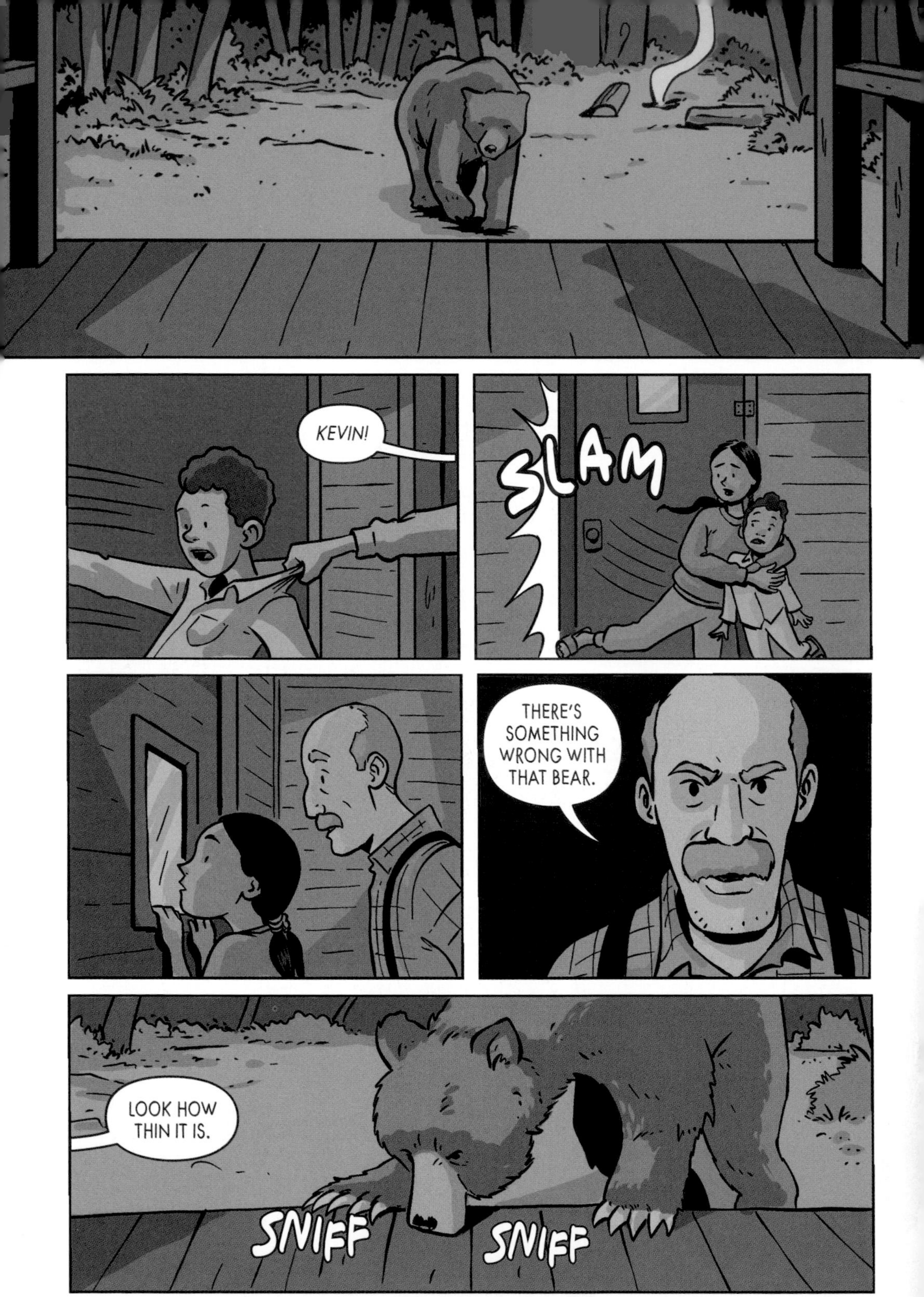
KEVIN!
SLAM
THERE'S SOMETHING WRONG WITH THAT BEAR.
LOOK HOW THIN IT IS.
SNIFF
SNIFF

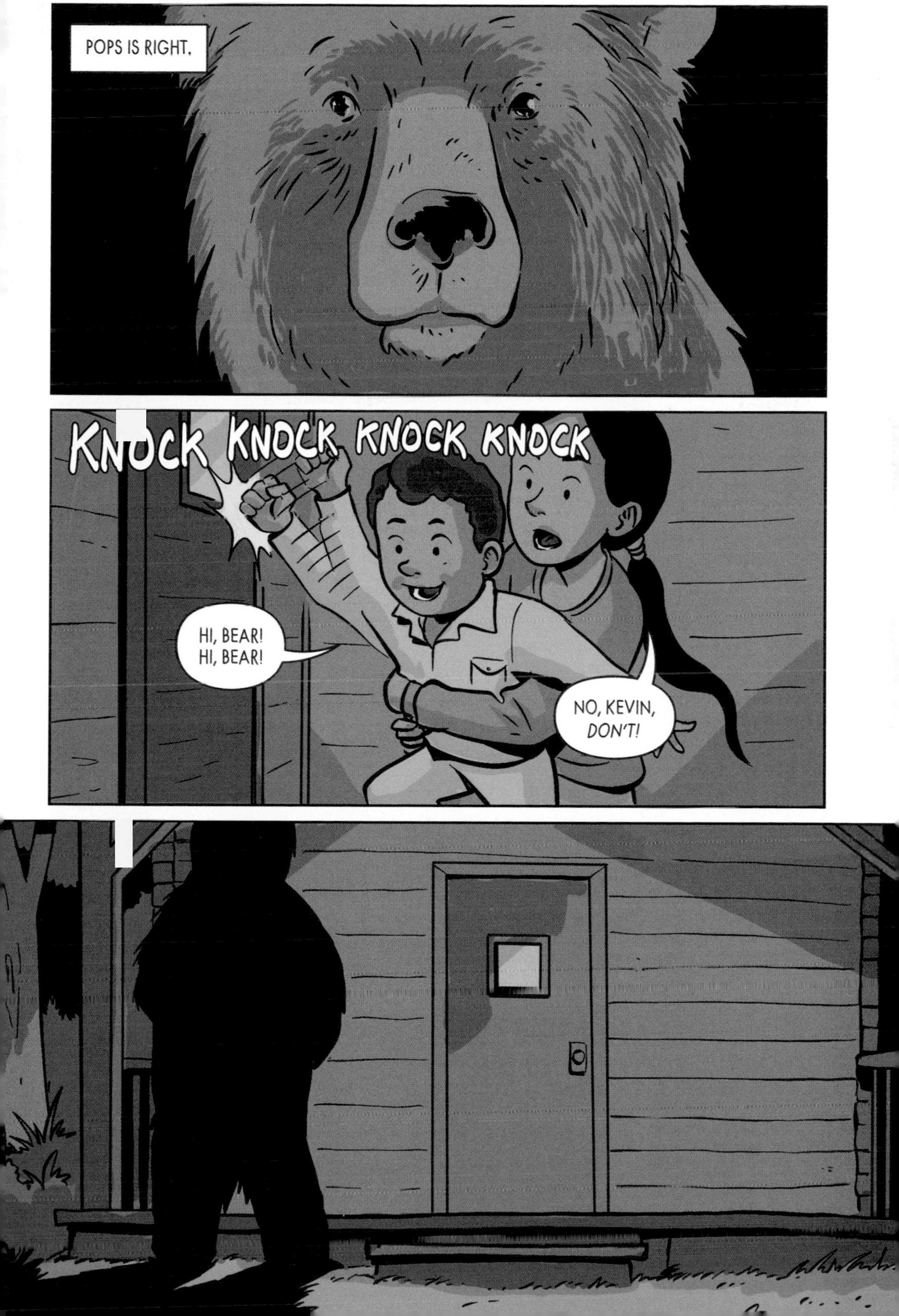
POPS IS RIGHT.
KNOCK KNOCK KNOCK KNOCK
HI, BEAR! HI, BEAR!
NO, KEVIN, DON'T!

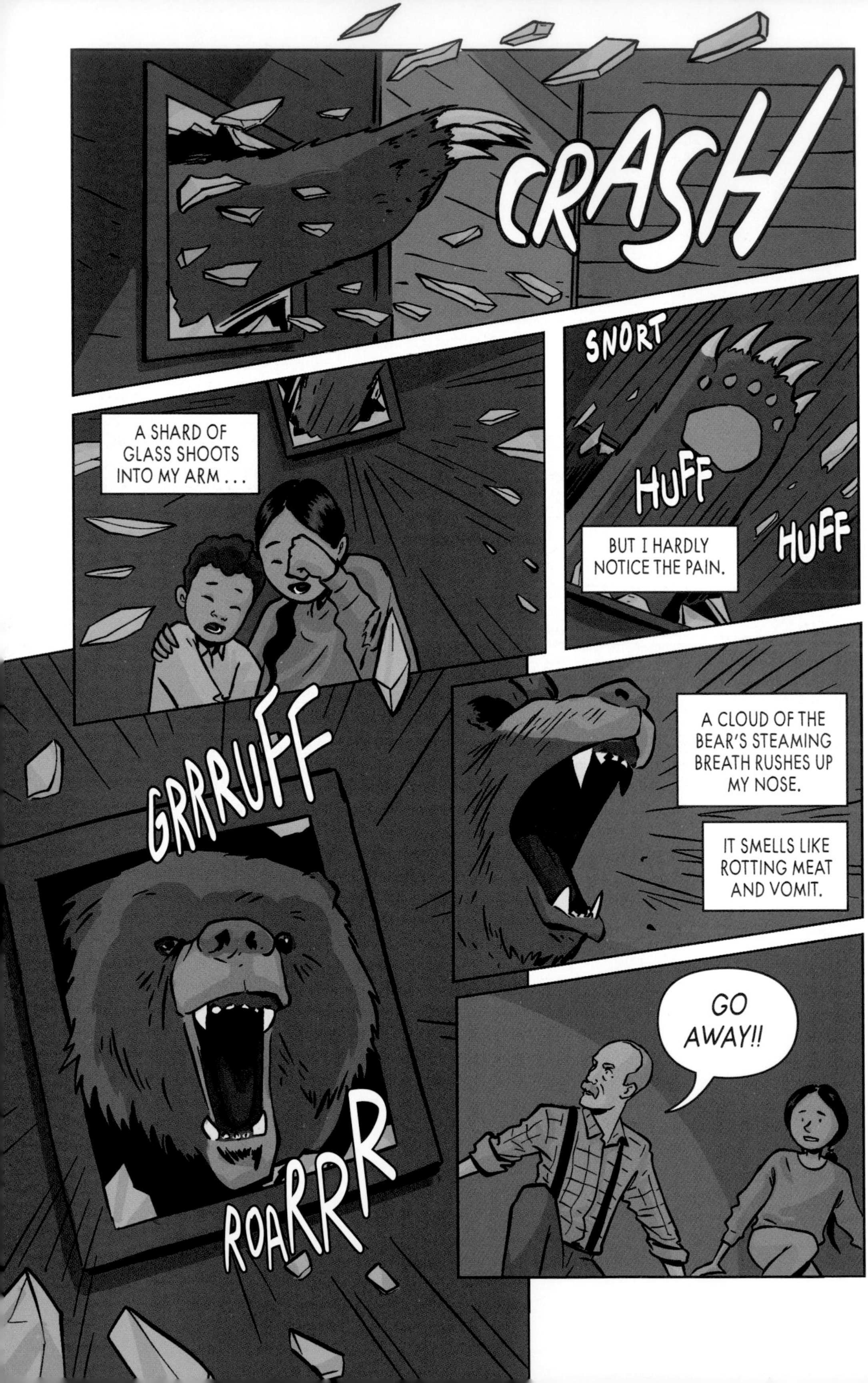
CRASH
A SHARD OF GLASS SHOOTS INTO MY ARM . . .
SNORT
HUFF
HUFF
BUT I HARDLY NOTICE THE PAIN.
GRRRUFF
ROARRR
A CLOUD OF THE BEAR'S STEAMING BREATH RUSHES UP MY NOSE.
IT SMELLS LIKE ROTTING MEAT AND VOMIT.
GO AWAY!!

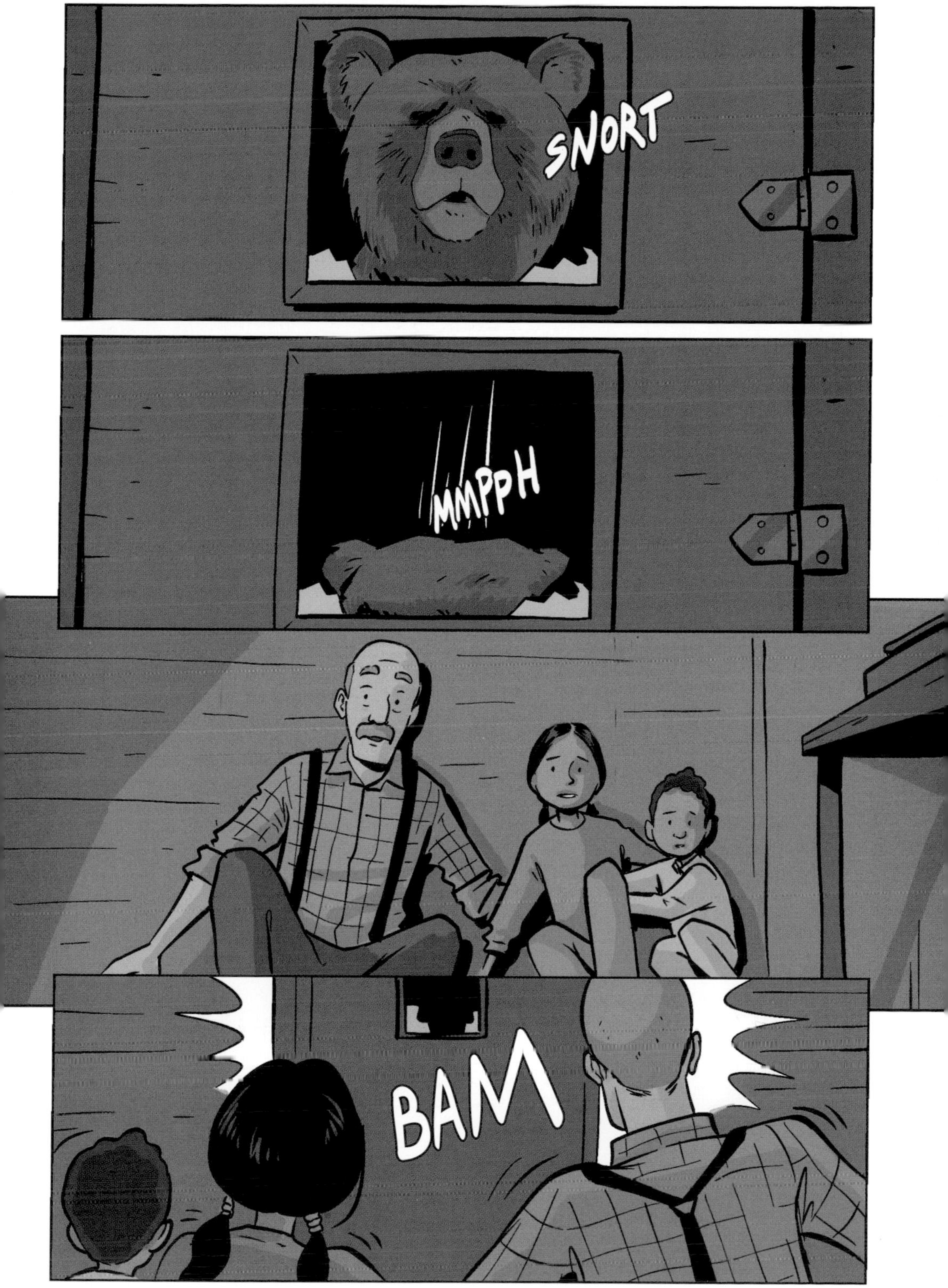
SNORT
MMPPH
BAM

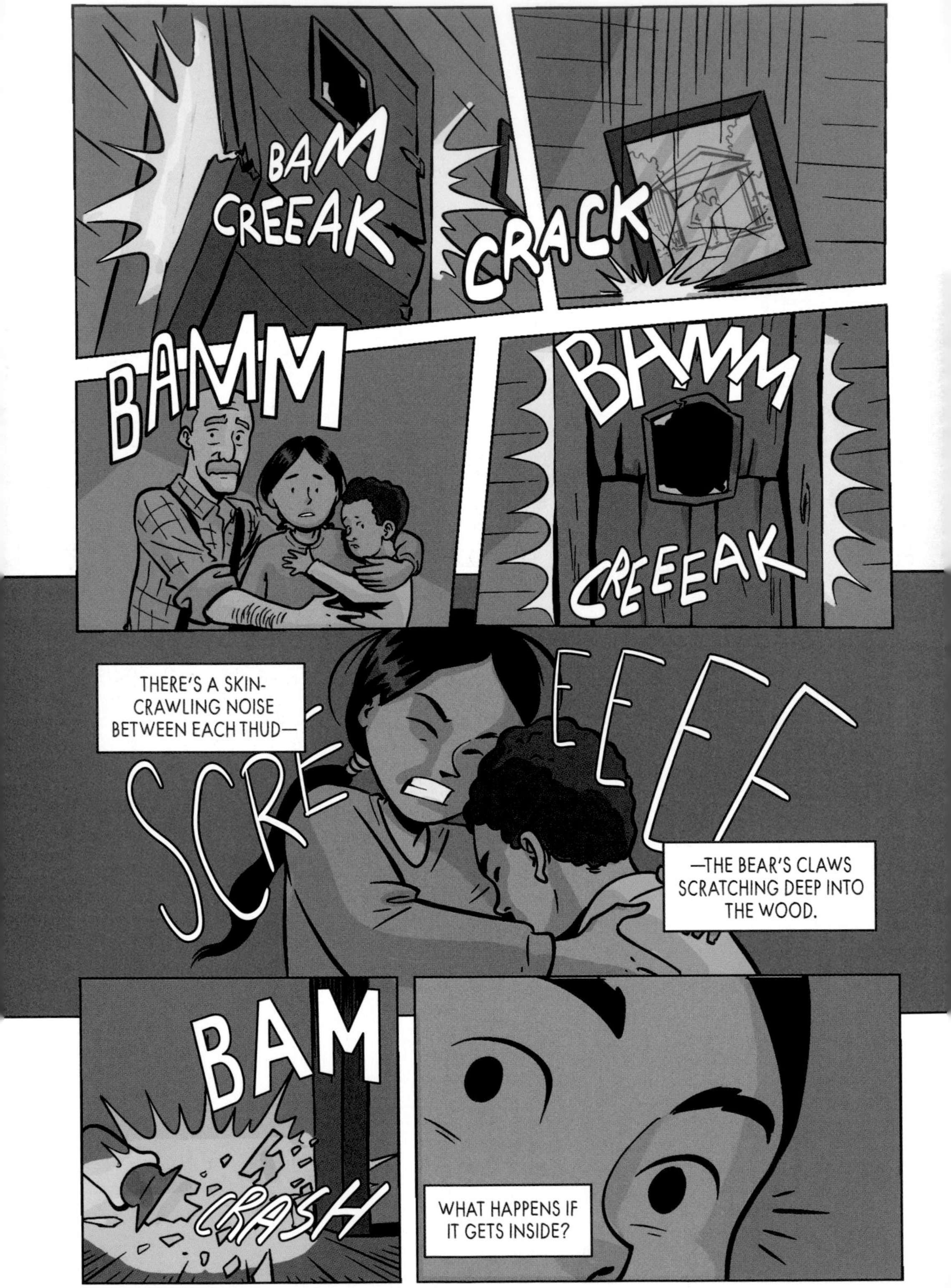
BAM
CREEAK
CRACK
BAMM
BAMM
CREEEAK
THERE'S A SKIN-CRAWLING NOISE BETWEEN EACH THUD—
SCREEEEE
—THE BEAR'S CLAWS SCRATCHING DEEP INTO THE WOOD.
BAM
CRASH
WHAT HAPPENS IF IT GETS INSIDE?

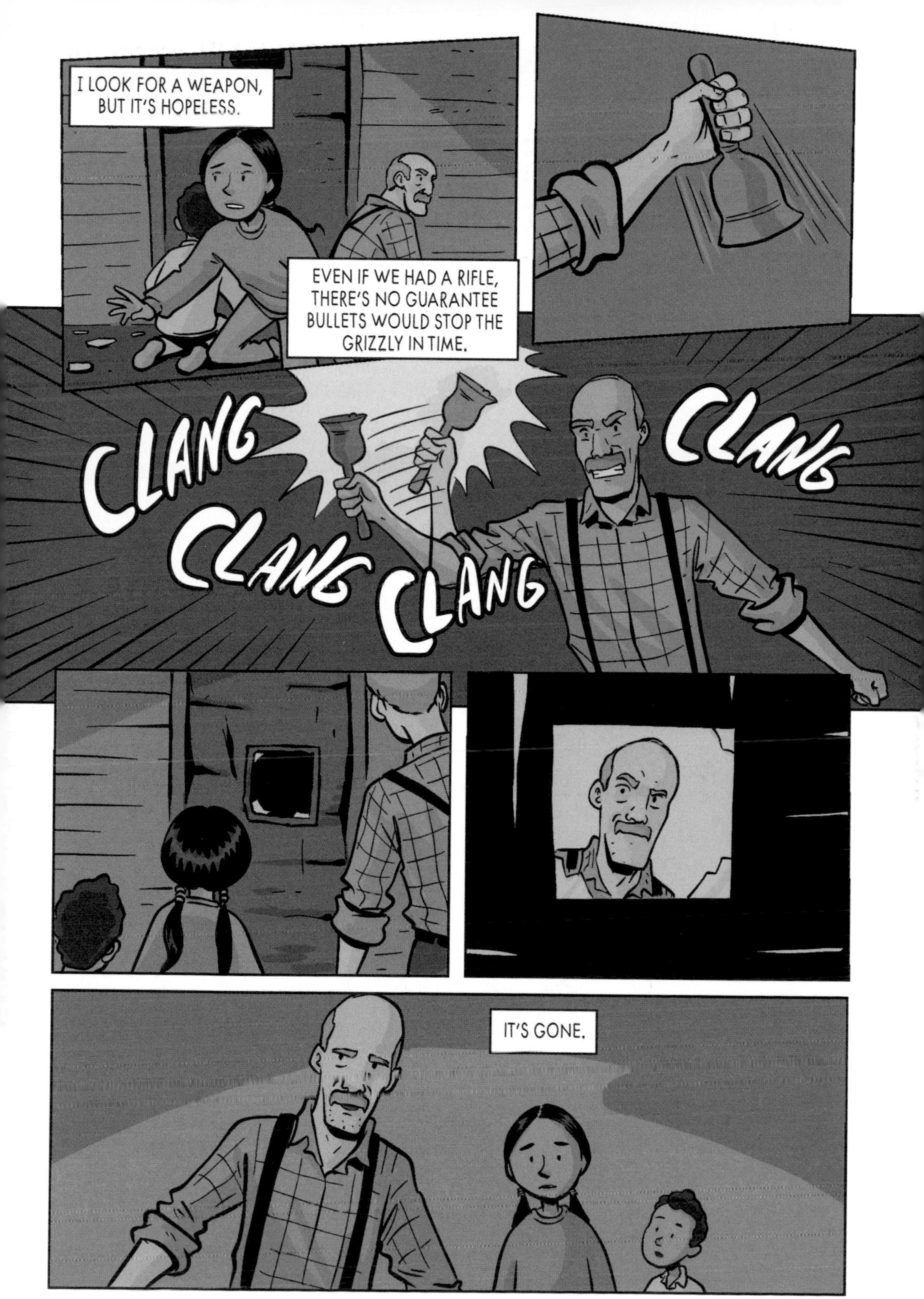
I LOOK FOR A WEAPON, BUT IT'S HOPELESS.
EVEN IF WE HAD A RIFLE, THERE'S NO GUARANTEE BULLETS WOULD STOP THE GRIZZLY IN TIME.
CLANG
CLANG
CLANG
CLANG
IT'S GONE.

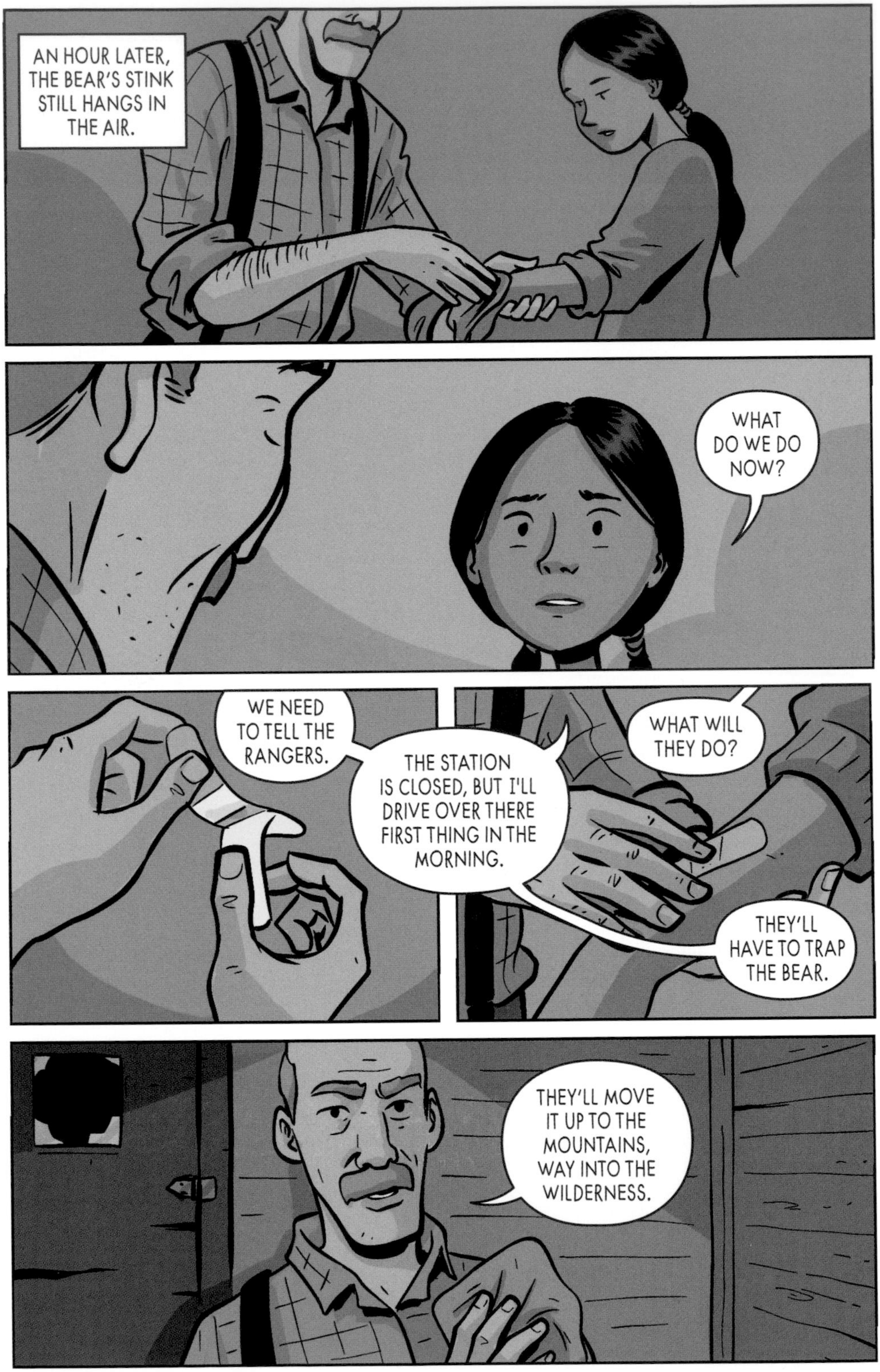
AN HOUR LATER, THE BEAR'S STINK STILL HANGS IN THE AIR.
WHAT DO WE DO NOW?
WE NEED TO TELL THE RANGERS.
THE STATION IS CLOSED, BUT I'LL DRIVE OVER THERE FIRST THING IN THE MORNING.
WHAT WILL THEY DO?
THEY'LL HAVE TO TRAP THE BEAR.
THEY'LL MOVE IT UP TO THE MOUNTAINS, WAY INTO THE WILDERNESS.

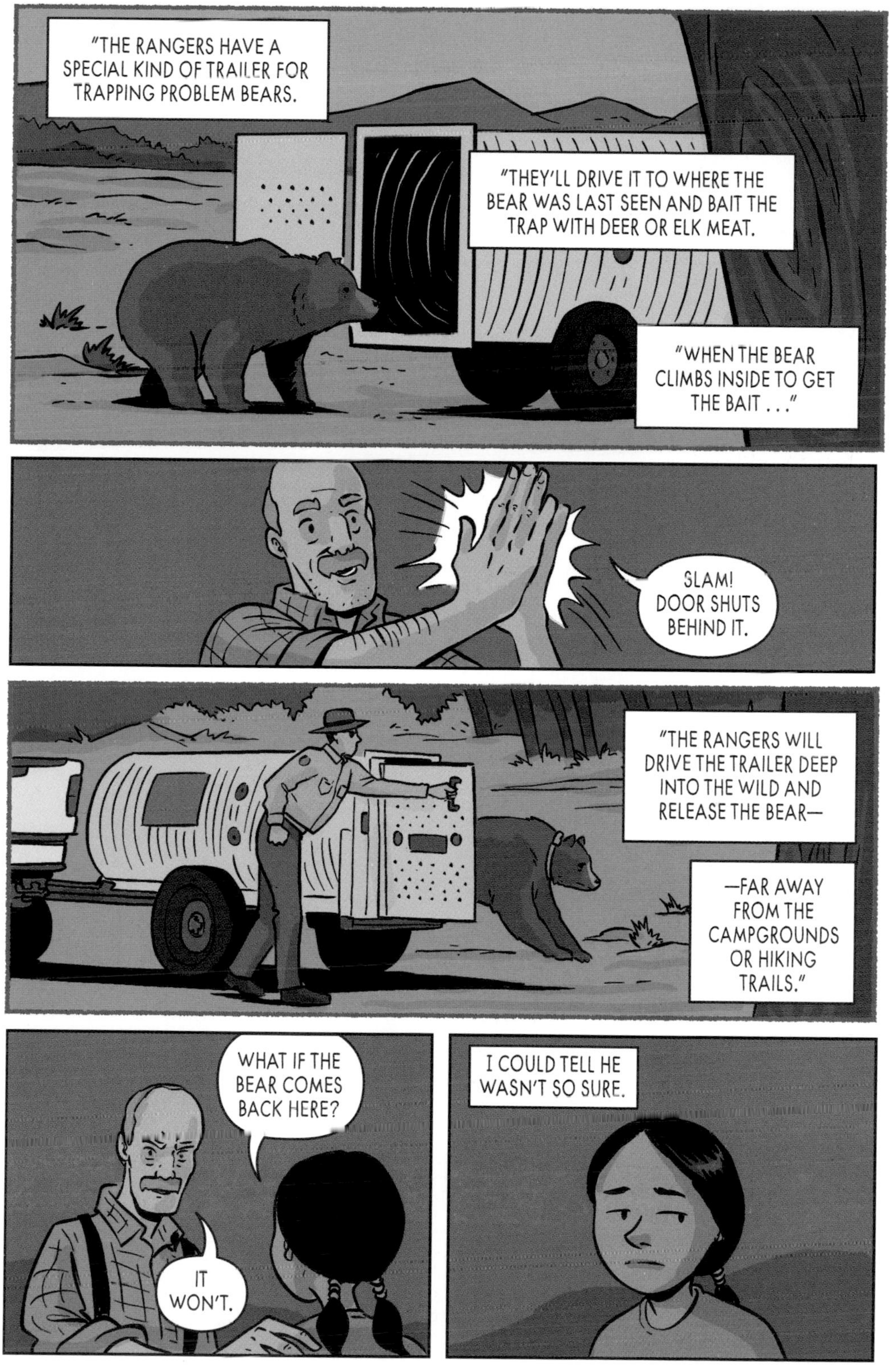
"THE RANGERS HAVE A SPECIAL KIND OF TRAILER FOR TRAPPING PROBLEM BEARS.
"THEY'LL DRIVE IT TO WHERE THE BEAR WAS LAST SEEN AND BAIT THE TRAP WITH DEER OR ELK MEAT.
"WHEN THE BEAR CLIMBS INSIDE TO GET THE BAIT . . ."
SLAM! DOOR SHUTS BEHIND IT.
"THE RANGERS WILL DRIVE THE TRAILER DEEP INTO THE WILD AND RELEASE THE BEAR—
—FAR AWAY FROM THE CAMPGROUNDS OR HIKING TRAILS."
WHAT IF THE BEAR COMES BACK HERE?
IT WON'T.
I COULD TELL HE WASN'T SO SURE.

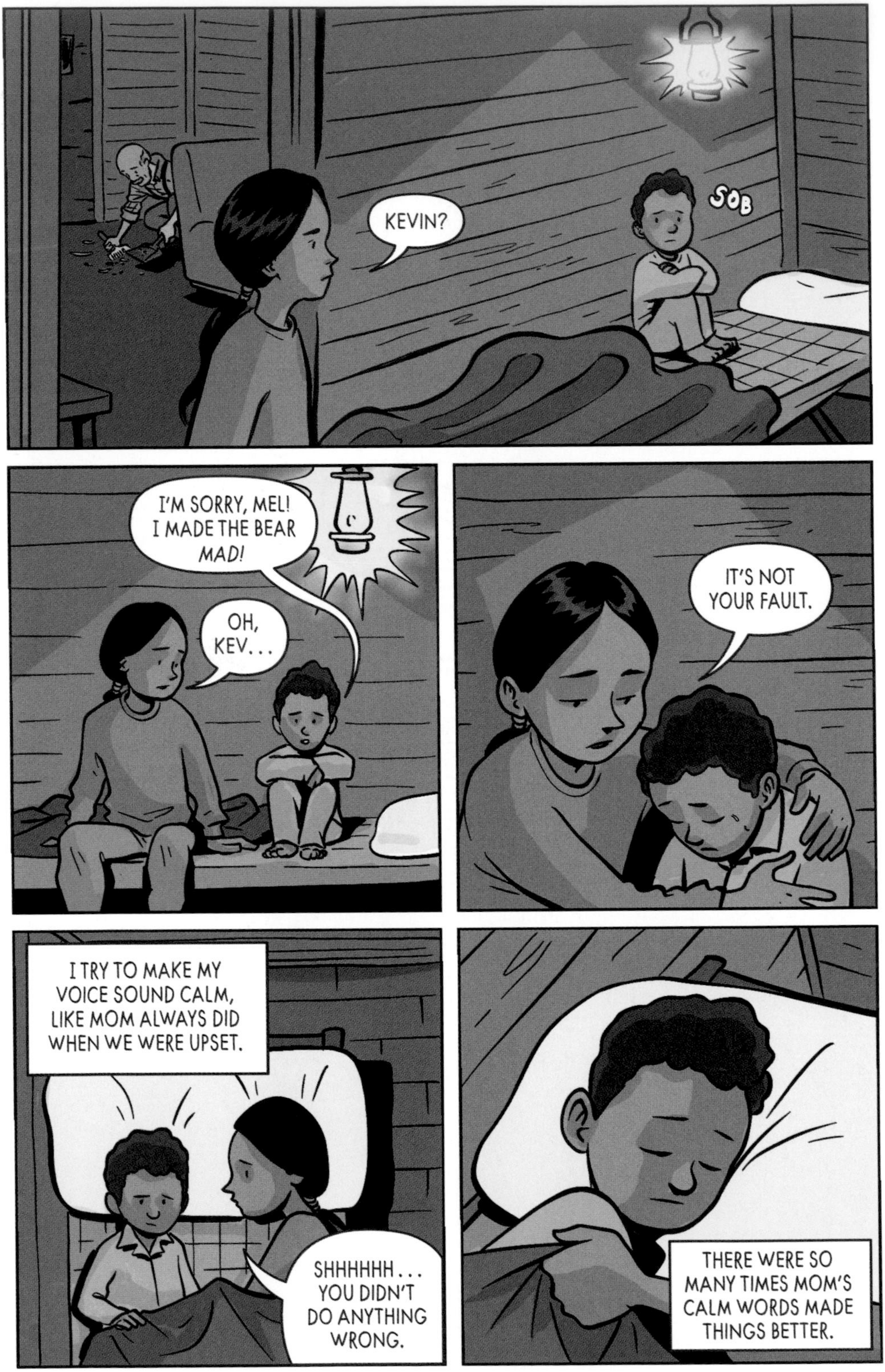
KEVIN?
SOB
I'M SORRY, MEL! I MADE THE BEAR *MAD!*
OH, KEV...
IT'S NOT YOUR FAULT.
I TRY TO MAKE MY VOICE SOUND CALM, LIKE MOM ALWAYS DID WHEN WE WERE UPSET.
SHHHHHH... YOU DIDN'T DO ANYTHING WRONG.
THERE WERE SO MANY TIMES MOM'S CALM WORDS MADE THINGS BETTER.

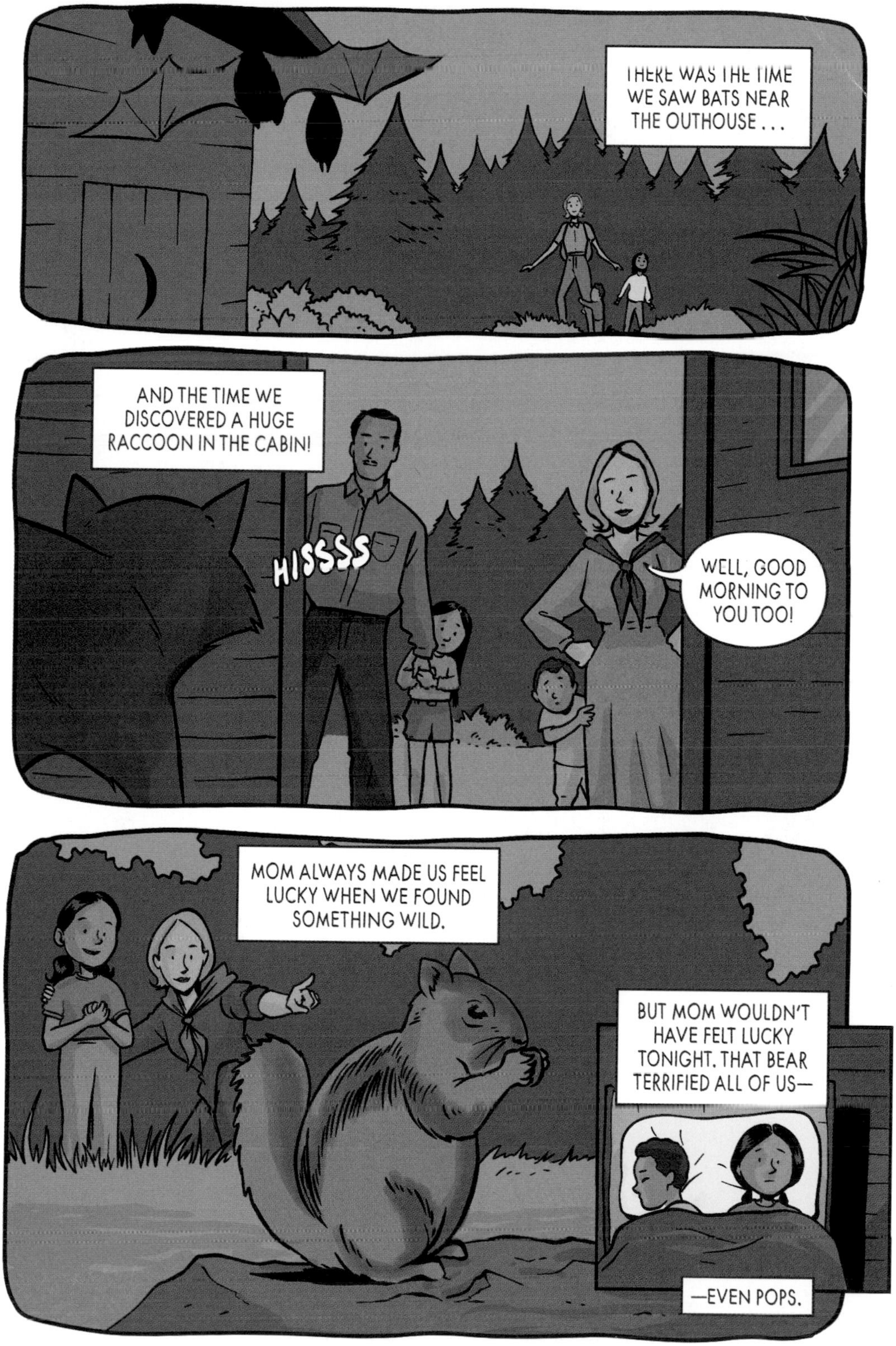
THERE WAS THE TIME WE SAW BATS NEAR THE OUTHOUSE . . .
AND THE TIME WE DISCOVERED A HUGE RACCOON IN THE CABIN!
HISSSS
WELL, GOOD MORNING TO YOU TOO!
MOM ALWAYS MADE US FEEL LUCKY WHEN WE FOUND SOMETHING WILD.
BUT MOM WOULDN'T HAVE FELT LUCKY TONIGHT. THAT BEAR TERRIFIED ALL OF US—
—EVEN POPS.

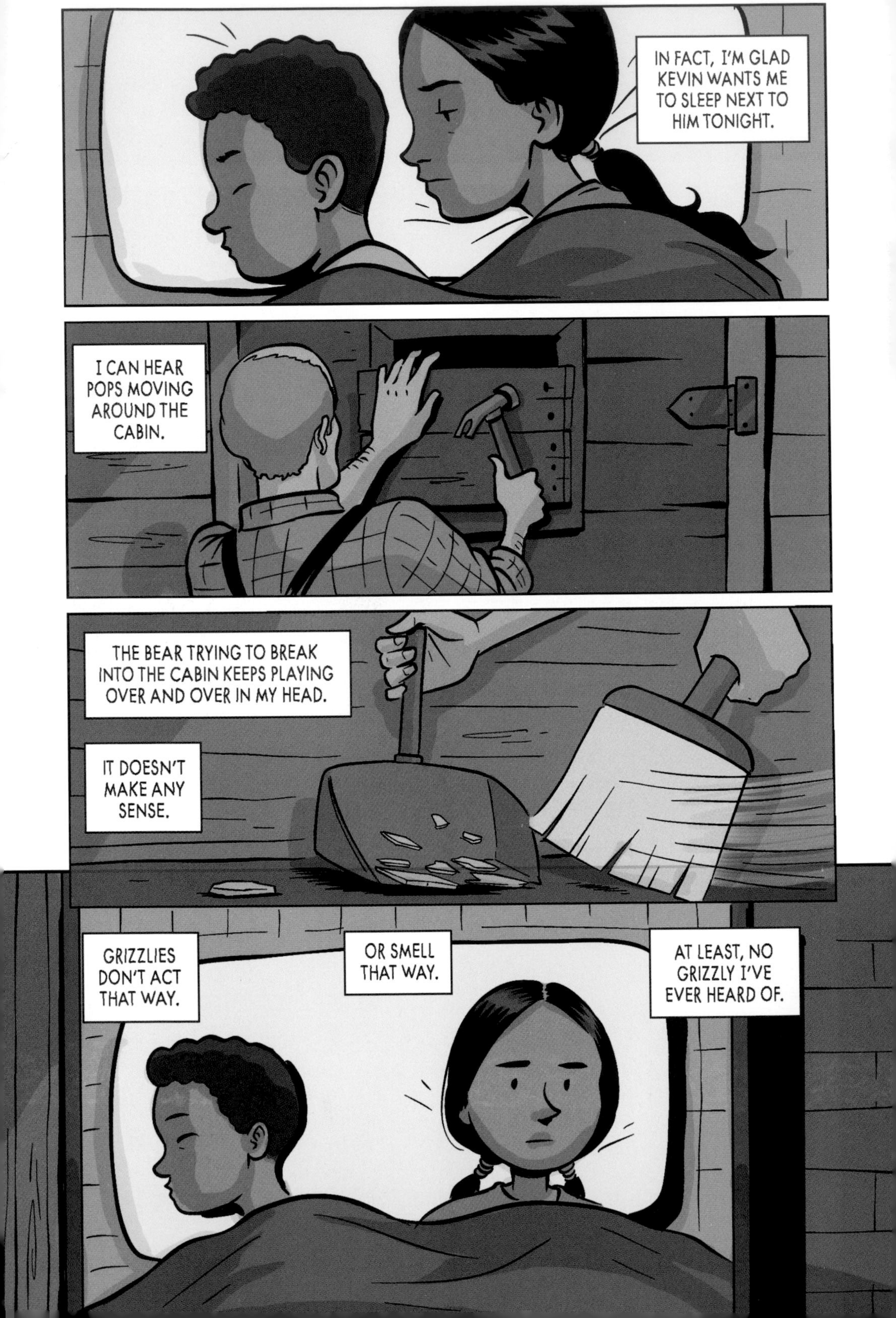
IN FACT, I'M GLAD KEVIN WANTS ME TO SLEEP NEXT TO HIM TONIGHT.
I CAN HEAR POPS MOVING AROUND THE CABIN.
THE BEAR TRYING TO BREAK INTO THE CABIN KEEPS PLAYING OVER AND OVER IN MY HEAD.
IT DOESN'T MAKE ANY SENSE.
GRIZZLIES DON'T ACT THAT WAY.
OR SMELL THAT WAY.
AT LEAST, NO GRIZZLY I'VE EVER HEARD OF.

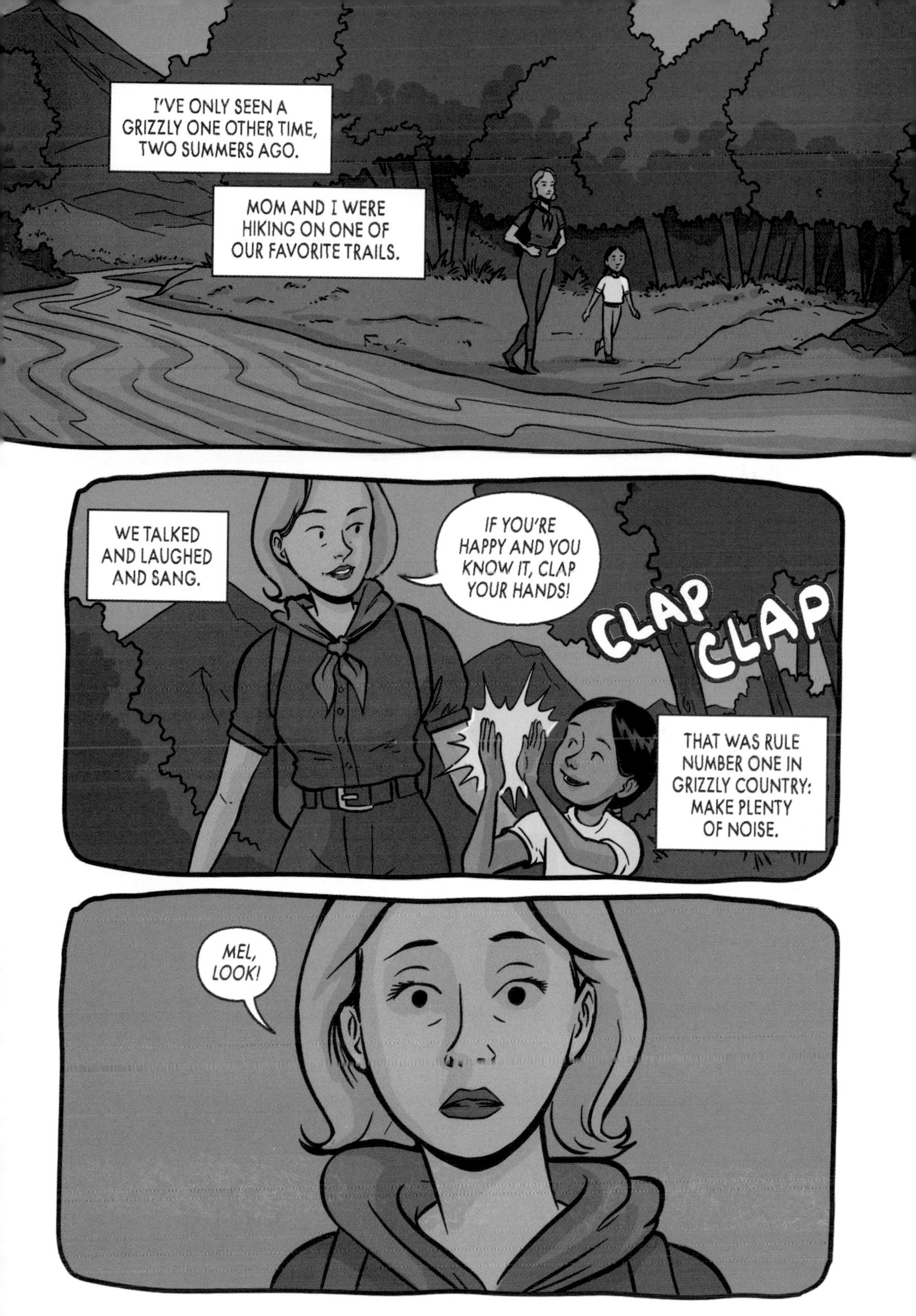
I'VE ONLY SEEN A GRIZZLY ONE OTHER TIME, TWO SUMMERS AGO.
MOM AND I WERE HIKING ON ONE OF OUR FAVORITE TRAILS.
WE TALKED AND LAUGHED AND SANG.
IF YOU'RE HAPPY AND YOU KNOW IT, CLAP YOUR HANDS!
CLAP CLAP
THAT WAS RULE NUMBER ONE IN GRIZZLY COUNTRY: MAKE PLENTY OF NOISE.
MEL, LOOK!

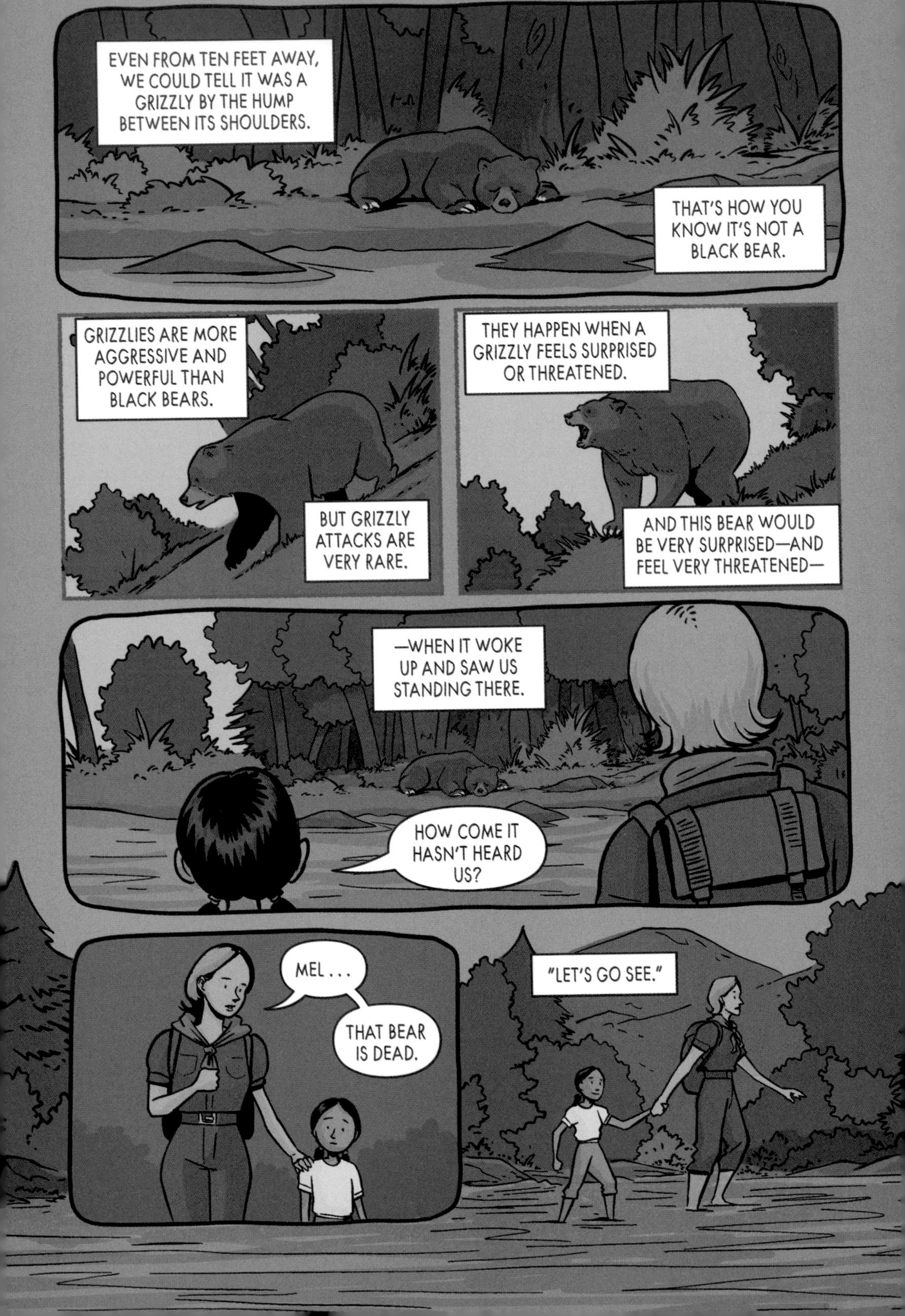
EVEN FROM TEN FEET AWAY, WE COULD TELL IT WAS A GRIZZLY BY THE HUMP BETWEEN ITS SHOULDERS.
THAT'S HOW YOU KNOW IT'S NOT A BLACK BEAR.
GRIZZLIES ARE MORE AGGRESSIVE AND POWERFUL THAN BLACK BEARS.
BUT GRIZZLY ATTACKS ARE VERY RARE.
THEY HAPPEN WHEN A GRIZZLY FEELS SURPRISED OR THREATENED.
AND THIS BEAR WOULD BE VERY SURPRISED—AND FEEL VERY THREATENED—
—WHEN IT WOKE UP AND SAW US STANDING THERE.
HOW COME IT HASN'T HEARD US?
MEL . . .
THAT BEAR IS DEAD.
"LET'S GO SEE."

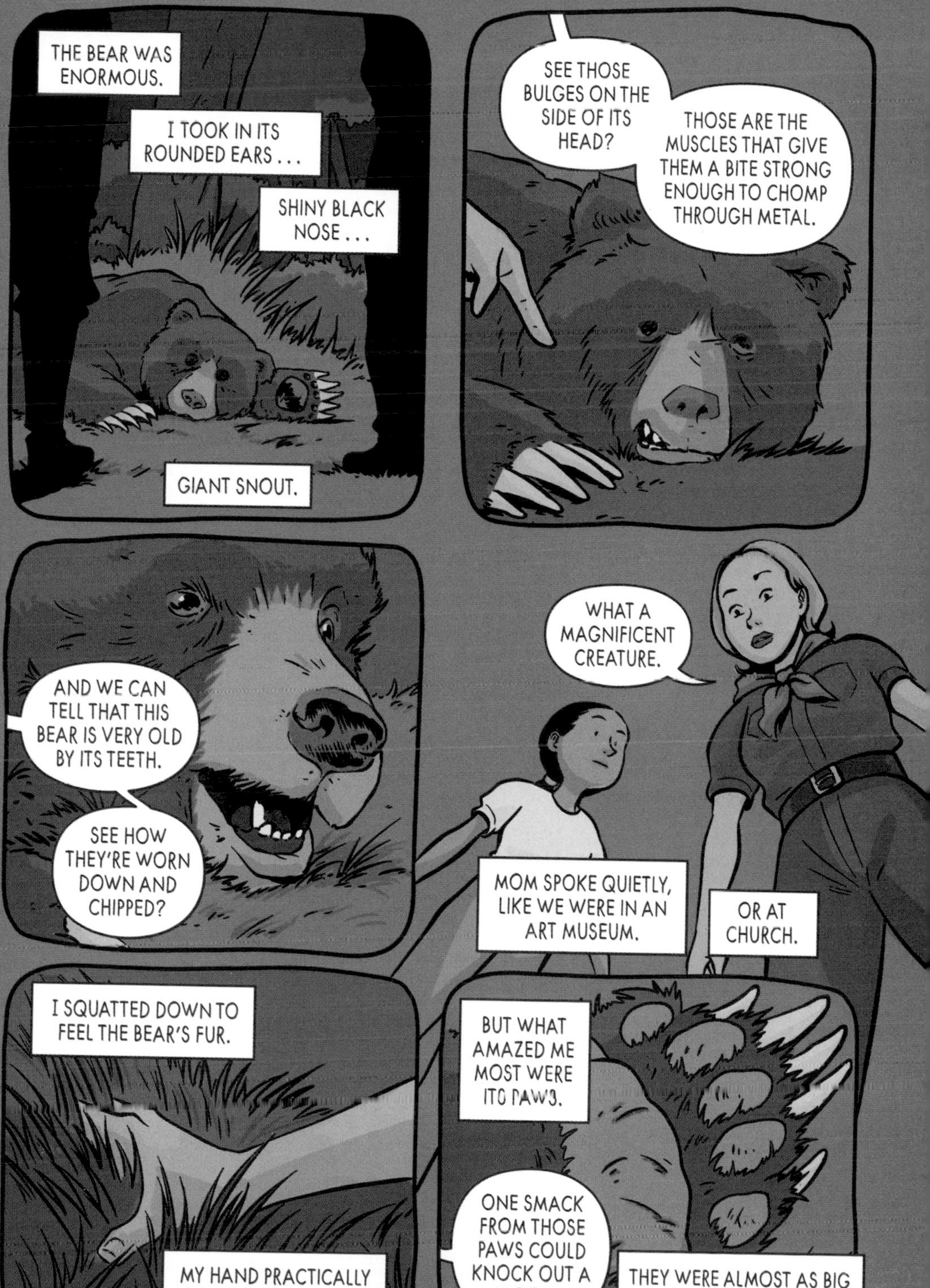
THE BEAR WAS ENORMOUS.
I TOOK IN ITS ROUNDED EARS . . .
SHINY BLACK NOSE . . .
GIANT SNOUT.
SEE THOSE BULGES ON THE SIDE OF ITS HEAD?
THOSE ARE THE MUSCLES THAT GIVE THEM A BITE STRONG ENOUGH TO CHOMP THROUGH METAL.
AND WE CAN TELL THAT THIS BEAR IS VERY OLD BY ITS TEETH.
SEE HOW THEY'RE WORN DOWN AND CHIPPED?
WHAT A MAGNIFICENT CREATURE.
MOM SPOKE QUIETLY, LIKE WE WERE IN AN ART MUSEUM.
OR AT CHURCH.
I SQUATTED DOWN TO FEEL THE BEAR'S FUR.
MY HAND PRACTICALLY DISAPPEARED INTO IT.
BUT WHAT AMAZED ME MOST WERE ITS PAWS.
ONE SMACK FROM THOSE PAWS COULD KNOCK OUT A MOOSE.
THEY WERE ALMOST AS BIG AS BASEBALL MITTS, WITH LONG, CURVED CLAWS.

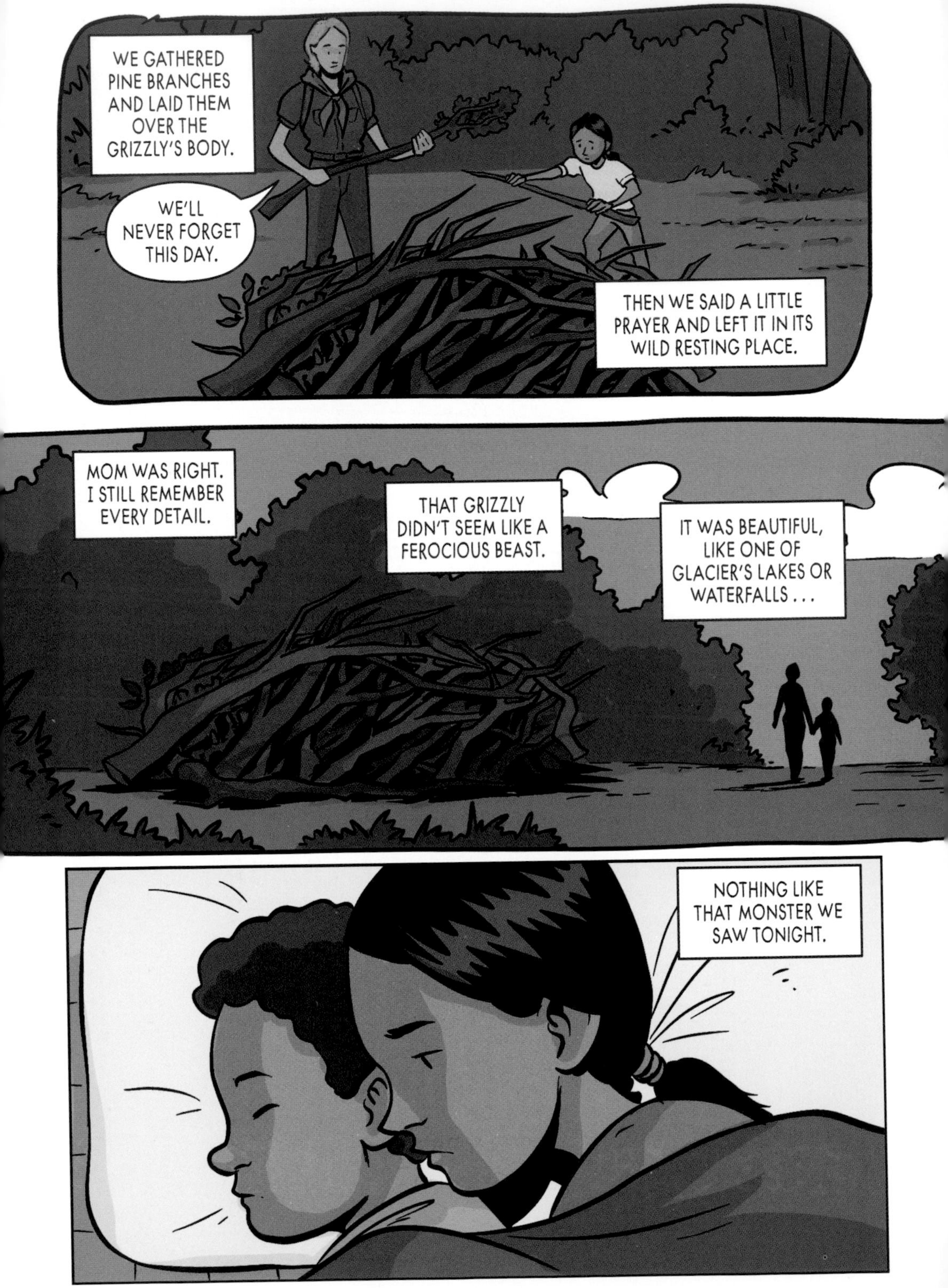
WE GATHERED PINE BRANCHES AND LAID THEM OVER THE GRIZZLY'S BODY.
WE'LL NEVER FORGET THIS DAY.
THEN WE SAID A LITTLE PRAYER AND LEFT IT IN ITS WILD RESTING PLACE.
MOM WAS RIGHT. I STILL REMEMBER EVERY DETAIL.
THAT GRIZZLY DIDN'T SEEM LIKE A FEROCIOUS BEAST.
IT WAS BEAUTIFUL, LIKE ONE OF GLACIER'S LAKES OR WATERFALLS . . .
NOTHING LIKE THAT MONSTER WE SAW TONIGHT.

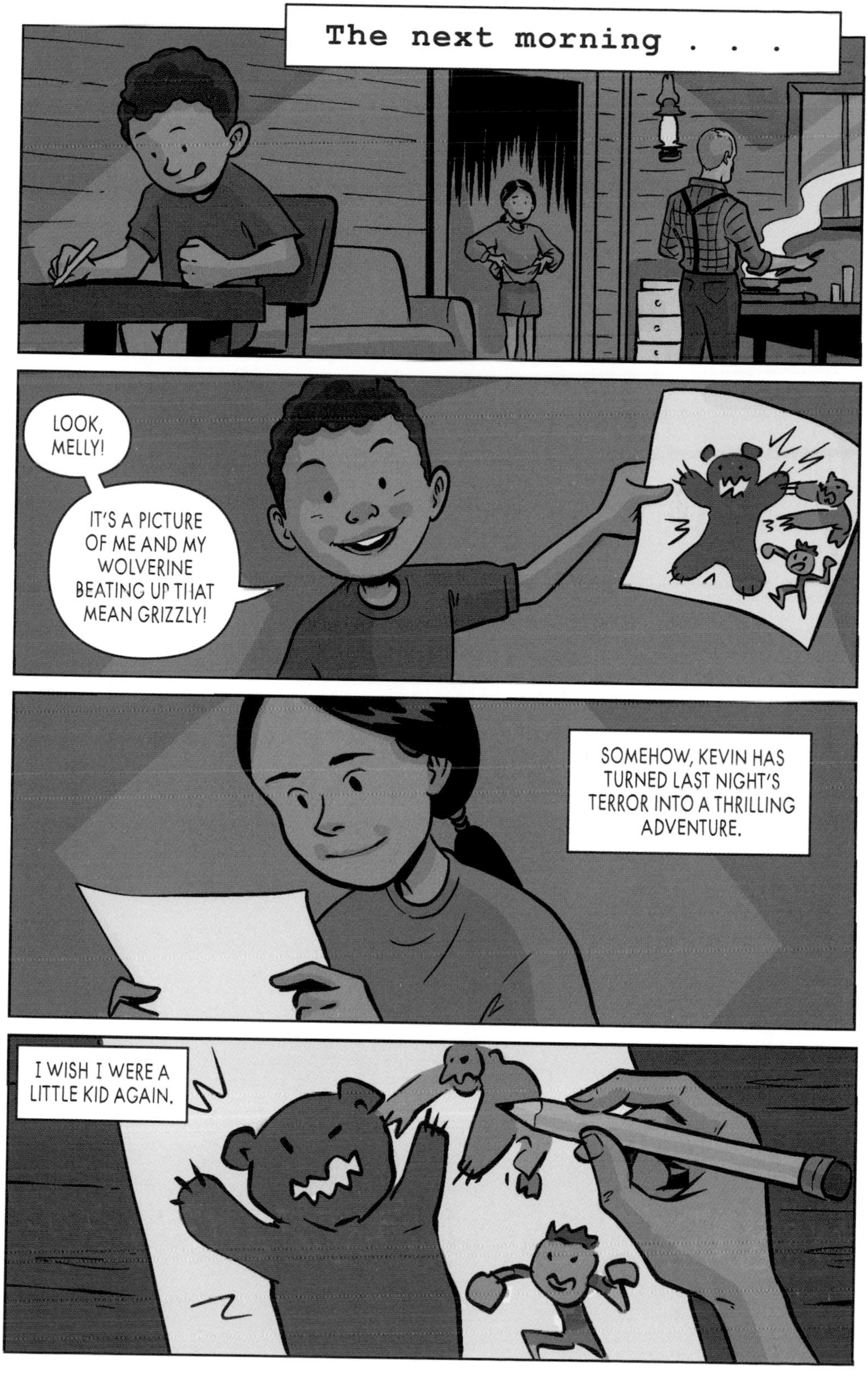
The next morning . . .
LOOK, MELLY!
IT'S A PICTURE OF ME AND MY WOLVERINE BEATING UP THAT MEAN GRIZZLY!
SOMEHOW, KEVIN HAS TURNED LAST NIGHT'S TERROR INTO A THRILLING ADVENTURE.
I WISH I WERE A LITTLE KID AGAIN.

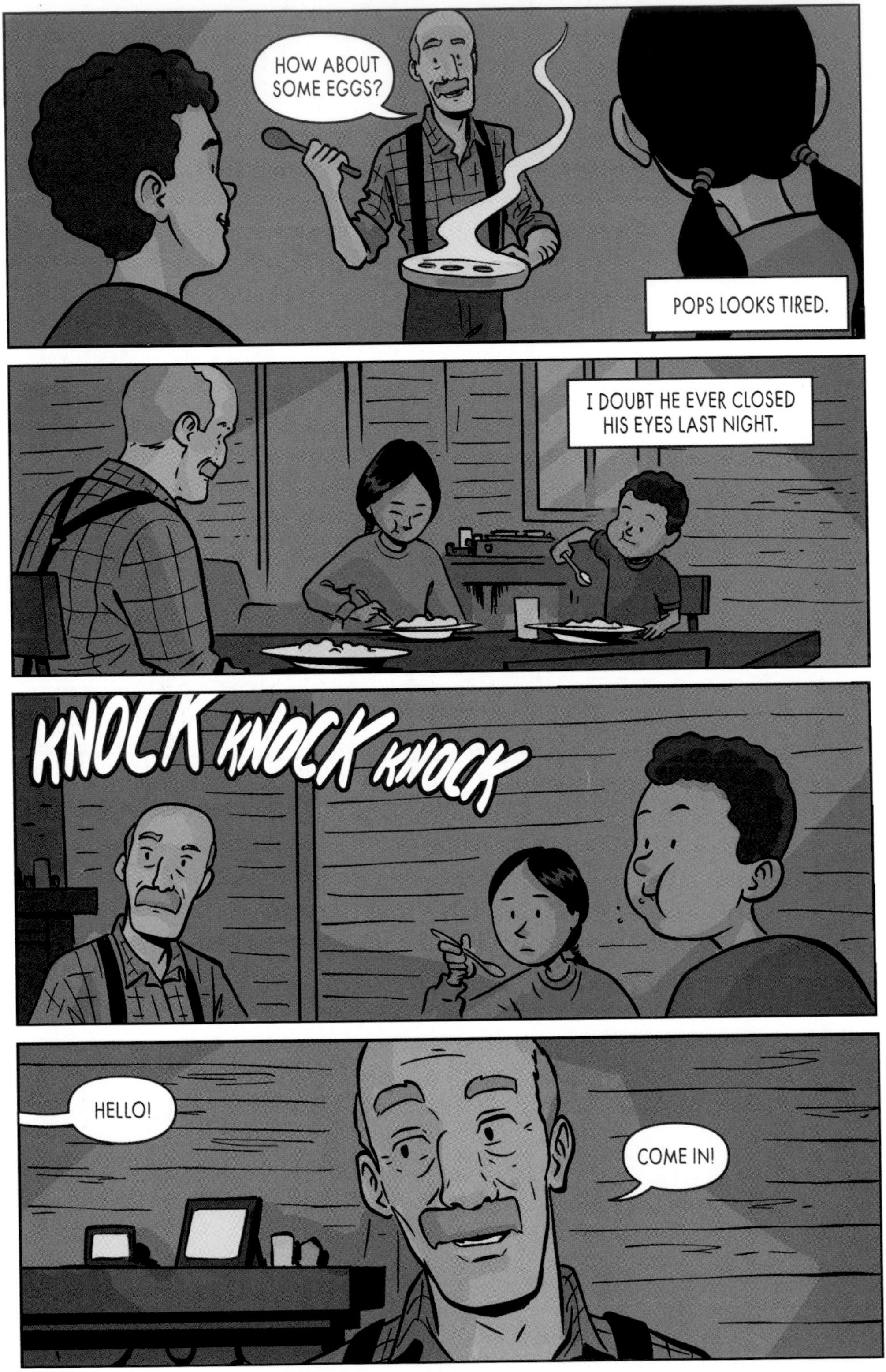
HOW ABOUT SOME EGGS?
POPS LOOKS TIRED.
I DOUBT HE EVER CLOSED HIS EYES LAST NIGHT.
KNOCK KNOCK KNOCK
HELLO!
COME IN!

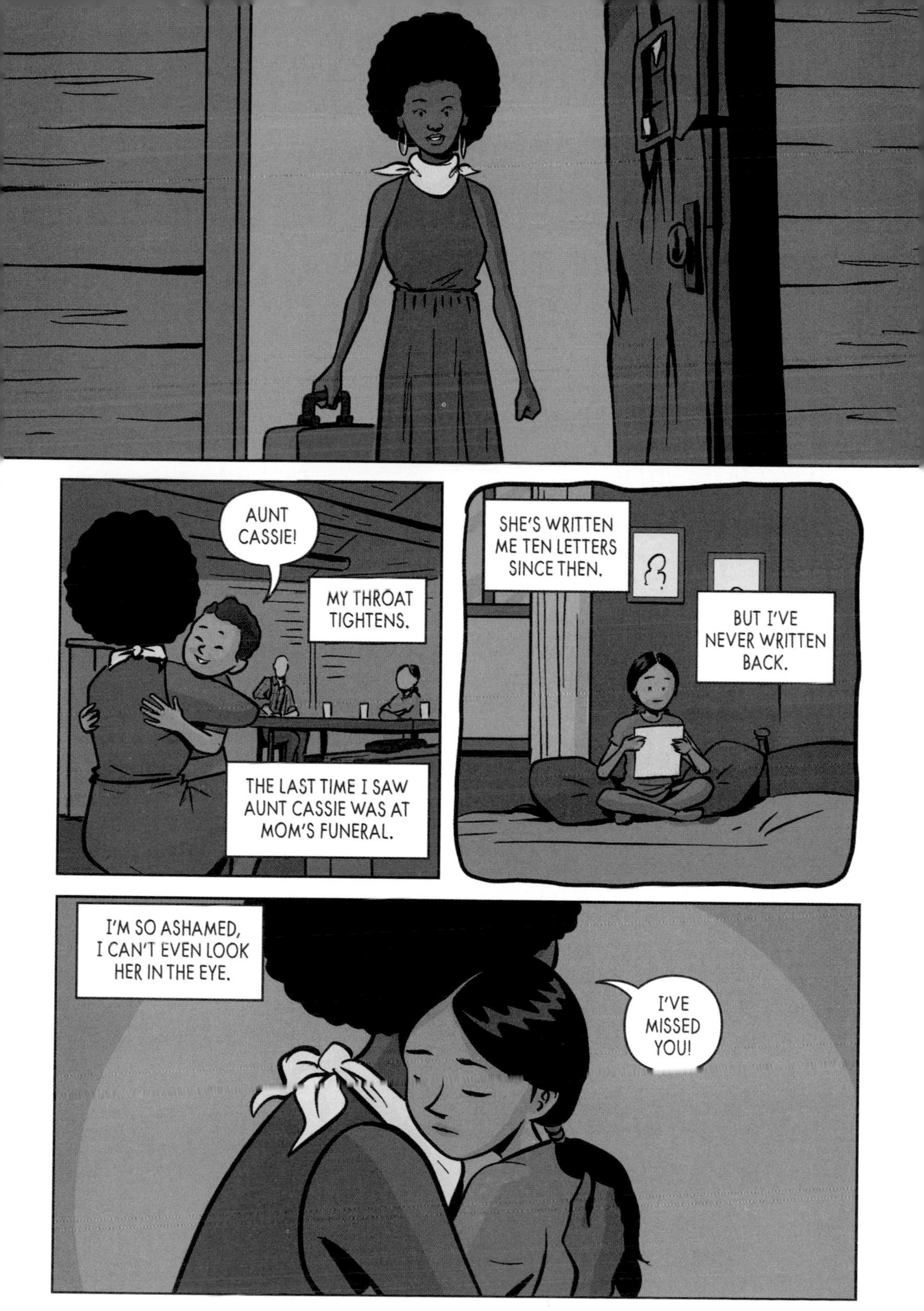
AUNT CASSIE!
MY THROAT TIGHTENS.
THE LAST TIME I SAW AUNT CASSIE WAS AT MOM'S FUNERAL.
SHE'S WRITTEN ME TEN LETTERS SINCE THEN.
BUT I'VE NEVER WRITTEN BACK.
I'M SO ASHAMED, I CAN'T EVEN LOOK HER IN THE EYE.
I'VE MISSED YOU!

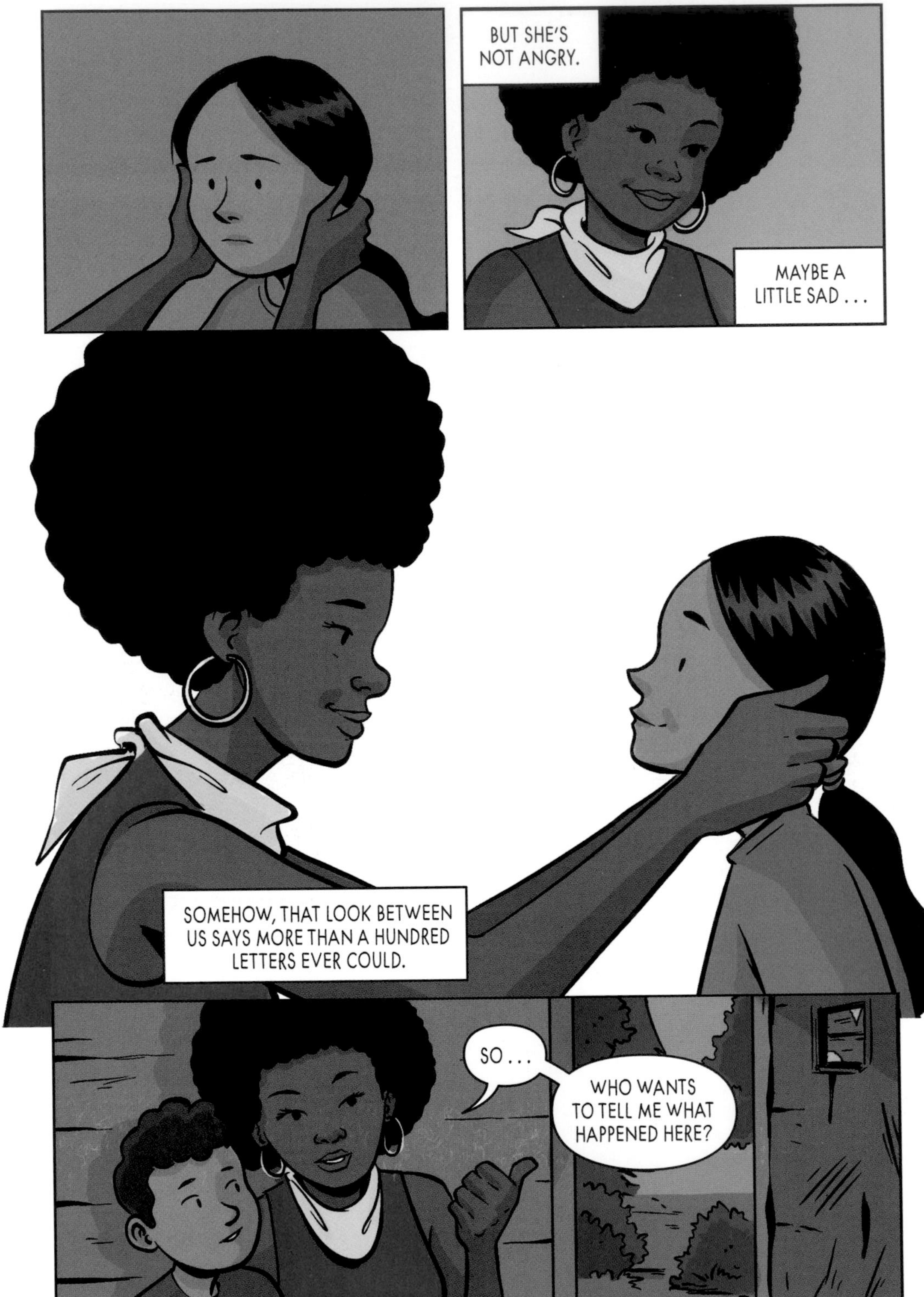
BUT SHE'S NOT ANGRY.
MAYBE A LITTLE SAD . . .
SOMEHOW, THAT LOOK BETWEEN US SAYS MORE THAN A HUNDRED LETTERS EVER COULD.
SO . . .
WHO WANTS TO TELL ME WHAT HAPPENED HERE?

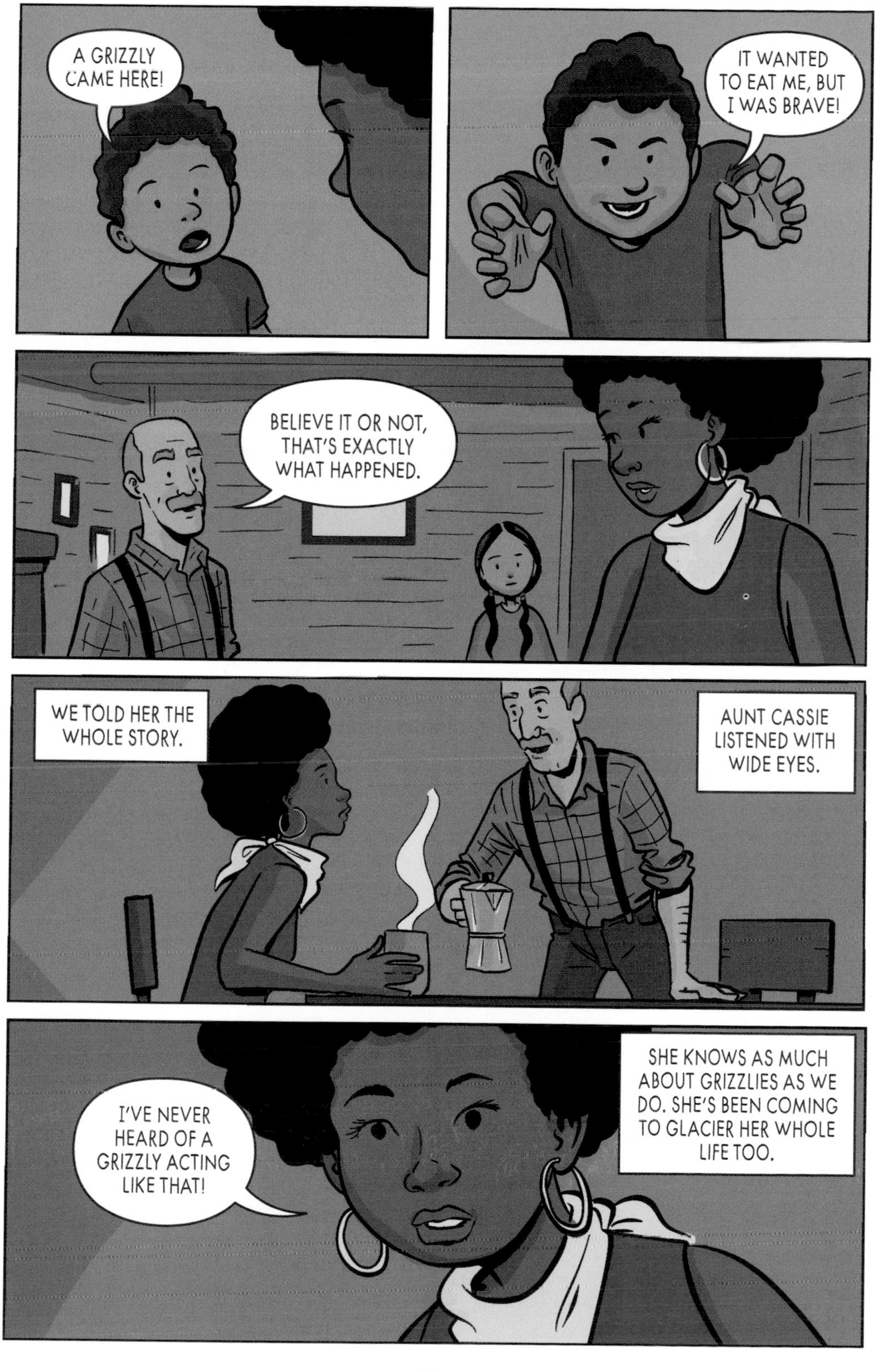
A GRIZZLY CAME HERE!
IT WANTED TO EAT ME, BUT I WAS BRAVE!
BELIEVE IT OR NOT, THAT'S EXACTLY WHAT HAPPENED.
WE TOLD HER THE WHOLE STORY.
AUNT CASSIE LISTENED WITH WIDE EYES.
SHE KNOWS AS MUCH ABOUT GRIZZLIES AS WE DO. SHE'S BEEN COMING TO GLACIER HER WHOLE LIFE TOO.
I'VE NEVER HEARD OF A GRIZZLY ACTING LIKE THAT!

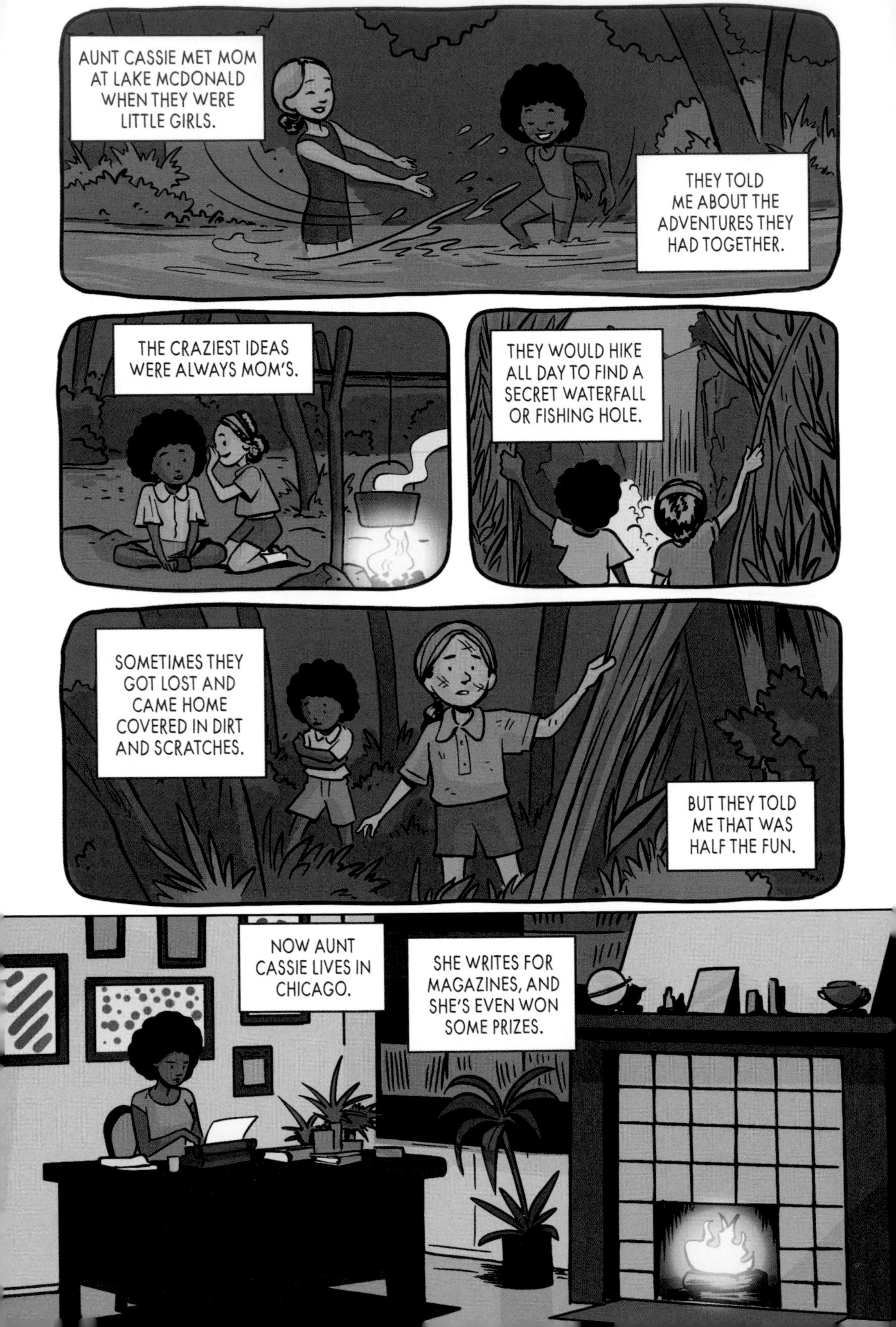
AUNT CASSIE MET MOM AT LAKE MCDONALD WHEN THEY WERE LITTLE GIRLS.
THEY TOLD ME ABOUT THE ADVENTURES THEY HAD TOGETHER.
THE CRAZIEST IDEAS WERE ALWAYS MOM'S.
THEY WOULD HIKE ALL DAY TO FIND A SECRET WATERFALL OR FISHING HOLE.
SOMETIMES THEY GOT LOST AND CAME HOME COVERED IN DIRT AND SCRATCHES.
BUT THEY TOLD ME THAT WAS HALF THE FUN.
NOW AUNT CASSIE LIVES IN CHICAGO.
SHE WRITES FOR MAGAZINES, AND SHE'S EVEN WON SOME PRIZES.

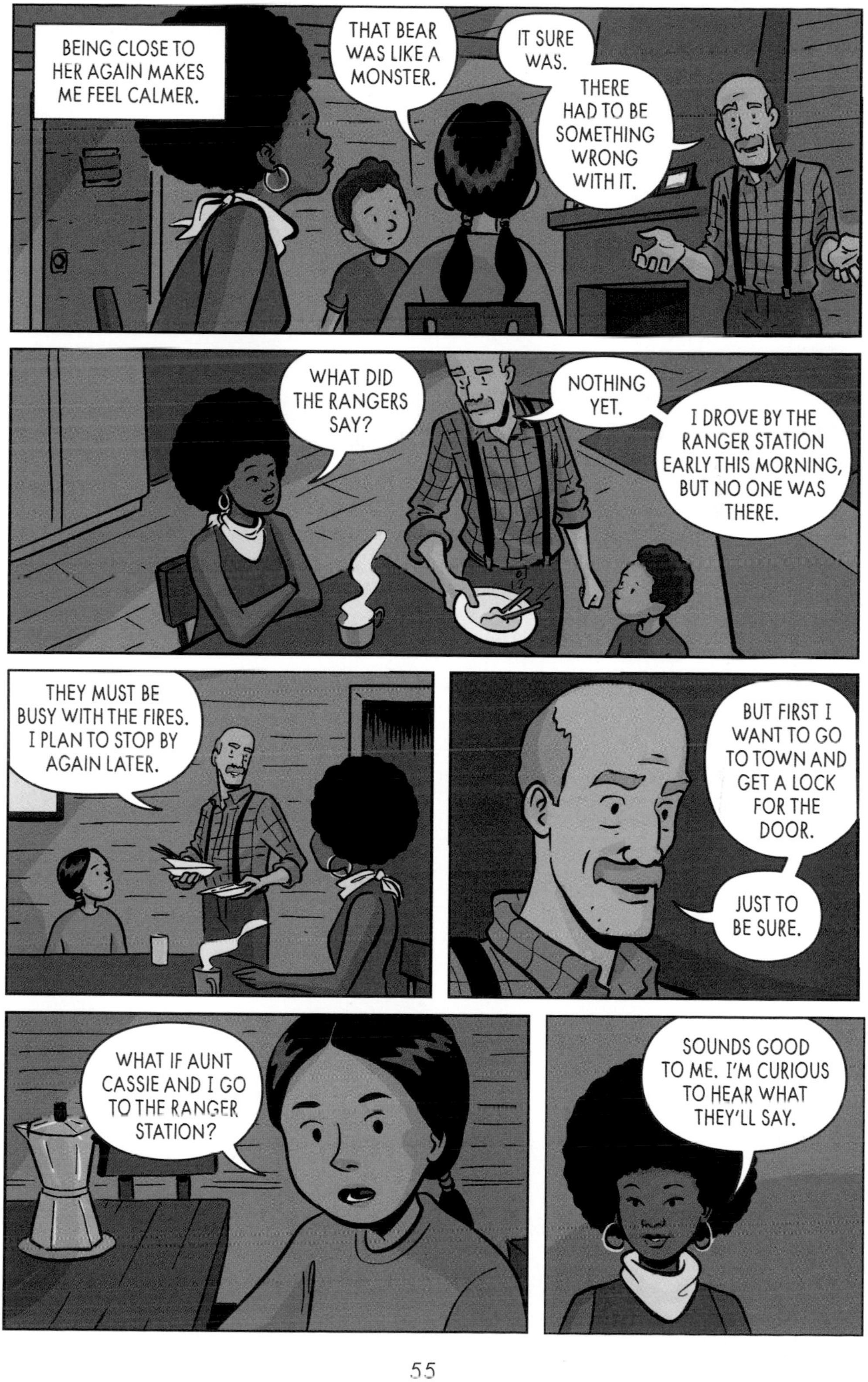
BEING CLOSE TO HER AGAIN MAKES ME FEEL CALMER.
THAT BEAR WAS LIKE A MONSTER.
IT SURE WAS.
THERE HAD TO BE SOMETHING WRONG WITH IT.
WHAT DID THE RANGERS SAY?
NOTHING YET.
I DROVE BY THE RANGER STATION EARLY THIS MORNING, BUT NO ONE WAS THERE.
THEY MUST BE BUSY WITH THE FIRES. I PLAN TO STOP BY AGAIN LATER.
BUT FIRST I WANT TO GO TO TOWN AND GET A LOCK FOR THE DOOR.
JUST TO BE SURE.
WHAT IF AUNT CASSIE AND I GO TO THE RANGER STATION?
SOUNDS GOOD TO ME. I'M CURIOUS TO HEAR WHAT THEY'LL SAY.

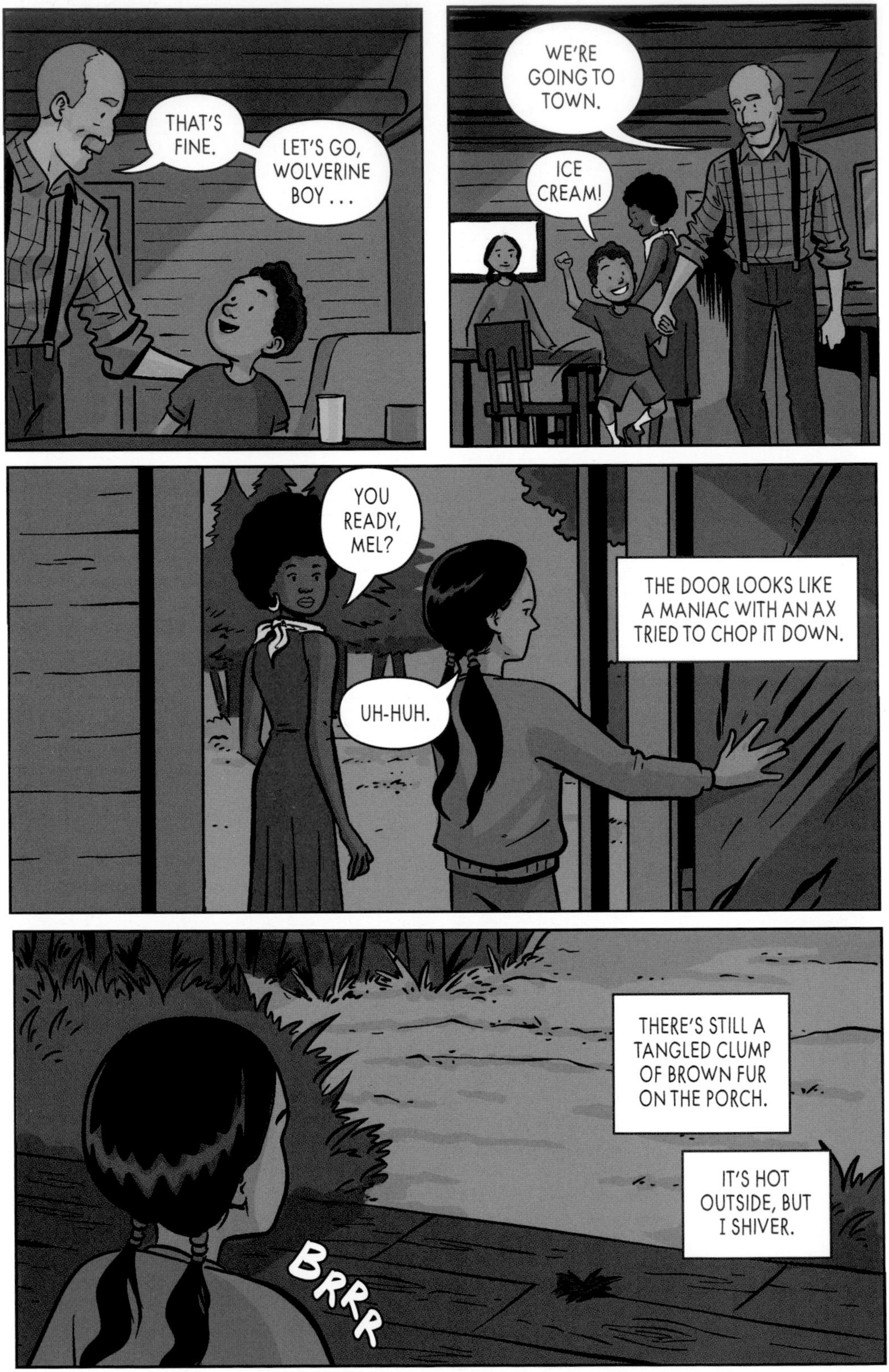
THAT'S FINE.
LET'S GO, WOLVERINE BOY . . .
WE'RE GOING TO TOWN.
ICE CREAM!
YOU READY, MEL?
UH-HUH.
THE DOOR LOOKS LIKE A MANIAC WITH AN AX TRIED TO CHOP IT DOWN.
THERE'S STILL A TANGLED CLUMP OF BROWN FUR ON THE PORCH.
IT'S HOT OUTSIDE, BUT I SHIVER.
BRRR

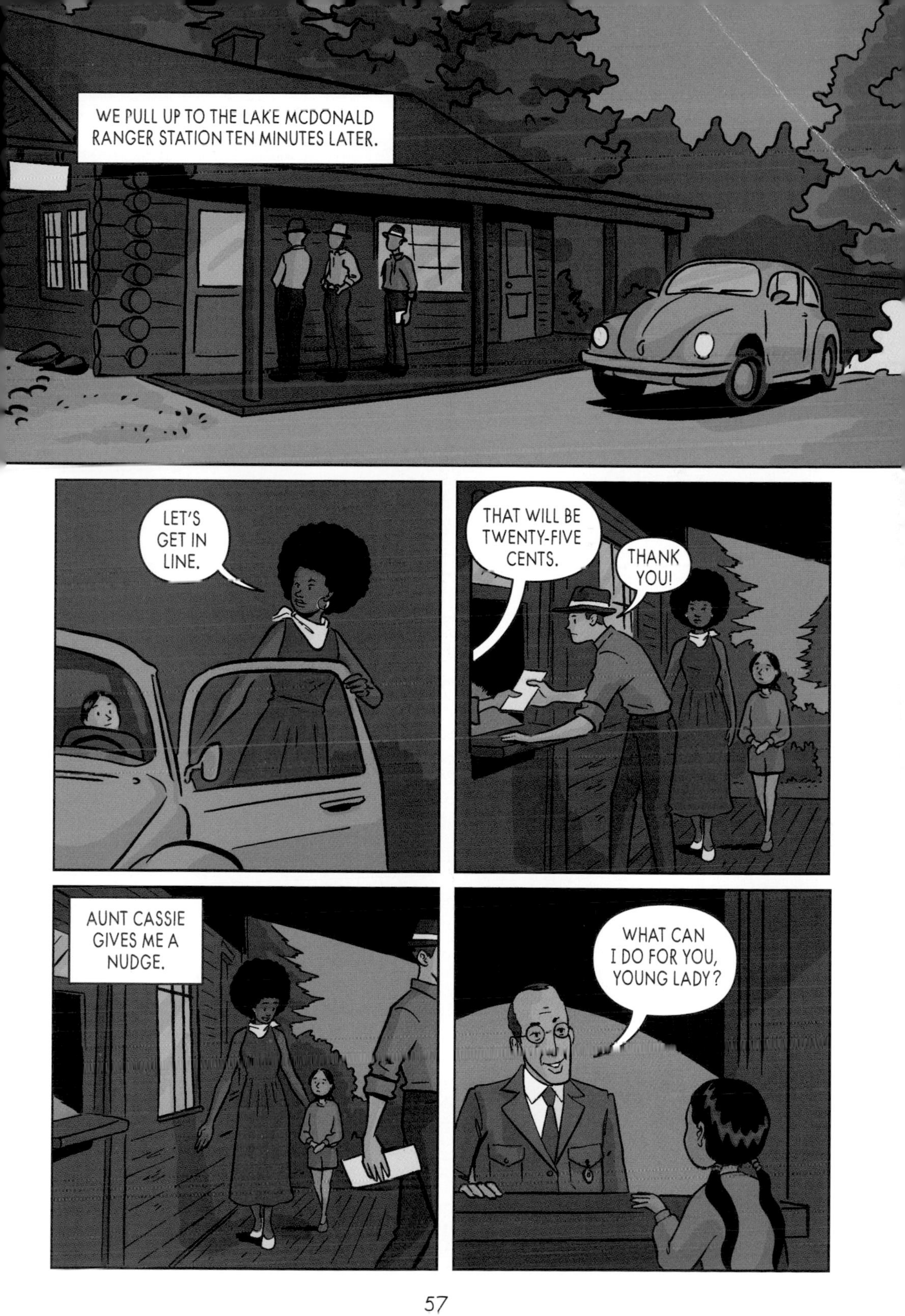
WE PULL UP TO THE LAKE MCDONALD RANGER STATION TEN MINUTES LATER.
LET'S GET IN LINE.
THAT WILL BE TWENTY-FIVE CENTS.
THANK YOU!
AUNT CASSIE GIVES ME A NUDGE.
WHAT CAN I DO FOR YOU, YOUNG LADY?

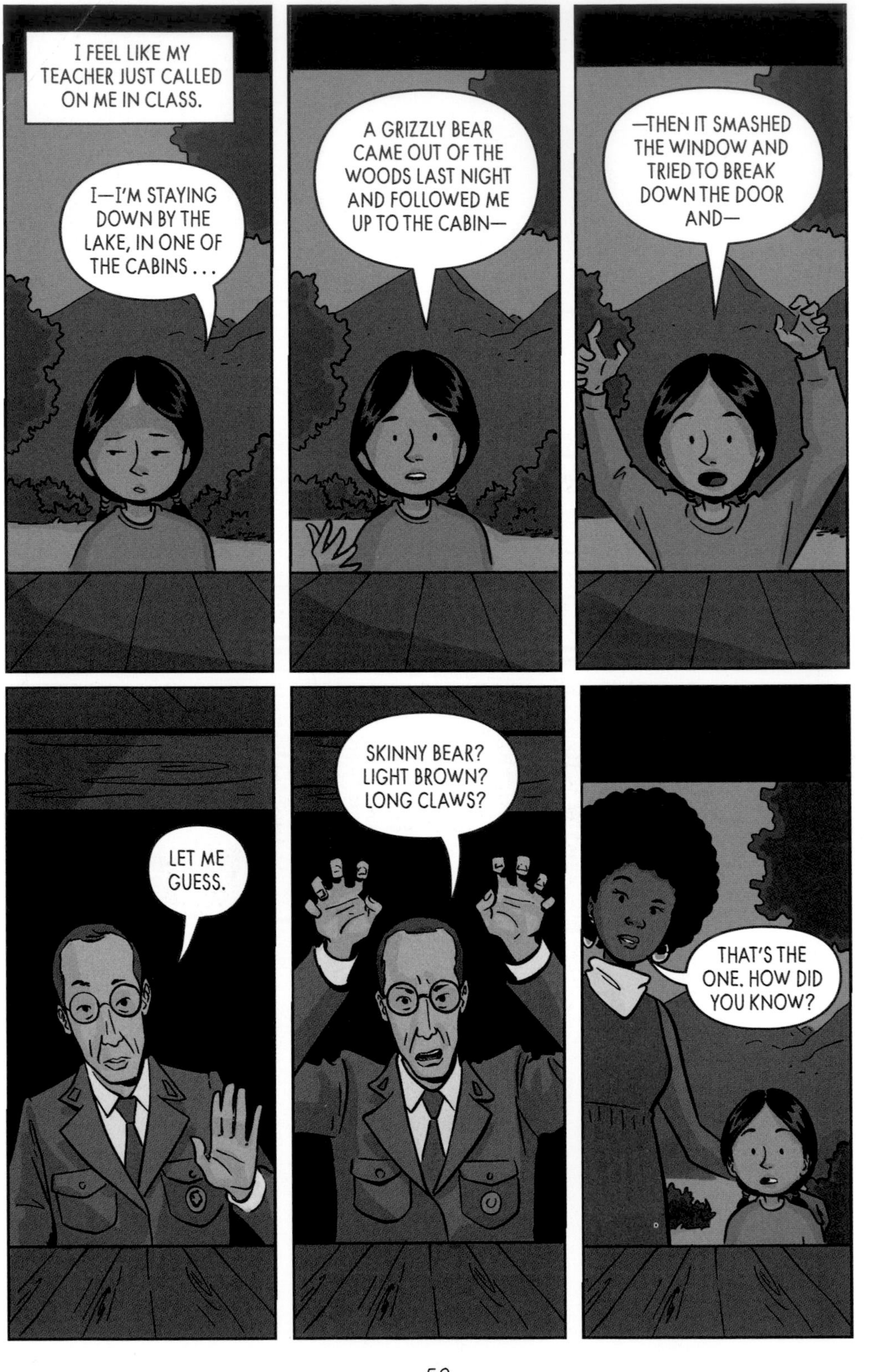
I FEEL LIKE MY TEACHER JUST CALLED ON ME IN CLASS.
I—I'M STAYING DOWN BY THE LAKE, IN ONE OF THE CABINS . . .
A GRIZZLY BEAR CAME OUT OF THE WOODS LAST NIGHT AND FOLLOWED ME UP TO THE CABIN—
—THEN IT SMASHED THE WINDOW AND TRIED TO BREAK DOWN THE DOOR AND—
LET ME GUESS.
SKINNY BEAR? LIGHT BROWN? LONG CLAWS?
THAT'S THE ONE. HOW DID YOU KNOW?

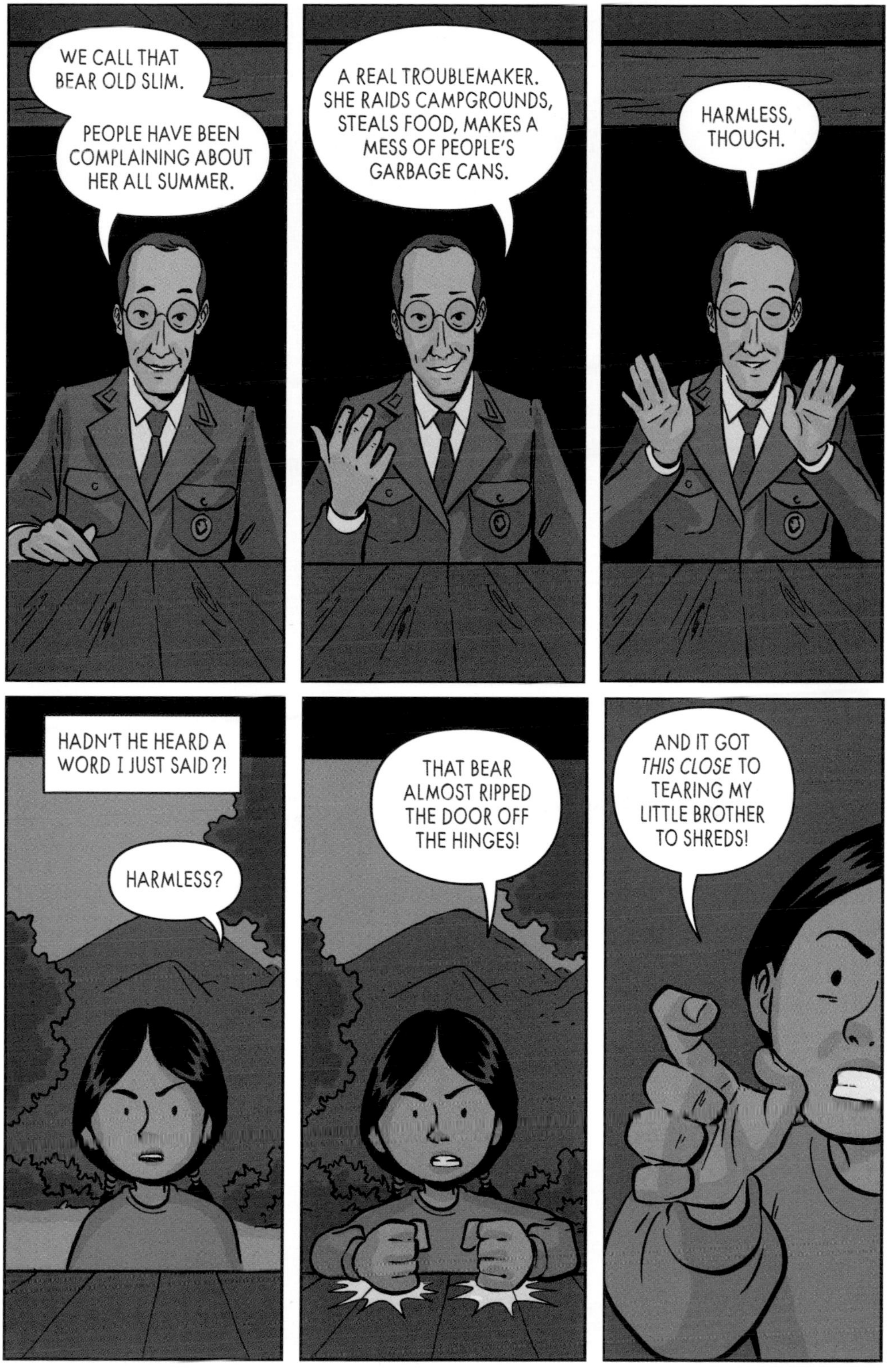
WE CALL THAT BEAR OLD SLIM.
PEOPLE HAVE BEEN COMPLAINING ABOUT HER ALL SUMMER.
A REAL TROUBLEMAKER. SHE RAIDS CAMPGROUNDS, STEALS FOOD, MAKES A MESS OF PEOPLE'S GARBAGE CANS.
HARMLESS, THOUGH.
HADN'T HE HEARD A WORD I JUST SAID?!
HARMLESS?
THAT BEAR ALMOST RIPPED THE DOOR OFF THE HINGES!
AND IT GOT *THIS CLOSE* TO TEARING MY LITTLE BROTHER TO SHREDS!

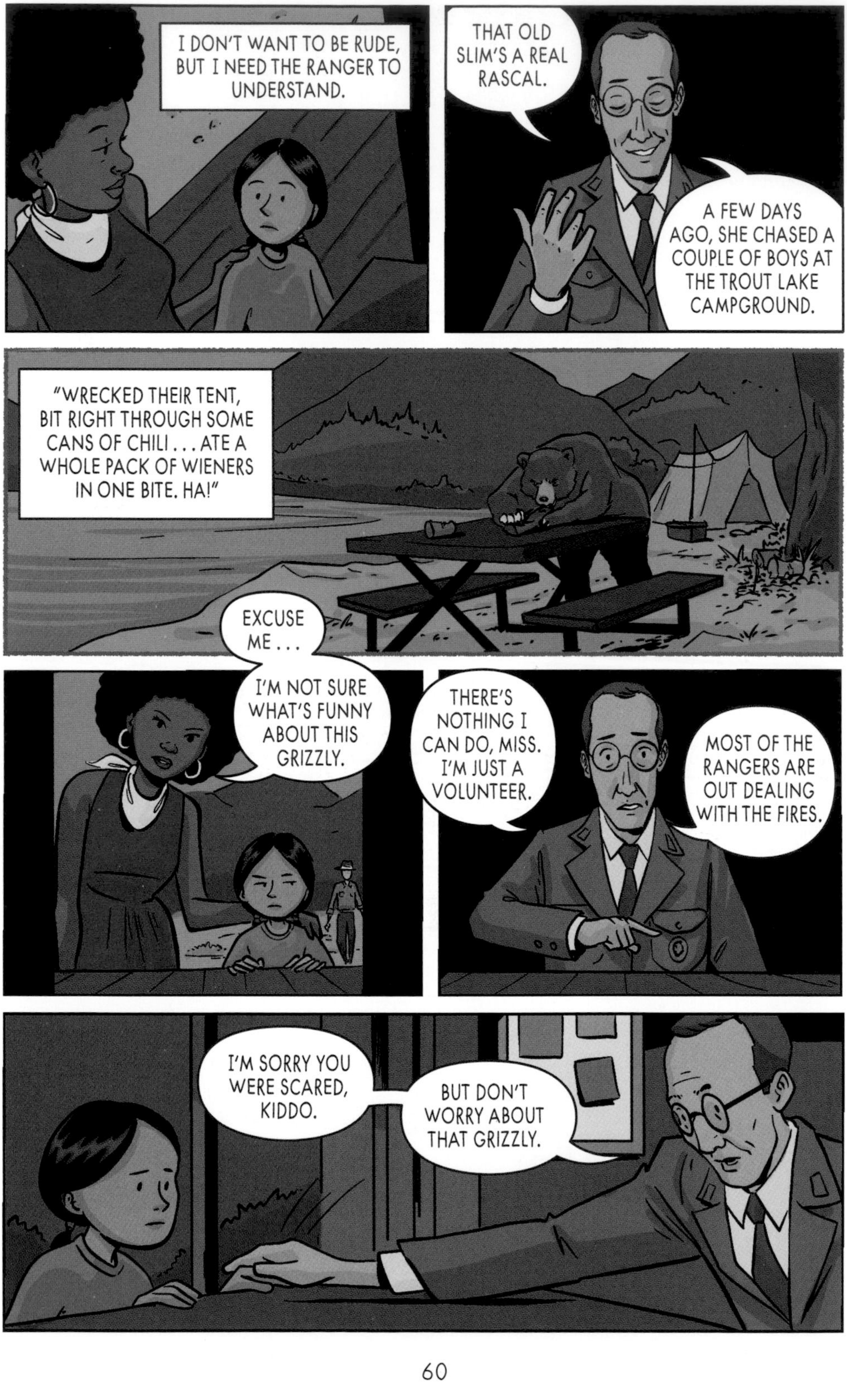
I DON'T WANT TO BE RUDE, BUT I NEED THE RANGER TO UNDERSTAND.
THAT OLD SLIM'S A REAL RASCAL.
A FEW DAYS AGO, SHE CHASED A COUPLE OF BOYS AT THE TROUT LAKE CAMPGROUND.
"WRECKED THEIR TENT, BIT RIGHT THROUGH SOME CANS OF CHILI . . . ATE A WHOLE PACK OF WIENERS IN ONE BITE. HA!"
EXCUSE ME . . .
I'M NOT SURE WHAT'S FUNNY ABOUT THIS GRIZZLY.
THERE'S NOTHING I CAN DO, MISS. I'M JUST A VOLUNTEER.
MOST OF THE RANGERS ARE OUT DEALING WITH THE FIRES.
I'M SORRY YOU WERE SCARED, KIDDO.
BUT DON'T WORRY ABOUT THAT GRIZZLY.

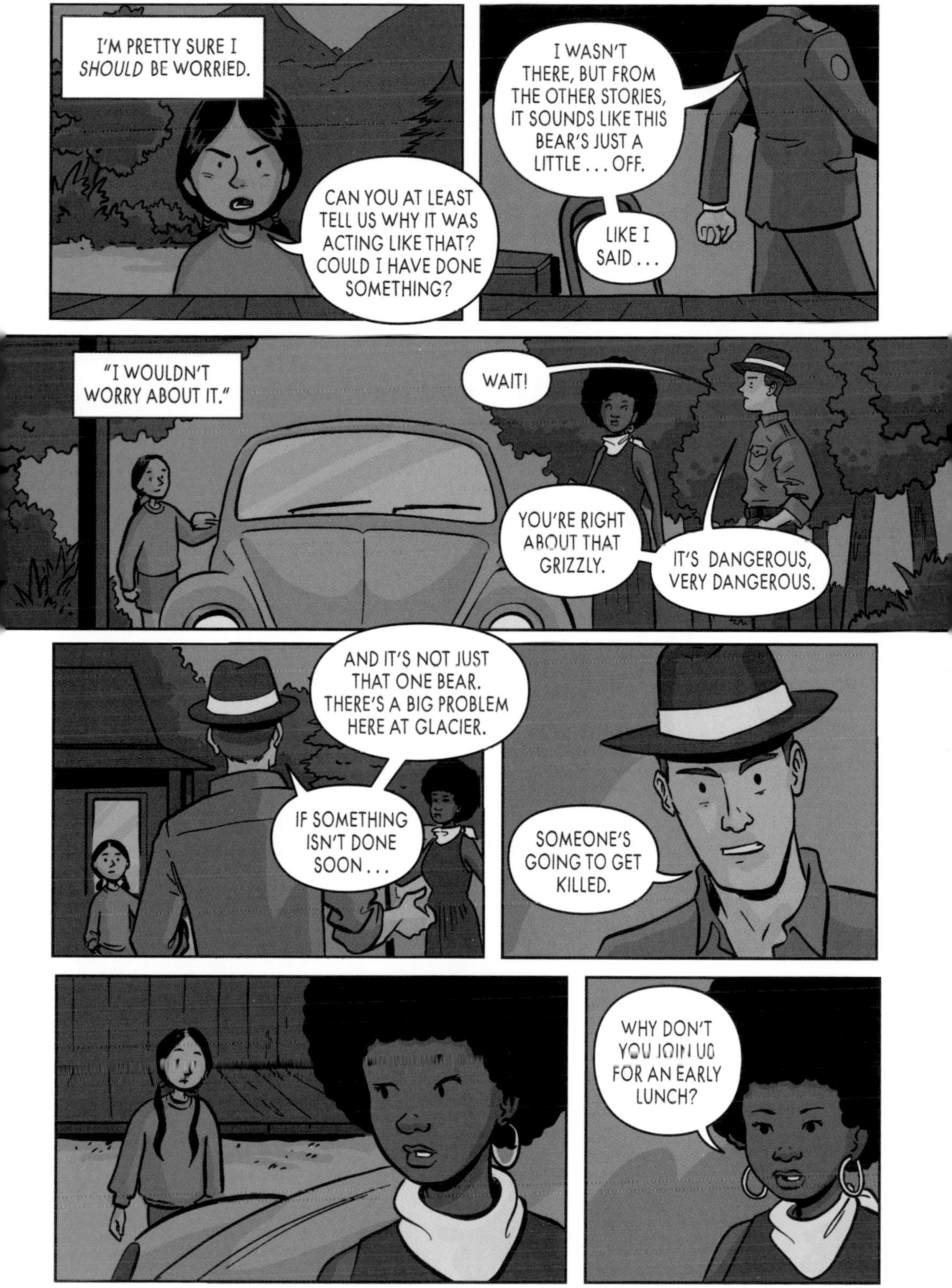
I'M PRETTY SURE I *SHOULD* BE WORRIED.
CAN YOU AT LEAST TELL US WHY IT WAS ACTING LIKE THAT? COULD I HAVE DONE SOMETHING?
I WASN'T THERE, BUT FROM THE OTHER STORIES, IT SOUNDS LIKE THIS BEAR'S JUST A LITTLE . . . OFF.
LIKE I SAID . . .
"I WOULDN'T WORRY ABOUT IT."
WAIT!
YOU'RE RIGHT ABOUT THAT GRIZZLY.
IT'S DANGEROUS, VERY DANGEROUS.
AND IT'S NOT JUST THAT ONE BEAR. THERE'S A BIG PROBLEM HERE AT GLACIER.
IF SOMETHING ISN'T DONE SOON . . .
SOMEONE'S GOING TO GET KILLED.
WHY DON'T YOU JOIN US FOR AN EARLY LUNCH?

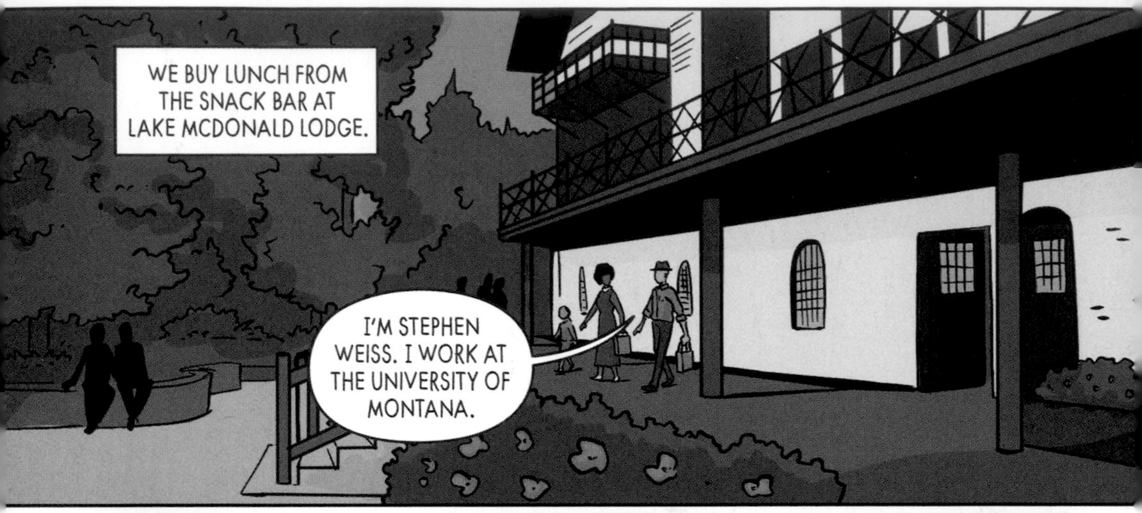
WE BUY LUNCH FROM THE SNACK BAR AT LAKE MCDONALD LODGE.
I'M STEPHEN WEISS. I WORK AT THE UNIVERSITY OF MONTANA.

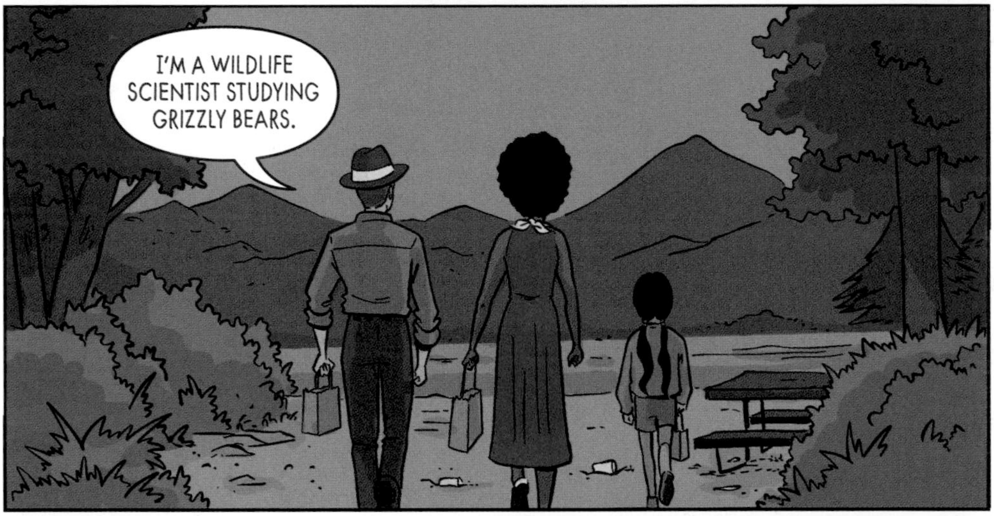
I'M A WILDLIFE SCIENTIST STUDYING GRIZZLY BEARS.

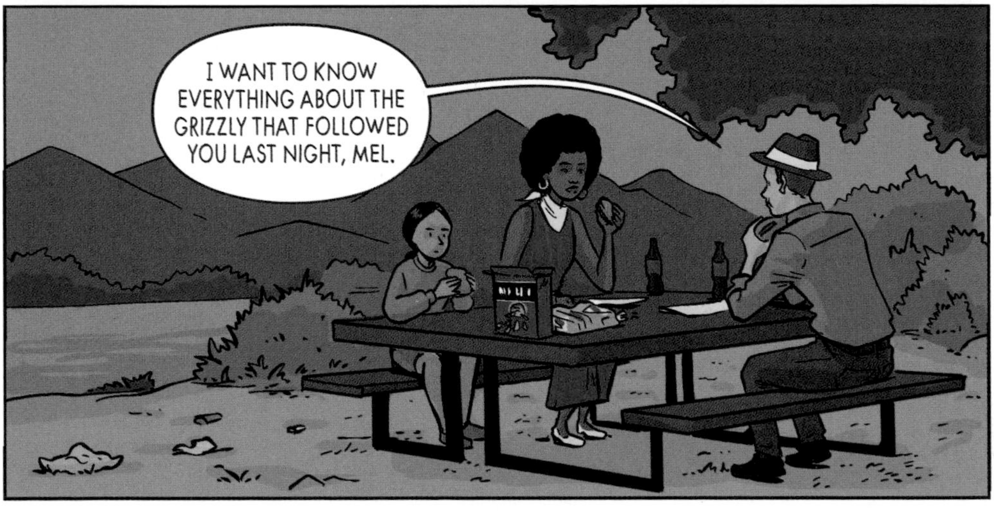
I WANT TO KNOW EVERYTHING ABOUT THE GRIZZLY THAT FOLLOWED YOU LAST NIGHT, MEL.

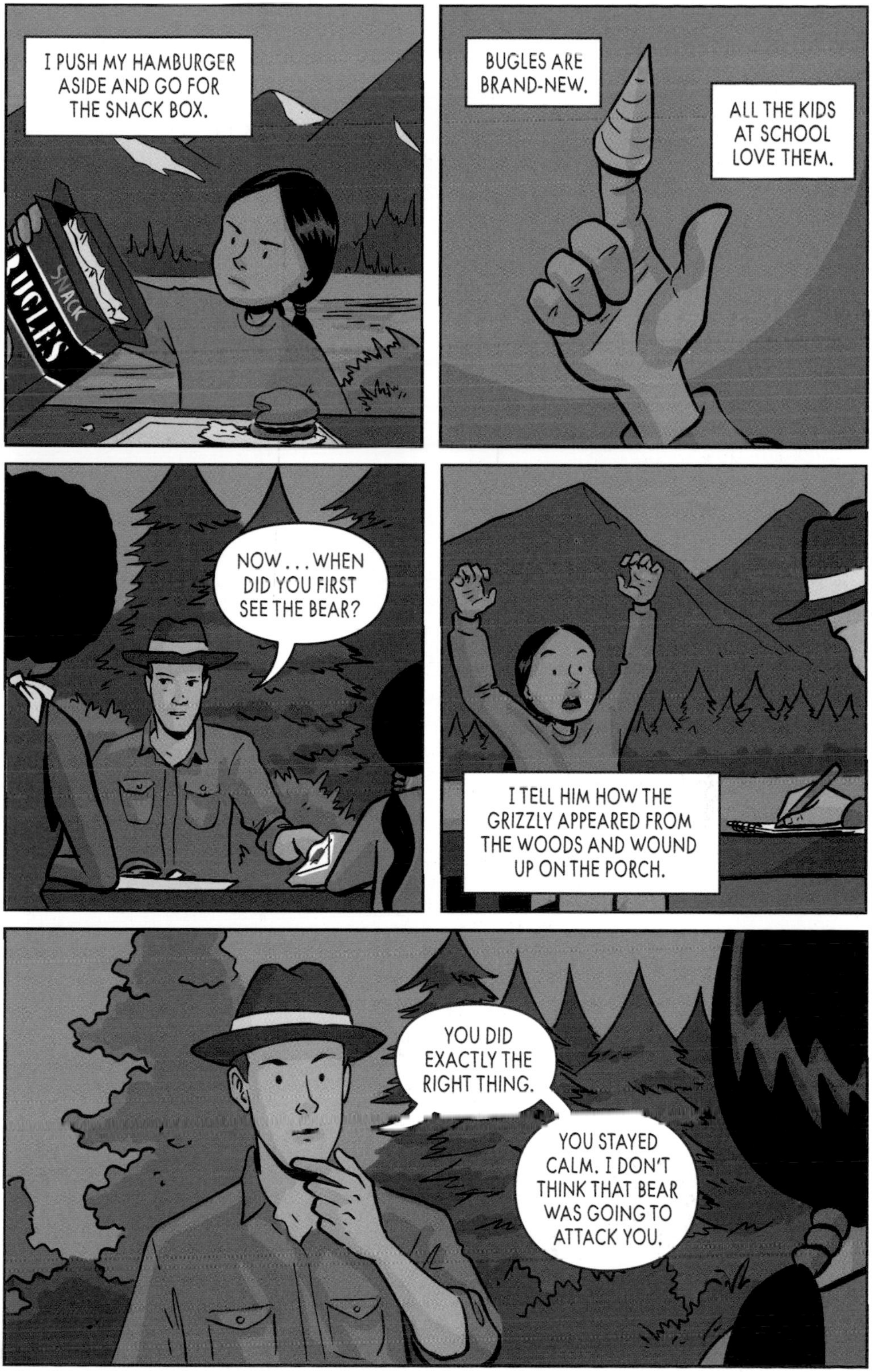
I PUSH MY HAMBURGER ASIDE AND GO FOR THE SNACK BOX.
BUGLES
SNACK
BUGLES ARE BRAND-NEW.
ALL THE KIDS AT SCHOOL LOVE THEM.
NOW . . . WHEN DID YOU FIRST SEE THE BEAR?
I TELL HIM HOW THE GRIZZLY APPEARED FROM THE WOODS AND WOUND UP ON THE PORCH.
YOU DID EXACTLY THE RIGHT THING.
YOU STAYED CALM. I DON'T THINK THAT BEAR WAS GOING TO ATTACK YOU.

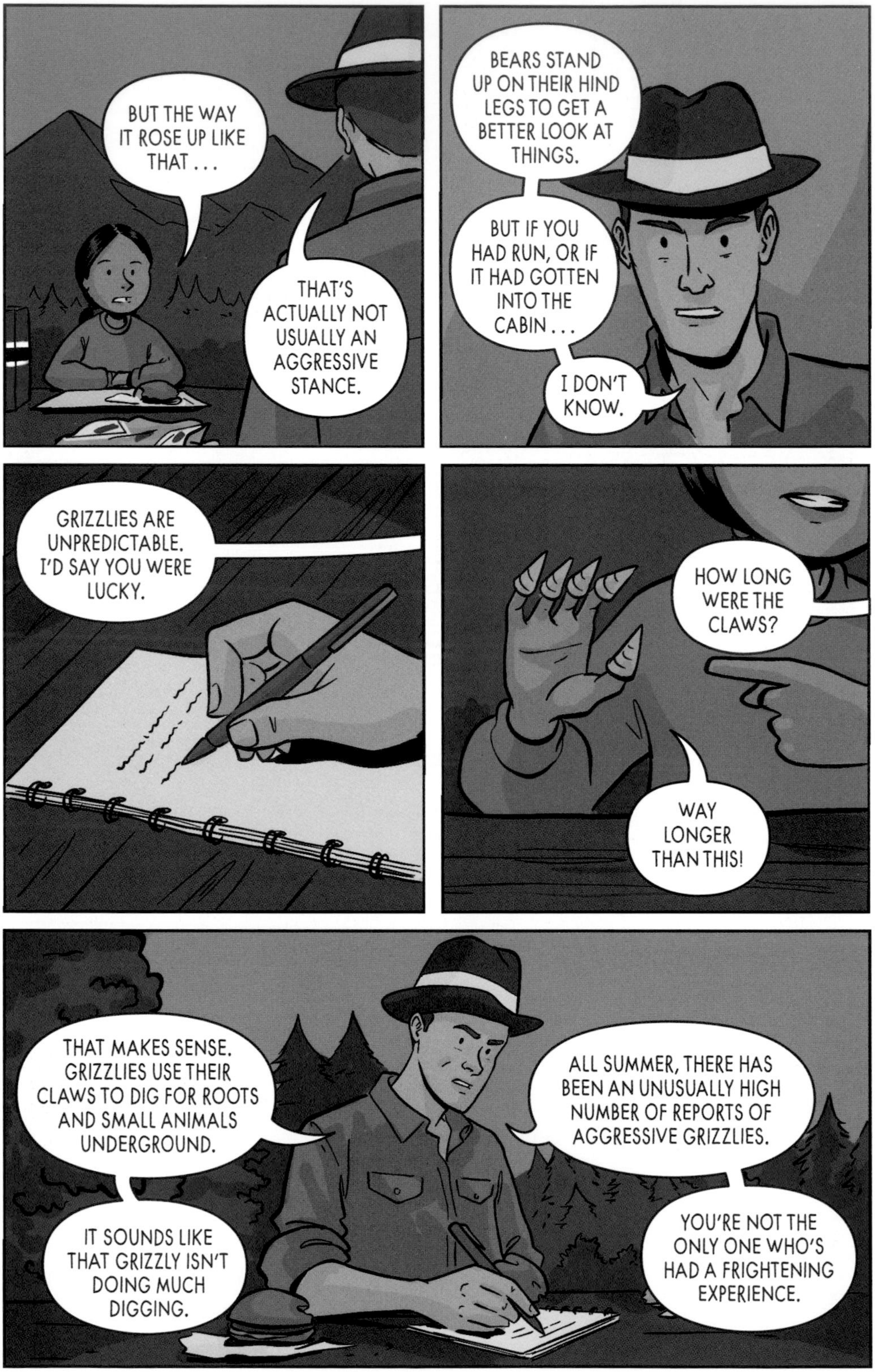
BUT THE WAY IT ROSE UP LIKE THAT . . .
THAT'S ACTUALLY NOT USUALLY AN AGGRESSIVE STANCE.
BEARS STAND UP ON THEIR HIND LEGS TO GET A BETTER LOOK AT THINGS.
BUT IF YOU HAD RUN, OR IF IT HAD GOTTEN INTO THE CABIN . . .
I DON'T KNOW.
GRIZZLIES ARE UNPREDICTABLE. I'D SAY YOU WERE LUCKY.
HOW LONG WERE THE CLAWS?
WAY LONGER THAN THIS!
THAT MAKES SENSE. GRIZZLIES USE THEIR CLAWS TO DIG FOR ROOTS AND SMALL ANIMALS UNDERGROUND.
IT SOUNDS LIKE THAT GRIZZLY ISN'T DOING MUCH DIGGING.
ALL SUMMER, THERE HAS BEEN AN UNUSUALLY HIGH NUMBER OF REPORTS OF AGGRESSIVE GRIZZLIES.
YOU'RE NOT THE ONLY ONE WHO'S HAD A FRIGHTENING EXPERIENCE.

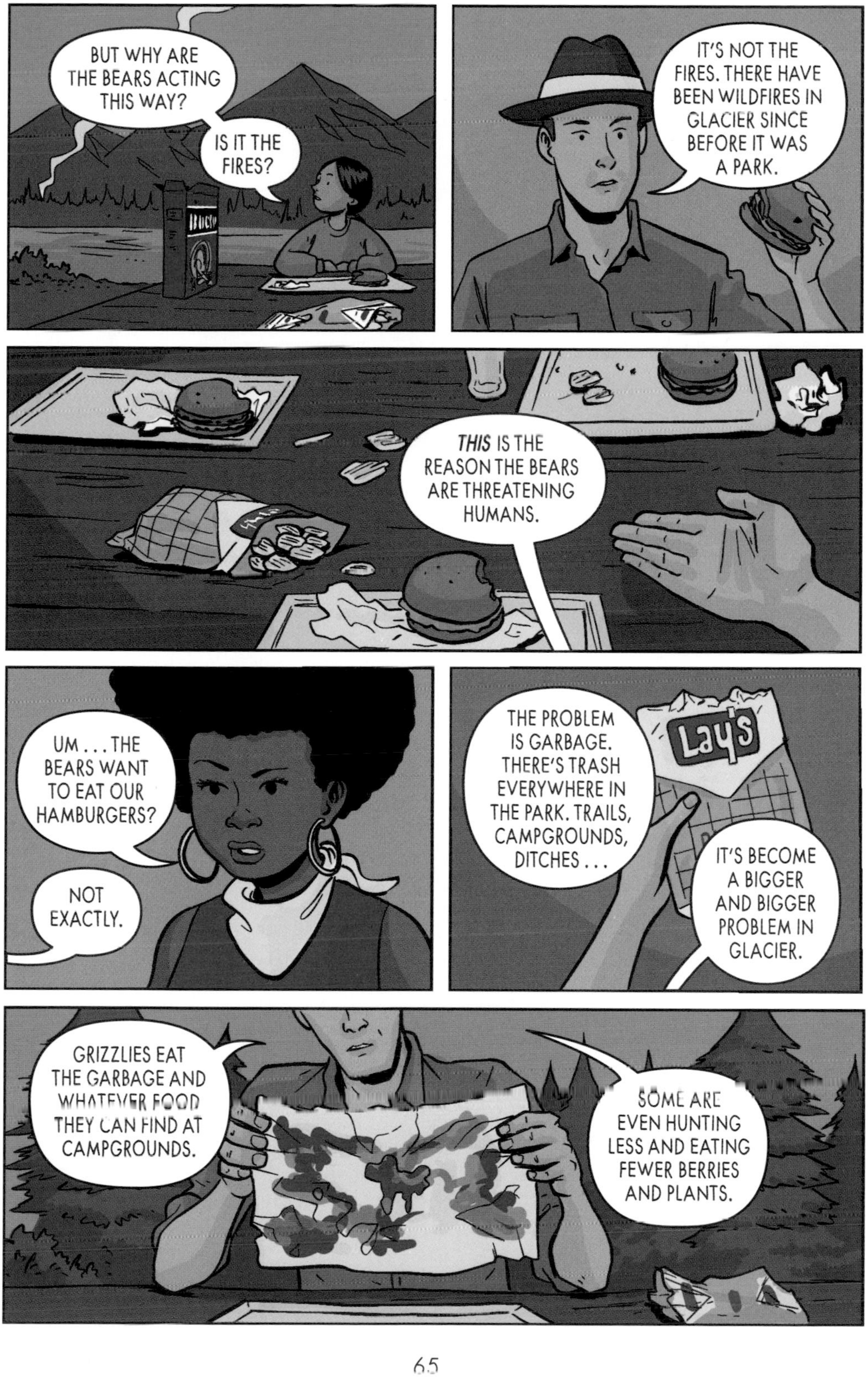
BUT WHY ARE THE BEARS ACTING THIS WAY?
IS IT THE FIRES?
IT'S NOT THE FIRES. THERE HAVE BEEN WILDFIRES IN GLACIER SINCE BEFORE IT WAS A PARK.
THIS IS THE REASON THE BEARS ARE THREATENING HUMANS.
UM . . . THE BEARS WANT TO EAT OUR HAMBURGERS?
NOT EXACTLY.
THE PROBLEM IS GARBAGE. THERE'S TRASH EVERYWHERE IN THE PARK. TRAILS, CAMPGROUNDS, DITCHES . . .
Lay's
IT'S BECOME A BIGGER AND BIGGER PROBLEM IN GLACIER.
GRIZZLIES EAT THE GARBAGE AND WHATEVER FOOD THEY CAN FIND AT CAMPGROUNDS.
SOME ARE EVEN HUNTING LESS AND EATING FEWER BERRIES AND PLANTS.

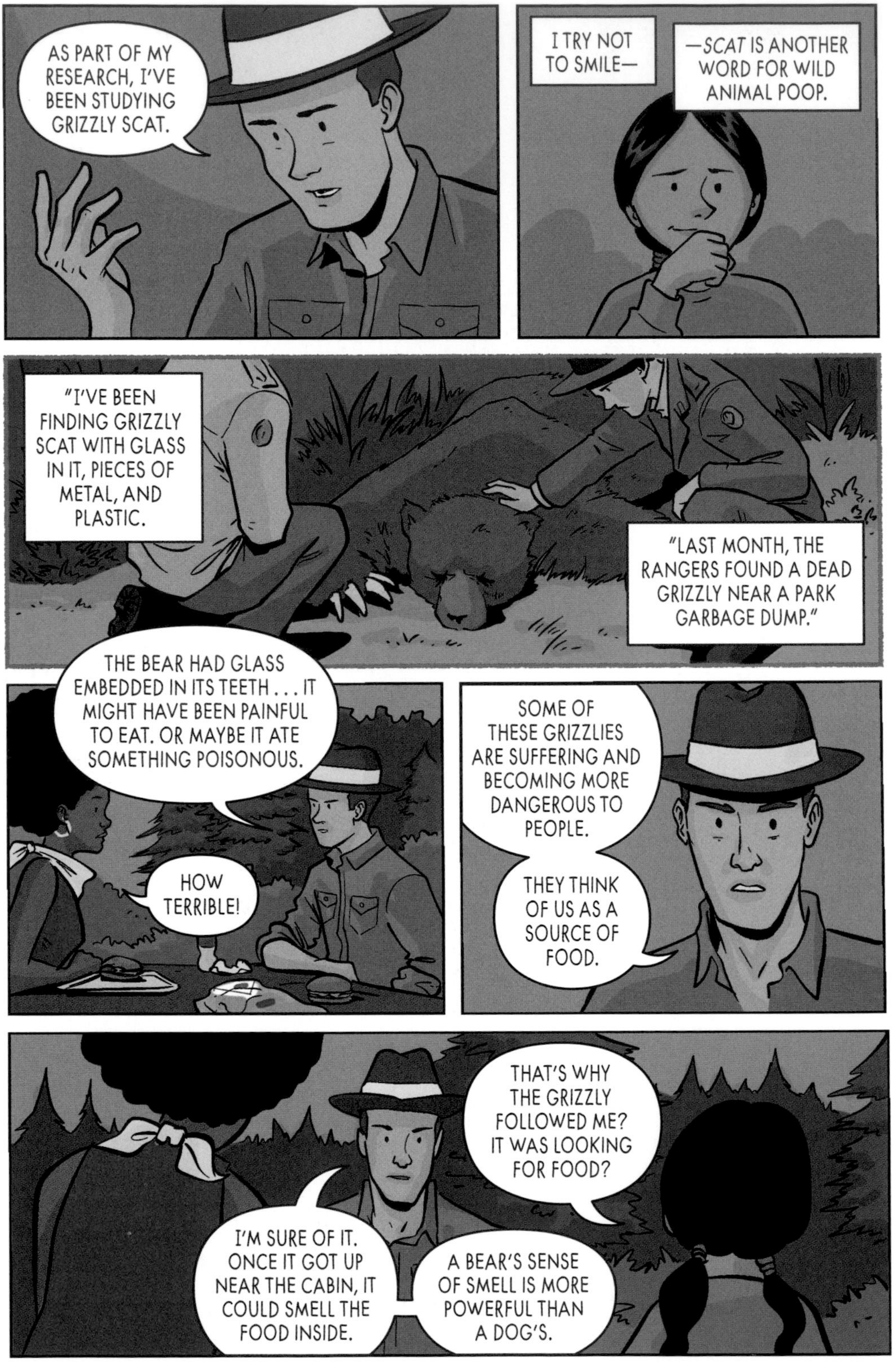
AS PART OF MY RESEARCH, I'VE BEEN STUDYING GRIZZLY SCAT.
I TRY NOT TO SMILE—
—*SCAT* IS ANOTHER WORD FOR WILD ANIMAL POOP.
"I'VE BEEN FINDING GRIZZLY SCAT WITH GLASS IN IT, PIECES OF METAL, AND PLASTIC.
"LAST MONTH, THE RANGERS FOUND A DEAD GRIZZLY NEAR A PARK GARBAGE DUMP."
THE BEAR HAD GLASS EMBEDDED IN ITS TEETH . . . IT MIGHT HAVE BEEN PAINFUL TO EAT. OR MAYBE IT ATE SOMETHING POISONOUS.
HOW TERRIBLE!
SOME OF THESE GRIZZLIES ARE SUFFERING AND BECOMING MORE DANGEROUS TO PEOPLE.
THEY THINK OF US AS A SOURCE OF FOOD.
THAT'S WHY THE GRIZZLY FOLLOWED ME? IT WAS LOOKING FOR FOOD?
I'M SURE OF IT. ONCE IT GOT UP NEAR THE CABIN, IT COULD SMELL THE FOOD INSIDE.
A BEAR'S SENSE OF SMELL IS MORE POWERFUL THAN A DOG'S.

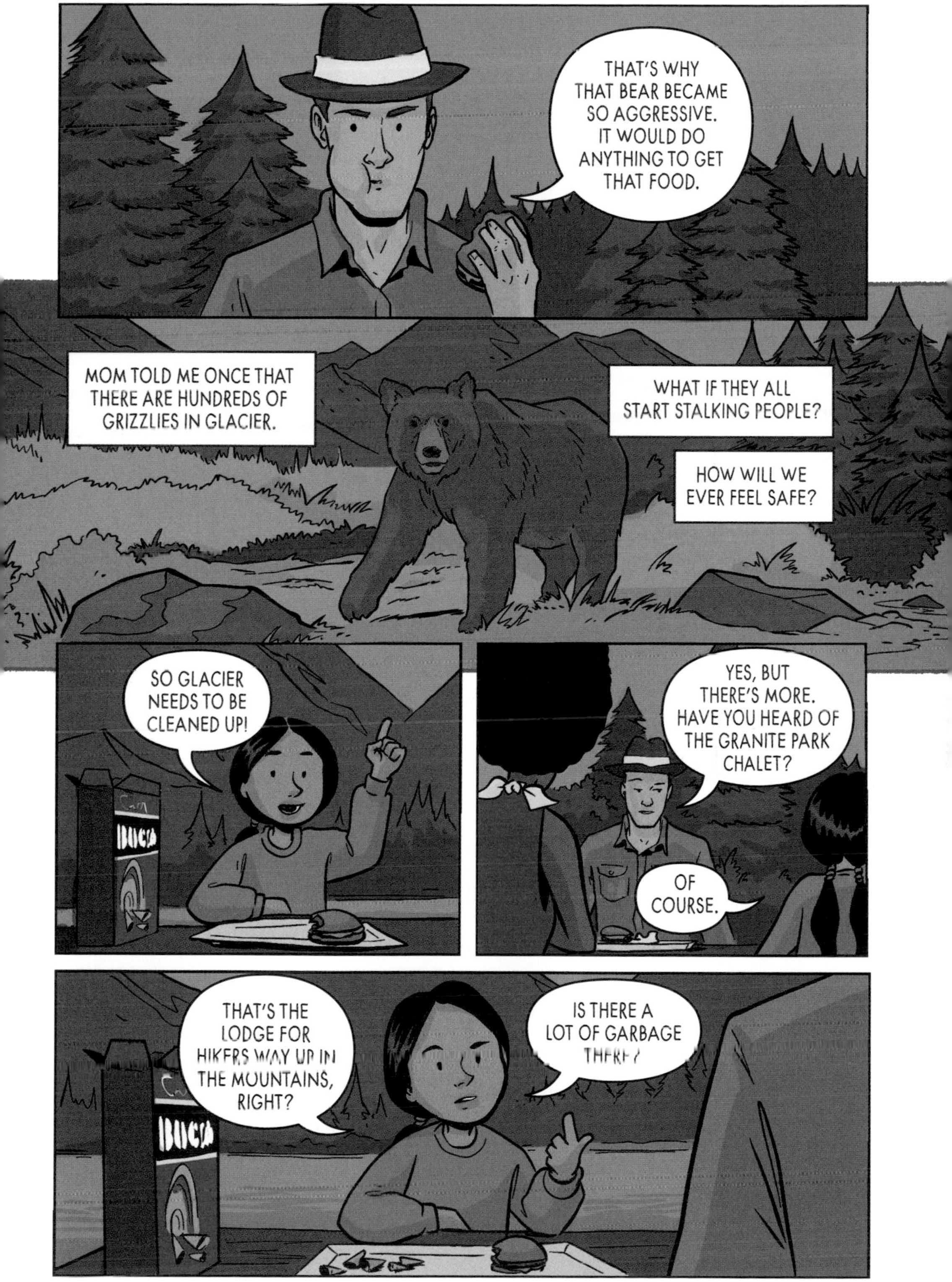
THAT'S WHY THAT BEAR BECAME SO AGGRESSIVE. IT WOULD DO ANYTHING TO GET THAT FOOD.
MOM TOLD ME ONCE THAT THERE ARE HUNDREDS OF GRIZZLIES IN GLACIER.
WHAT IF THEY ALL START STALKING PEOPLE?
HOW WILL WE EVER FEEL SAFE?
SO GLACIER NEEDS TO BE CLEANED UP!
YES, BUT THERE'S MORE. HAVE YOU HEARD OF THE GRANITE PARK CHALET?
OF COURSE.
THAT'S THE LODGE FOR HIKERS WAY UP IN THE MOUNTAINS, RIGHT?
IS THERE A LOT OF GARBAGE THERE?

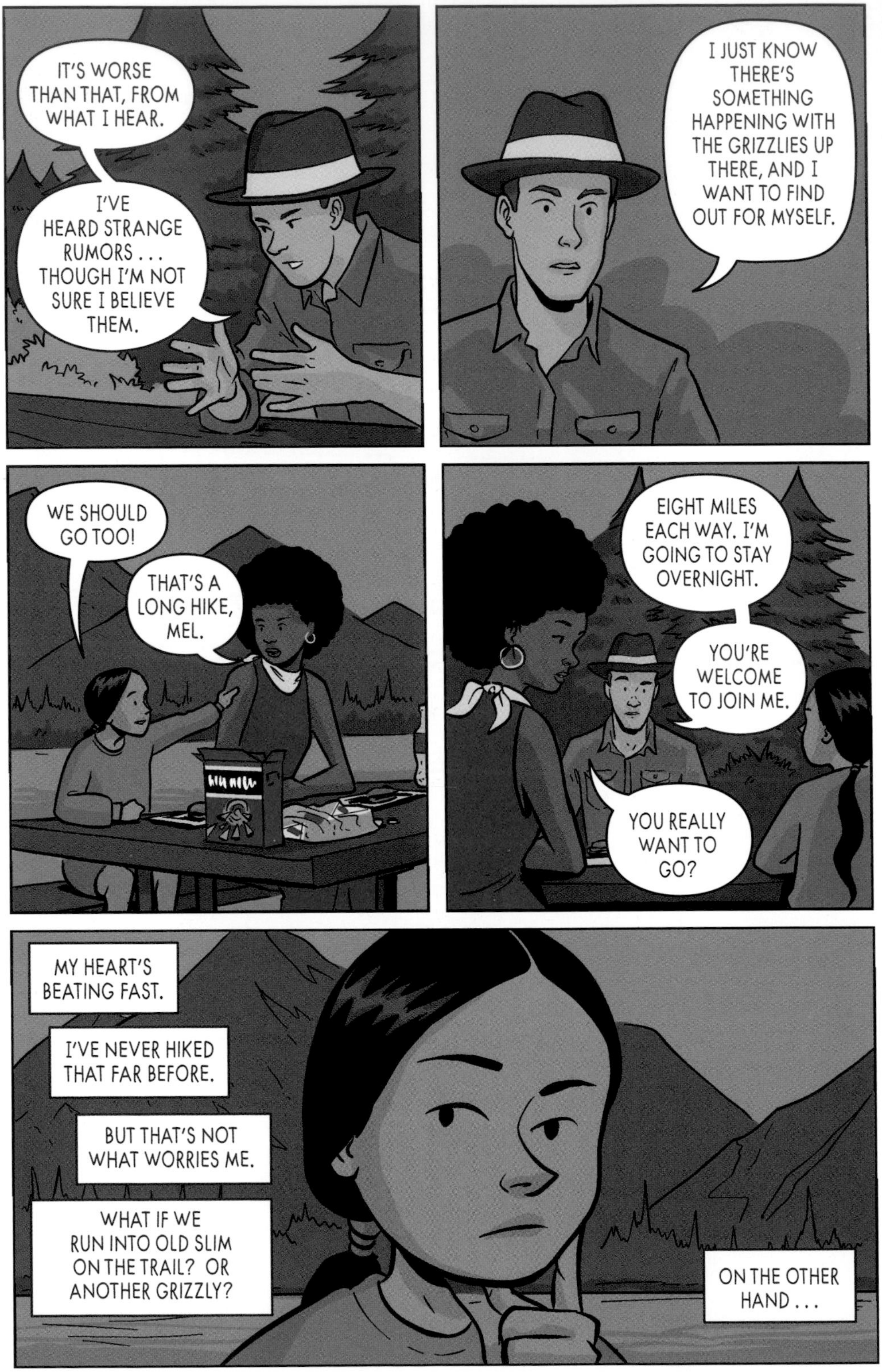
IT'S WORSE THAN THAT, FROM WHAT I HEAR.
I'VE HEARD STRANGE RUMORS . . . THOUGH I'M NOT SURE I BELIEVE THEM.
I JUST KNOW THERE'S SOMETHING HAPPENING WITH THE GRIZZLIES UP THERE, AND I WANT TO FIND OUT FOR MYSELF.
WE SHOULD GO TOO!
THAT'S A LONG HIKE, MEL.
EIGHT MILES EACH WAY. I'M GOING TO STAY OVERNIGHT.
YOU'RE WELCOME TO JOIN ME.
YOU REALLY WANT TO GO?
MY HEART'S BEATING FAST.
I'VE NEVER HIKED THAT FAR BEFORE.
BUT THAT'S NOT WHAT WORRIES ME.
WHAT IF WE RUN INTO OLD SLIM ON THE TRAIL? OR ANOTHER GRIZZLY?
ON THE OTHER HAND . . .

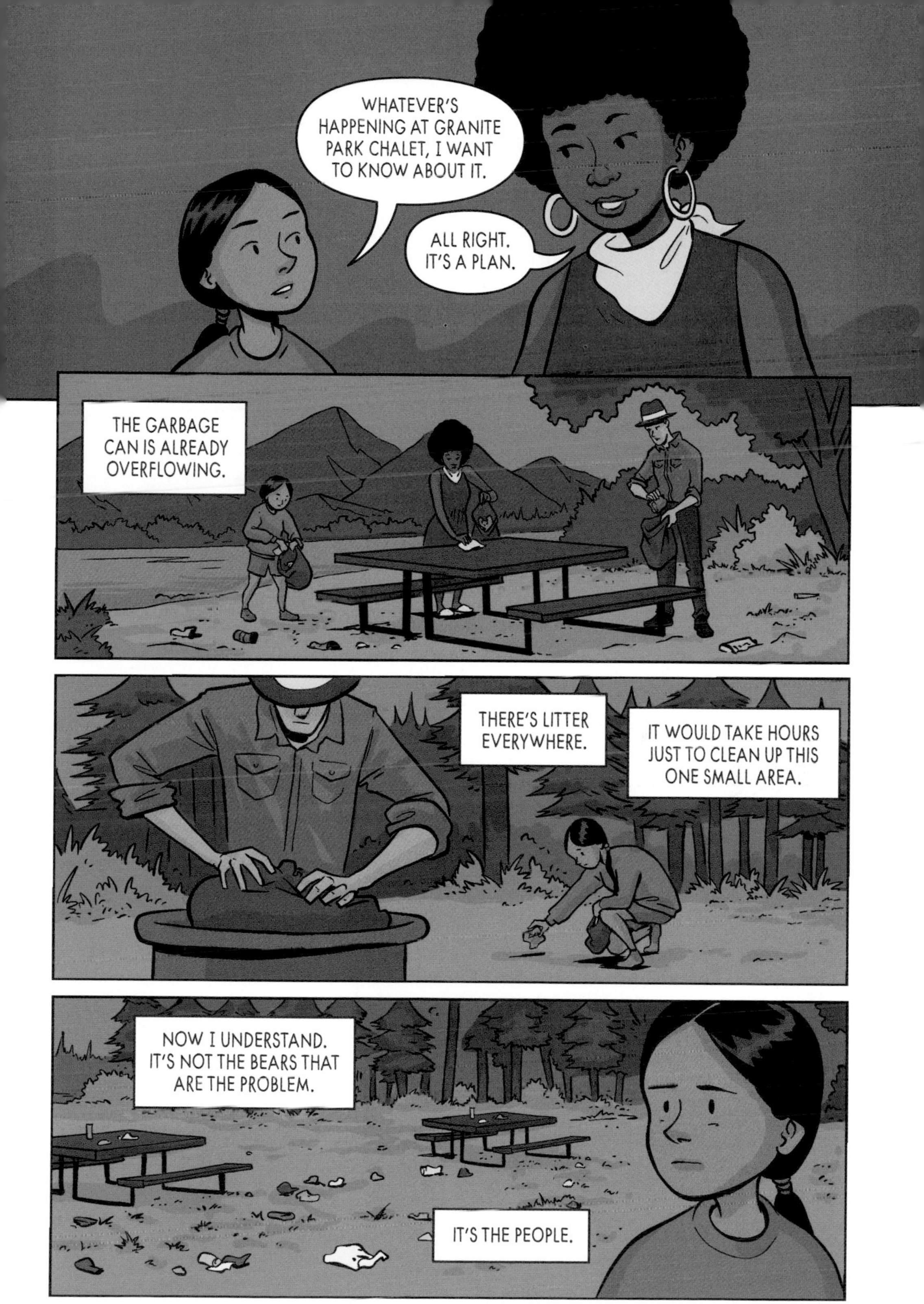
WHATEVER'S HAPPENING AT GRANITE PARK CHALET, I WANT TO KNOW ABOUT IT.
ALL RIGHT. IT'S A PLAN.
THE GARBAGE CAN IS ALREADY OVERFLOWING.
THERE'S LITTER EVERYWHERE.
IT WOULD TAKE HOURS JUST TO CLEAN UP THIS ONE SMALL AREA.
NOW I UNDERSTAND. IT'S NOT THE BEARS THAT ARE THE PROBLEM.
IT'S THE PEOPLE.

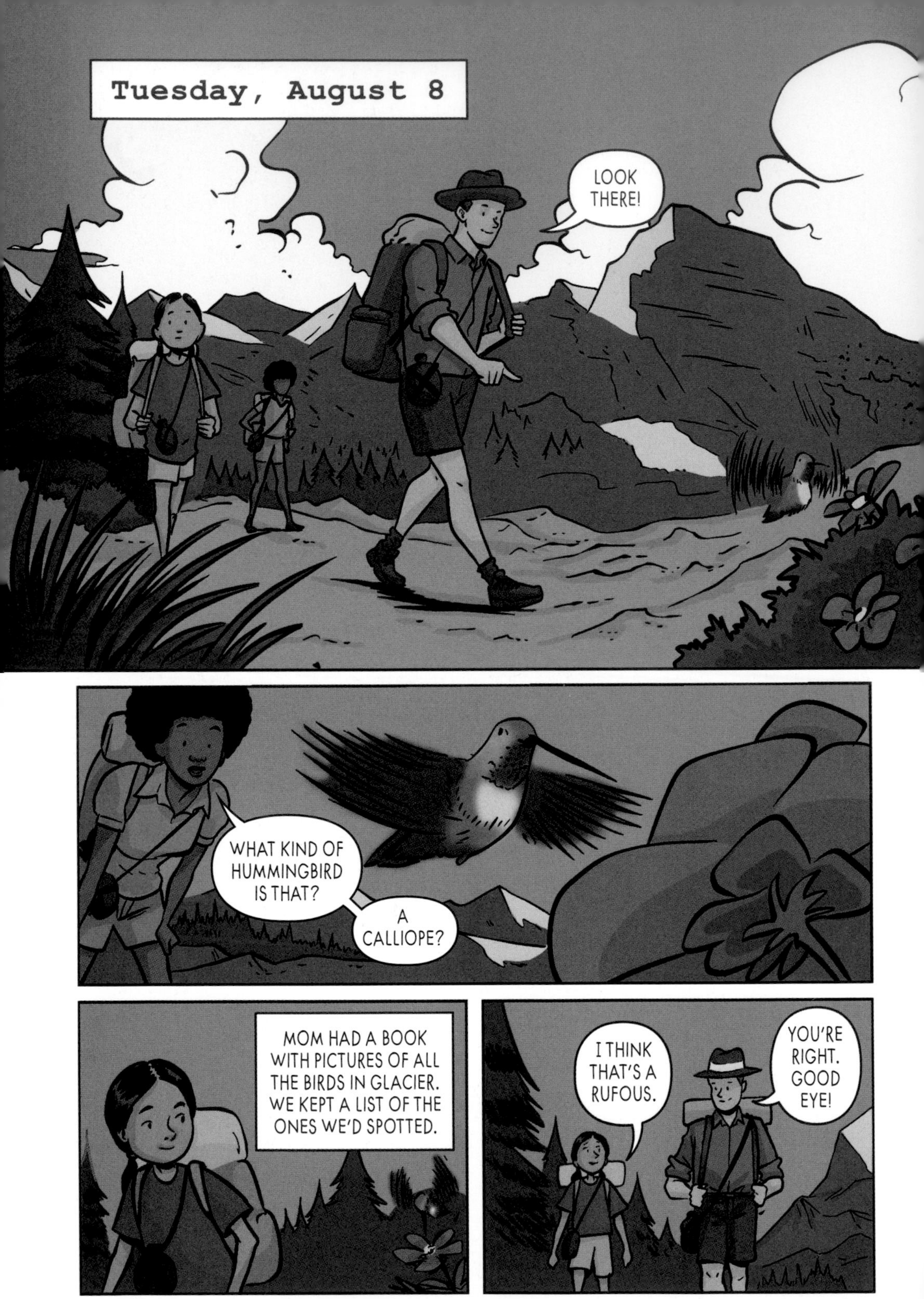
Tuesday, August 8
LOOK THERE!
WHAT KIND OF HUMMINGBIRD IS THAT?
A CALLIOPE?
MOM HAD A BOOK WITH PICTURES OF ALL THE BIRDS IN GLACIER. WE KEPT A LIST OF THE ONES WE'D SPOTTED.
I THINK THAT'S A RUFOUS.
YOU'RE RIGHT. GOOD EYE!

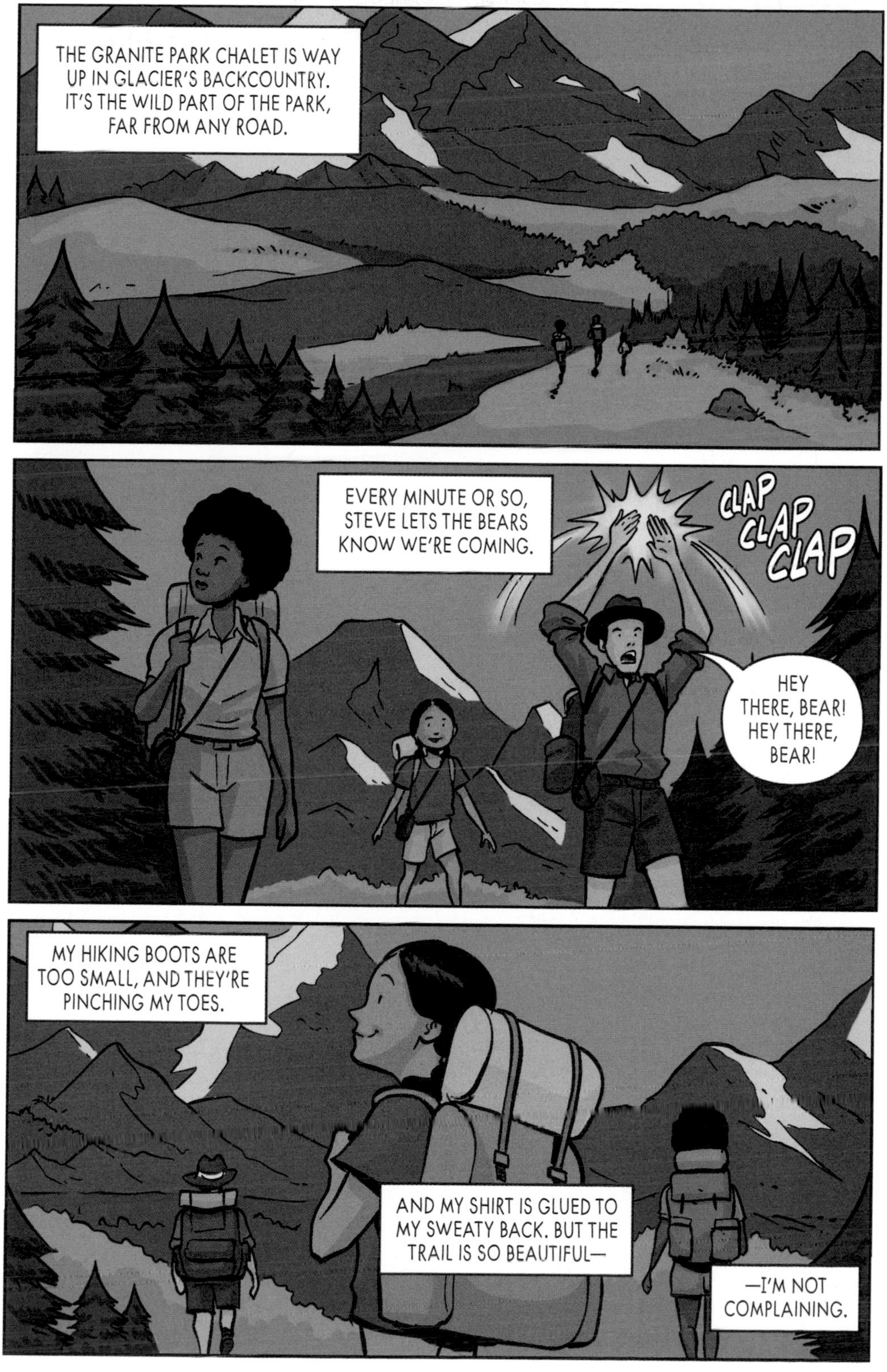
THE GRANITE PARK CHALET IS WAY UP IN GLACIER'S BACKCOUNTRY. IT'S THE WILD PART OF THE PARK, FAR FROM ANY ROAD.
EVERY MINUTE OR SO, STEVE LETS THE BEARS KNOW WE'RE COMING.
CLAP CLAP CLAP
HEY THERE, BEAR! HEY THERE, BEAR!
MY HIKING BOOTS ARE TOO SMALL, AND THEY'RE PINCHING MY TOES.
AND MY SHIRT IS GLUED TO MY SWEATY BACK. BUT THE TRAIL IS SO BEAUTIFUL—
—I'M NOT COMPLAINING.

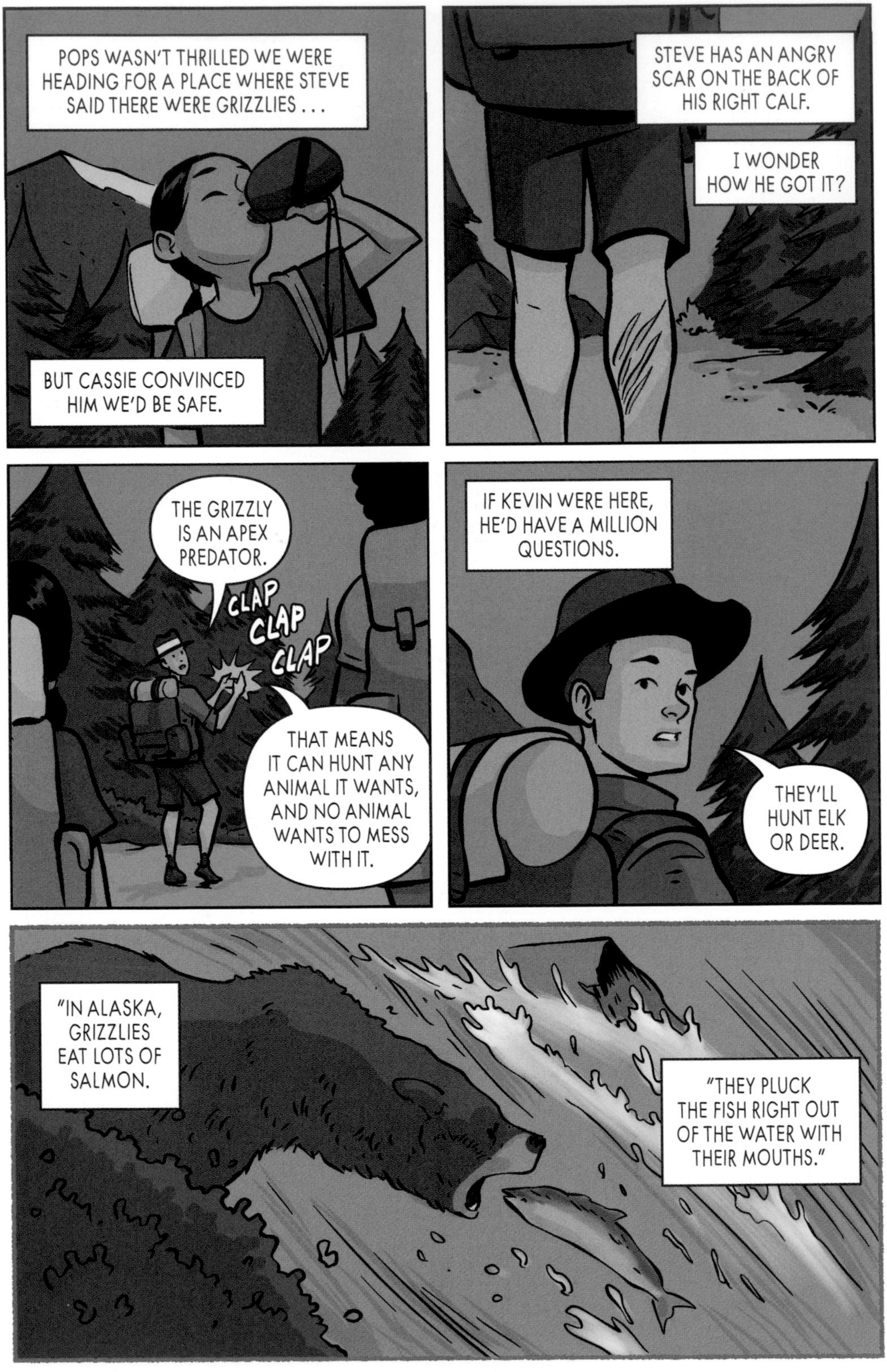
POPS WASN'T THRILLED WE WERE HEADING FOR A PLACE WHERE STEVE SAID THERE WERE GRIZZLIES . . .
BUT CASSIE CONVINCED HIM WE'D BE SAFE.
STEVE HAS AN ANGRY SCAR ON THE BACK OF HIS RIGHT CALF.
I WONDER HOW HE GOT IT?
THE GRIZZLY IS AN APEX PREDATOR.
CLAP CLAP CLAP
THAT MEANS IT CAN HUNT ANY ANIMAL IT WANTS, AND NO ANIMAL WANTS TO MESS WITH IT.
IF KEVIN WERE HERE, HE'D HAVE A MILLION QUESTIONS.
THEY'LL HUNT ELK OR DEER.
"IN ALASKA, GRIZZLIES EAT LOTS OF SALMON.
"THEY PLUCK THE FISH RIGHT OUT OF THE WATER WITH THEIR MOUTHS."

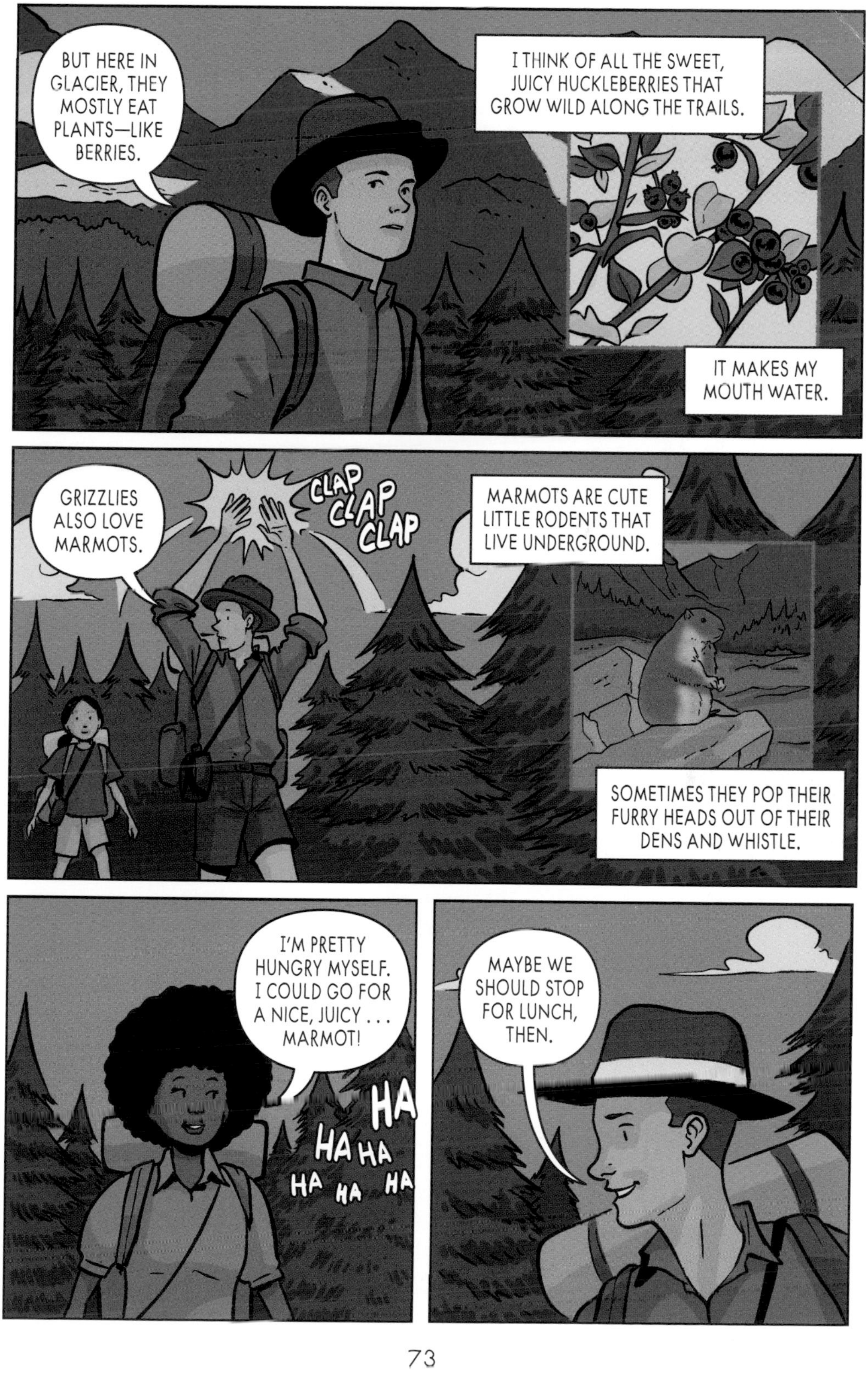
BUT HERE IN GLACIER, THEY MOSTLY EAT PLANTS—LIKE BERRIES.
I THINK OF ALL THE SWEET, JUICY HUCKLEBERRIES THAT GROW WILD ALONG THE TRAILS.
IT MAKES MY MOUTH WATER.
GRIZZLIES ALSO LOVE MARMOTS.
CLAP CLAP CLAP
MARMOTS ARE CUTE LITTLE RODENTS THAT LIVE UNDERGROUND.
SOMETIMES THEY POP THEIR FURRY HEADS OUT OF THEIR DENS AND WHISTLE.
I'M PRETTY HUNGRY MYSELF. I COULD GO FOR A NICE, JUICY . . . MARMOT!
HA HA HA HA HA HA
MAYBE WE SHOULD STOP FOR LUNCH, THEN.

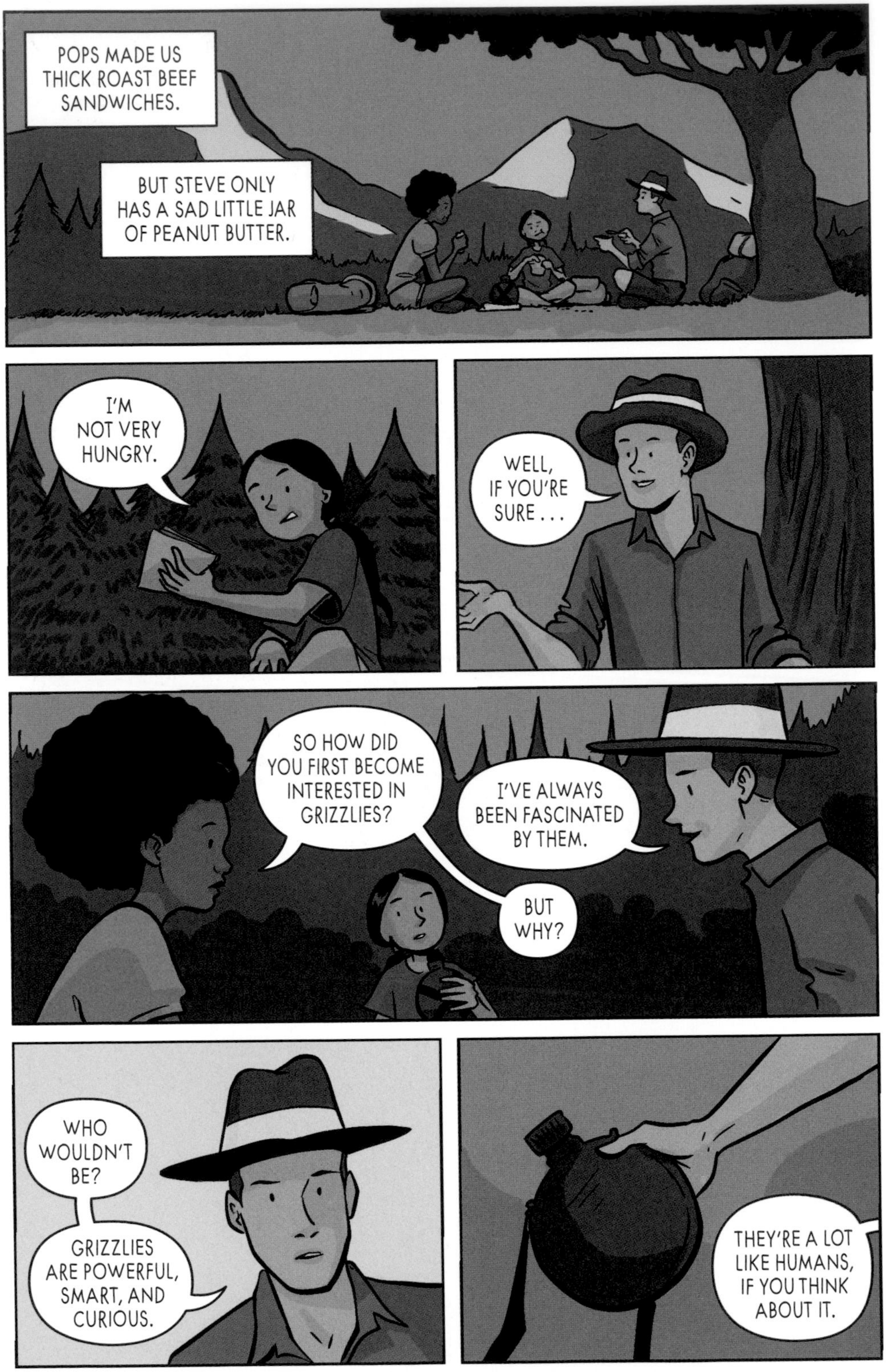
POPS MADE US THICK ROAST BEEF SANDWICHES.
BUT STEVE ONLY HAS A SAD LITTLE JAR OF PEANUT BUTTER.
I'M NOT VERY HUNGRY.
WELL, IF YOU'RE SURE . . .
SO HOW DID YOU FIRST BECOME INTERESTED IN GRIZZLIES?
I'VE ALWAYS BEEN FASCINATED BY THEM.
BUT WHY?
WHO WOULDN'T BE?
GRIZZLIES ARE POWERFUL, SMART, AND CURIOUS.
THEY'RE A LOT LIKE HUMANS, IF YOU THINK ABOUT IT.

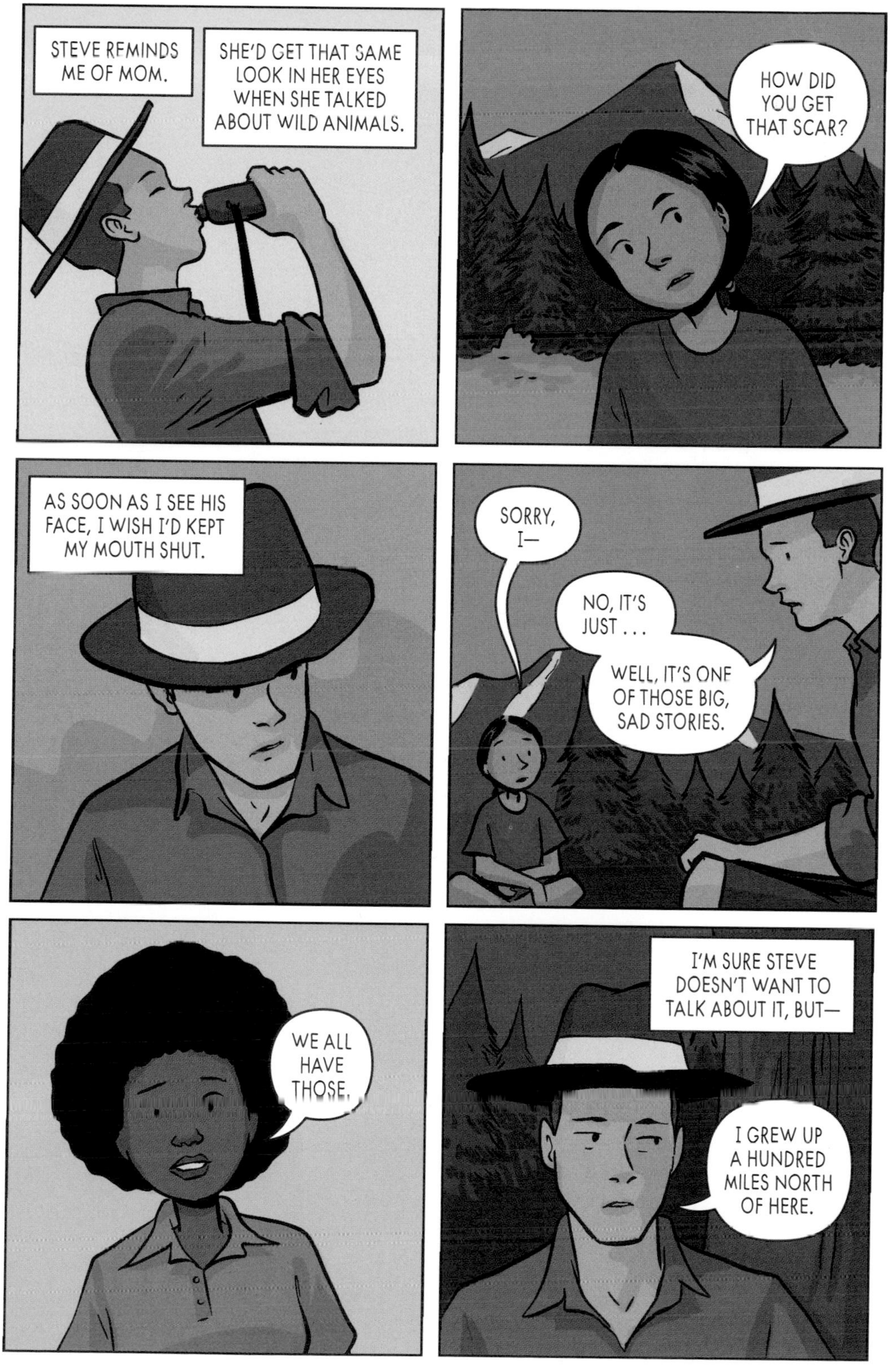
STEVE REMINDS ME OF MOM.
SHE'D GET THAT SAME LOOK IN HER EYES WHEN SHE TALKED ABOUT WILD ANIMALS.
HOW DID YOU GET THAT SCAR?
AS SOON AS I SEE HIS FACE, I WISH I'D KEPT MY MOUTH SHUT.
SORRY, I—
NO, IT'S JUST . . .
WELL, IT'S ONE OF THOSE BIG, SAD STORIES.
WE ALL HAVE THOSE.
I'M SURE STEVE DOESN'T WANT TO TALK ABOUT IT, BUT—
I GREW UP A HUNDRED MILES NORTH OF HERE.

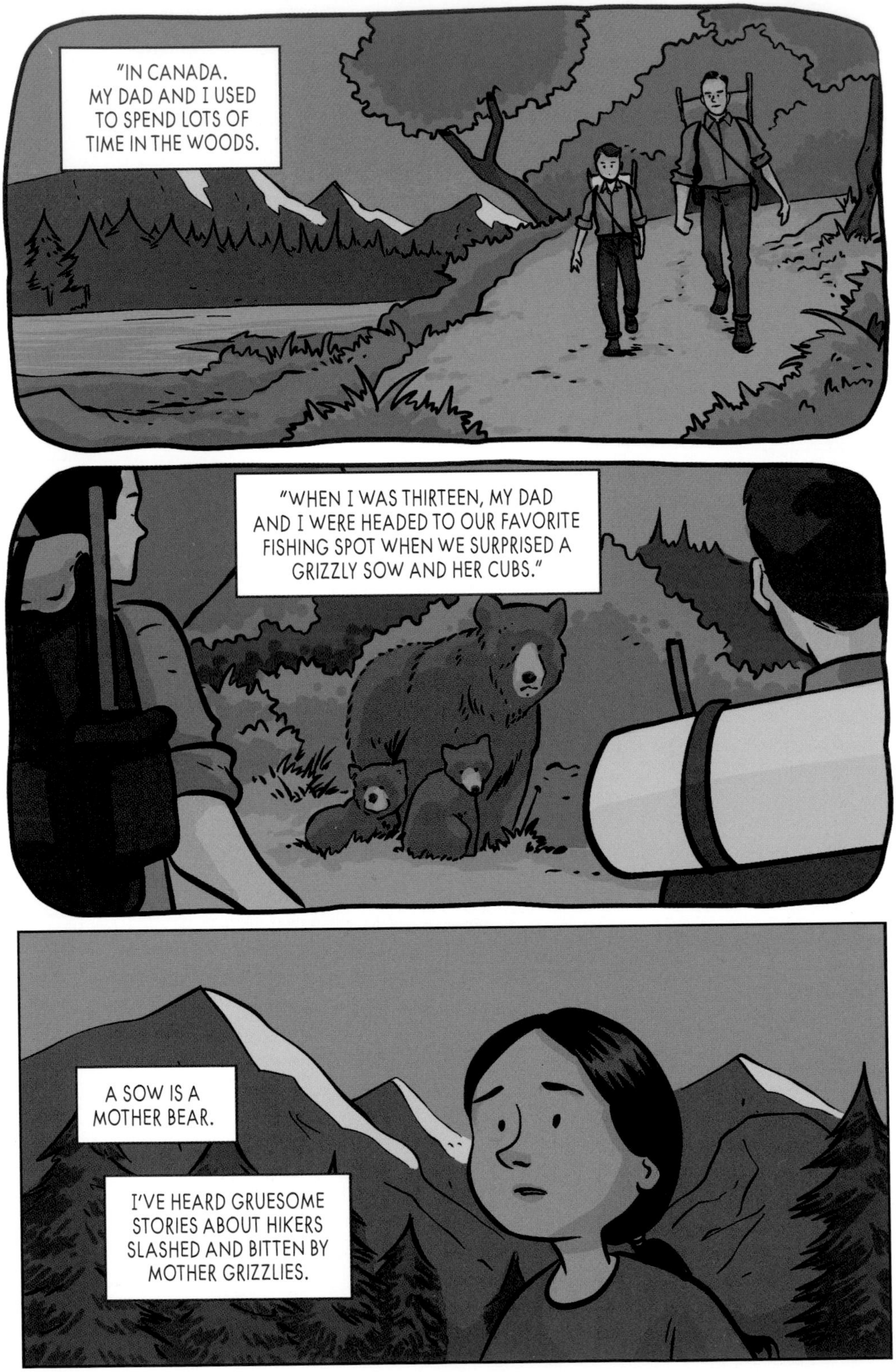
"IN CANADA.
MY DAD AND I USED
TO SPEND LOTS OF
TIME IN THE WOODS.
"WHEN I WAS THIRTEEN, MY DAD
AND I WERE HEADED TO OUR FAVORITE
FISHING SPOT WHEN WE SURPRISED A
GRIZZLY SOW AND HER CUBS."
A SOW IS A
MOTHER BEAR.
I'VE HEARD GRUESOME
STORIES ABOUT HIKERS
SLASHED AND BITTEN BY
MOTHER GRIZZLIES.

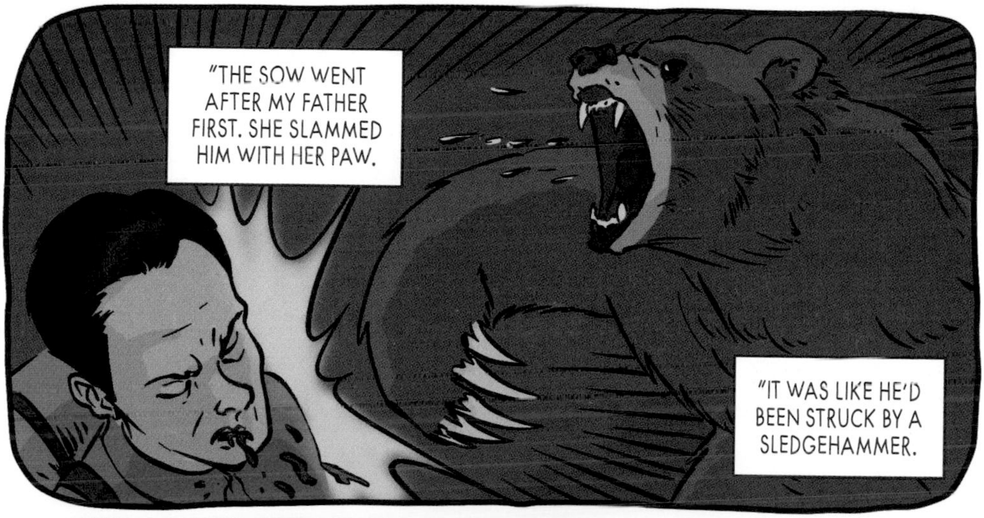
"THE SOW WENT AFTER MY FATHER FIRST. SHE SLAMMED HIM WITH HER PAW.
"IT WAS LIKE HE'D BEEN STRUCK BY A SLEDGEHAMMER.

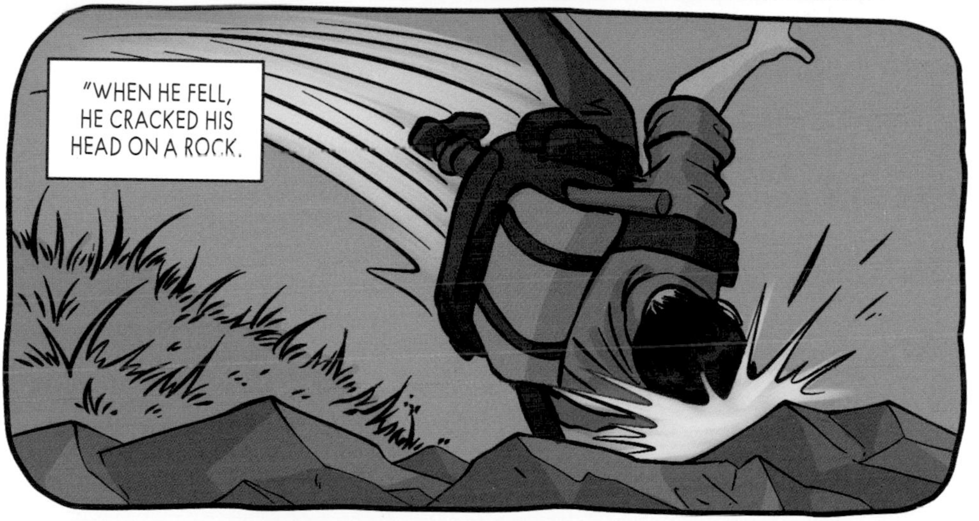
"WHEN HE FELL, HE CRACKED HIS HEAD ON A ROCK.

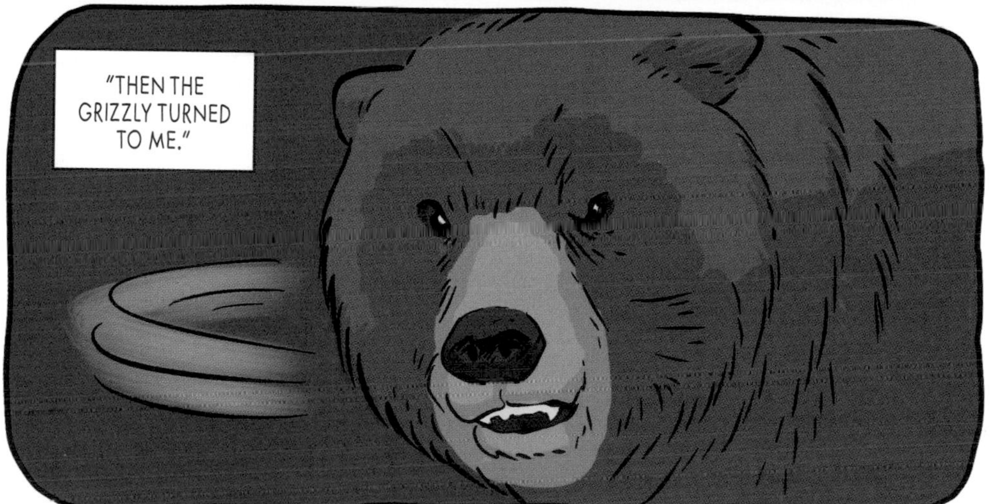
"THEN THE GRIZZLY TURNED TO ME."

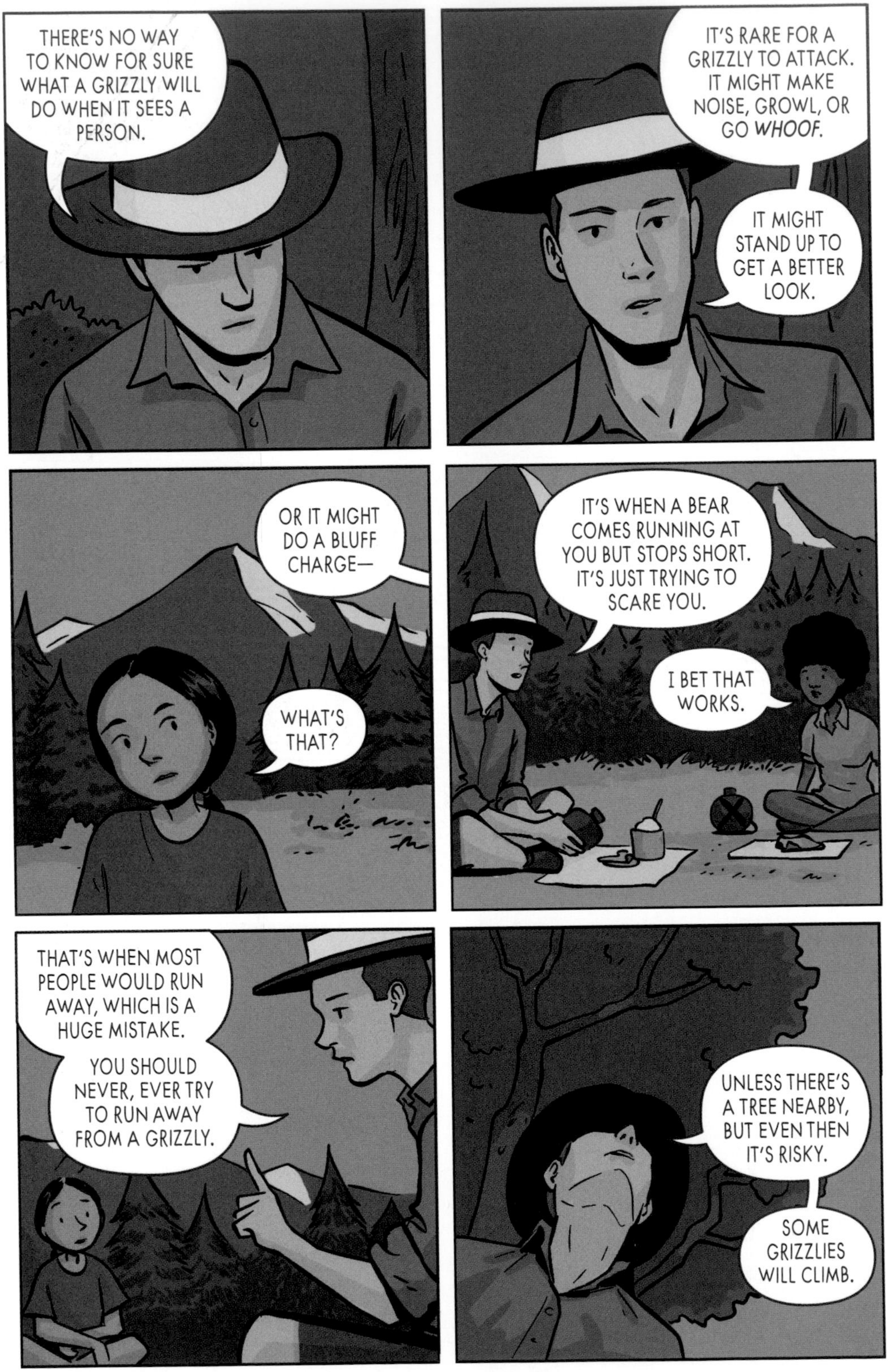
THERE'S NO WAY TO KNOW FOR SURE WHAT A GRIZZLY WILL DO WHEN IT SEES A PERSON.
IT'S RARE FOR A GRIZZLY TO ATTACK. IT MIGHT MAKE NOISE, GROWL, OR GO *WHOOF*.
IT MIGHT STAND UP TO GET A BETTER LOOK.
OR IT MIGHT DO A BLUFF CHARGE—
WHAT'S THAT?
IT'S WHEN A BEAR COMES RUNNING AT YOU BUT STOPS SHORT. IT'S JUST TRYING TO SCARE YOU.
I BET THAT WORKS.
THAT'S WHEN MOST PEOPLE WOULD RUN AWAY, WHICH IS A HUGE MISTAKE.
YOU SHOULD NEVER, EVER TRY TO RUN AWAY FROM A GRIZZLY.
UNLESS THERE'S A TREE NEARBY, BUT EVEN THEN IT'S RISKY.
SOME GRIZZLIES WILL CLIMB.

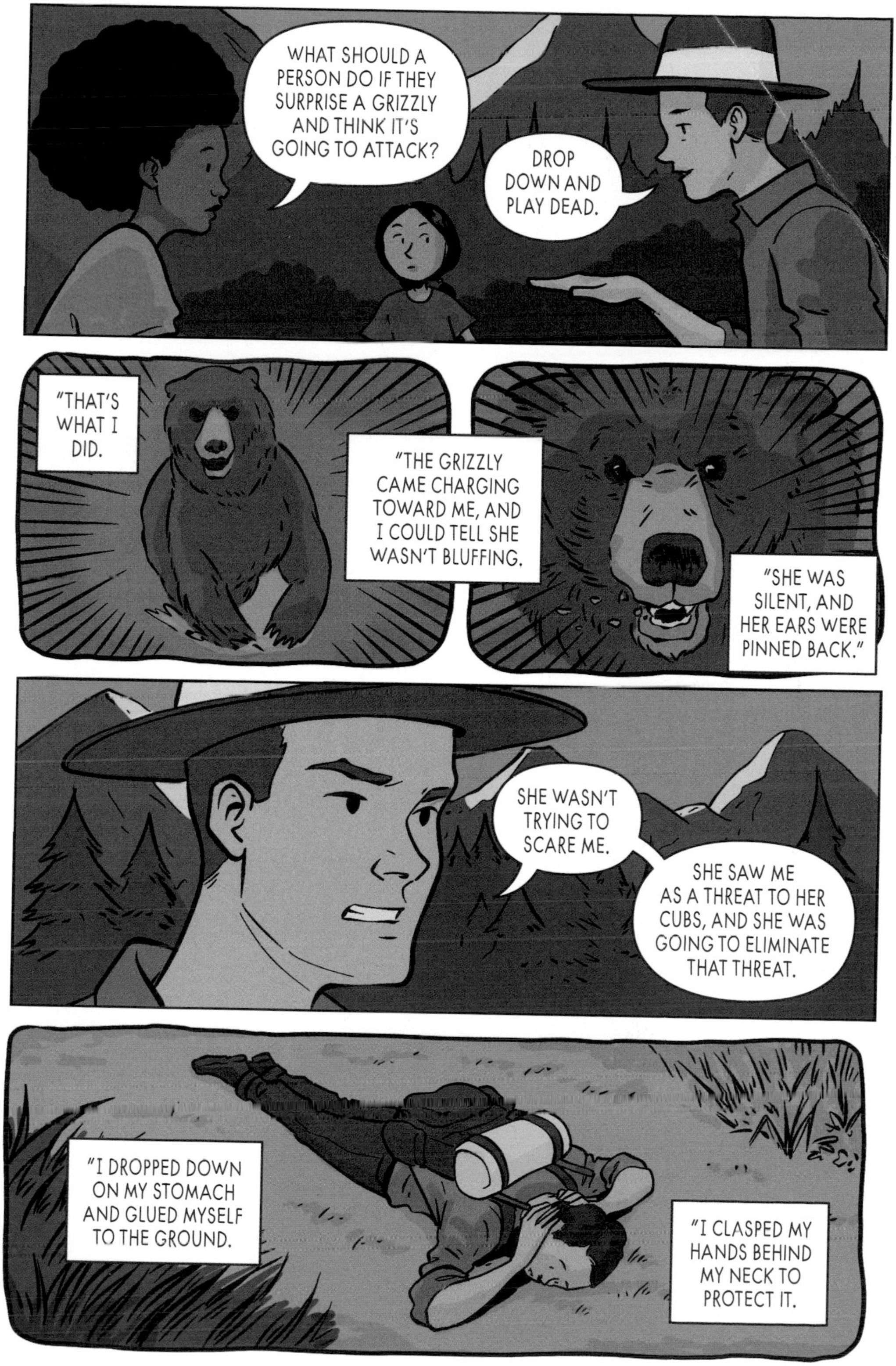
WHAT SHOULD A PERSON DO IF THEY SURPRISE A GRIZZLY AND THINK IT'S GOING TO ATTACK?
DROP DOWN AND PLAY DEAD.
"THAT'S WHAT I DID.
"THE GRIZZLY CAME CHARGING TOWARD ME, AND I COULD TELL SHE WASN'T BLUFFING.
"SHE WAS SILENT, AND HER EARS WERE PINNED BACK."
SHE WASN'T TRYING TO SCARE ME.
SHE SAW ME AS A THREAT TO HER CUBS, AND SHE WAS GOING TO ELIMINATE THAT THREAT.
"I DROPPED DOWN ON MY STOMACH AND GLUED MYSELF TO THE GROUND.
"I CLASPED MY HANDS BEHIND MY NECK TO PROTECT IT.

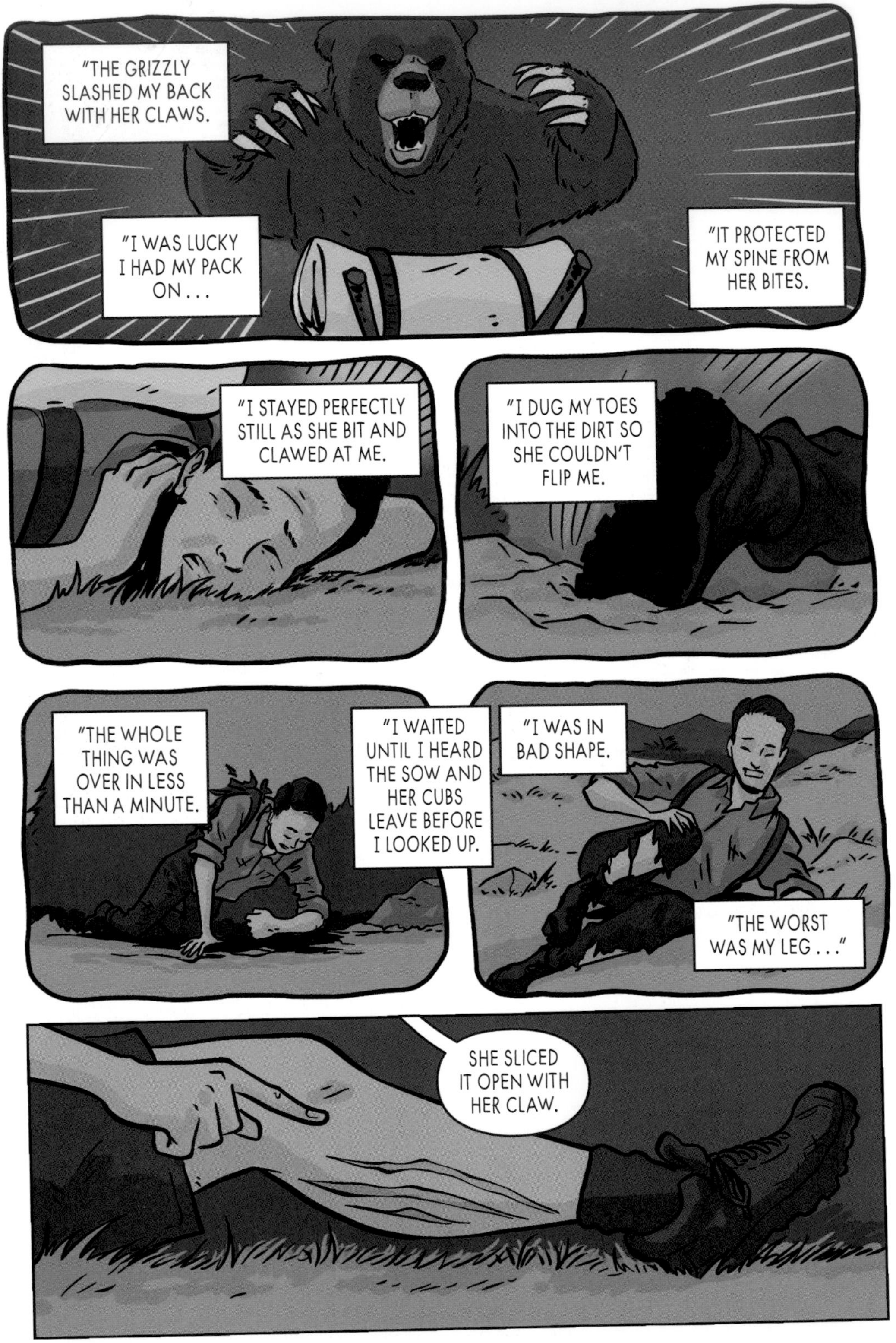
"THE GRIZZLY SLASHED MY BACK WITH HER CLAWS.
"I WAS LUCKY I HAD MY PACK ON . . .
"IT PROTECTED MY SPINE FROM HER BITES.
"I STAYED PERFECTLY STILL AS SHE BIT AND CLAWED AT ME.
"I DUG MY TOES INTO THE DIRT SO SHE COULDN'T FLIP ME.
"THE WHOLE THING WAS OVER IN LESS THAN A MINUTE.
"I WAITED UNTIL I HEARD THE SOW AND HER CUBS LEAVE BEFORE I LOOKED UP.
"I WAS IN BAD SHAPE.
"THE WORST WAS MY LEG . . ."
SHE SLICED IT OPEN WITH HER CLAW.

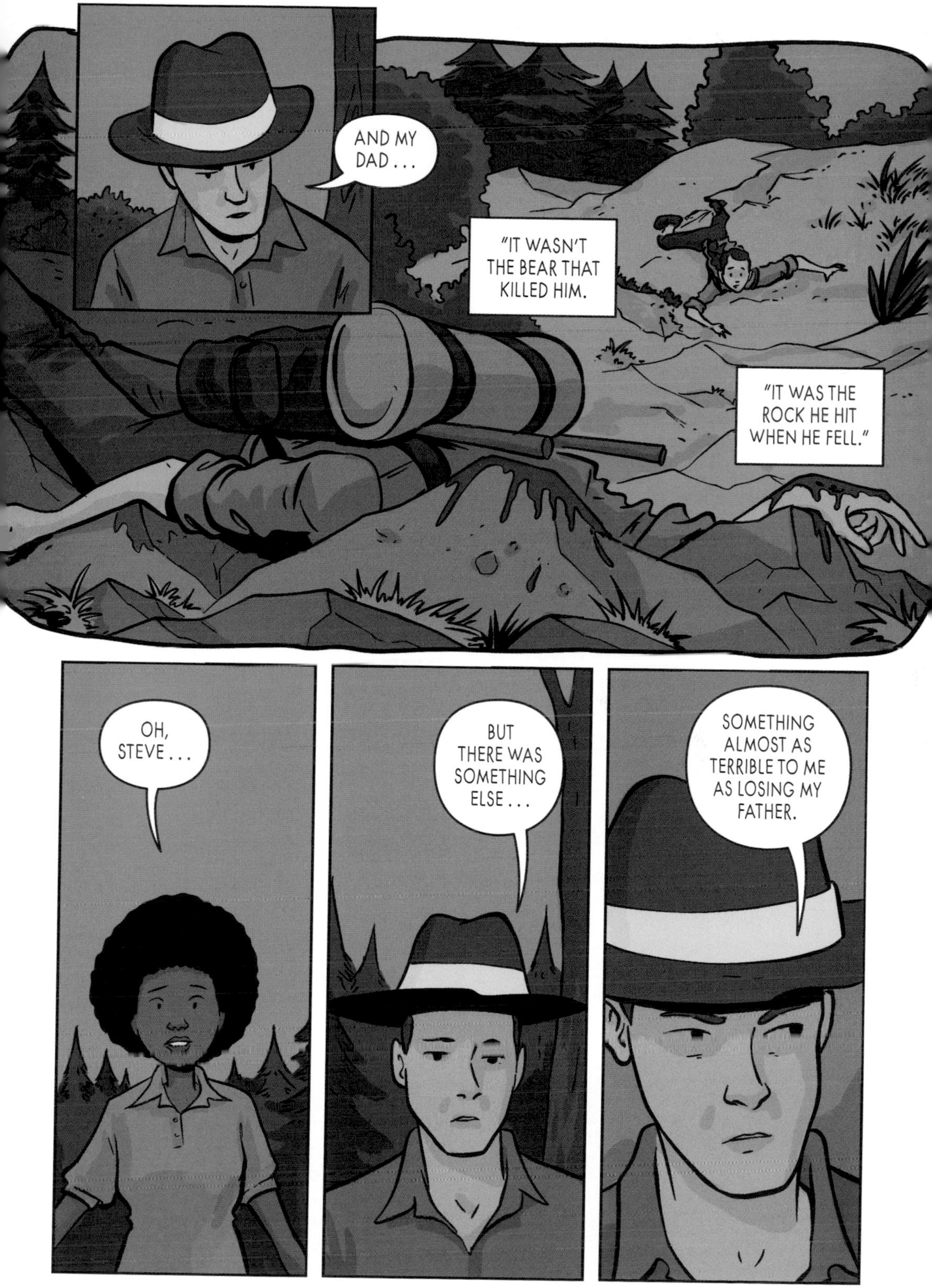
AND MY DAD . . .
"IT WASN'T THE BEAR THAT KILLED HIM.
"IT WAS THE ROCK HE HIT WHEN HE FELL."
OH, STEVE . . .
BUT THERE WAS SOMETHING ELSE . . .
SOMETHING ALMOST AS TERRIBLE TO ME AS LOSING MY FATHER.

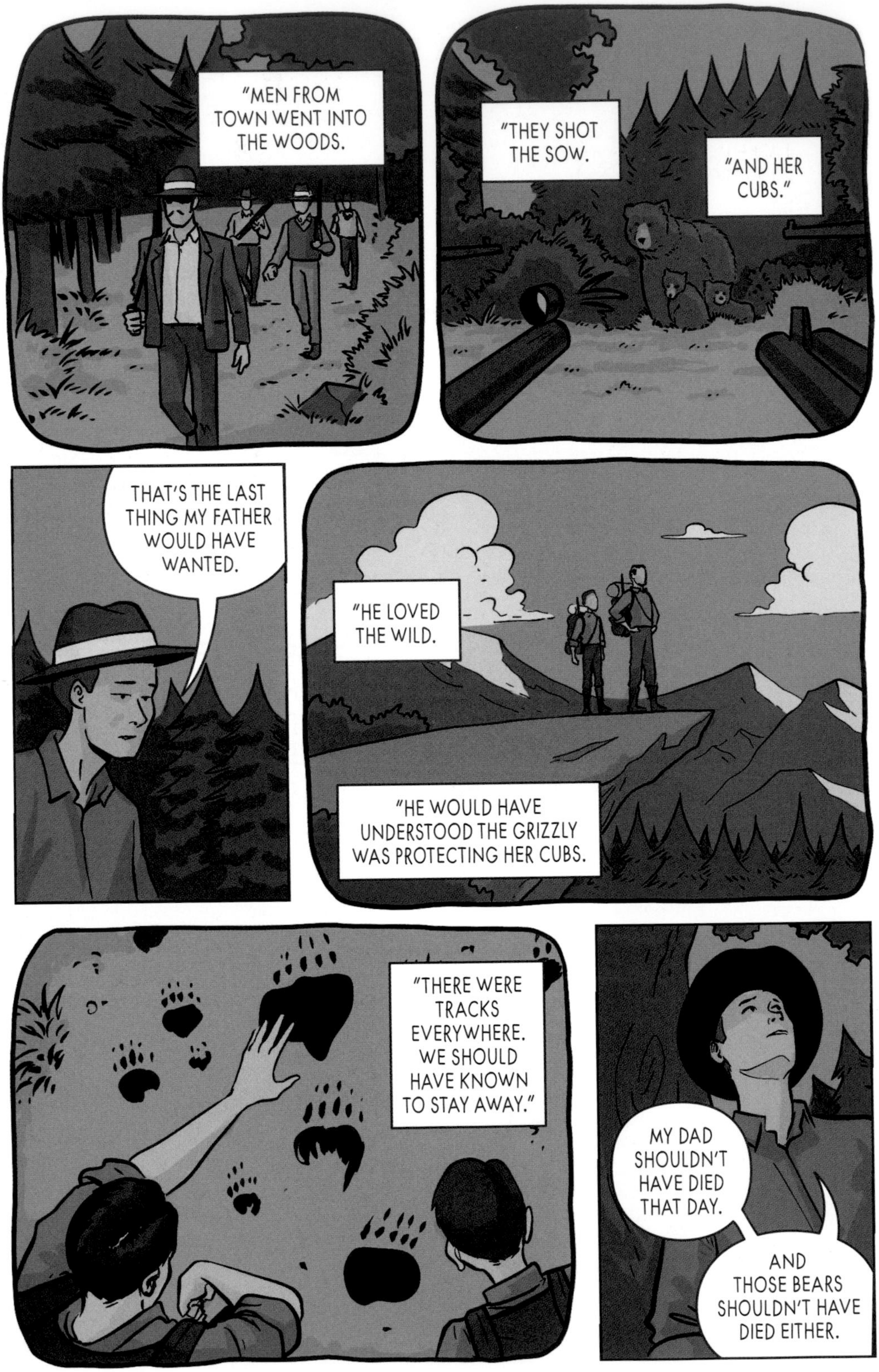
"MEN FROM TOWN WENT INTO THE WOODS.
"THEY SHOT THE SOW.
"AND HER CUBS."
THAT'S THE LAST THING MY FATHER WOULD HAVE WANTED.
"HE LOVED THE WILD.
"HE WOULD HAVE UNDERSTOOD THE GRIZZLY WAS PROTECTING HER CUBS.
"THERE WERE TRACKS EVERYWHERE. WE SHOULD HAVE KNOWN TO STAY AWAY."
MY DAD SHOULDN'T HAVE DIED THAT DAY.
AND THOSE BEARS SHOULDN'T HAVE DIED EITHER.

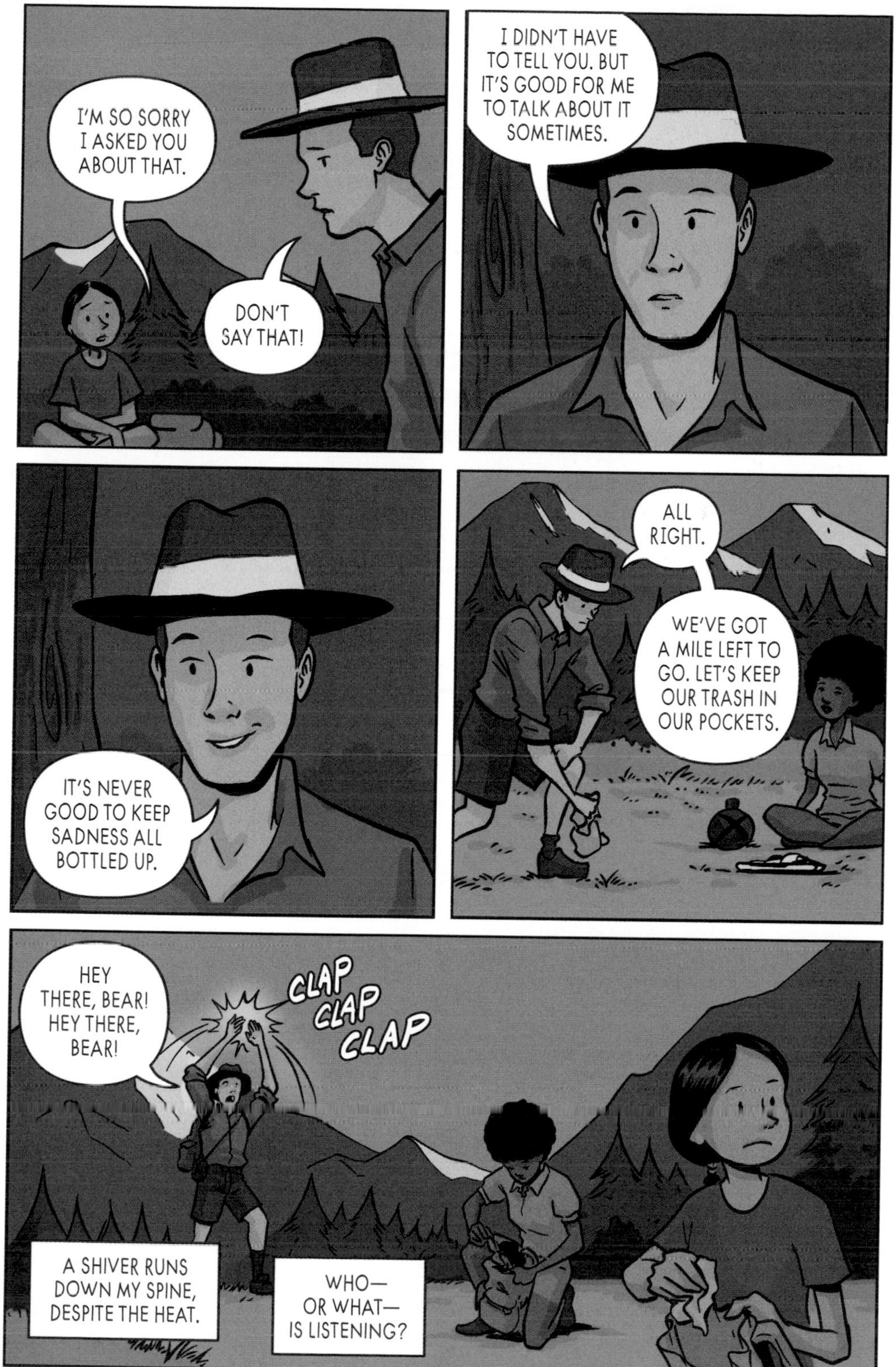
I'M SO SORRY I ASKED YOU ABOUT THAT.
DON'T SAY THAT!
I DIDN'T HAVE TO TELL YOU. BUT IT'S GOOD FOR ME TO TALK ABOUT IT SOMETIMES.
IT'S NEVER GOOD TO KEEP SADNESS ALL BOTTLED UP.
ALL RIGHT.
WE'VE GOT A MILE LEFT TO GO. LET'S KEEP OUR TRASH IN OUR POCKETS.
HEY THERE, BEAR! HEY THERE, BEAR!
CLAP CLAP CLAP
A SHIVER RUNS DOWN MY SPINE, DESPITE THE HEAT.
WHO— OR WHAT— IS LISTENING?

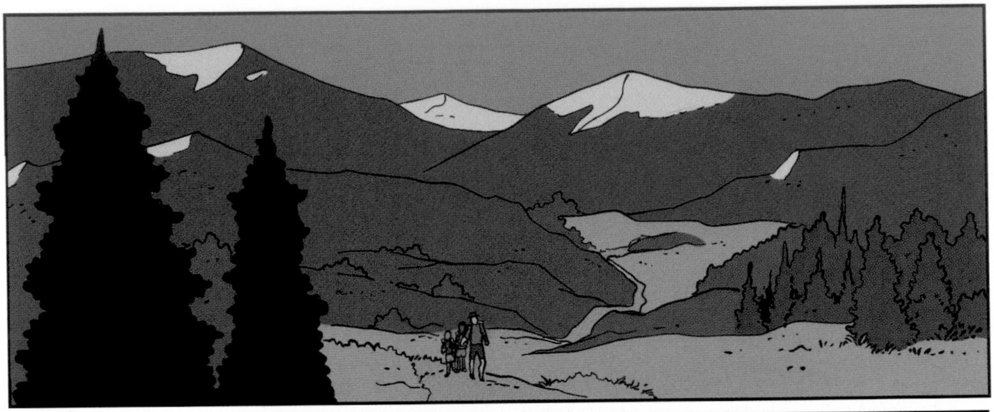

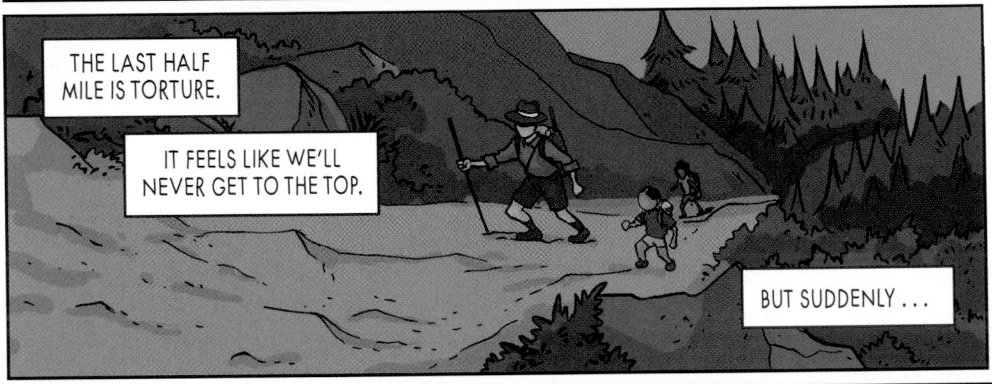
THE LAST HALF MILE IS TORTURE.
IT FEELS LIKE WE'LL NEVER GET TO THE TOP.
BUT SUDDENLY . . .

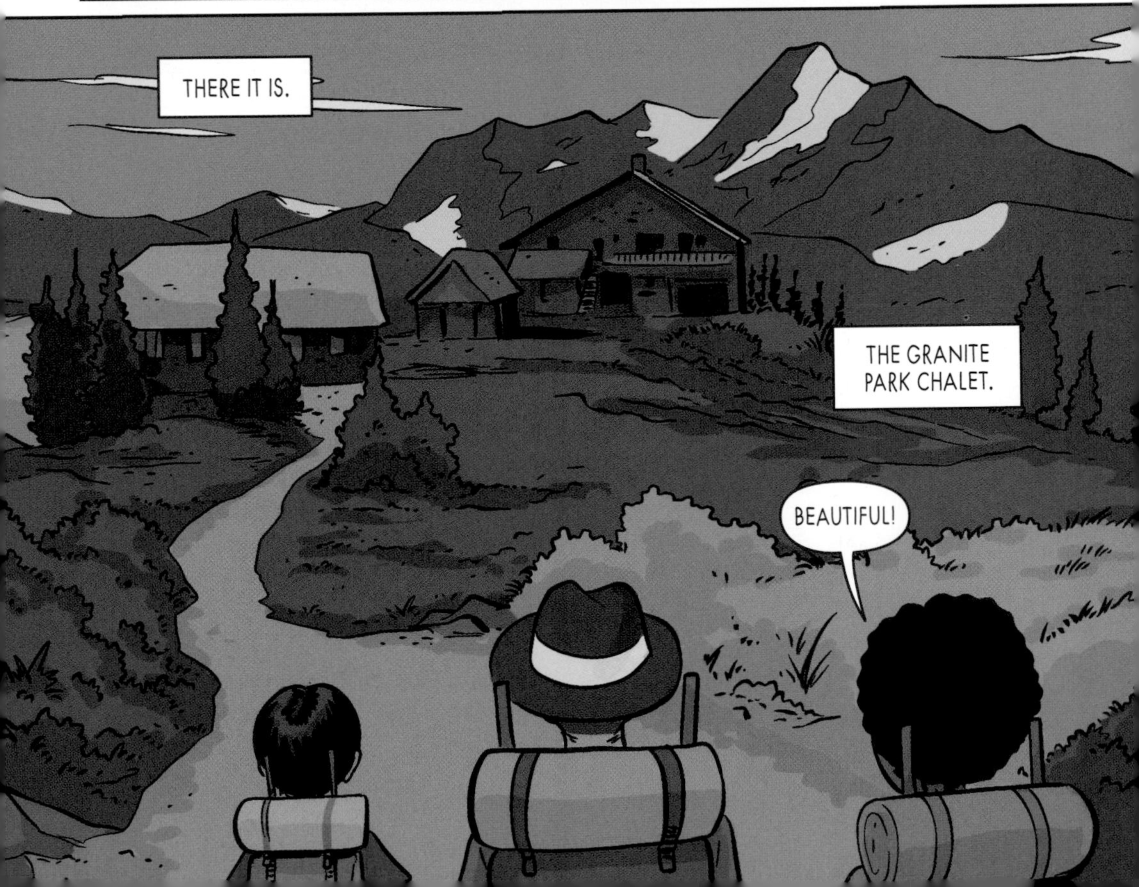
THERE IT IS.
THE GRANITE PARK CHALET.
BEAUTIFUL!

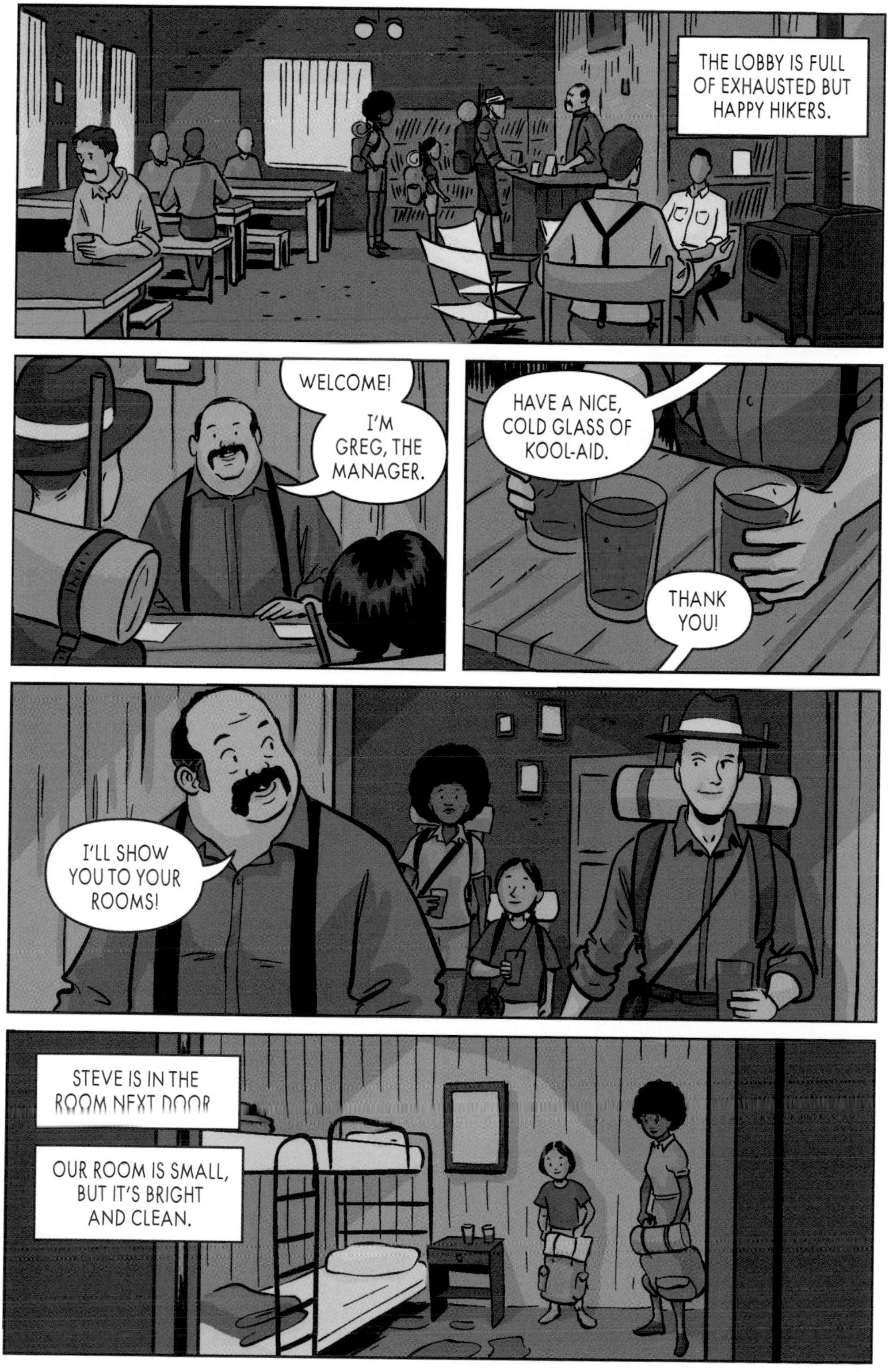

THE LOBBY IS FULL OF EXHAUSTED BUT HAPPY HIKERS.
WELCOME!
I'M GREG, THE MANAGER.
HAVE A NICE, COLD GLASS OF KOOL-AID.
THANK YOU!
I'LL SHOW YOU TO YOUR ROOMS!
STEVE IS IN THE ROOM NEXT DOOR
OUR ROOM IS SMALL, BUT IT'S BRIGHT AND CLEAN.

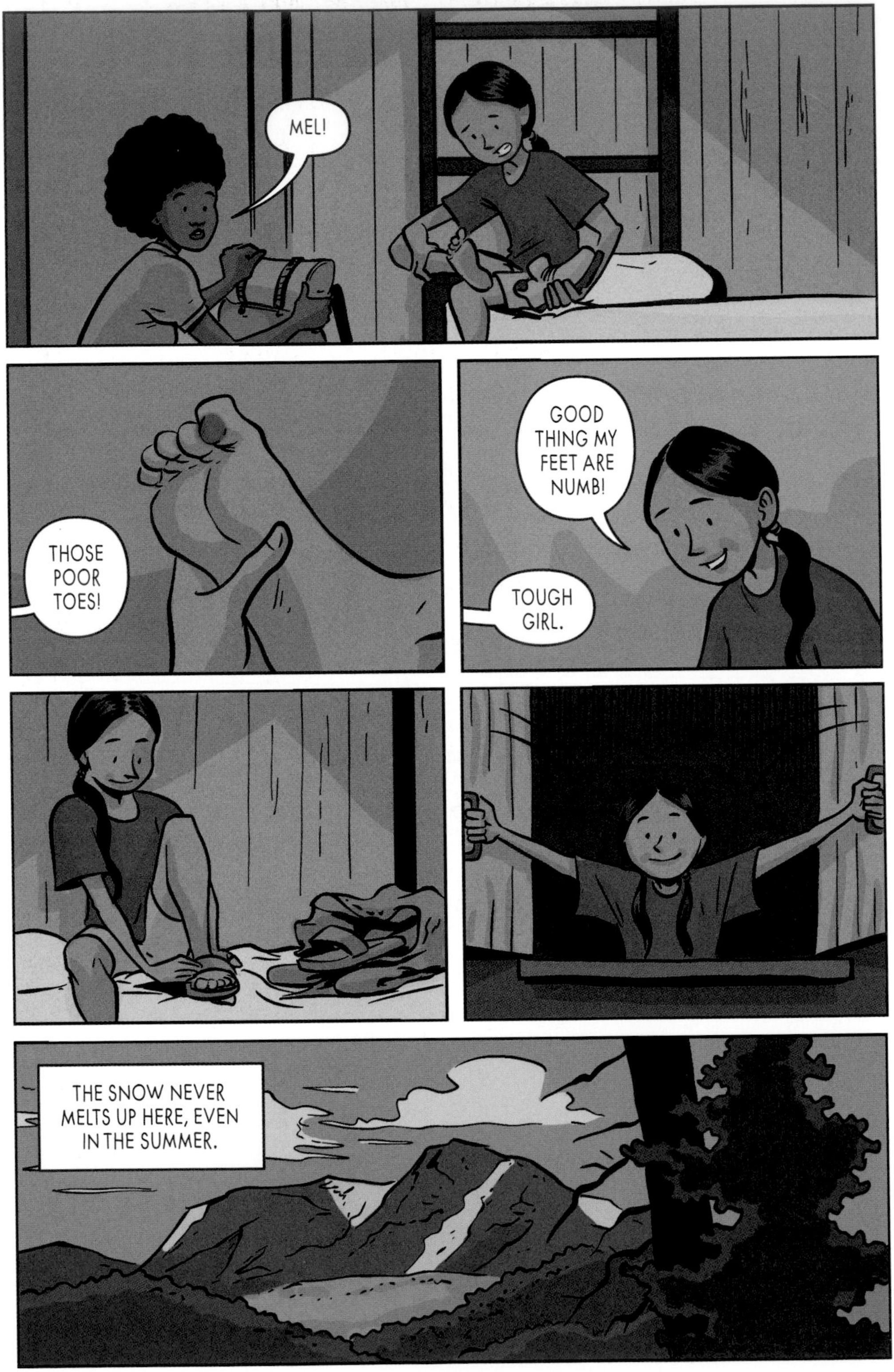
MEL!
THOSE POOR TOES!
GOOD THING MY FEET ARE NUMB!
TOUGH GIRL.
THE SNOW NEVER MELTS UP HERE, EVEN IN THE SUMMER.

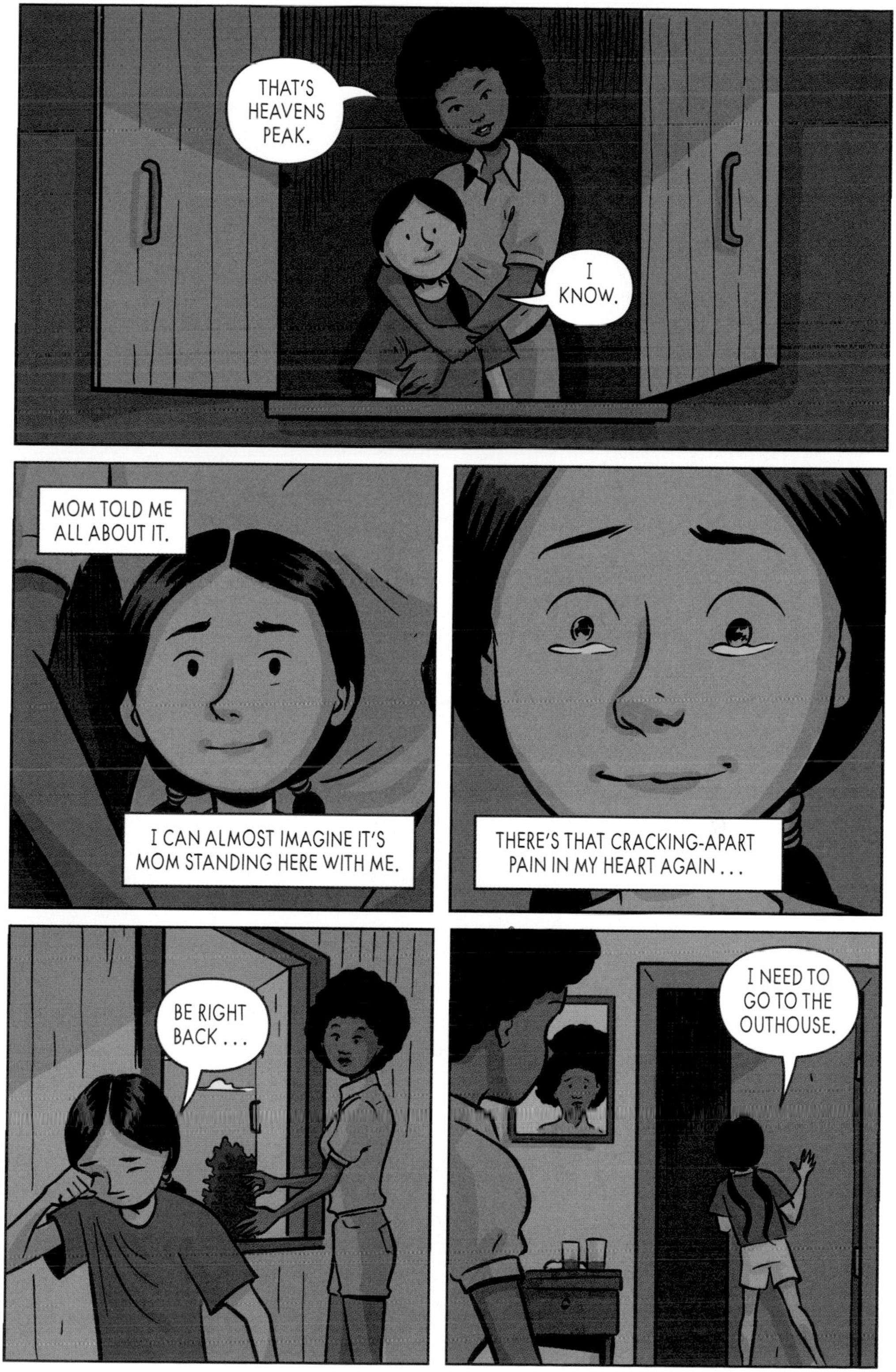
THAT'S HEAVENS PEAK.
I KNOW.
MOM TOLD ME ALL ABOUT IT.
I CAN ALMOST IMAGINE IT'S MOM STANDING HERE WITH ME.
THERE'S THAT CRACKING-APART PAIN IN MY HEART AGAIN . . .
BE RIGHT BACK . . .
I NEED TO GO TO THE OUTHOUSE.

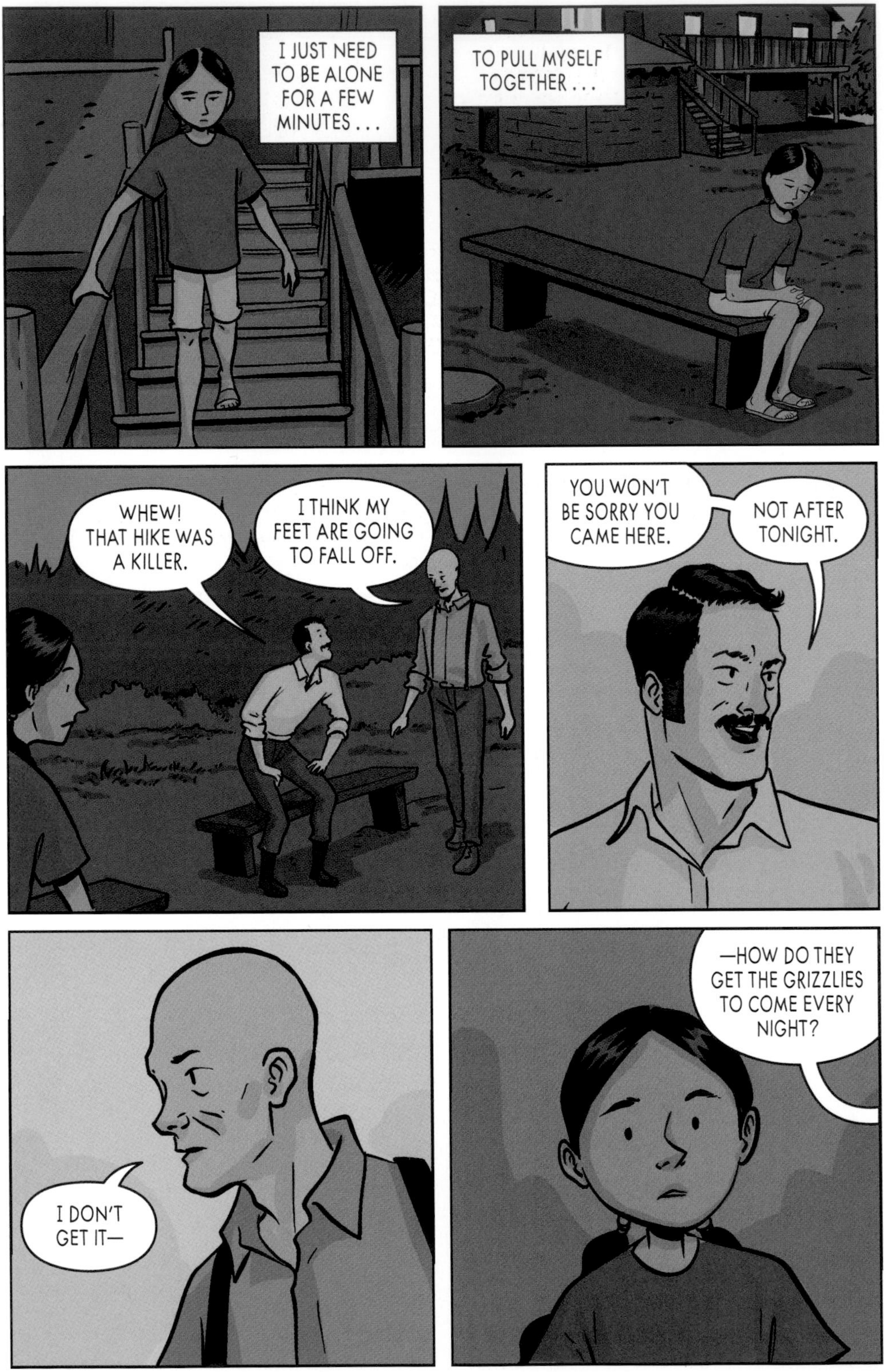
I JUST NEED TO BE ALONE FOR A FEW MINUTES . . .
TO PULL MYSELF TOGETHER . . .
WHEW! THAT HIKE WAS A KILLER.
I THINK MY FEET ARE GOING TO FALL OFF.
YOU WON'T BE SORRY YOU CAME HERE.
NOT AFTER TONIGHT.
I DON'T GET IT—
—HOW DO THEY GET THE GRIZZLIES TO COME EVERY NIGHT?

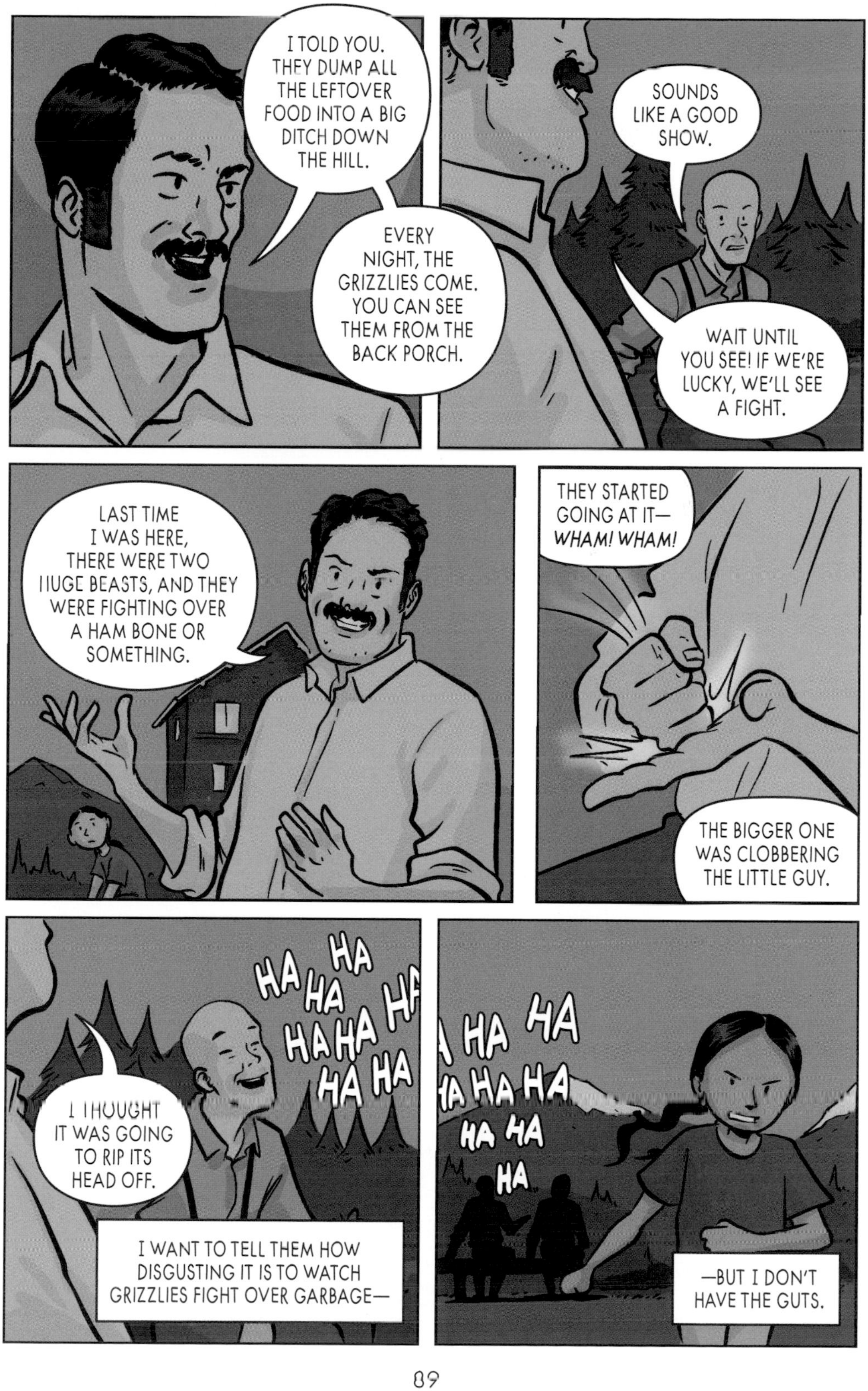
I TOLD YOU. THEY DUMP ALL THE LEFTOVER FOOD INTO A BIG DITCH DOWN THE HILL.
EVERY NIGHT, THE GRIZZLIES COME. YOU CAN SEE THEM FROM THE BACK PORCH.
SOUNDS LIKE A GOOD SHOW.
WAIT UNTIL YOU SEE! IF WE'RE LUCKY, WE'LL SEE A FIGHT.
LAST TIME I WAS HERE, THERE WERE TWO HUGE BEASTS, AND THEY WERE FIGHTING OVER A HAM BONE OR SOMETHING.
THEY STARTED GOING AT IT—*WHAM! WHAM!*
THE BIGGER ONE WAS CLOBBERING THE LITTLE GUY.
HA HA HA HA HA HA HA HA HA
I THOUGHT IT WAS GOING TO RIP ITS HEAD OFF.
I WANT TO TELL THEM HOW DISGUSTING IT IS TO WATCH GRIZZLIES FIGHT OVER GARBAGE—
HA HA HA HA HA HA HA HA
—BUT I DON'T HAVE THE GUTS.

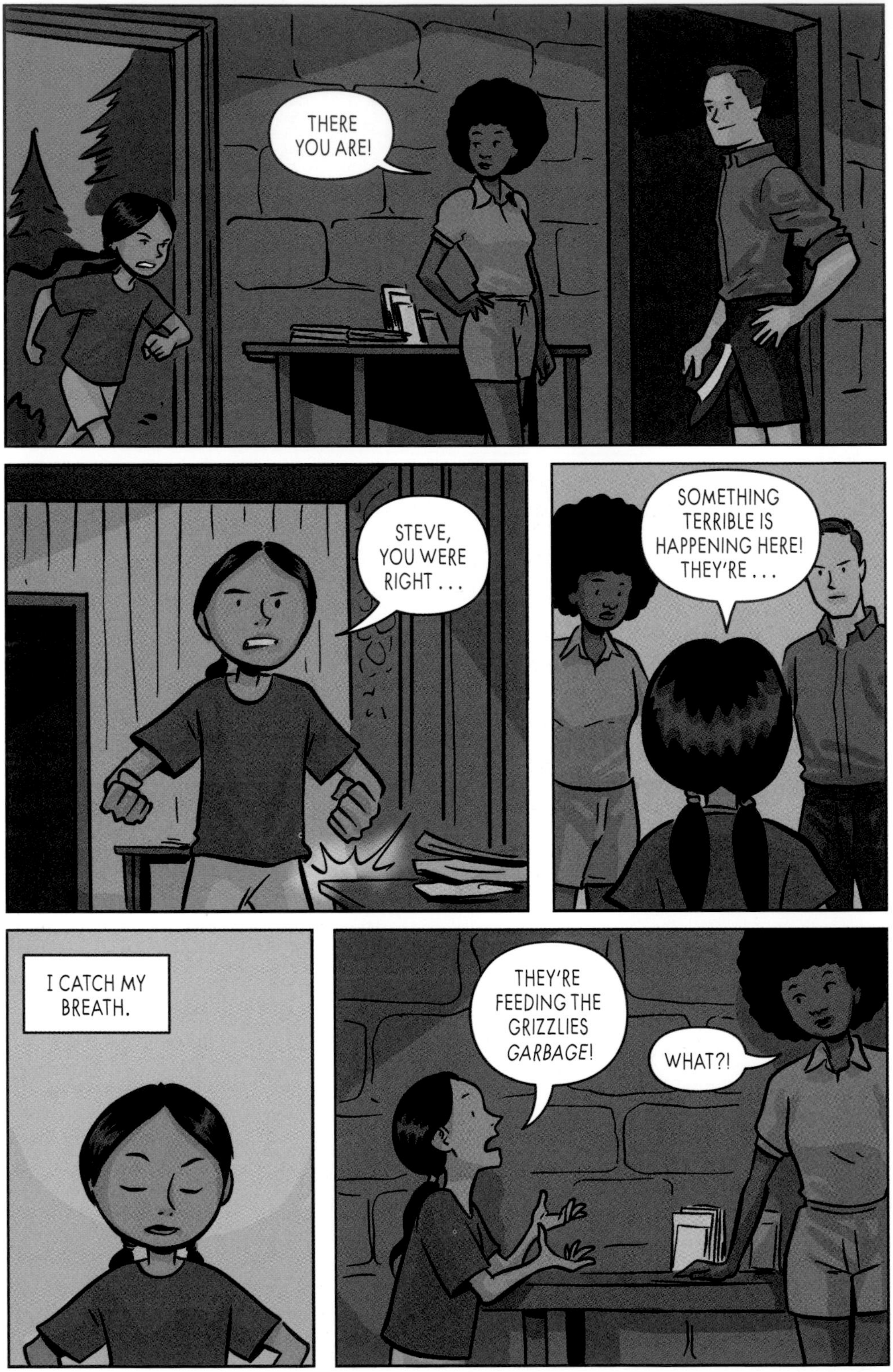
THERE YOU ARE!
STEVE, YOU WERE RIGHT . . .
SOMETHING TERRIBLE IS HAPPENING HERE! THEY'RE . . .
I CATCH MY BREATH.
THEY'RE FEEDING THE GRIZZLIES *GARBAGE*!
WHAT?!

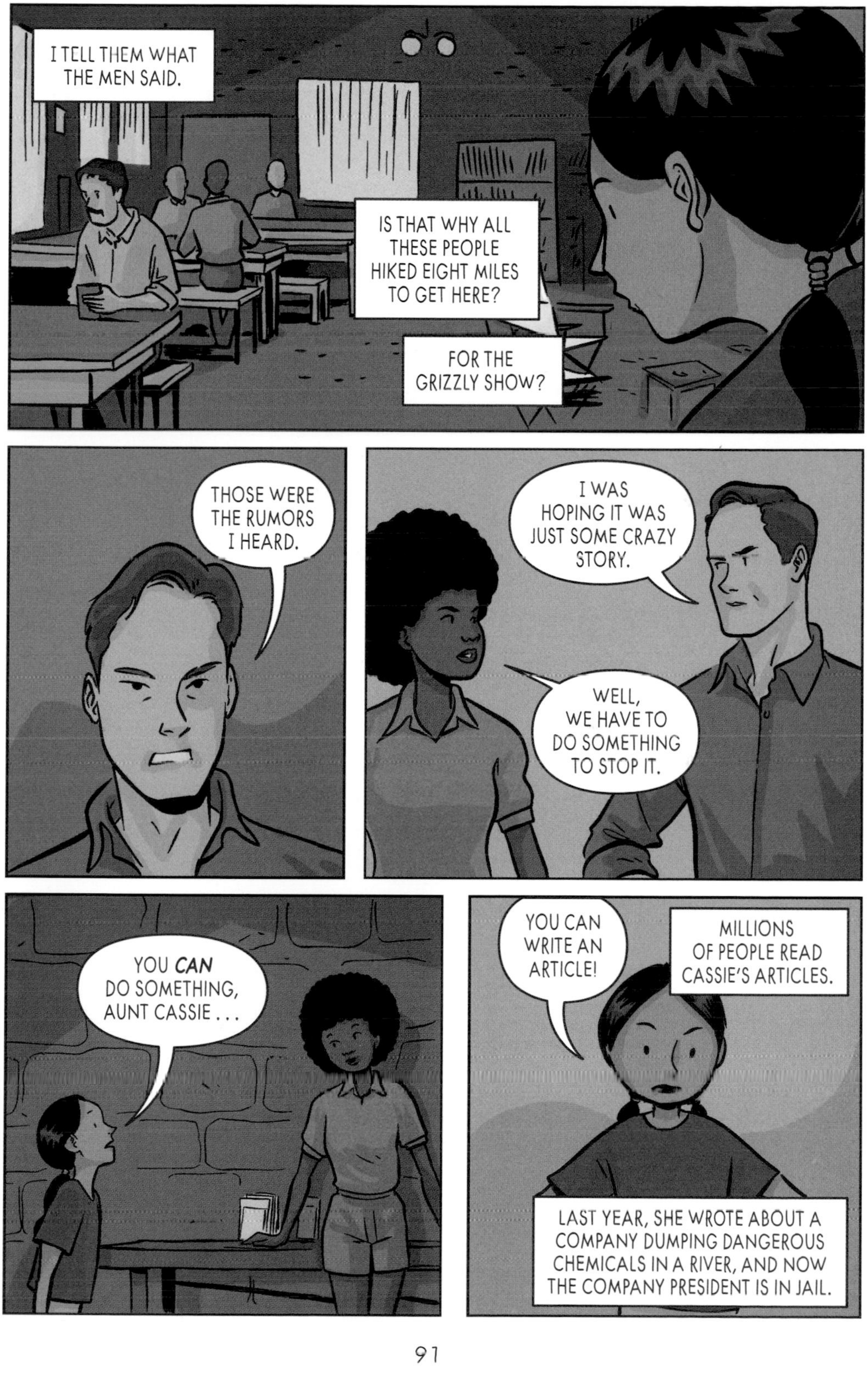
I TELL THEM WHAT THE MEN SAID.
IS THAT WHY ALL THESE PEOPLE HIKED EIGHT MILES TO GET HERE?
FOR THE GRIZZLY SHOW?
THOSE WERE THE RUMORS I HEARD.
I WAS HOPING IT WAS JUST SOME CRAZY STORY.
WELL, WE HAVE TO DO SOMETHING TO STOP IT.
YOU **CAN** DO SOMETHING, AUNT CASSIE . . .
YOU CAN WRITE AN ARTICLE!
MILLIONS OF PEOPLE READ CASSIE'S ARTICLES.
LAST YEAR, SHE WROTE ABOUT A COMPANY DUMPING DANGEROUS CHEMICALS IN A RIVER, AND NOW THE COMPANY PRESIDENT IS IN JAIL.

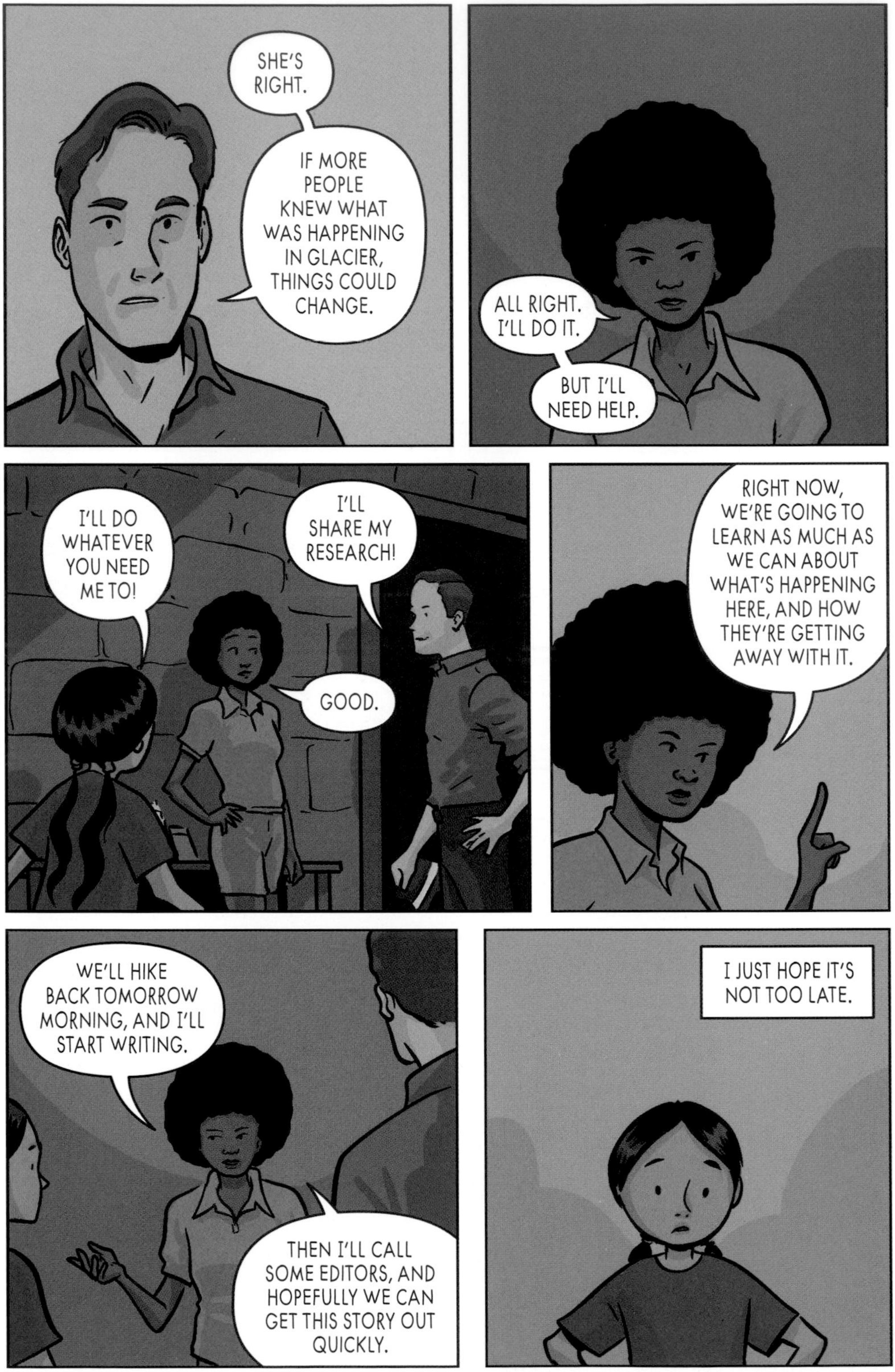
SHE'S RIGHT.
IF MORE PEOPLE KNEW WHAT WAS HAPPENING IN GLACIER, THINGS COULD CHANGE.
ALL RIGHT. I'LL DO IT.
BUT I'LL NEED HELP.
I'LL DO WHATEVER YOU NEED ME TO!
I'LL SHARE MY RESEARCH!
GOOD.
RIGHT NOW, WE'RE GOING TO LEARN AS MUCH AS WE CAN ABOUT WHAT'S HAPPENING HERE, AND HOW THEY'RE GETTING AWAY WITH IT.
WE'LL HIKE BACK TOMORROW MORNING, AND I'LL START WRITING.
THEN I'LL CALL SOME EDITORS, AND HOPEFULLY WE CAN GET THIS STORY OUT QUICKLY.
I JUST HOPE IT'S NOT TOO LATE.

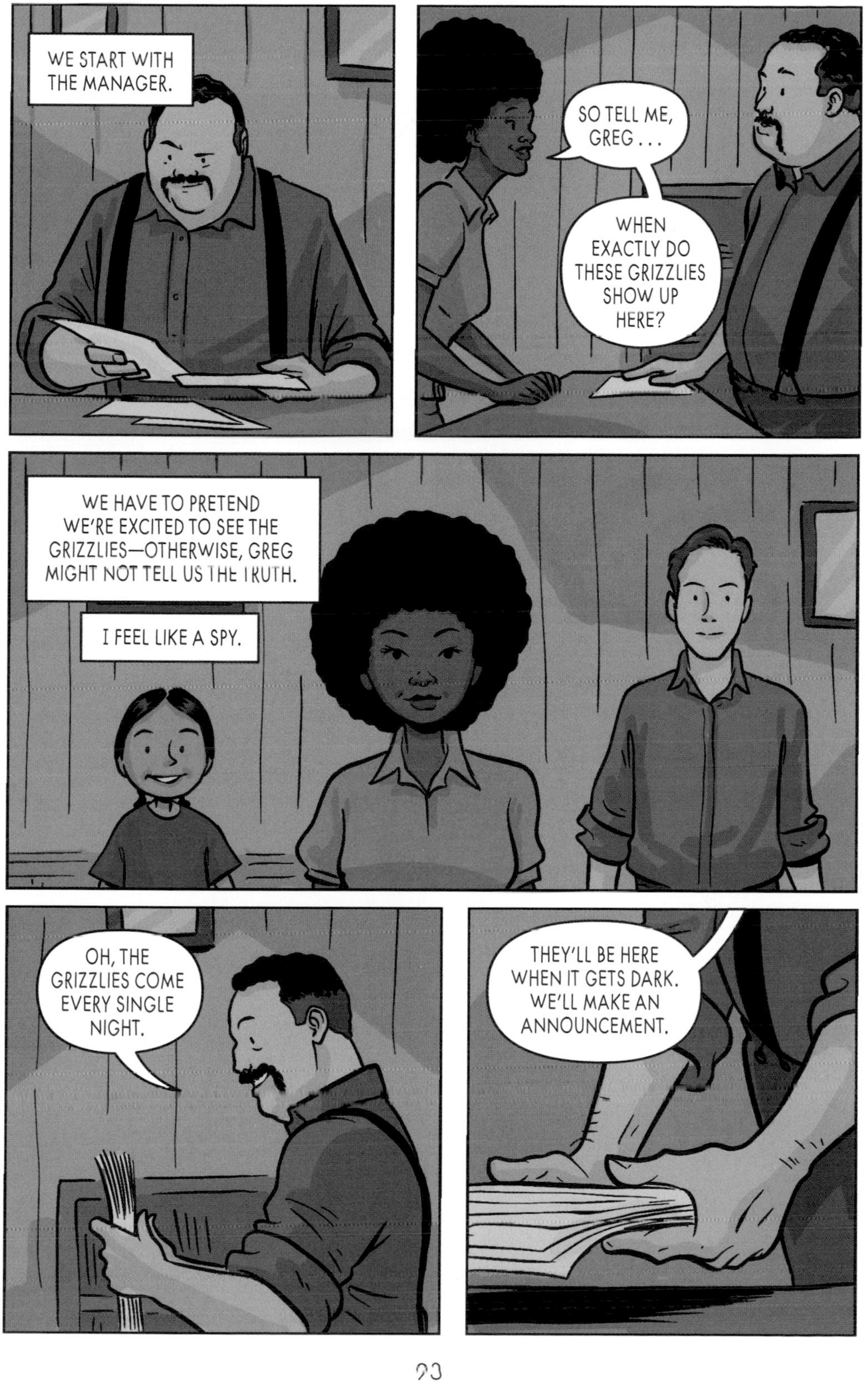
WE START WITH THE MANAGER.
SO TELL ME, GREG . . .
WHEN EXACTLY DO THESE GRIZZLIES SHOW UP HERE?
WE HAVE TO PRETEND WE'RE EXCITED TO SEE THE GRIZZLIES—OTHERWISE, GREG MIGHT NOT TELL US THE TRUTH.
I FEEL LIKE A SPY.
OH, THE GRIZZLIES COME EVERY SINGLE NIGHT.
THEY'LL BE HERE WHEN IT GETS DARK. WE'LL MAKE AN ANNOUNCEMENT.

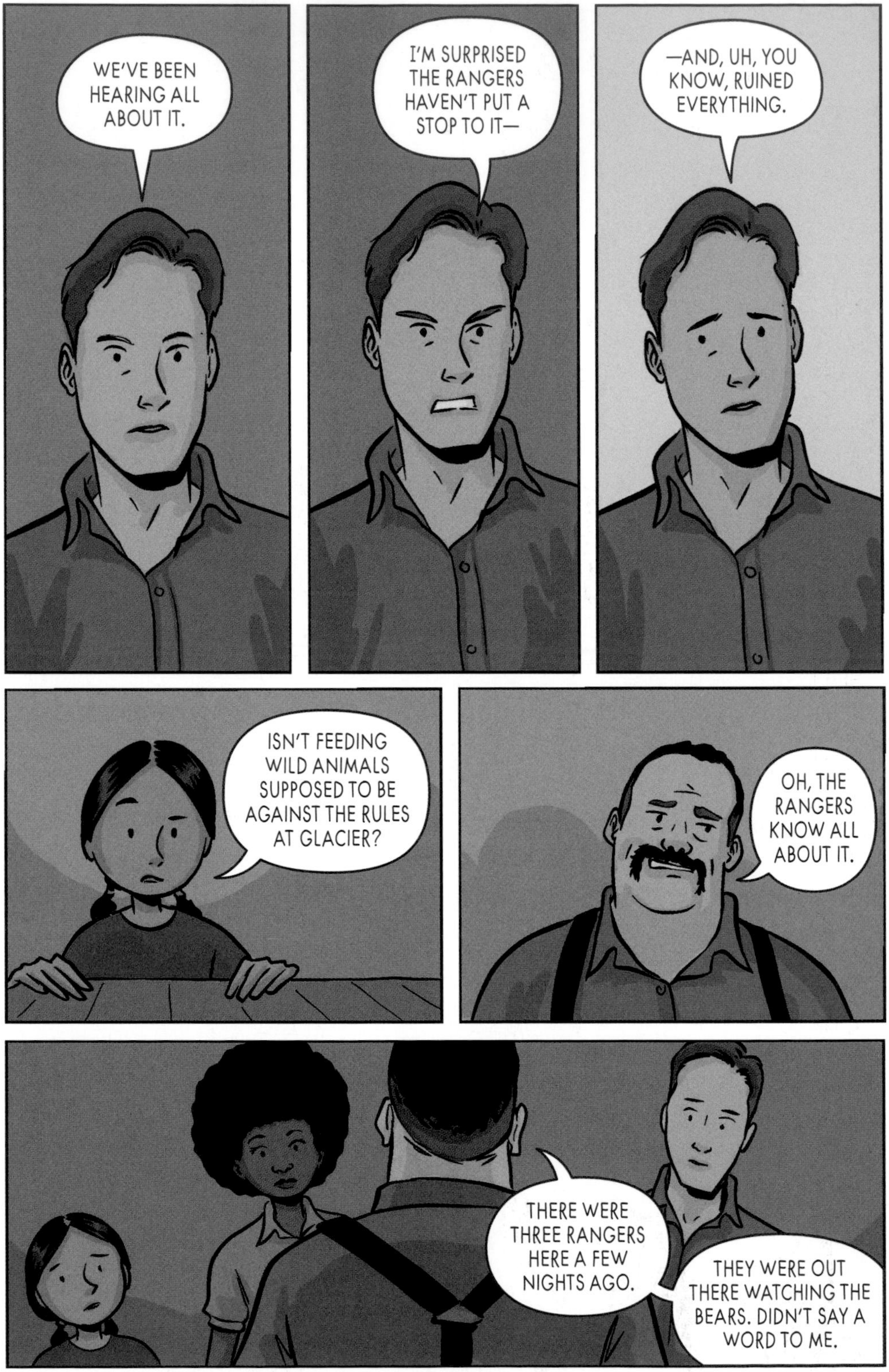
WE'VE BEEN HEARING ALL ABOUT IT.
I'M SURPRISED THE RANGERS HAVEN'T PUT A STOP TO IT—
—AND, UH, YOU KNOW, RUINED EVERYTHING.
ISN'T FEEDING WILD ANIMALS SUPPOSED TO BE AGAINST THE RULES AT GLACIER?
OH, THE RANGERS KNOW ALL ABOUT IT.
THERE WERE THREE RANGERS HERE A FEW NIGHTS AGO.
THEY WERE OUT THERE WATCHING THE BEARS. DIDN'T SAY A WORD TO ME.

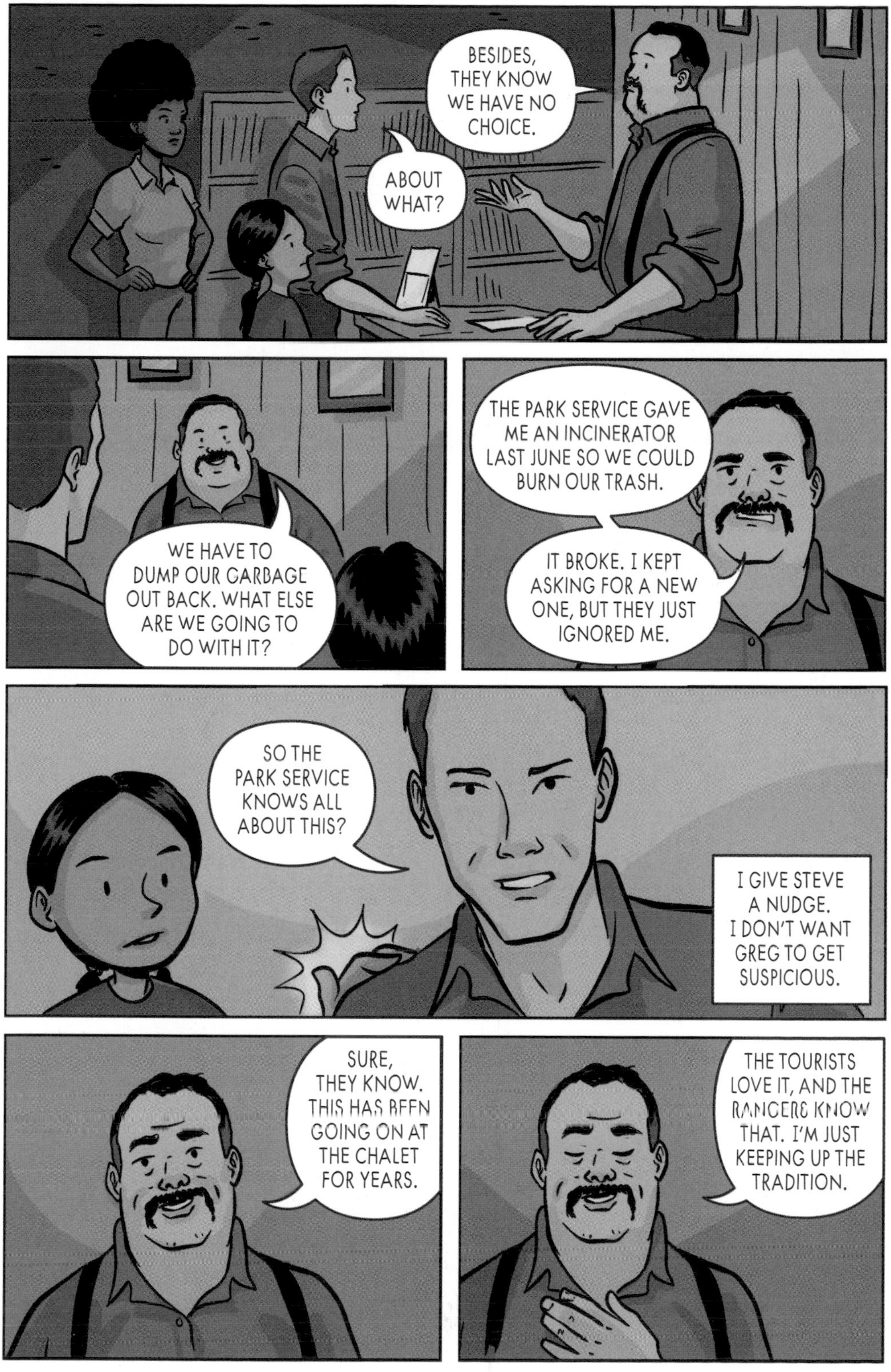
BESIDES, THEY KNOW WE HAVE NO CHOICE.
ABOUT WHAT?
WE HAVE TO DUMP OUR GARBAGE OUT BACK. WHAT ELSE ARE WE GOING TO DO WITH IT?
THE PARK SERVICE GAVE ME AN INCINERATOR LAST JUNE SO WE COULD BURN OUR TRASH.
IT BROKE. I KEPT ASKING FOR A NEW ONE, BUT THEY JUST IGNORED ME.
SO THE PARK SERVICE KNOWS ALL ABOUT THIS?
I GIVE STEVE A NUDGE. I DON'T WANT GREG TO GET SUSPICIOUS.
SURE, THEY KNOW. THIS HAS BEEN GOING ON AT THE CHALET FOR YEARS.
THE TOURISTS LOVE IT, AND THE RANGERS KNOW THAT. I'M JUST KEEPING UP THE TRADITION.

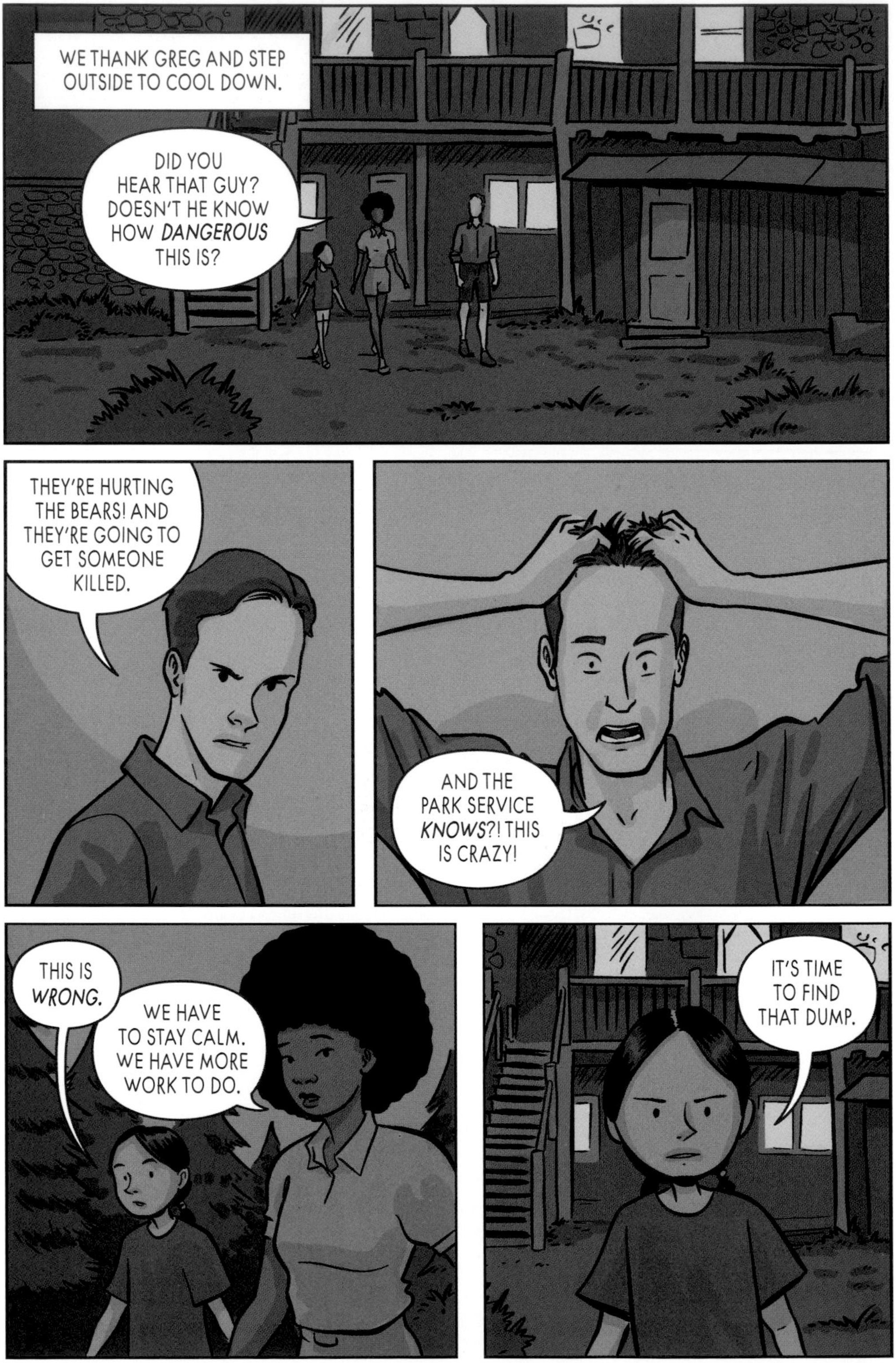
WE THANK GREG AND STEP OUTSIDE TO COOL DOWN.
DID YOU HEAR THAT GUY? DOESN'T HE KNOW HOW *DANGEROUS* THIS IS?
THEY'RE HURTING THE BEARS! AND THEY'RE GOING TO GET SOMEONE KILLED.
AND THE PARK SERVICE *KNOWS*?! THIS IS CRAZY!
THIS IS *WRONG.*
WE HAVE TO STAY CALM. WE HAVE MORE WORK TO DO.
IT'S TIME TO FIND THAT DUMP.

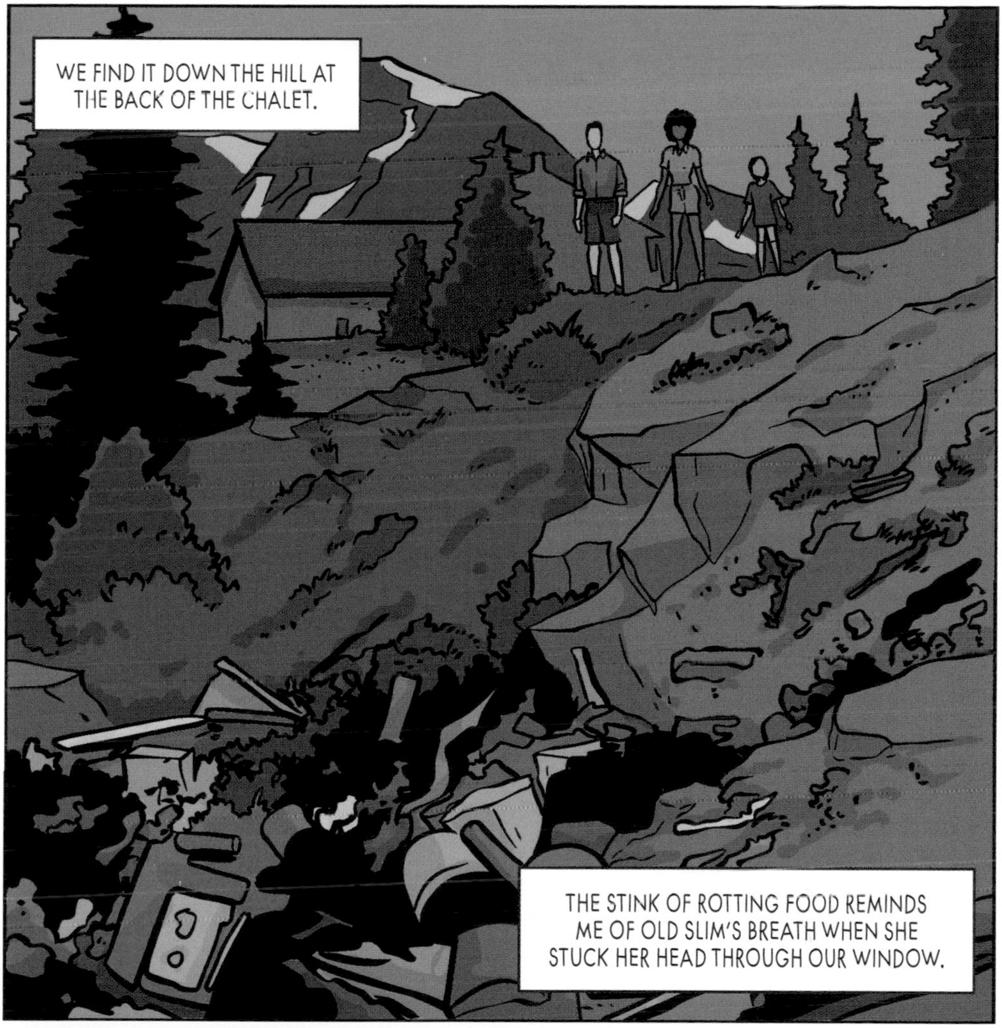
WE FIND IT DOWN THE HILL AT THE BACK OF THE CHALET.
THE STINK OF ROTTING FOOD REMINDS ME OF OLD SLIM'S BREATH WHEN SHE STUCK HER HEAD THROUGH OUR WINDOW.

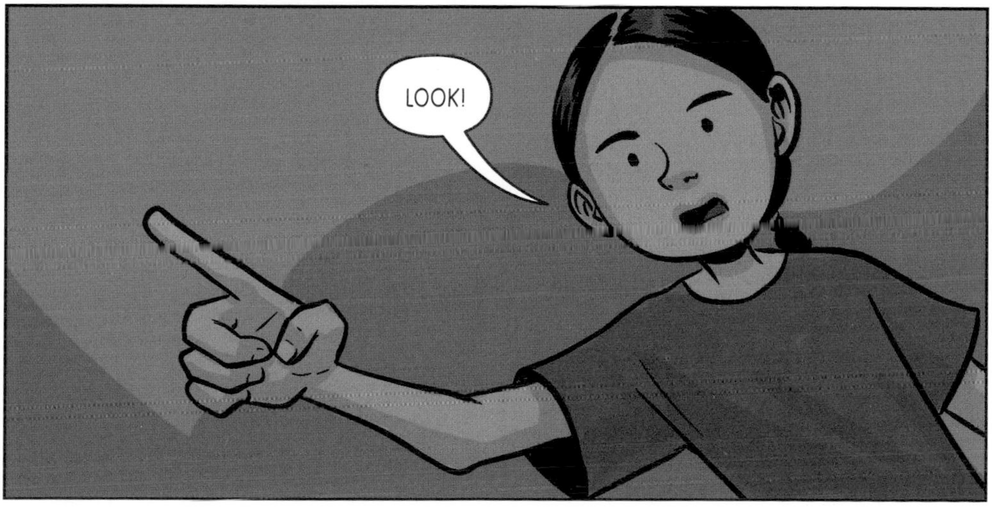
LOOK!

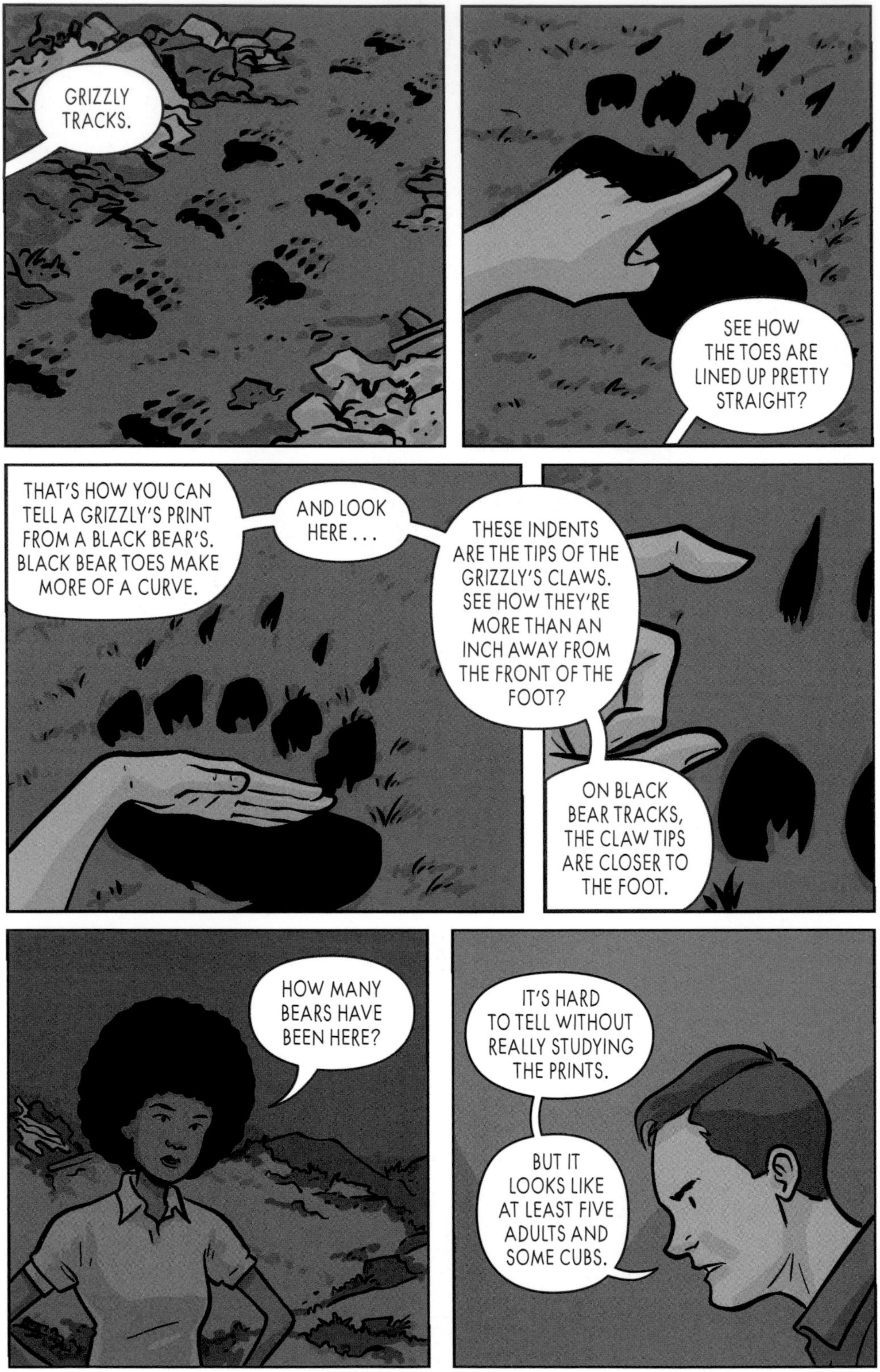
GRIZZLY TRACKS.
SEE HOW THE TOES ARE LINED UP PRETTY STRAIGHT?
THAT'S HOW YOU CAN TELL A GRIZZLY'S PRINT FROM A BLACK BEAR'S. BLACK BEAR TOES MAKE MORE OF A CURVE.
AND LOOK HERE . . .
THESE INDENTS ARE THE TIPS OF THE GRIZZLY'S CLAWS. SEE HOW THEY'RE MORE THAN AN INCH AWAY FROM THE FRONT OF THE FOOT?
ON BLACK BEAR TRACKS, THE CLAW TIPS ARE CLOSER TO THE FOOT.
HOW MANY BEARS HAVE BEEN HERE?
IT'S HARD TO TELL WITHOUT REALLY STUDYING THE PRINTS.
BUT IT LOOKS LIKE AT LEAST FIVE ADULTS AND SOME CUBS.

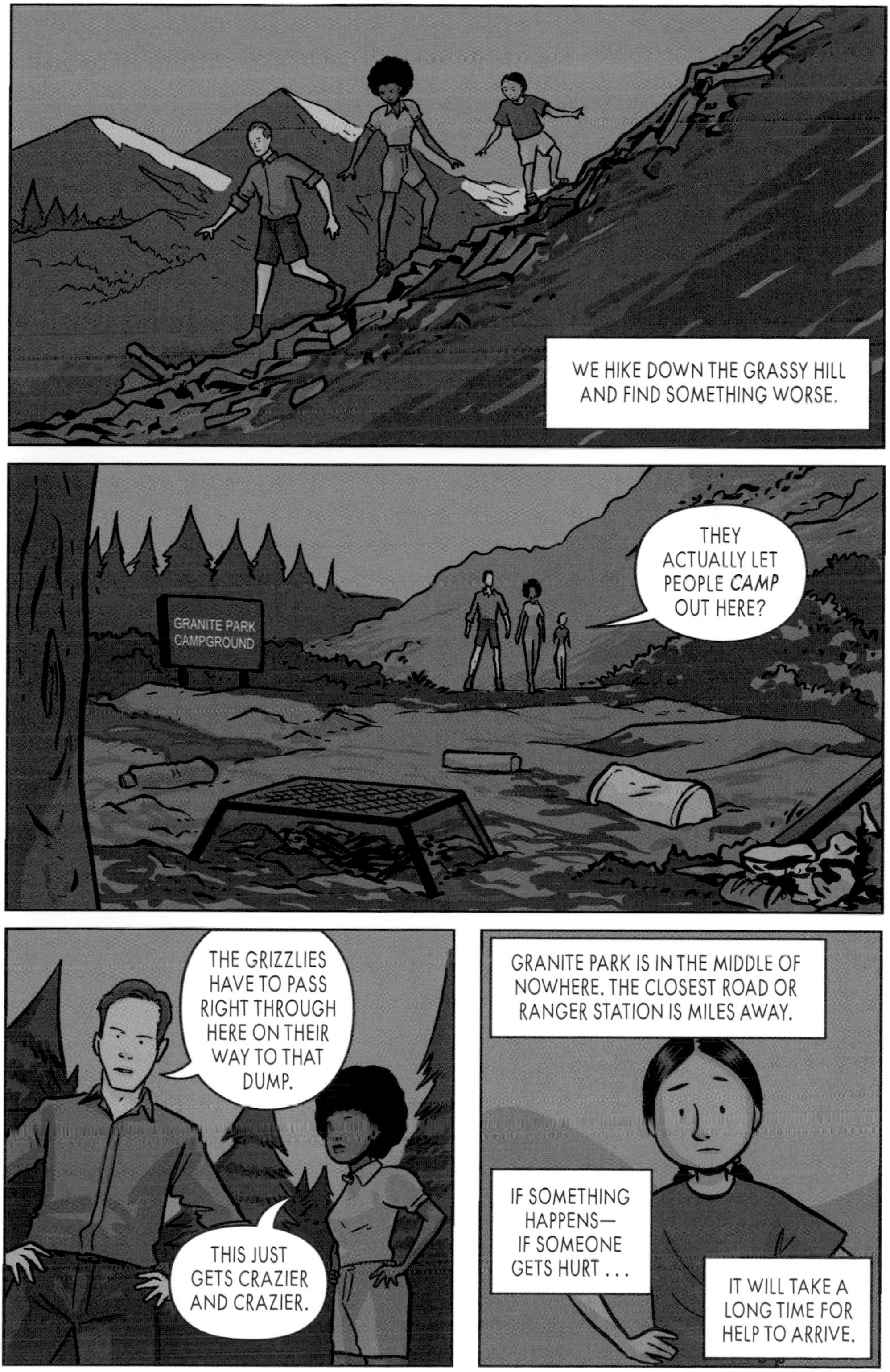
WE HIKE DOWN THE GRASSY HILL AND FIND SOMETHING WORSE.
GRANITE PARK CAMPGROUND
THEY ACTUALLY LET PEOPLE *CAMP* OUT HERE?
THE GRIZZLIES HAVE TO PASS RIGHT THROUGH HERE ON THEIR WAY TO THAT DUMP.
THIS JUST GETS CRAZIER AND CRAZIER.
GRANITE PARK IS IN THE MIDDLE OF NOWHERE. THE CLOSEST ROAD OR RANGER STATION IS MILES AWAY.
IF SOMETHING HAPPENS— IF SOMEONE GETS HURT . . .
IT WILL TAKE A LONG TIME FOR HELP TO ARRIVE.

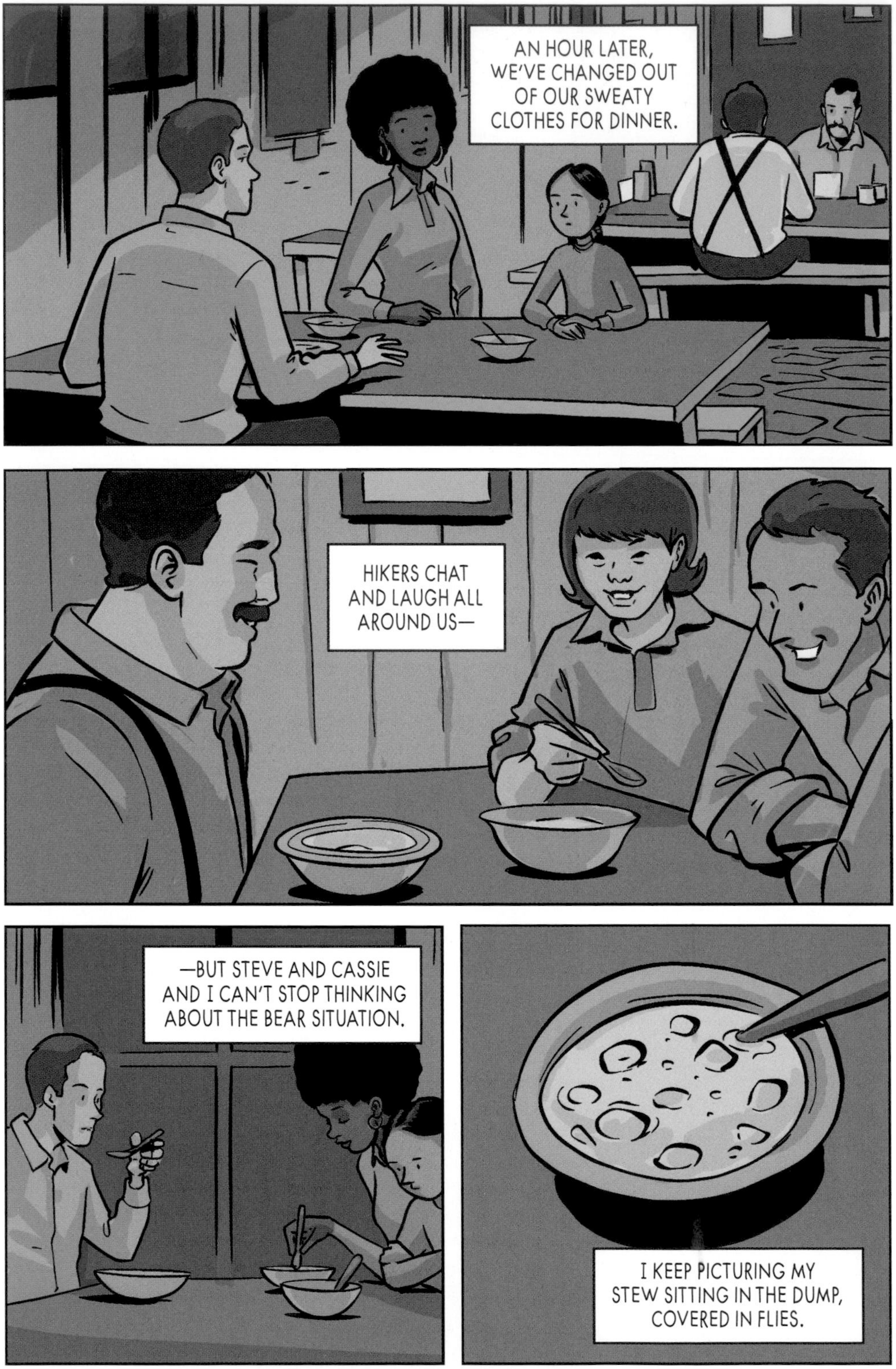
AN HOUR LATER, WE'VE CHANGED OUT OF OUR SWEATY CLOTHES FOR DINNER.
HIKERS CHAT AND LAUGH ALL AROUND US—
—BUT STEVE AND CASSIE AND I CAN'T STOP THINKING ABOUT THE BEAR SITUATION.
I KEEP PICTURING MY STEW SITTING IN THE DUMP, COVERED IN FLIES.

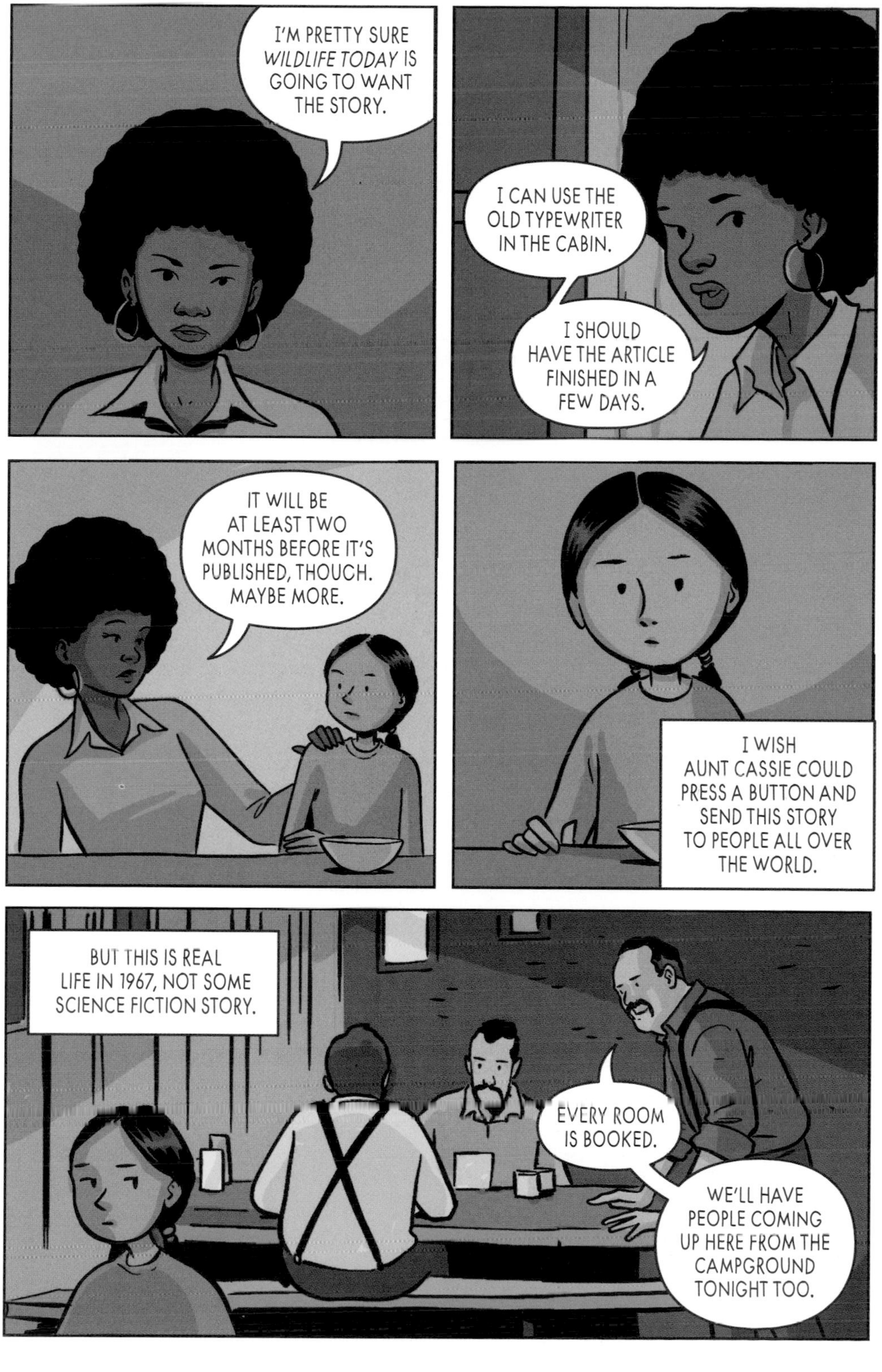
I'M PRETTY SURE *WILDLIFE TODAY* IS GOING TO WANT THE STORY.
I CAN USE THE OLD TYPEWRITER IN THE CABIN.
I SHOULD HAVE THE ARTICLE FINISHED IN A FEW DAYS.
IT WILL BE AT LEAST TWO MONTHS BEFORE IT'S PUBLISHED, THOUGH. MAYBE MORE.
I WISH AUNT CASSIE COULD PRESS A BUTTON AND SEND THIS STORY TO PEOPLE ALL OVER THE WORLD.
BUT THIS IS REAL LIFE IN 1967, NOT SOME SCIENCE FICTION STORY.
EVERY ROOM IS BOOKED.
WE'LL HAVE PEOPLE COMING UP HERE FROM THE CAMPGROUND TONIGHT TOO.

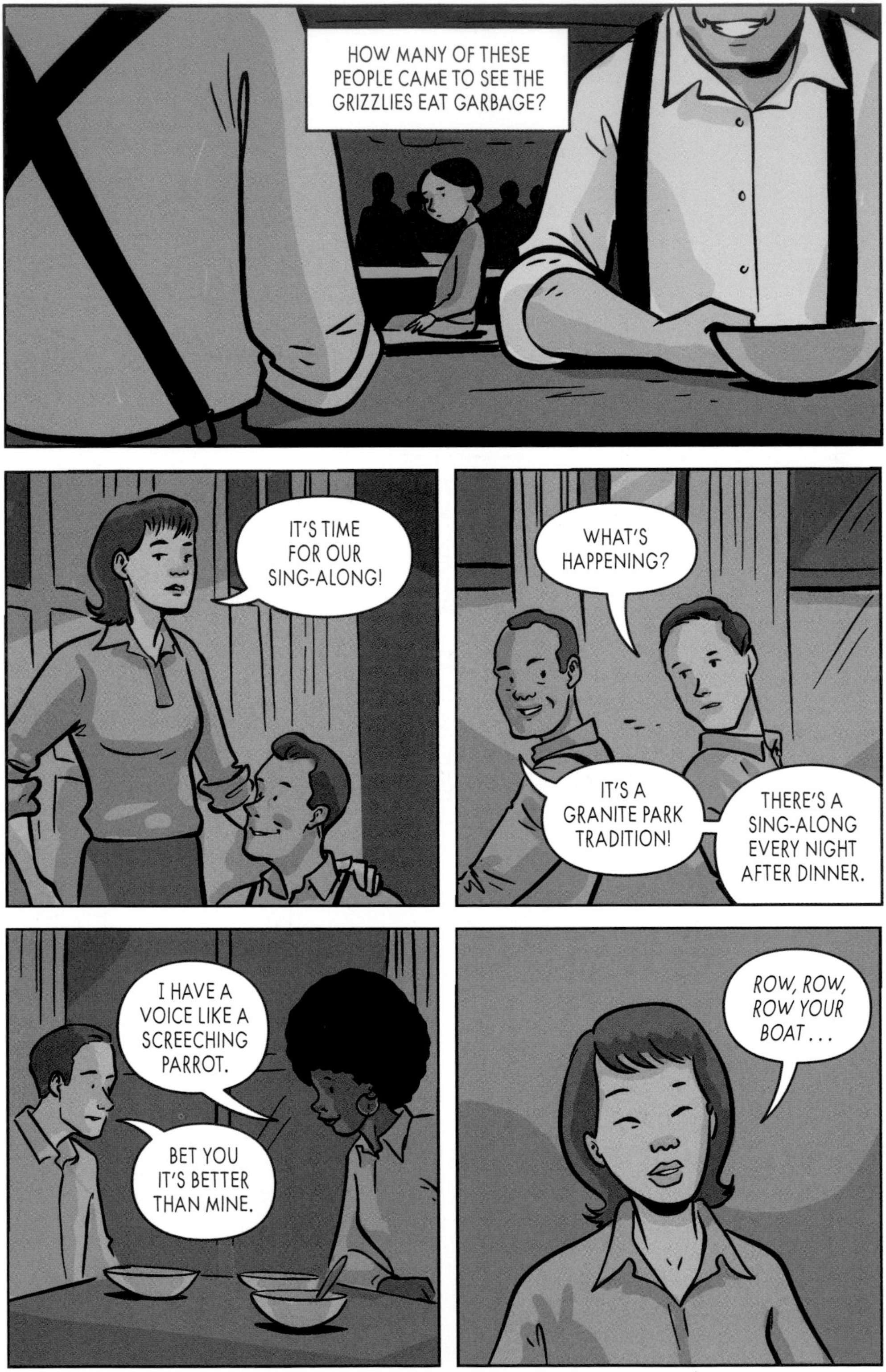

HOW MANY OF THESE PEOPLE CAME TO SEE THE GRIZZLIES EAT GARBAGE?
IT'S TIME FOR OUR SING-ALONG!
WHAT'S HAPPENING?
IT'S A GRANITE PARK TRADITION!
THERE'S A SING-ALONG EVERY NIGHT AFTER DINNER.
I HAVE A VOICE LIKE A SCREECHING PARROT.
BET YOU IT'S BETTER THAN MINE.
ROW, ROW, ROW YOUR BOAT . . .

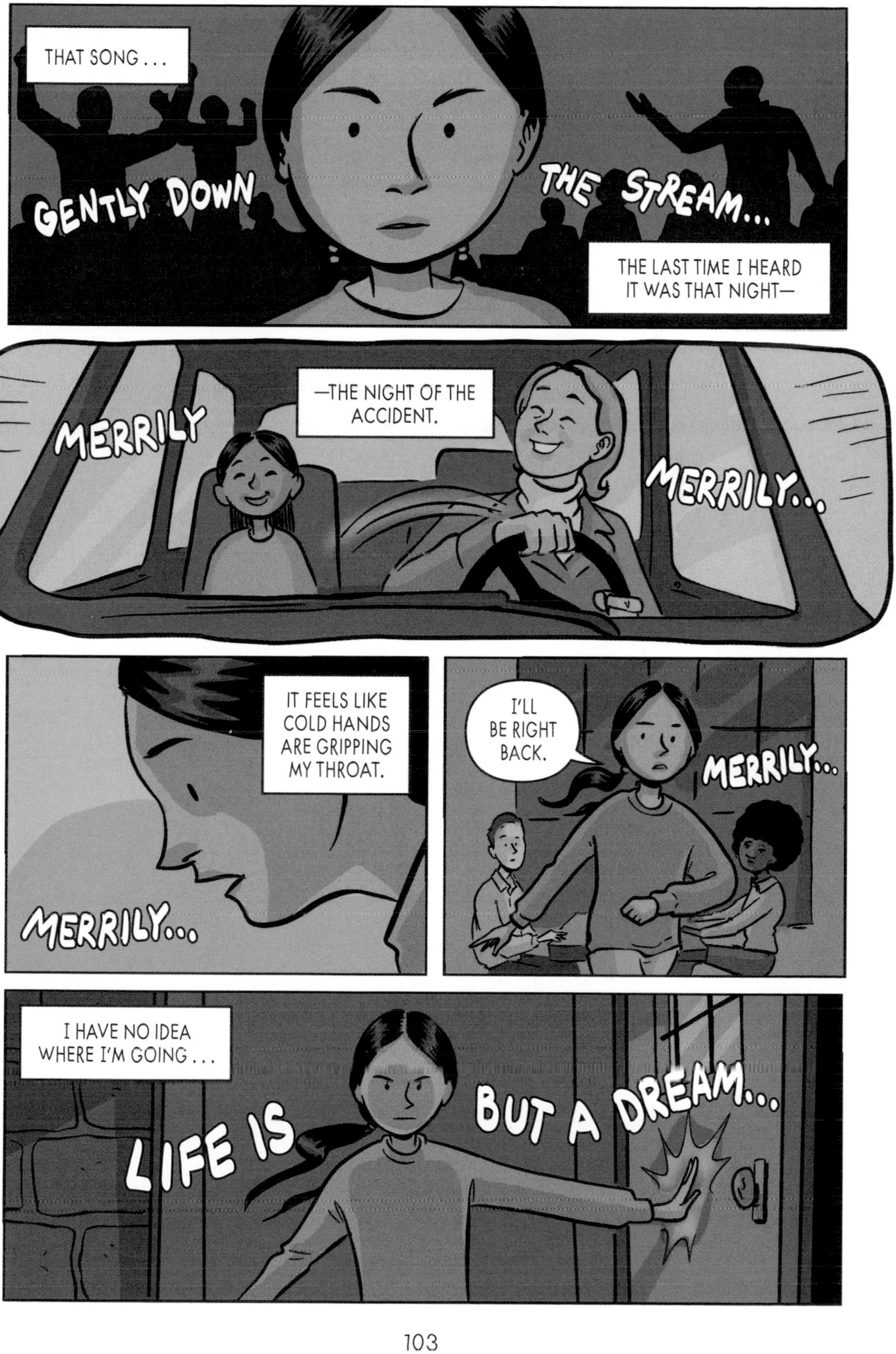

THAT SONG . . .
GENTLY DOWN
THE STREAM...
THE LAST TIME I HEARD IT WAS THAT NIGHT—
—THE NIGHT OF THE ACCIDENT.
MERRILY
MERRILY...
IT FEELS LIKE COLD HANDS ARE GRIPPING MY THROAT.
MERRILY...
I'LL BE RIGHT BACK.
MERRILY...
I HAVE NO IDEA WHERE I'M GOING . . .
LIFE IS
BUT A DREAM...

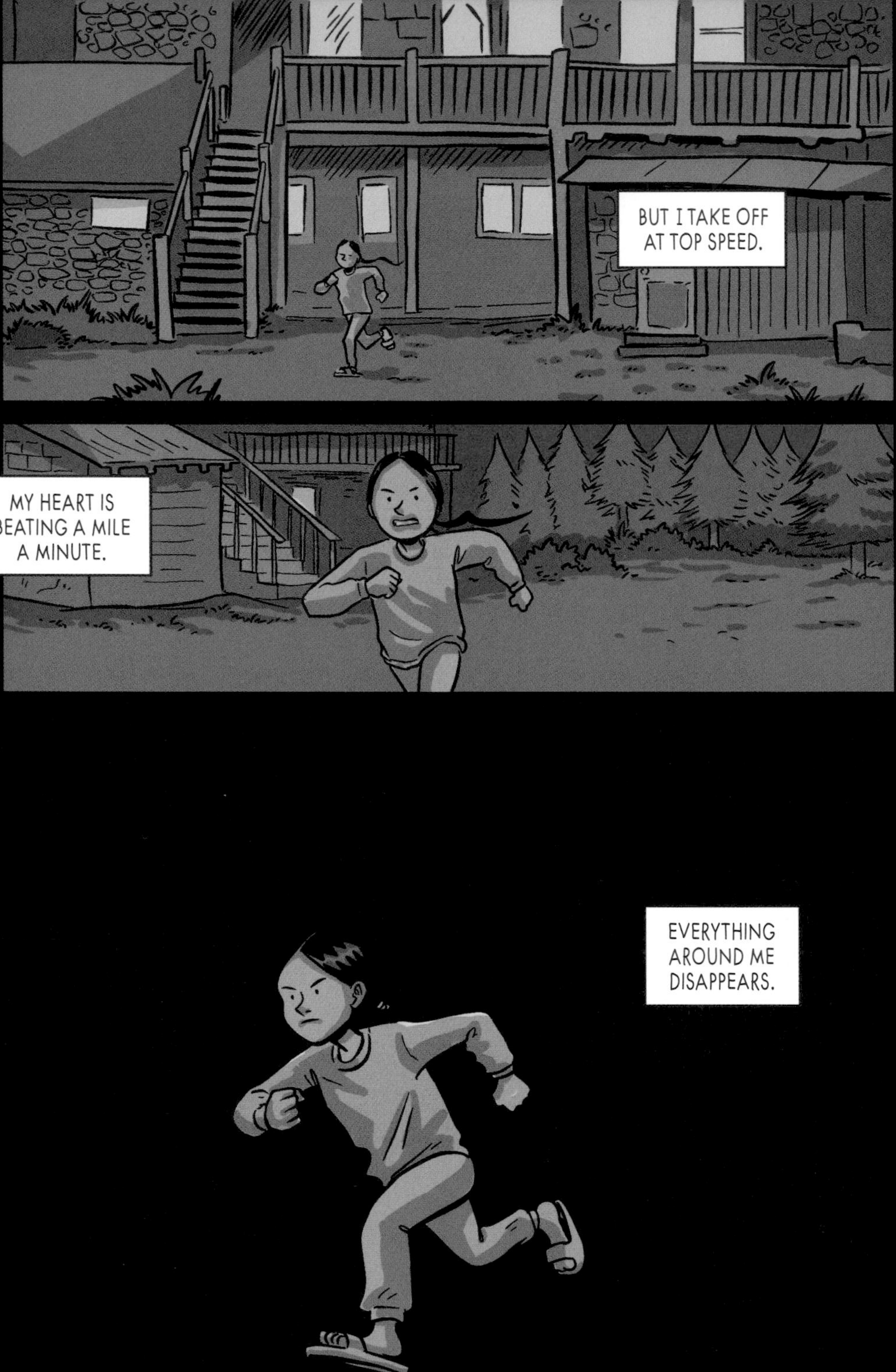
BUT I TAKE OFF AT TOP SPEED.
MY HEART IS BEATING A MILE A MINUTE.
EVERYTHING AROUND ME DISAPPEARS.

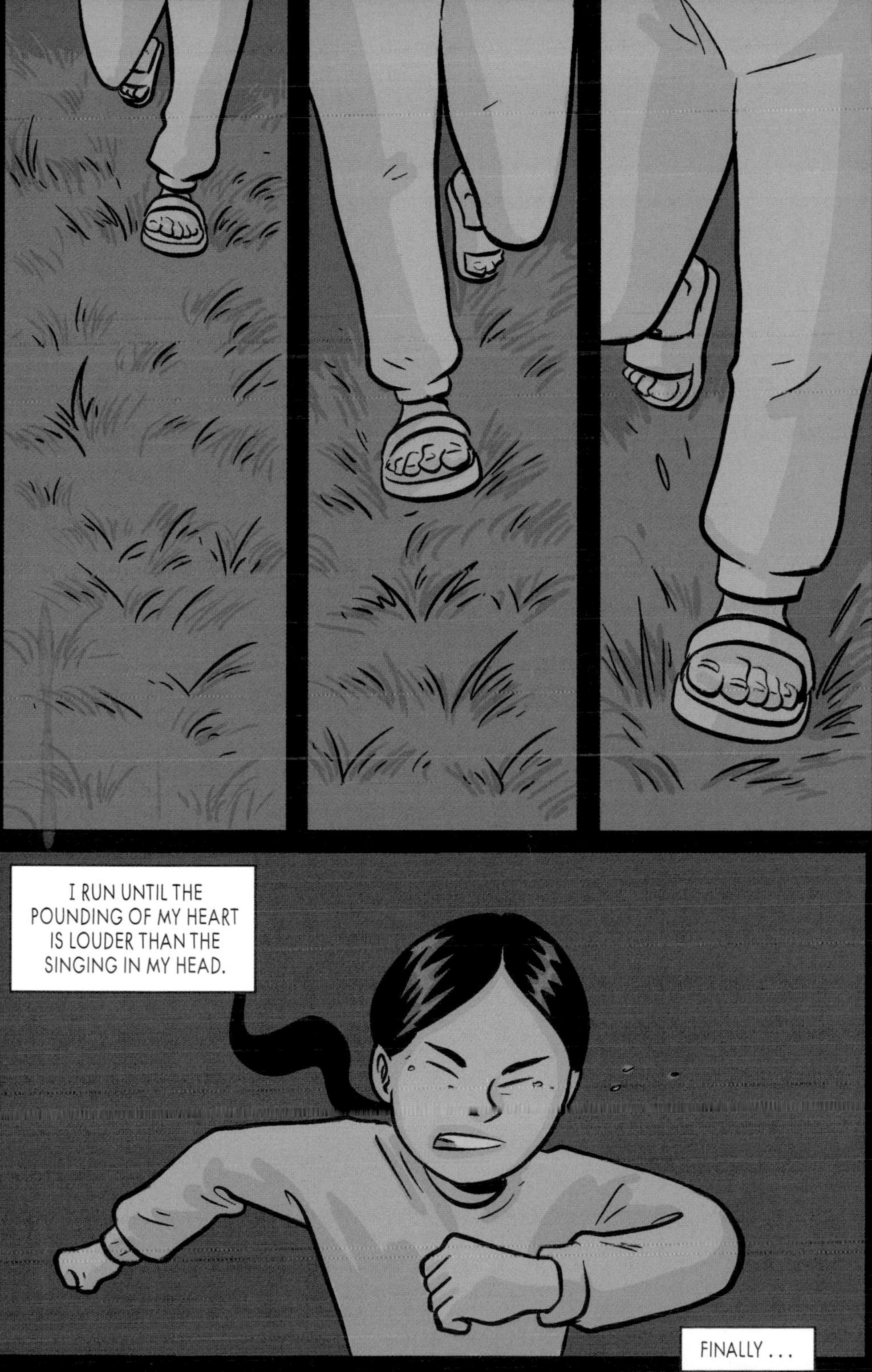
I RUN UNTIL THE POUNDING OF MY HEART IS LOUDER THAN THE SINGING IN MY HEAD.
FINALLY . . .

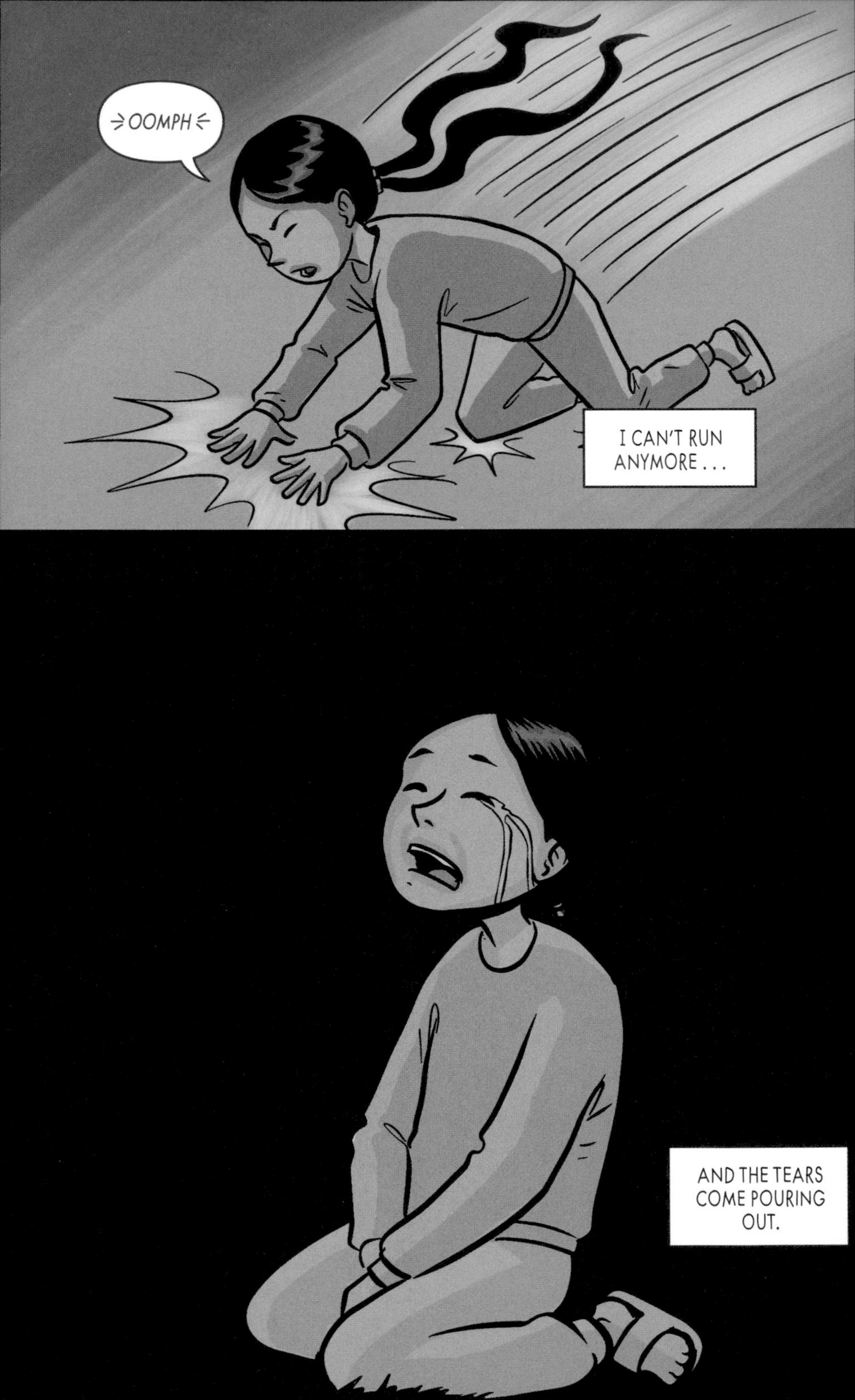
OOMPH
I CAN'T RUN ANYMORE . . .
AND THE TEARS COME POURING OUT.

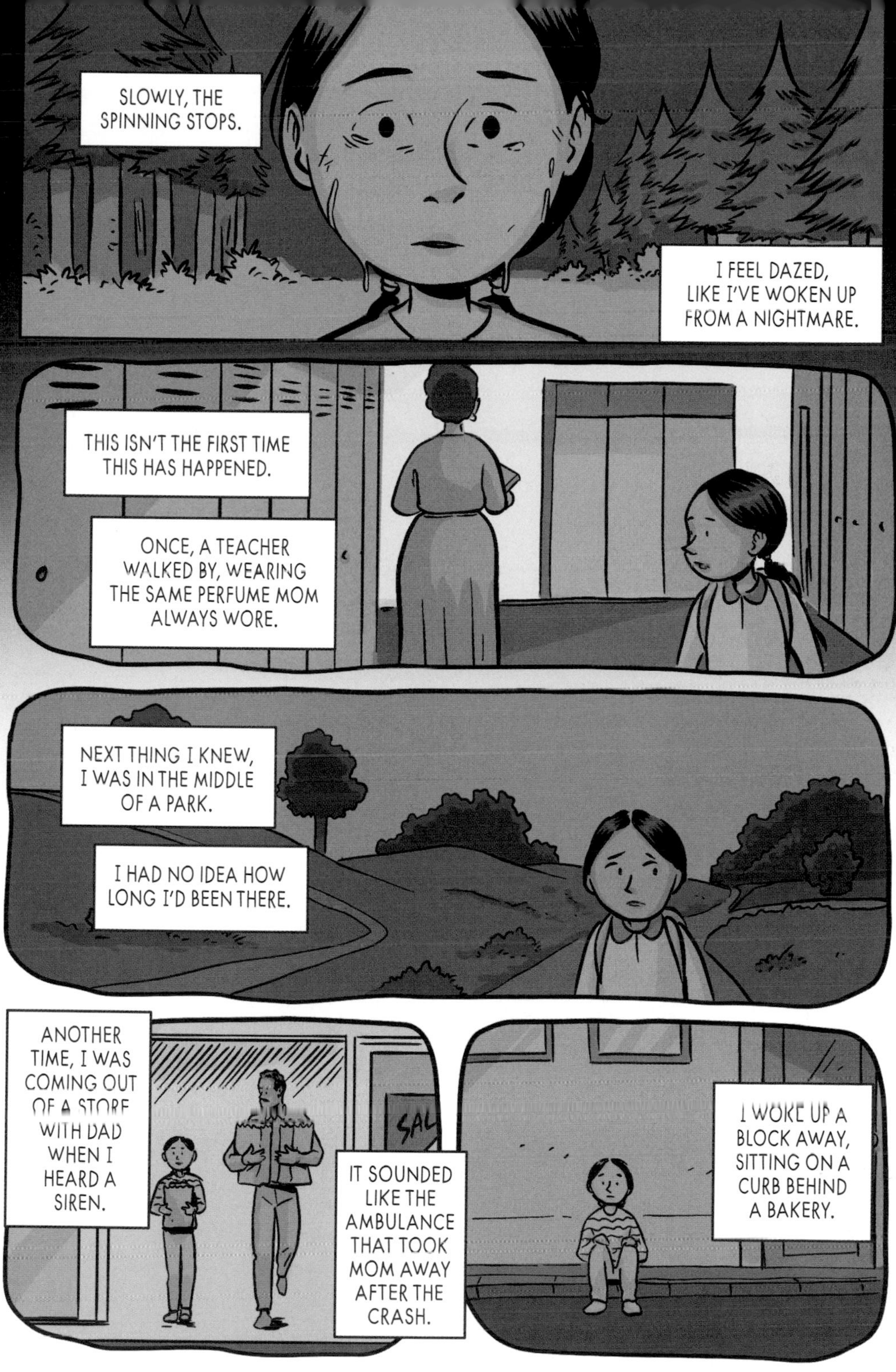
SLOWLY, THE SPINNING STOPS.
I FEEL DAZED, LIKE I'VE WOKEN UP FROM A NIGHTMARE.
THIS ISN'T THE FIRST TIME THIS HAS HAPPENED.
ONCE, A TEACHER WALKED BY, WEARING THE SAME PERFUME MOM ALWAYS WORE.
NEXT THING I KNEW, I WAS IN THE MIDDLE OF A PARK.
I HAD NO IDEA HOW LONG I'D BEEN THERE.
ANOTHER TIME, I WAS COMING OUT OF A STORE WITH DAD WHEN I HEARD A SIREN.
IT SOUNDED LIKE THE AMBULANCE THAT TOOK MOM AWAY AFTER THE CRASH.
I WOKE UP A BLOCK AWAY, SITTING ON A CURB BEHIND A BAKERY.

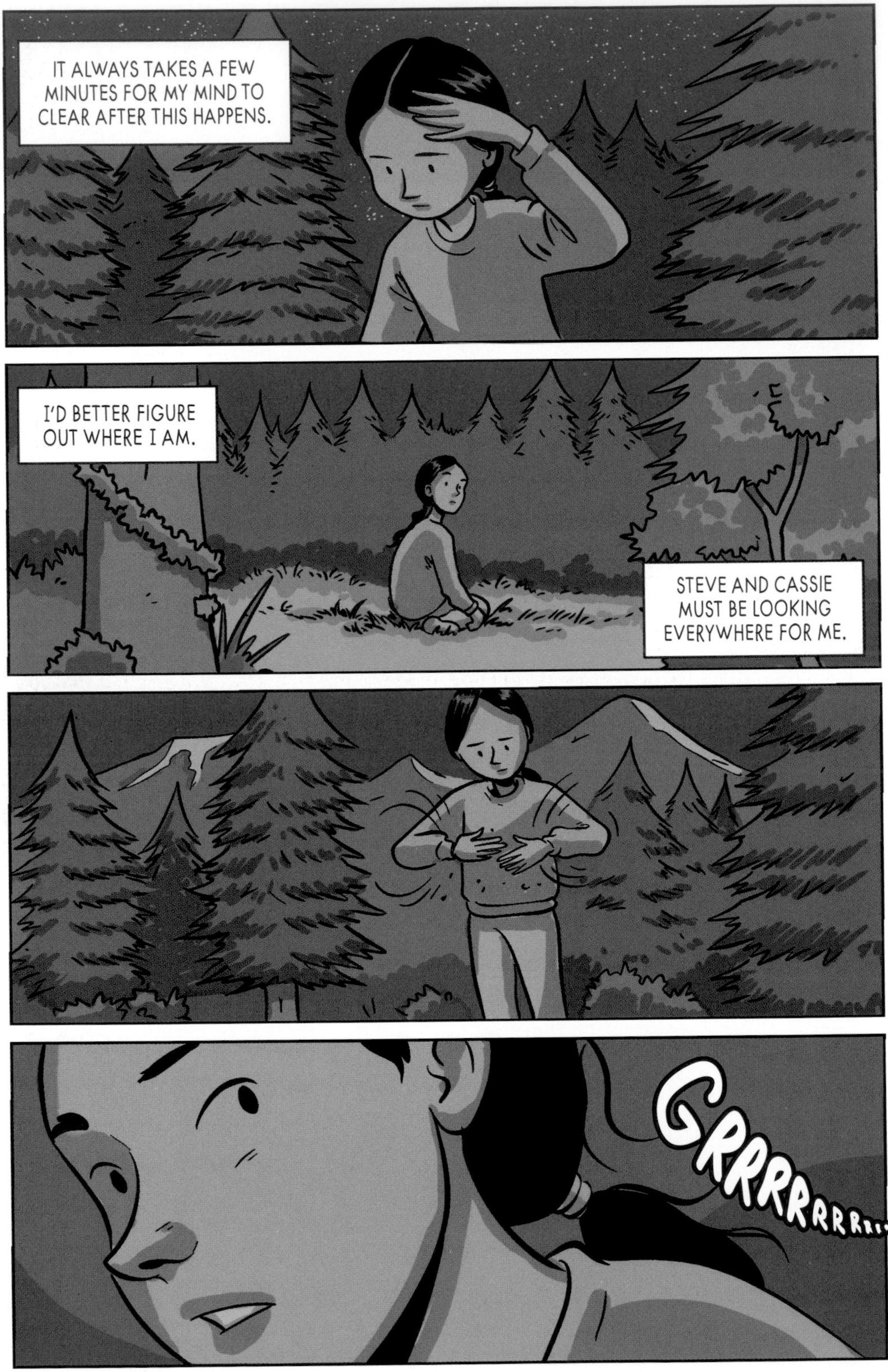
IT ALWAYS TAKES A FEW MINUTES FOR MY MIND TO CLEAR AFTER THIS HAPPENS.
I'D BETTER FIGURE OUT WHERE I AM.
STEVE AND CASSIE MUST BE LOOKING EVERYWHERE FOR ME.
GRRRRRRRR...

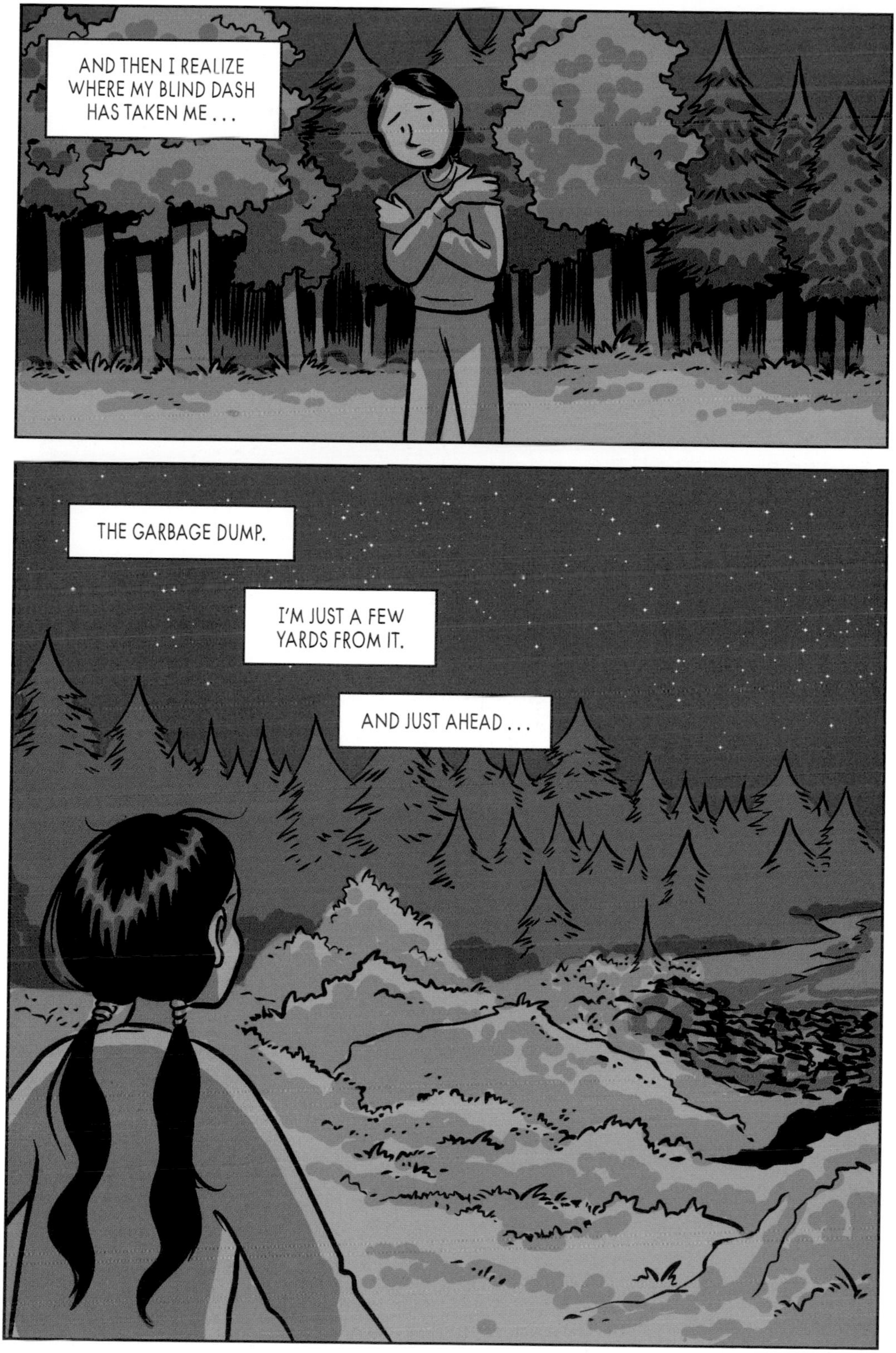
AND THEN I REALIZE WHERE MY BLIND DASH HAS TAKEN ME . . .
THE GARBAGE DUMP.
I'M JUST A FEW YARDS FROM IT.
AND JUST AHEAD . . .

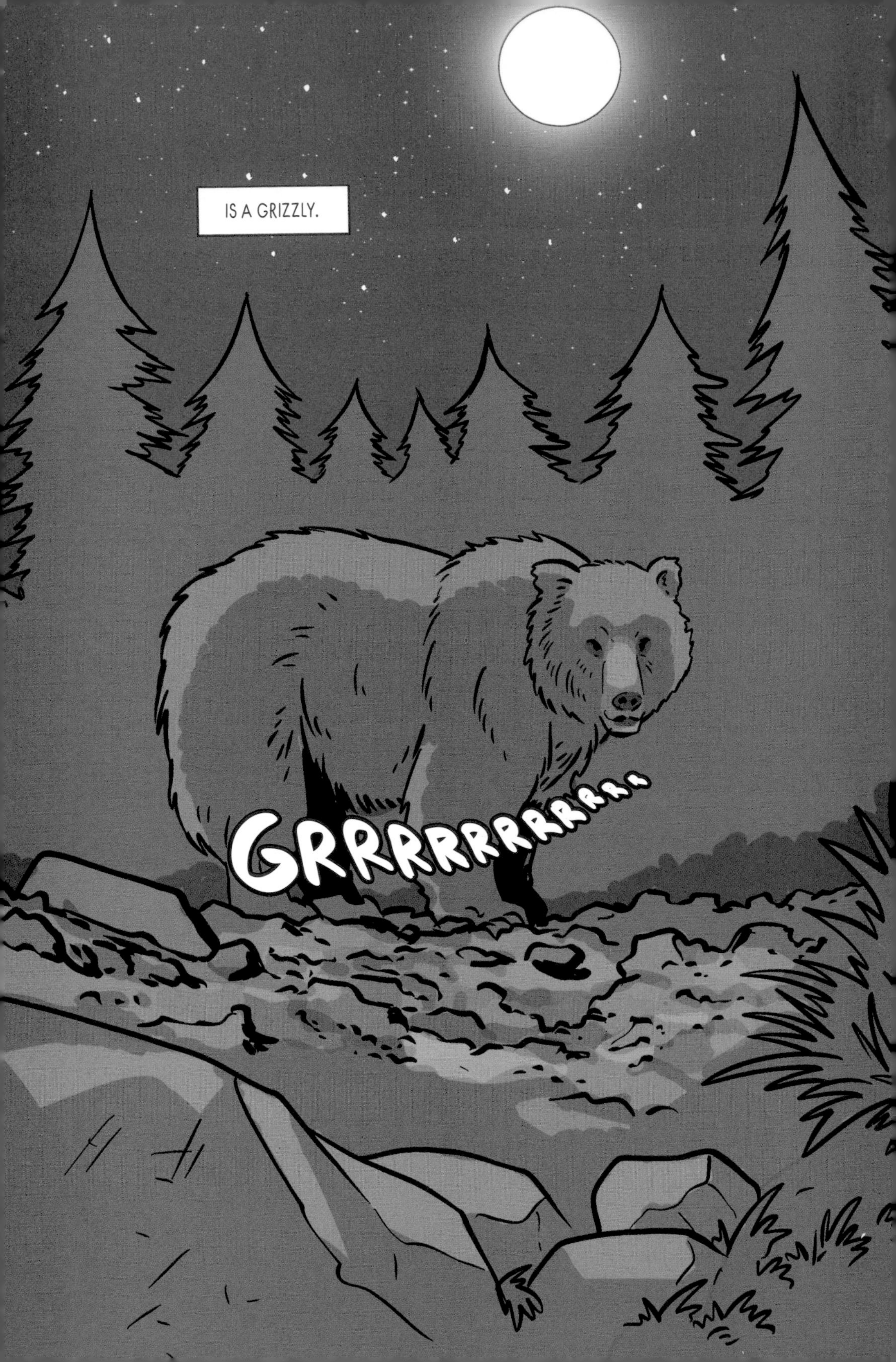
IS A GRIZZLY.
GRRRRRRRRRRr...

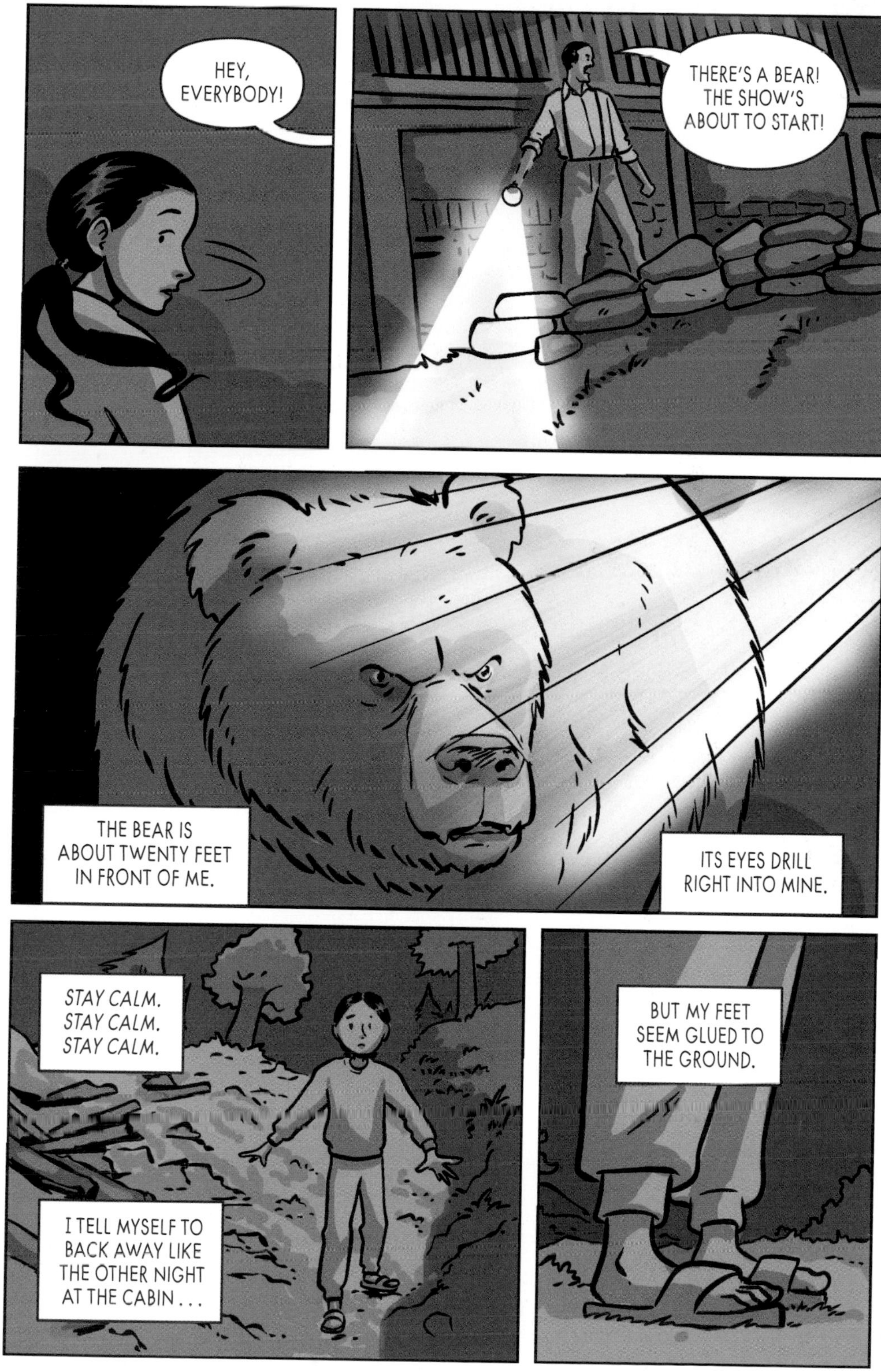
HEY, EVERYBODY!
THERE'S A BEAR! THE SHOW'S ABOUT TO START!
THE BEAR IS ABOUT TWENTY FEET IN FRONT OF ME.
ITS EYES DRILL RIGHT INTO MINE.
STAY CALM. STAY CALM. STAY CALM.
I TELL MYSELF TO BACK AWAY LIKE THE OTHER NIGHT AT THE CABIN . . .
BUT MY FEET SEEM GLUED TO THE GROUND.

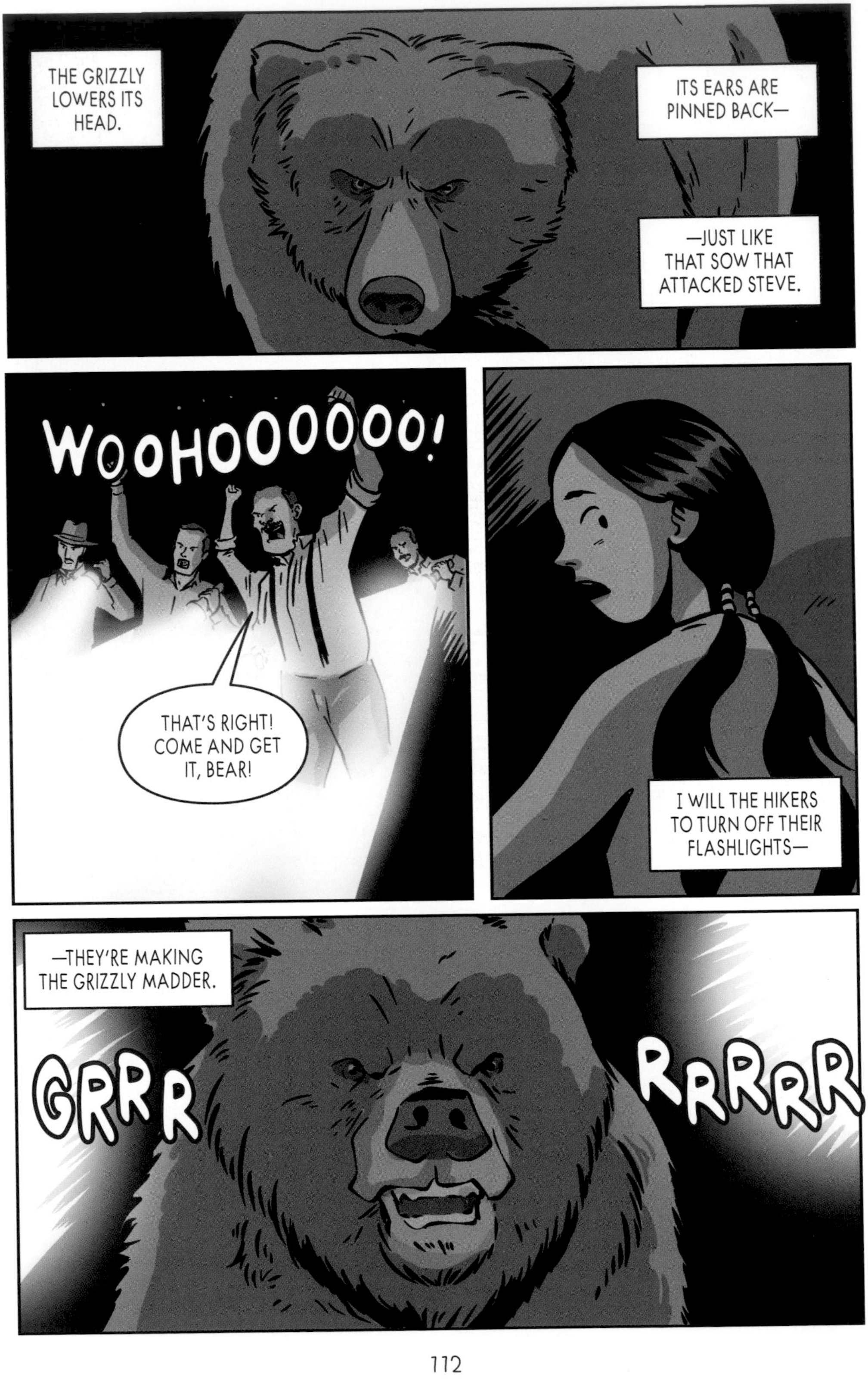
THE GRIZZLY LOWERS ITS HEAD.
ITS EARS ARE PINNED BACK—
—JUST LIKE THAT SOW THAT ATTACKED STEVE.
WOOHOOOOOO!
THAT'S RIGHT! COME AND GET IT, BEAR!
I WILL THE HIKERS TO TURN OFF THEIR FLASHLIGHTS—
—THEY'RE MAKING THE GRIZZLY MADDER.
GRRR
RRRRR

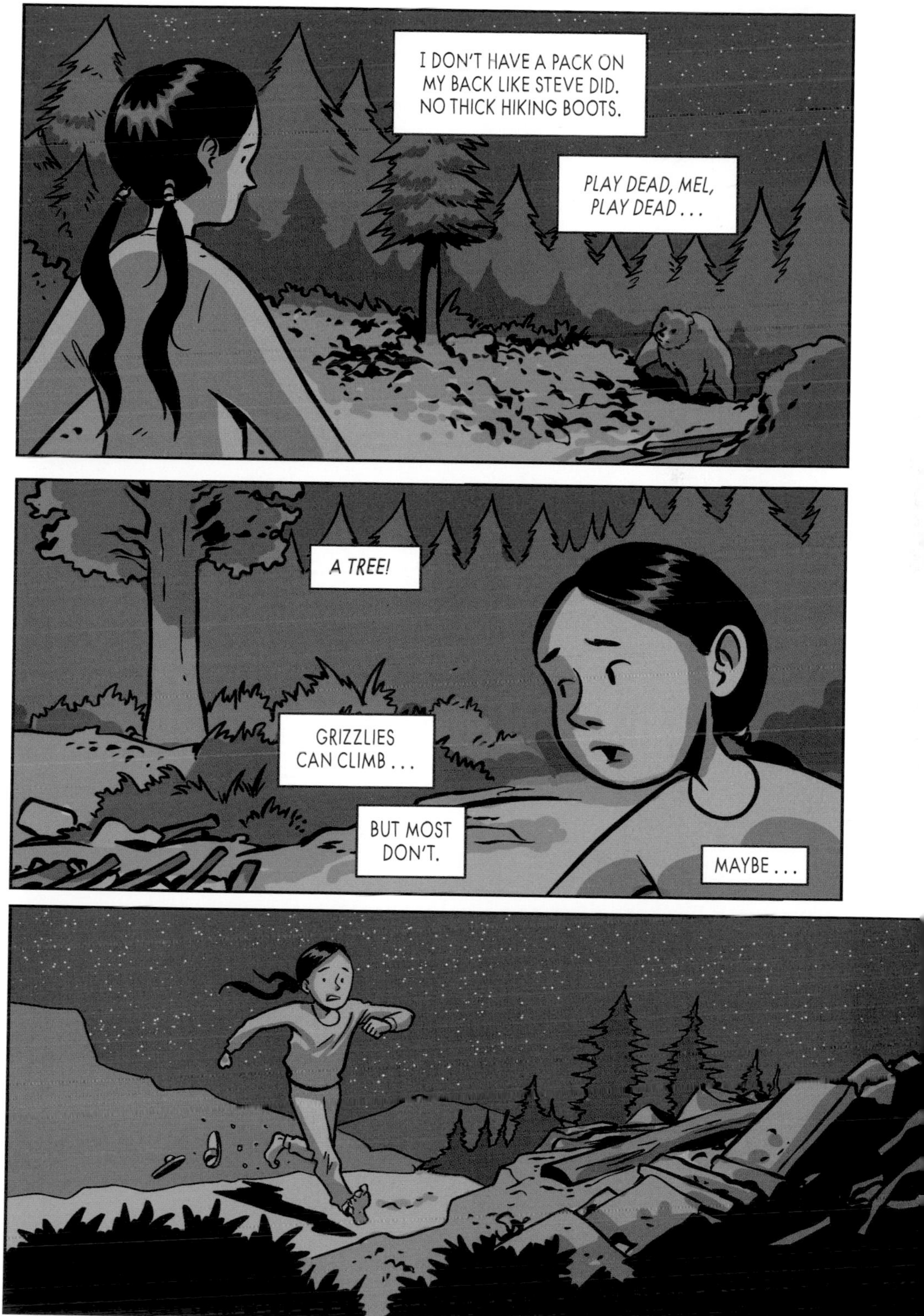
I DON'T HAVE A PACK ON MY BACK LIKE STEVE DID. NO THICK HIKING BOOTS.
PLAY DEAD, MEL, PLAY DEAD . . .
A TREE!
GRIZZLIES CAN CLIMB . . .
BUT MOST DON'T.
MAYBE . . .

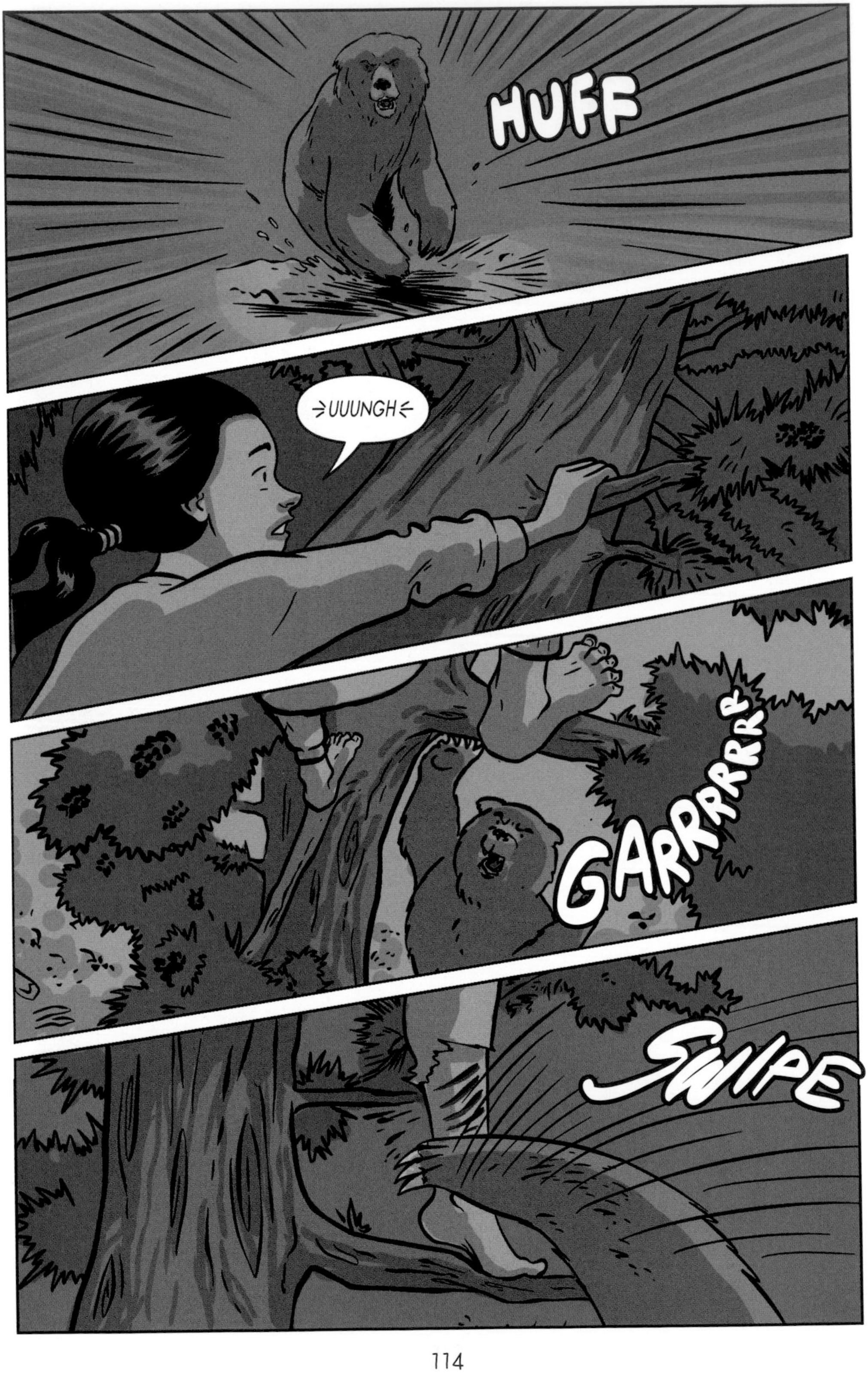
HUFF
UUUNGH
GARRRRRRR
SWIPE

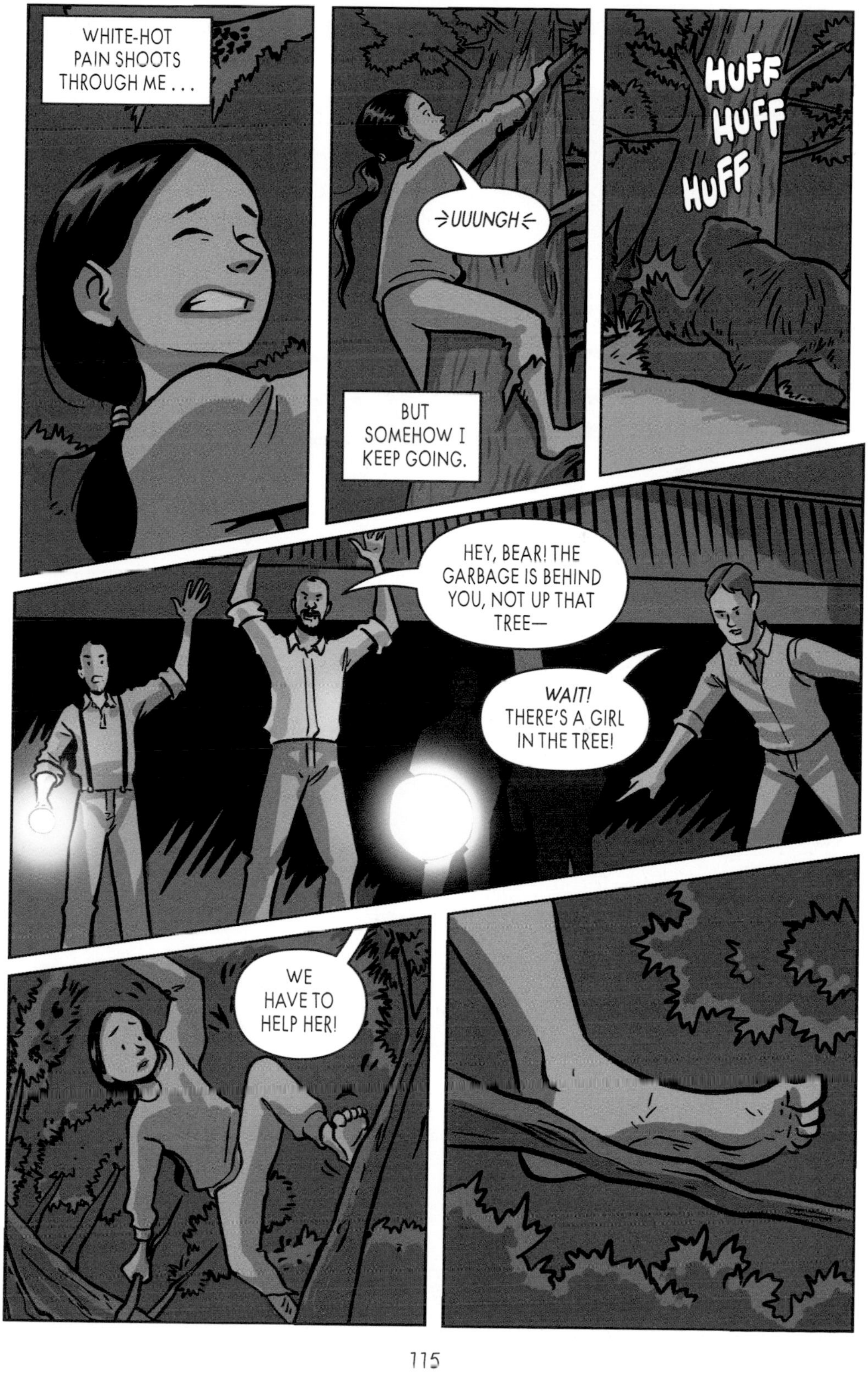
WHITE-HOT PAIN SHOOTS THROUGH ME . . .
UUUNGH
BUT SOMEHOW I KEEP GOING.
HUFF HUFF HUFF
HEY, BEAR! THE GARBAGE IS BEHIND YOU, NOT UP THAT TREE—
WAIT! THERE'S A GIRL IN THE TREE!
WE HAVE TO HELP HER!

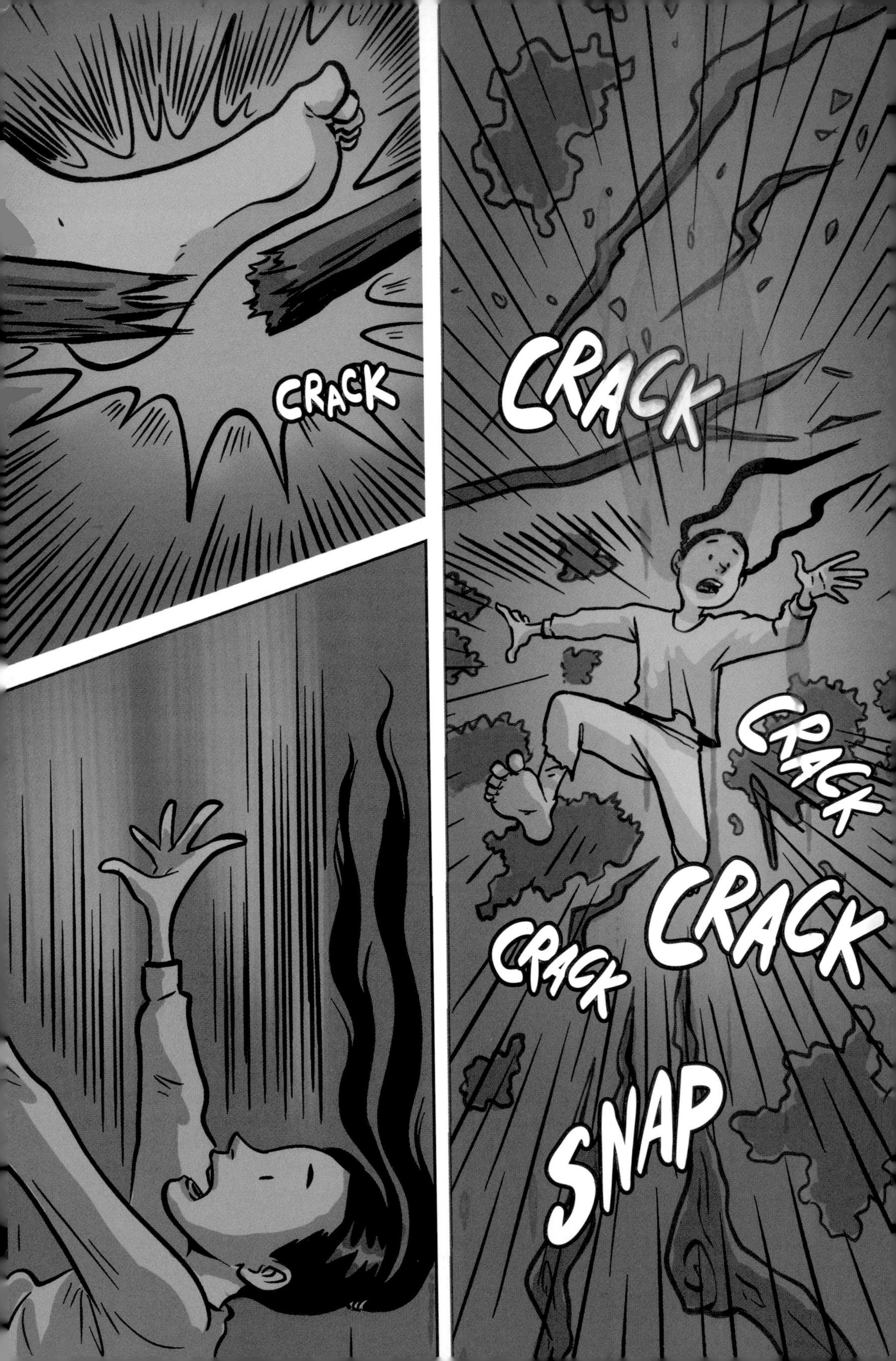
CRACK
CRACK
CRACK
CRACK
CRACK
SNAP

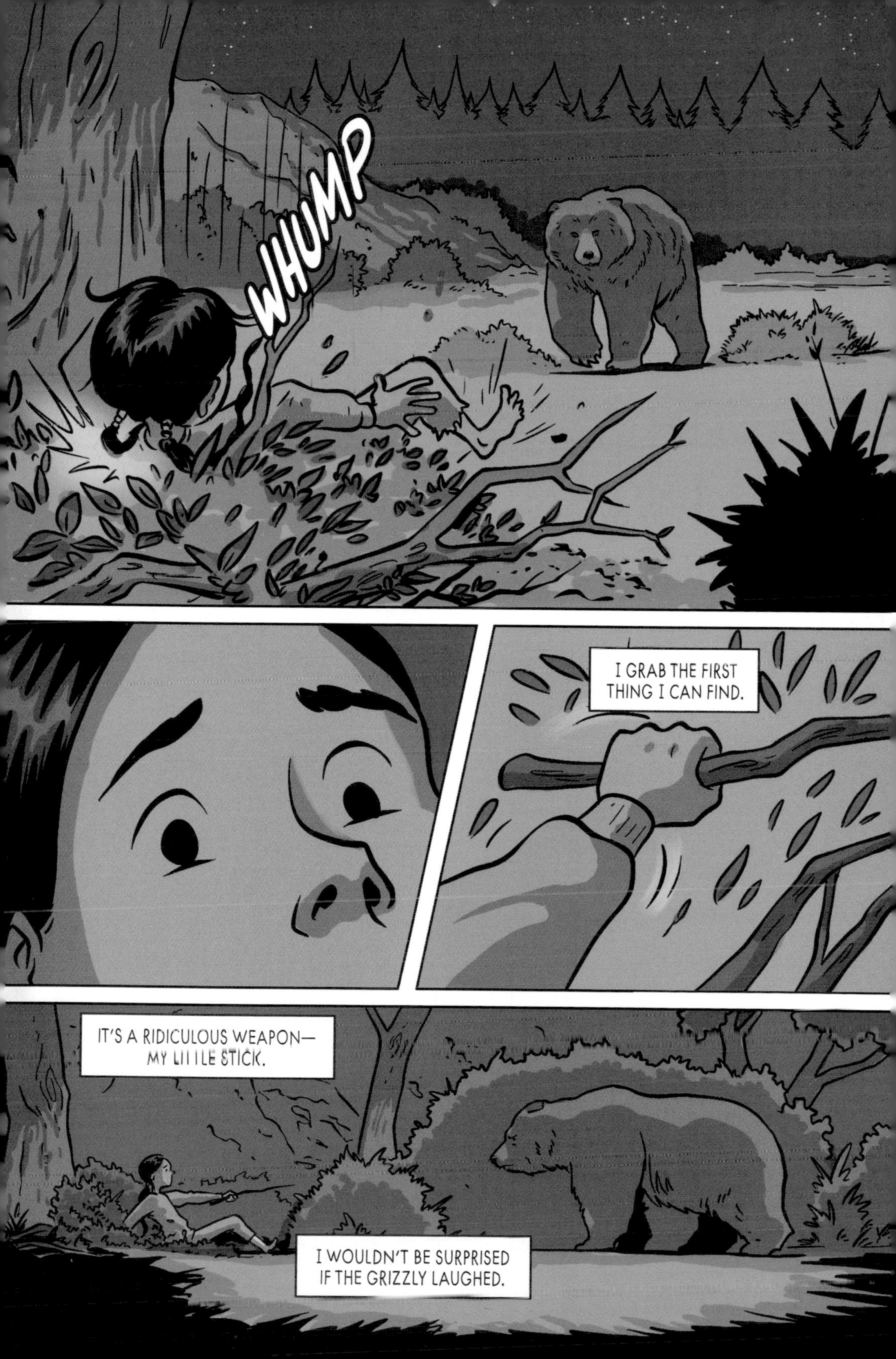
WHUMP
I GRAB THE FIRST THING I CAN FIND.
IT'S A RIDICULOUS WEAPON— MY LITTLE STICK.
I WOULDN'T BE SURPRISED IF THE GRIZZLY LAUGHED.

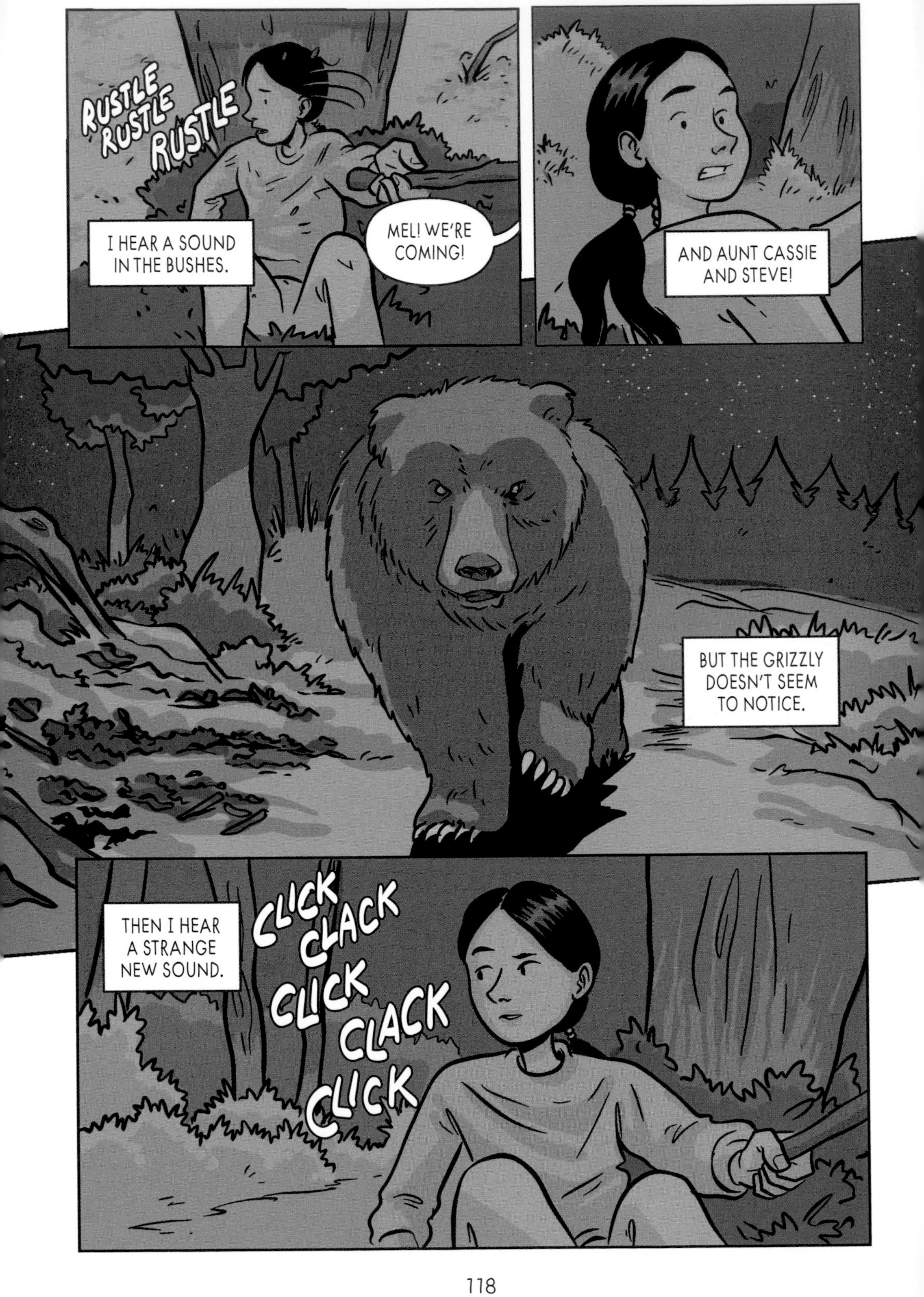
RUSTLE
RUSTLE
RUSTLE
I HEAR A SOUND IN THE BUSHES.
MEL! WE'RE COMING!
AND AUNT CASSIE AND STEVE!
BUT THE GRIZZLY DOESN'T SEEM TO NOTICE.
THEN I HEAR A STRANGE NEW SOUND.
CLICK
CLACK
CLICK
CLACK
CLICK

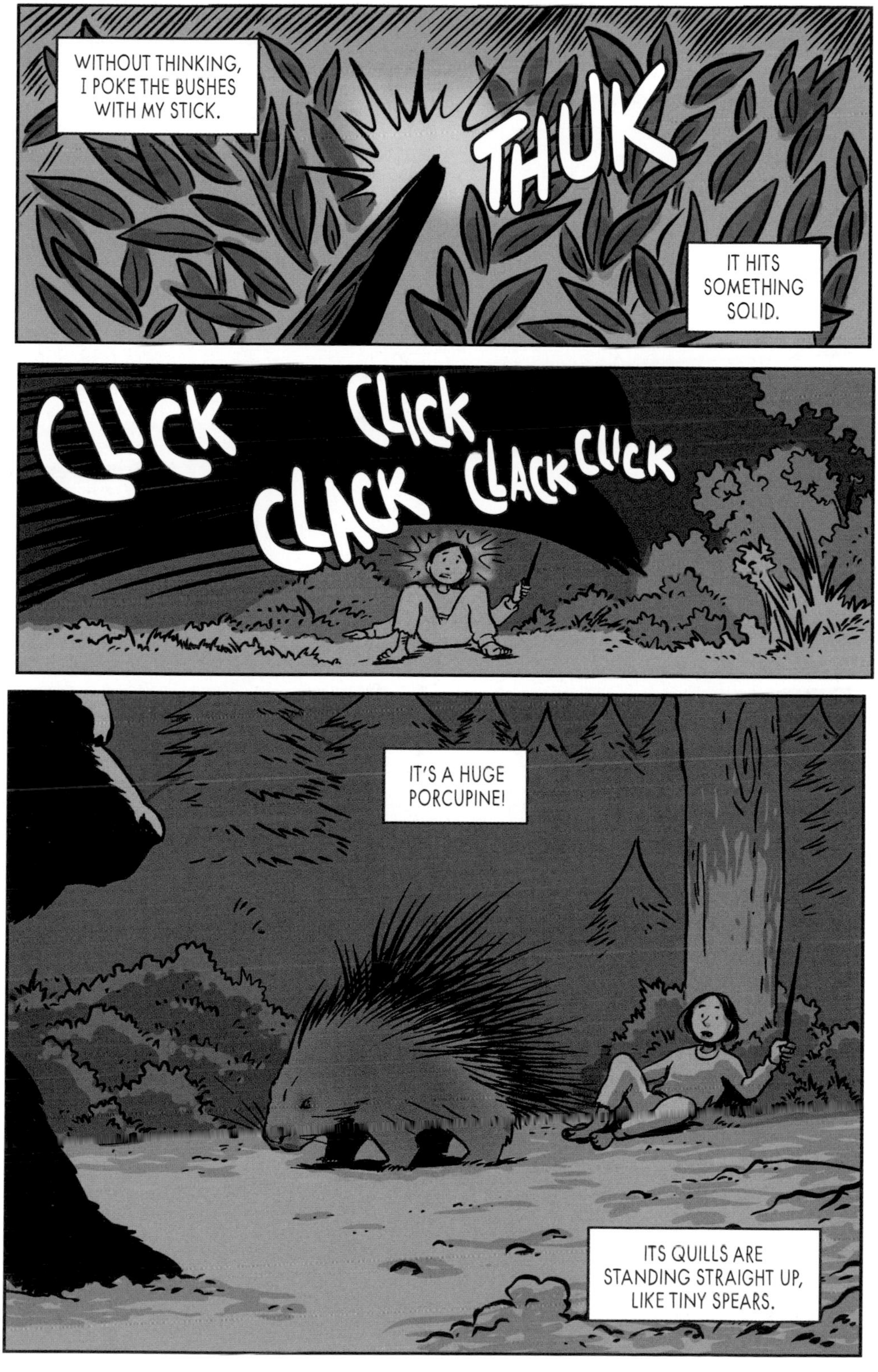

WITHOUT THINKING, I POKE THE BUSHES WITH MY STICK.
THUK
IT HITS SOMETHING SOLID.
CLICK
CLICK
CLACK
CLACK CLICK
IT'S A HUGE PORCUPINE!
ITS QUILLS ARE STANDING STRAIGHT UP, LIKE TINY SPEARS.

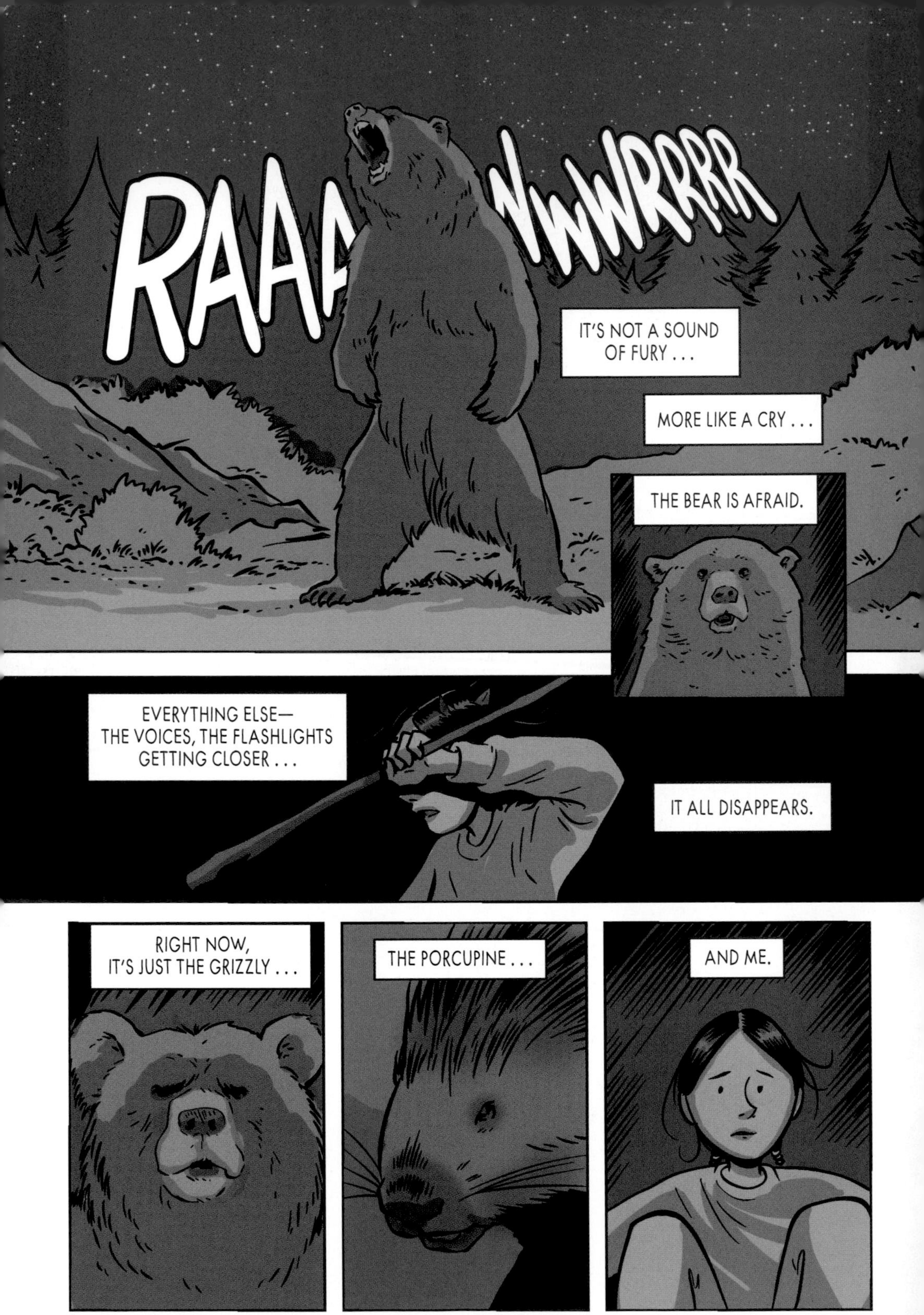
RAAAWWWRRRR
IT'S NOT A SOUND OF FURY . . .
MORE LIKE A CRY . . .
THE BEAR IS AFRAID.
EVERYTHING ELSE— THE VOICES, THE FLASHLIGHTS GETTING CLOSER . . .
IT ALL DISAPPEARS.
RIGHT NOW, IT'S JUST THE GRIZZLY . . .
THE PORCUPINE . . .
AND ME.

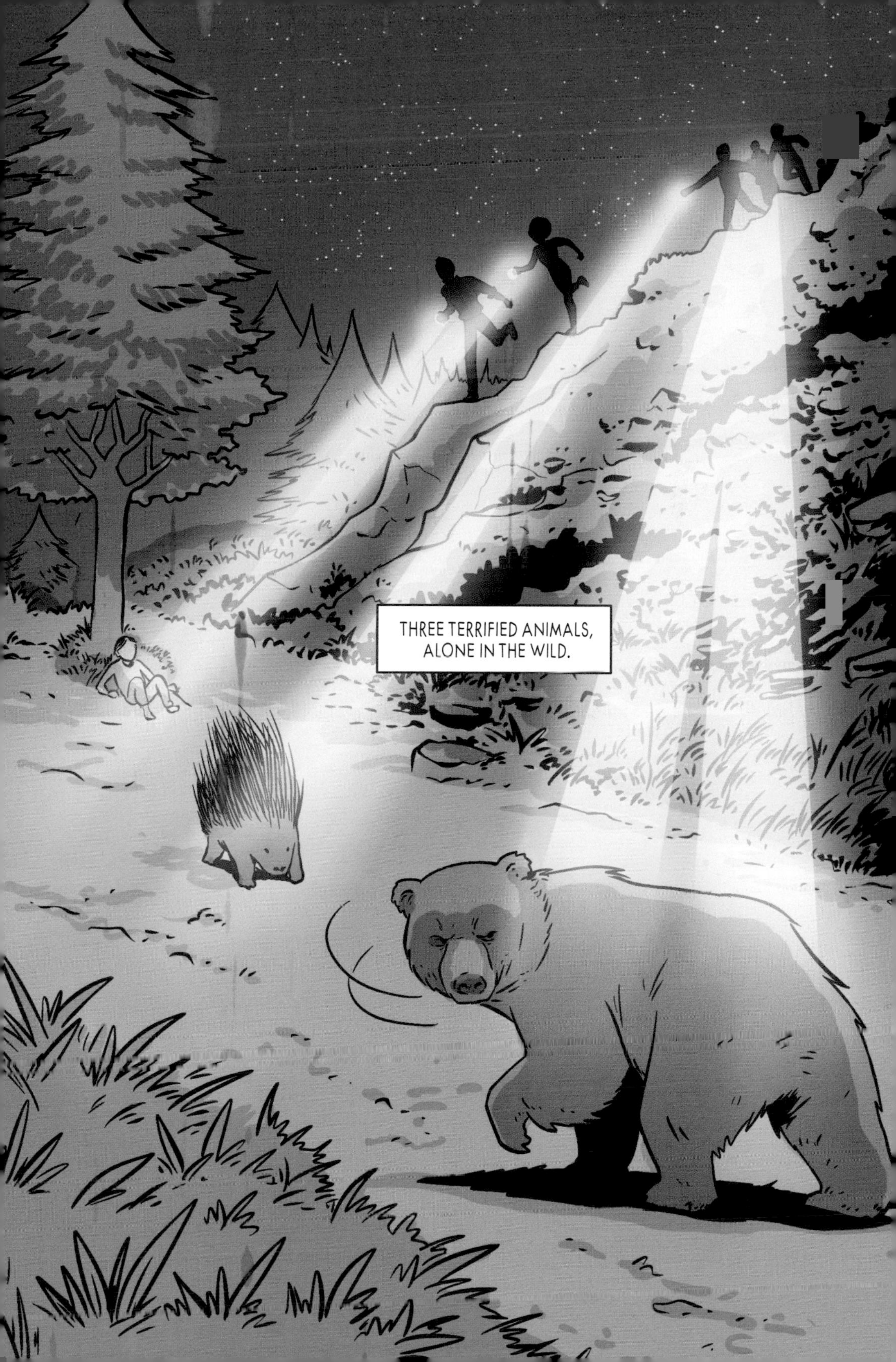
THREE TERRIFIED ANIMALS, ALONE IN THE WILD.

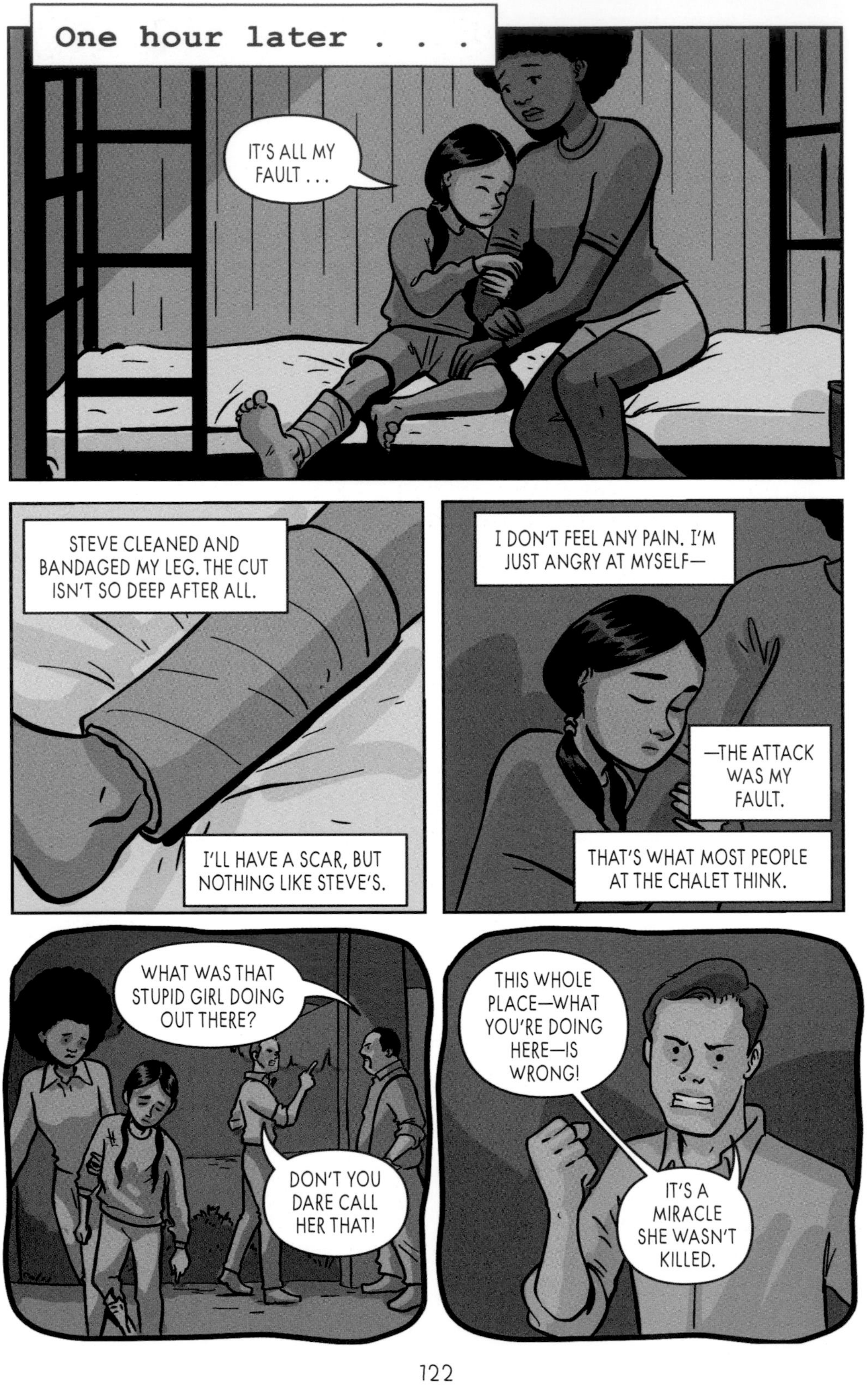
One hour later . . .
IT'S ALL MY FAULT . . .
STEVE CLEANED AND BANDAGED MY LEG. THE CUT ISN'T SO DEEP AFTER ALL.
I'LL HAVE A SCAR, BUT NOTHING LIKE STEVE'S.
I DON'T FEEL ANY PAIN. I'M JUST ANGRY AT MYSELF—
—THE ATTACK WAS MY FAULT.
THAT'S WHAT MOST PEOPLE AT THE CHALET THINK.
WHAT WAS THAT STUPID GIRL DOING OUT THERE?
DON'T YOU DARE CALL HER THAT!
THIS WHOLE PLACE—WHAT YOU'RE DOING HERE—IS WRONG!
IT'S A MIRACLE SHE WASN'T KILLED.

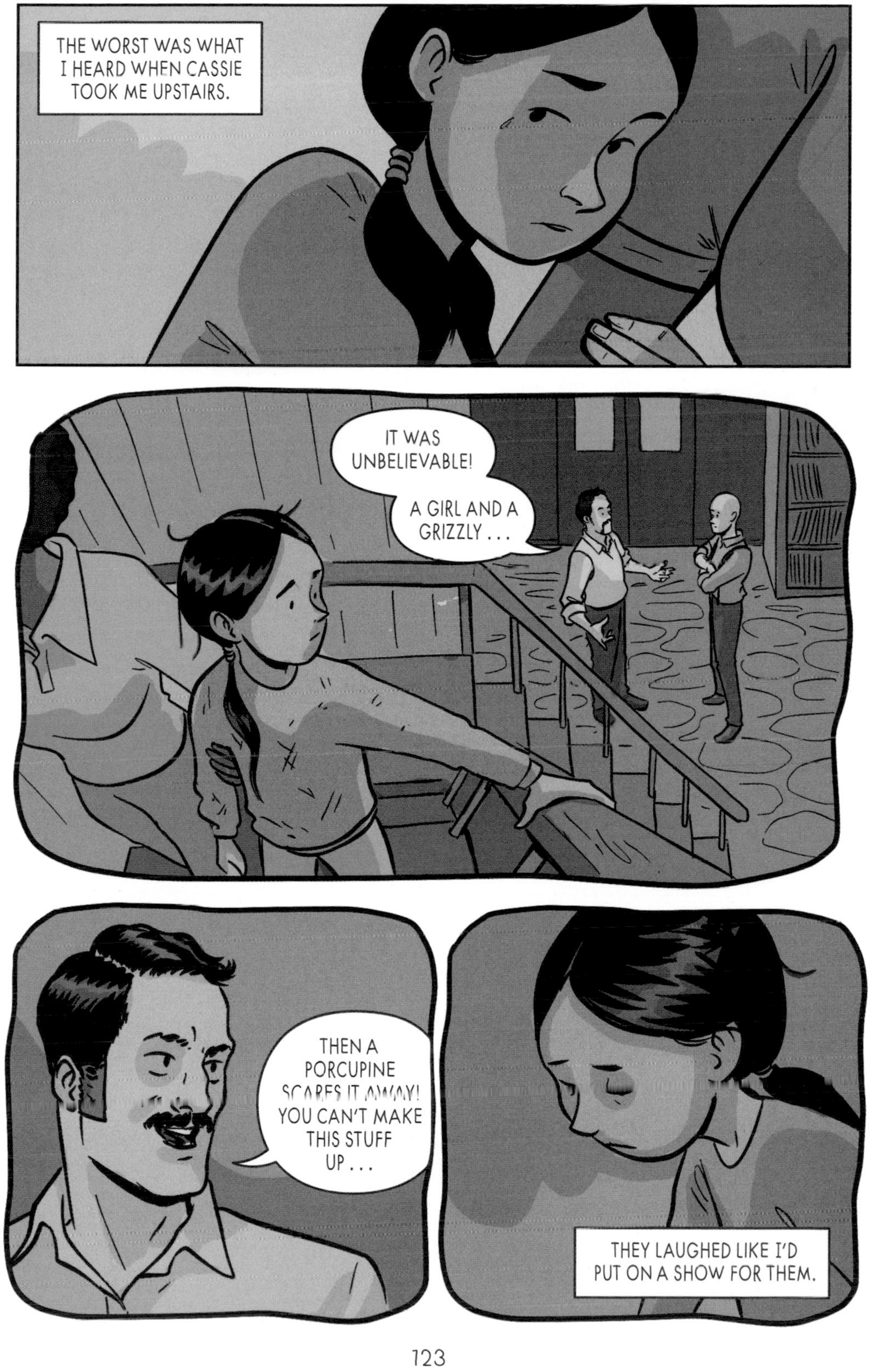
THE WORST WAS WHAT I HEARD WHEN CASSIE TOOK ME UPSTAIRS.
IT WAS UNBELIEVABLE!
A GIRL AND A GRIZZLY . . .
THEN A PORCUPINE SCARES IT AWAY! YOU CAN'T MAKE THIS STUFF UP . . .
THEY LAUGHED LIKE I'D PUT ON A SHOW FOR THEM.

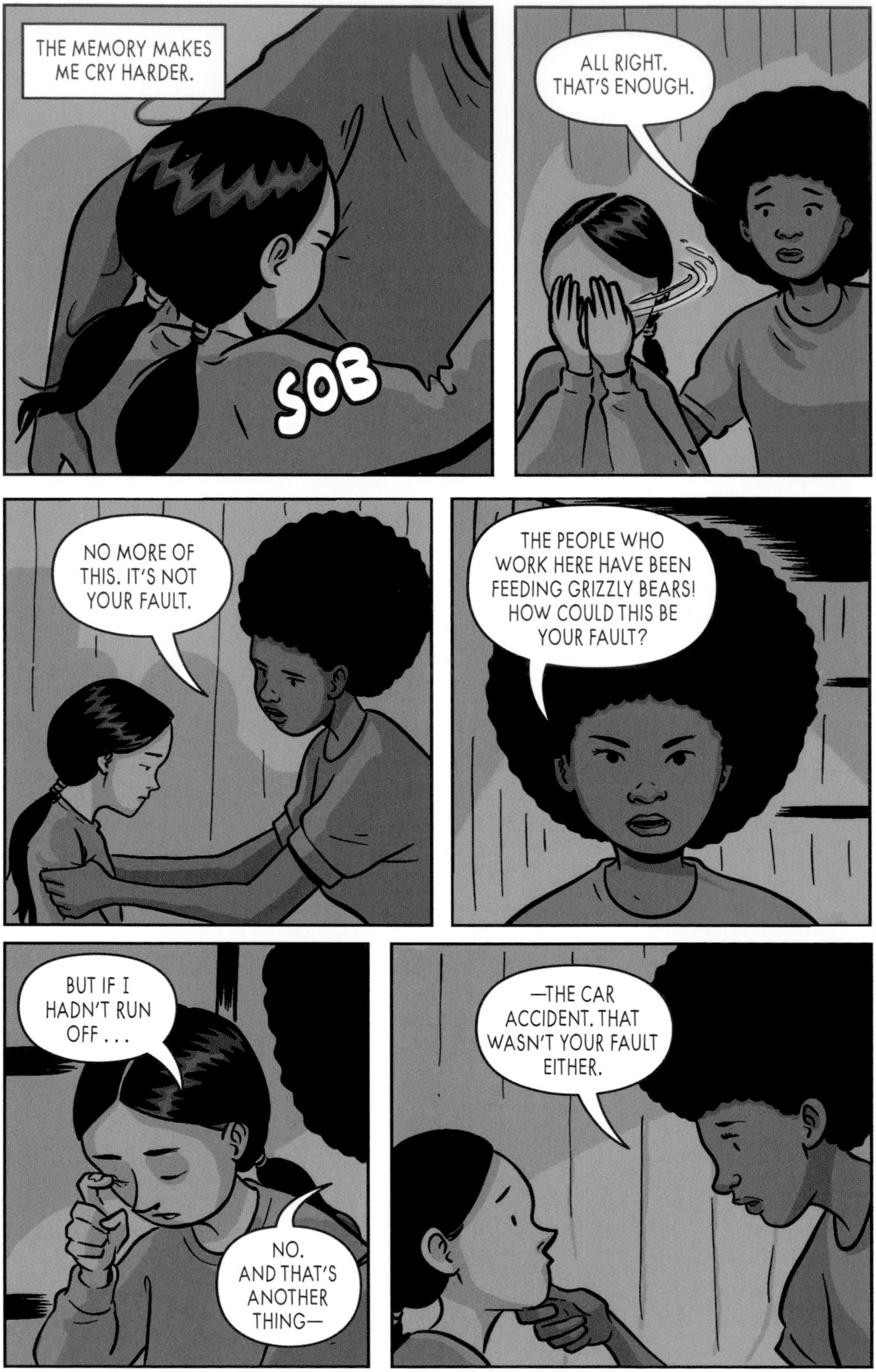
THE MEMORY MAKES ME CRY HARDER.
SOB
ALL RIGHT. THAT'S ENOUGH.
NO MORE OF THIS. IT'S NOT YOUR FAULT.
THE PEOPLE WHO WORK HERE HAVE BEEN FEEDING GRIZZLY BEARS! HOW COULD THIS BE YOUR FAULT?
BUT IF I HADN'T RUN OFF . . .
NO. AND THAT'S ANOTHER THING—
—THE CAR ACCIDENT. THAT WASN'T YOUR FAULT EITHER.

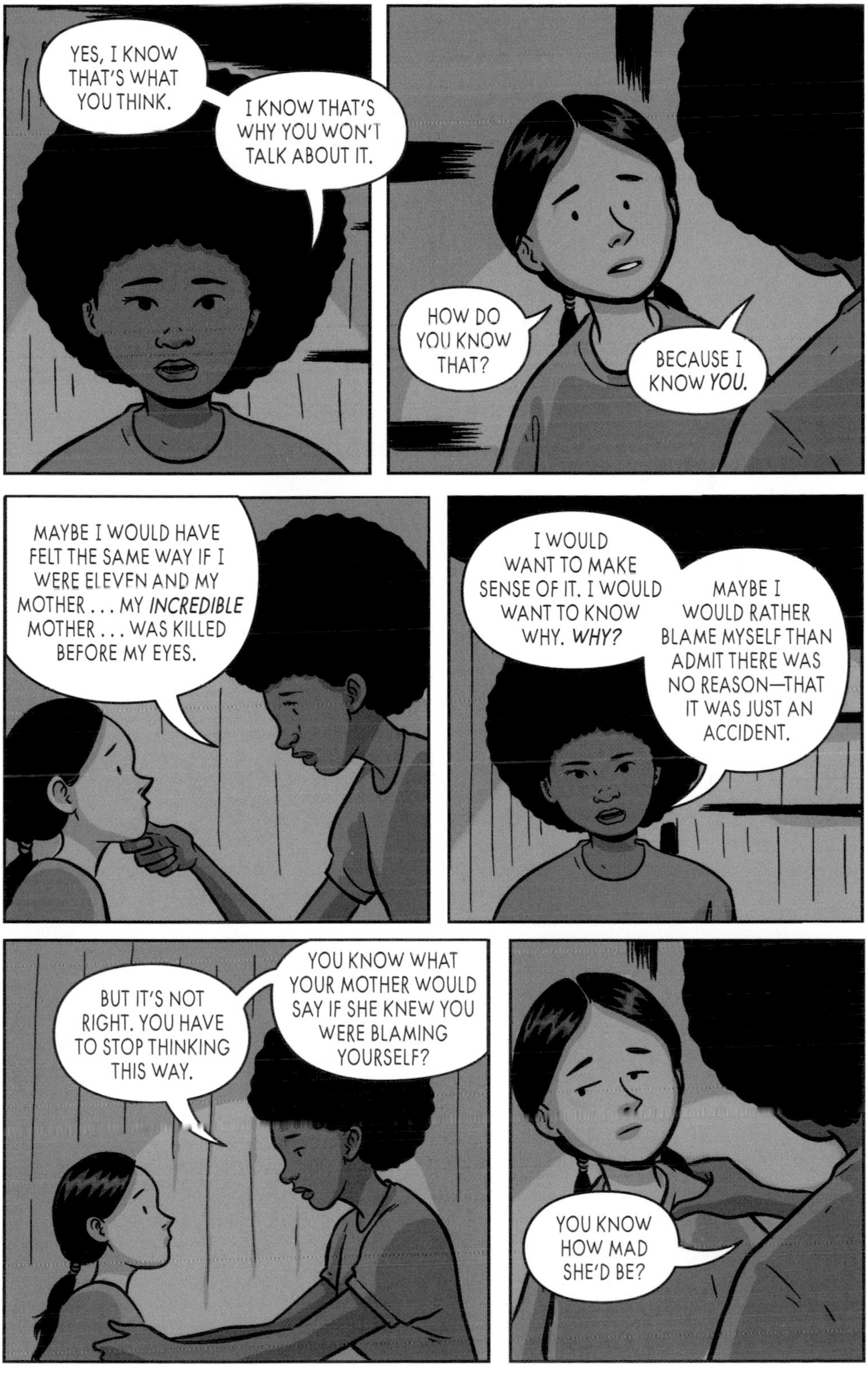
YES, I KNOW THAT'S WHAT YOU THINK.
I KNOW THAT'S WHY YOU WON'T TALK ABOUT IT.
HOW DO YOU KNOW THAT?
BECAUSE I KNOW *YOU.*
MAYBE I WOULD HAVE FELT THE SAME WAY IF I WERE ELEVEN AND MY MOTHER . . . MY *INCREDIBLE* MOTHER . . . WAS KILLED BEFORE MY EYES.
I WOULD WANT TO MAKE SENSE OF IT. I WOULD WANT TO KNOW WHY. *WHY?*
MAYBE I WOULD RATHER BLAME MYSELF THAN ADMIT THERE WAS NO REASON—THAT IT WAS JUST AN ACCIDENT.
BUT IT'S NOT RIGHT. YOU HAVE TO STOP THINKING THIS WAY.
YOU KNOW WHAT YOUR MOTHER WOULD SAY IF SHE KNEW YOU WERE BLAMING YOURSELF?
YOU KNOW HOW MAD SHE'D BE?

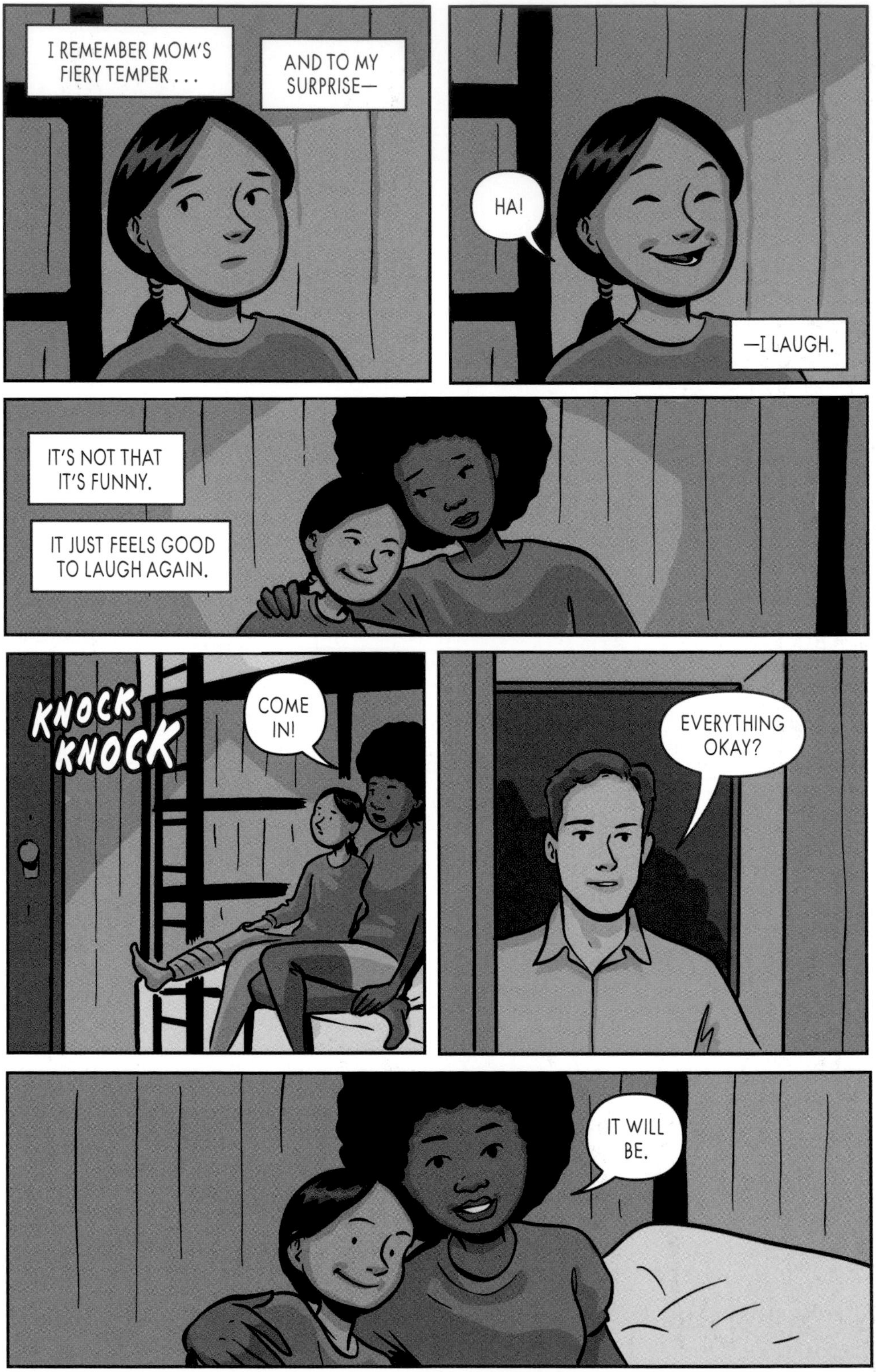
I REMEMBER MOM'S FIERY TEMPER . . .
AND TO MY SURPRISE—
HA!
—I LAUGH.
IT'S NOT THAT IT'S FUNNY.
IT JUST FEELS GOOD TO LAUGH AGAIN.
KNOCK KNOCK
COME IN!
EVERYTHING OKAY?
IT WILL BE.

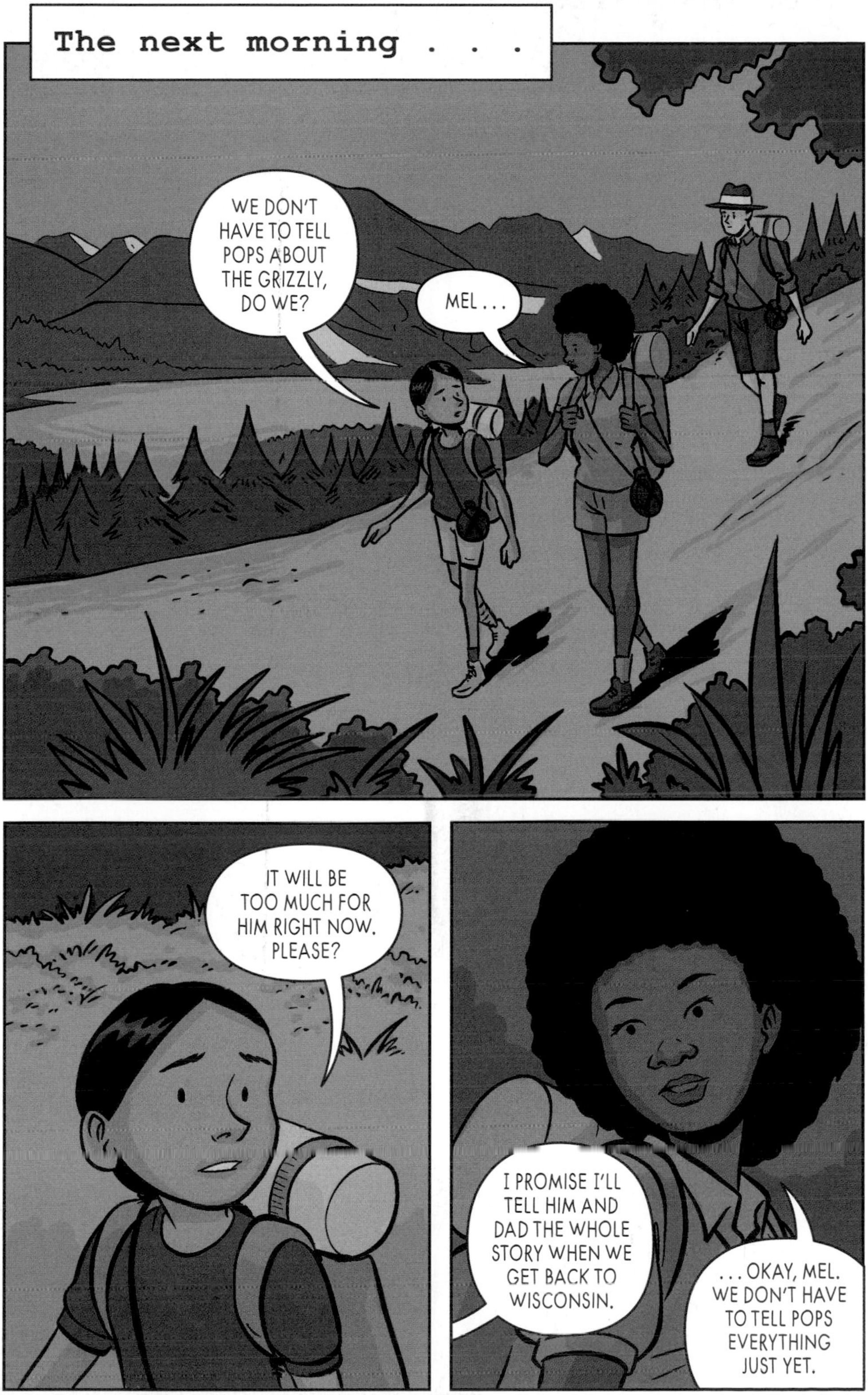
The next morning . . .
WE DON'T HAVE TO TELL POPS ABOUT THE GRIZZLY, DO WE?
MEL . . .
IT WILL BE TOO MUCH FOR HIM RIGHT NOW. PLEASE?
I PROMISE I'LL TELL HIM AND DAD THE WHOLE STORY WHEN WE GET BACK TO WISCONSIN.
. . . OKAY, MEL. WE DON'T HAVE TO TELL POPS EVERYTHING JUST YET.

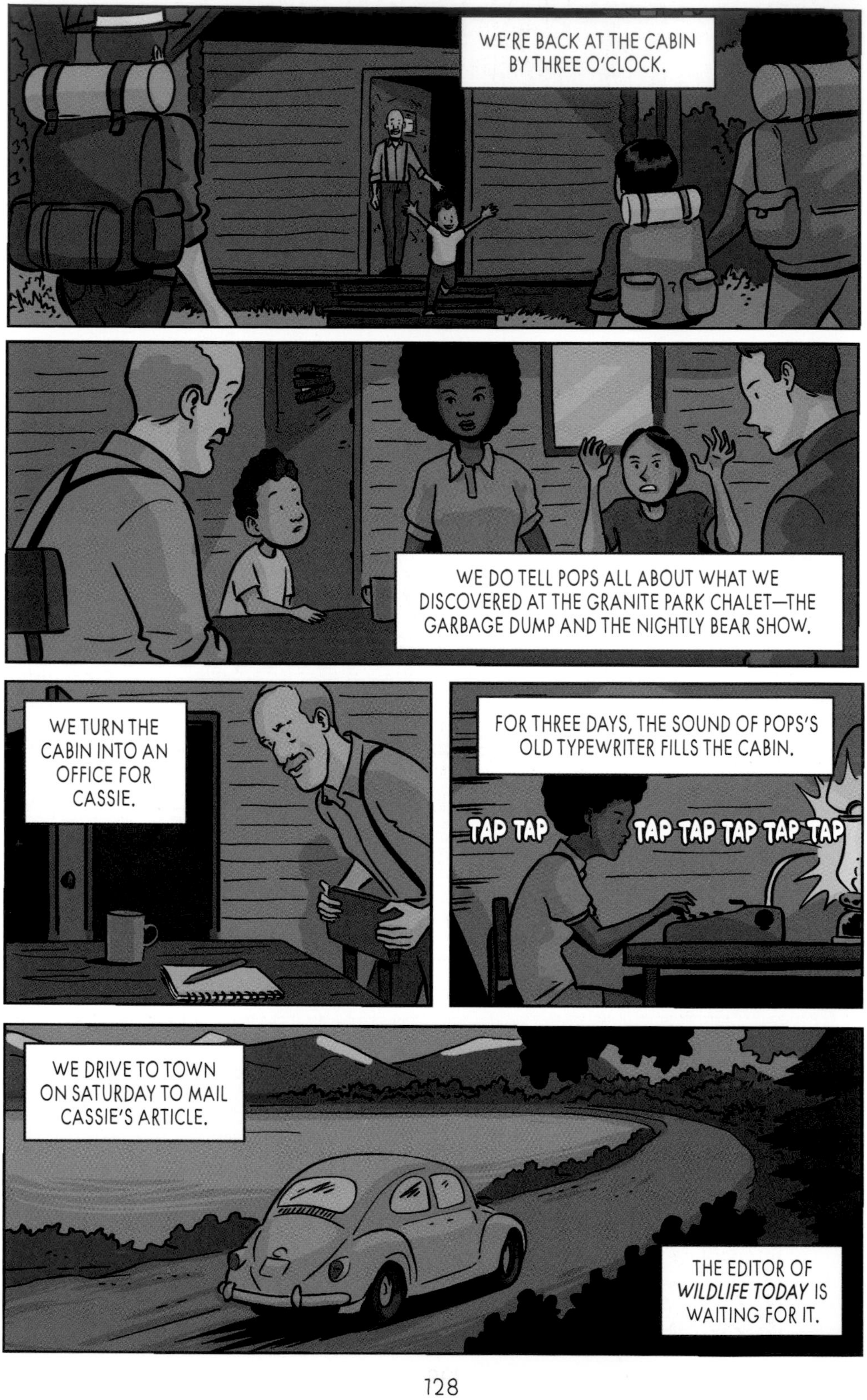

WE'RE BACK AT THE CABIN BY THREE O'CLOCK.
WE DO TELL POPS ALL ABOUT WHAT WE DISCOVERED AT THE GRANITE PARK CHALET—THE GARBAGE DUMP AND THE NIGHTLY BEAR SHOW.
WE TURN THE CABIN INTO AN OFFICE FOR CASSIE.
FOR THREE DAYS, THE SOUND OF POPS'S OLD TYPEWRITER FILLS THE CABIN.
TAP TAP
TAP TAP TAP TAP TAP
WE DRIVE TO TOWN ON SATURDAY TO MAIL CASSIE'S ARTICLE.
THE EDITOR OF *WILDLIFE TODAY* IS WAITING FOR IT.

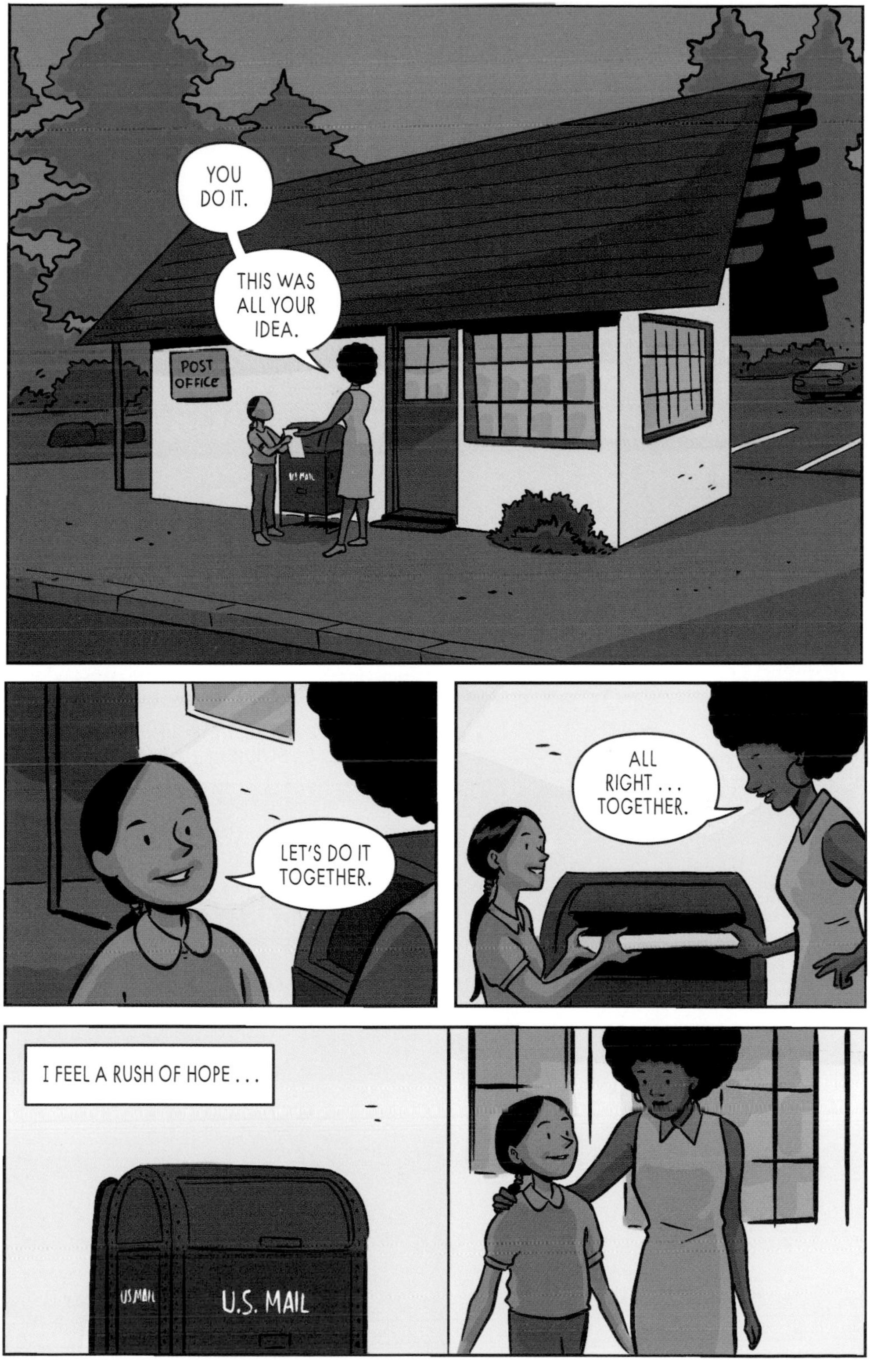
YOU DO IT.
THIS WAS ALL YOUR IDEA.
POST OFFICE
U.S. MAIL
LET'S DO IT TOGETHER.
ALL RIGHT . . . TOGETHER.
I FEEL A RUSH OF HOPE . . .
U.S. MAIL
U.S. MAIL

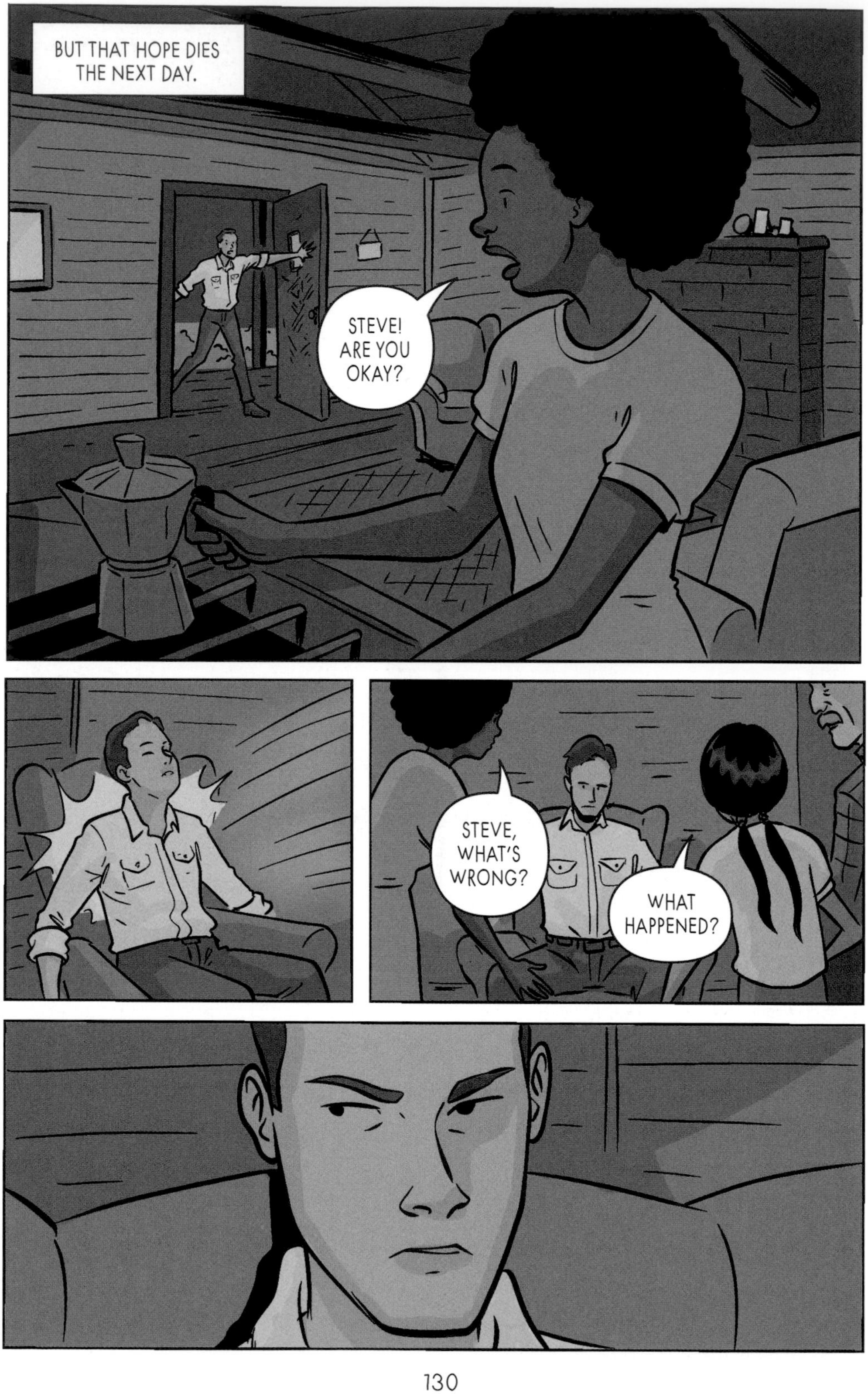
BUT THAT HOPE DIES THE NEXT DAY.
STEVE! ARE YOU OKAY?
STEVE, WHAT'S WRONG?
WHAT HAPPENED?

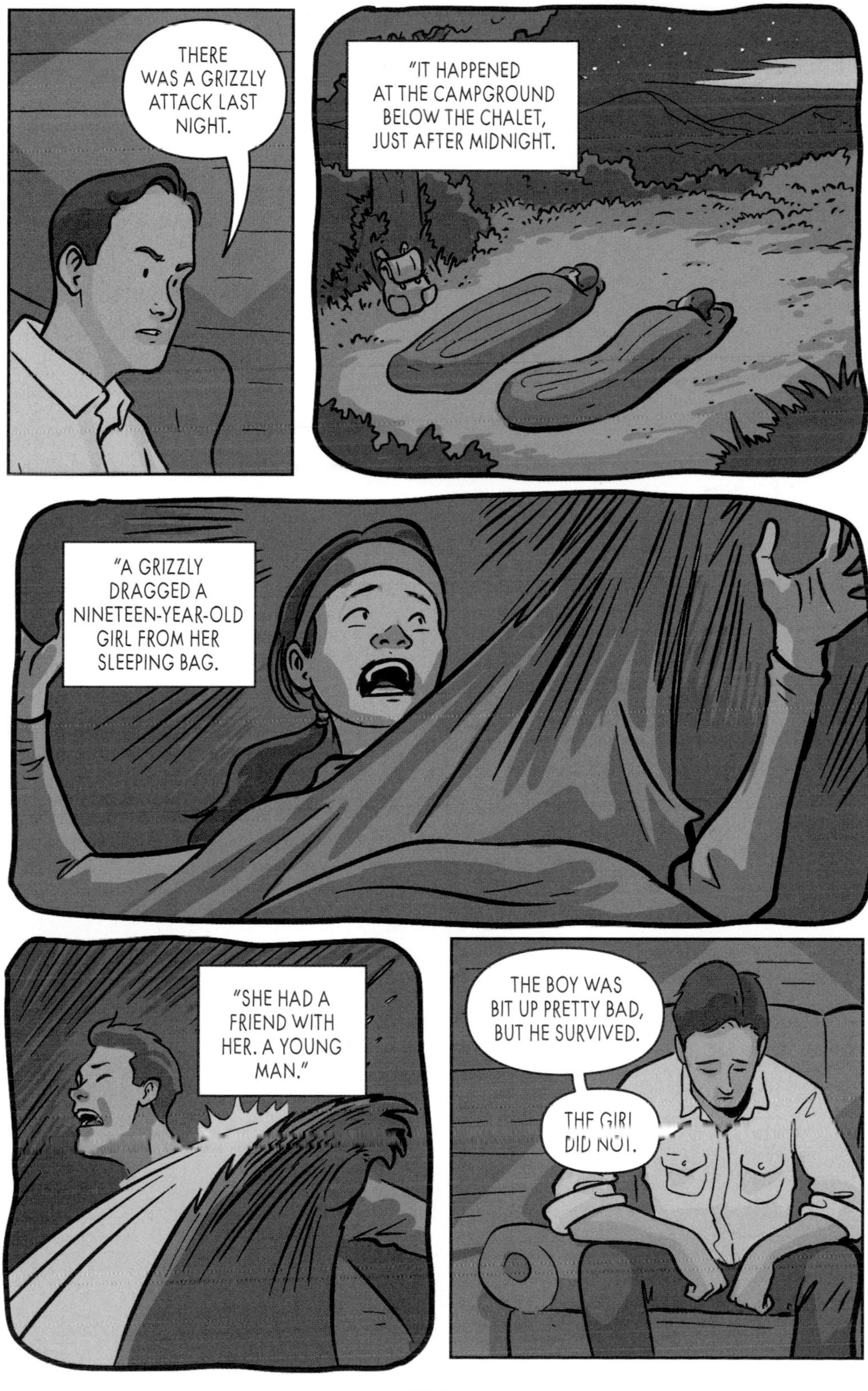
THERE WAS A GRIZZLY ATTACK LAST NIGHT.
"IT HAPPENED AT THE CAMPGROUND BELOW THE CHALET, JUST AFTER MIDNIGHT.
"A GRIZZLY DRAGGED A NINETEEN-YEAR-OLD GIRL FROM HER SLEEPING BAG.
"SHE HAD A FRIEND WITH HER. A YOUNG MAN."
THE BOY WAS BIT UP PRETTY BAD, BUT HE SURVIVED.
THE GIRL DID NOT.

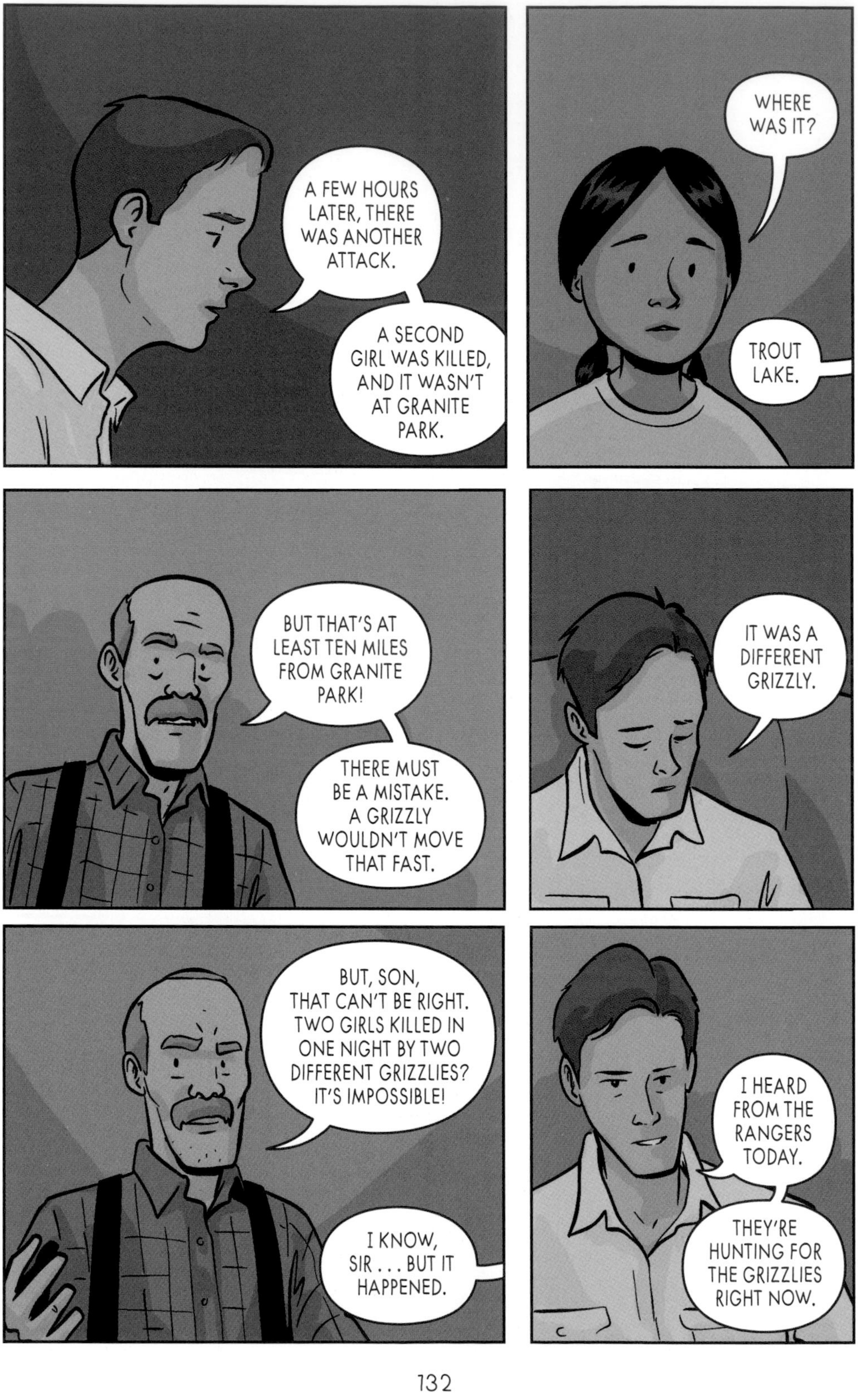
A FEW HOURS LATER, THERE WAS ANOTHER ATTACK.
A SECOND GIRL WAS KILLED, AND IT WASN'T AT GRANITE PARK.
WHERE WAS IT?
TROUT LAKE.
BUT THAT'S AT LEAST TEN MILES FROM GRANITE PARK!
THERE MUST BE A MISTAKE. A GRIZZLY WOULDN'T MOVE THAT FAST.
IT WAS A DIFFERENT GRIZZLY.
BUT, SON, THAT CAN'T BE RIGHT. TWO GIRLS KILLED IN ONE NIGHT BY TWO DIFFERENT GRIZZLIES? IT'S IMPOSSIBLE!
I KNOW, SIR . . . BUT IT HAPPENED.
I HEARD FROM THE RANGERS TODAY.
THEY'RE HUNTING FOR THE GRIZZLIES RIGHT NOW.

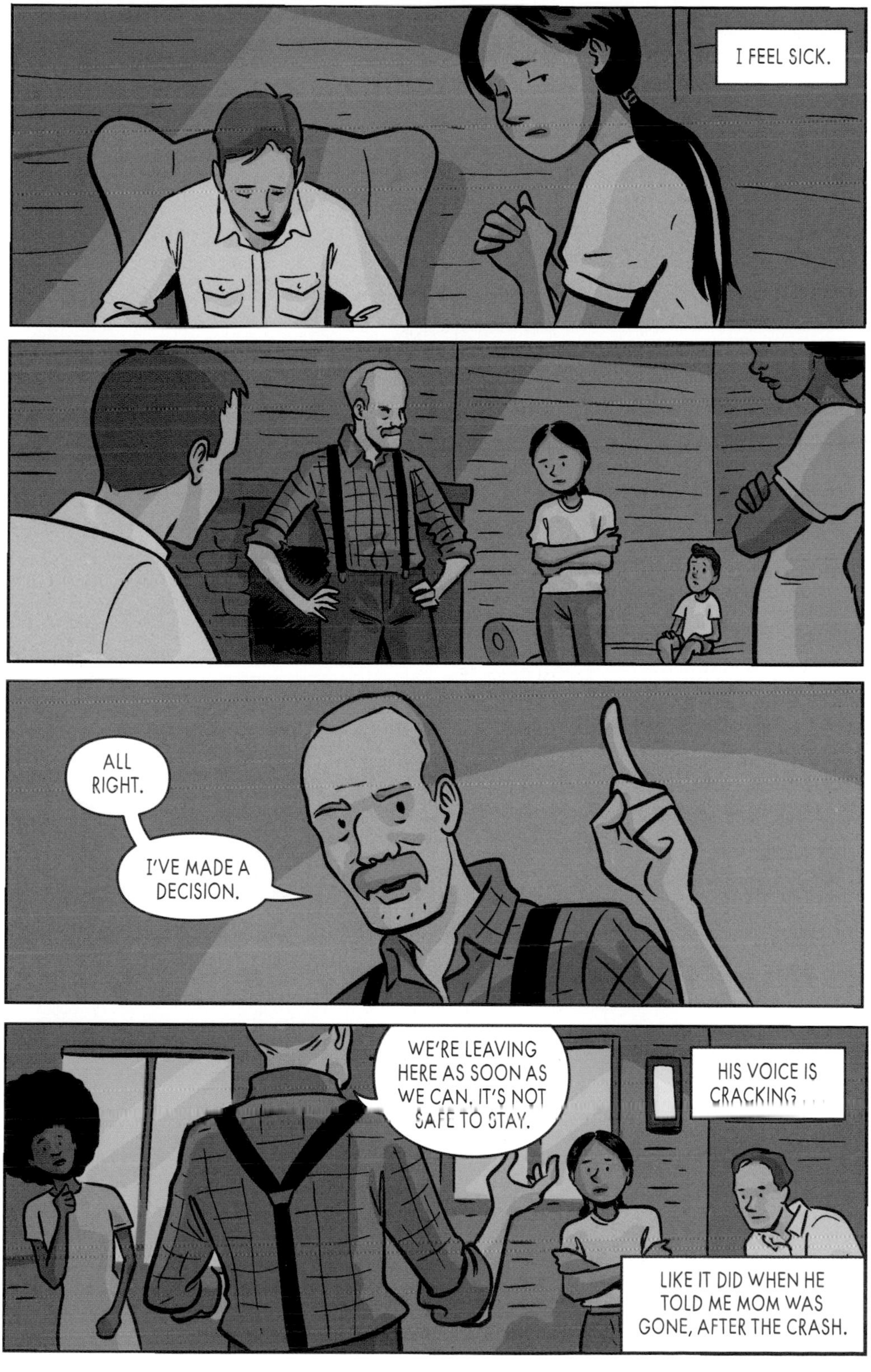
I FEEL SICK.
ALL RIGHT.
I'VE MADE A DECISION.
WE'RE LEAVING HERE AS SOON AS WE CAN. IT'S NOT SAFE TO STAY.
HIS VOICE IS CRACKING . . .
LIKE IT DID WHEN HE TOLD ME MOM WAS GONE, AFTER THE CRASH.

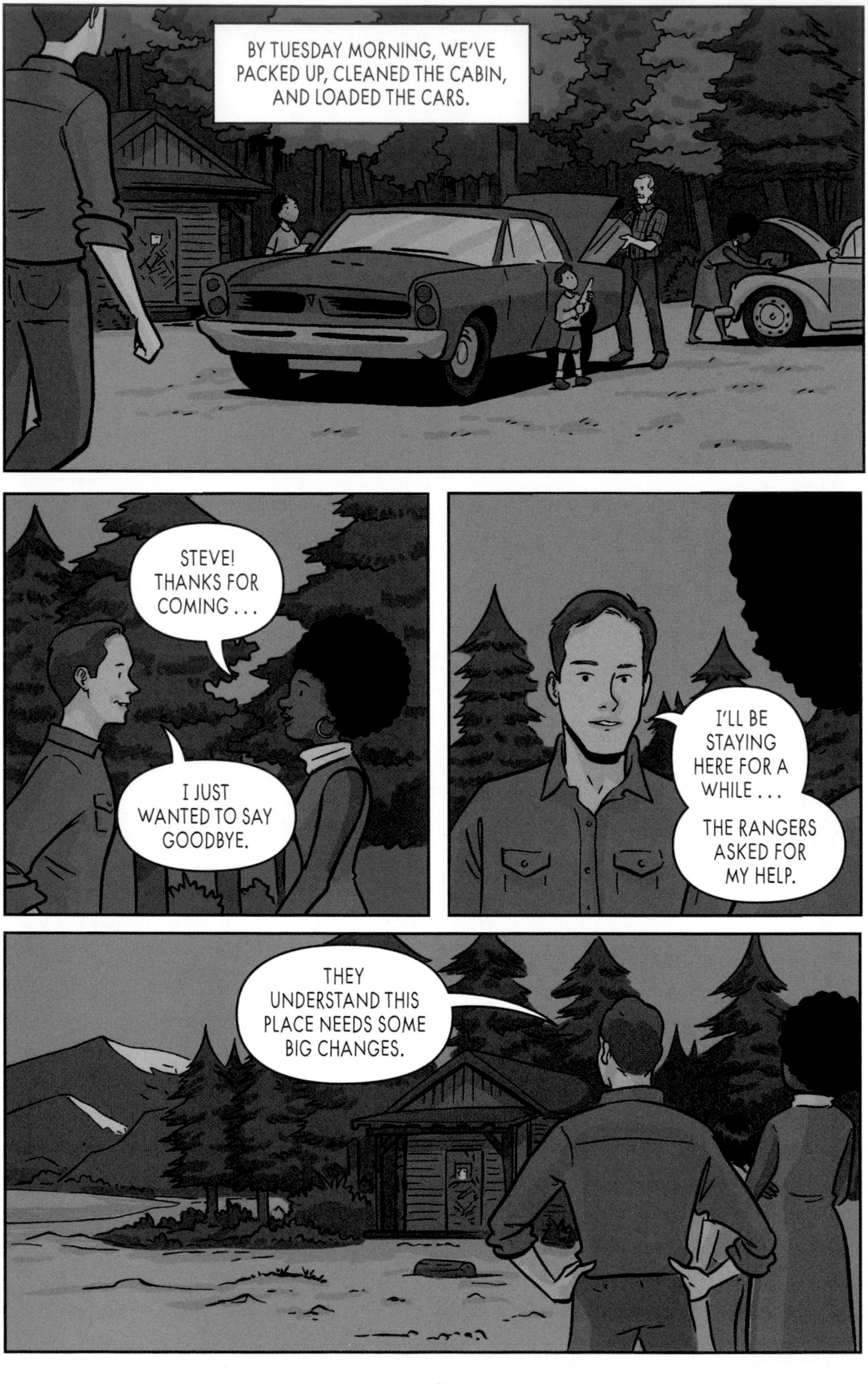
BY TUESDAY MORNING, WE'VE PACKED UP, CLEANED THE CABIN, AND LOADED THE CARS.
STEVE! THANKS FOR COMING . . .
I JUST WANTED TO SAY GOODBYE.
I'LL BE STAYING HERE FOR A WHILE . . .
THE RANGERS ASKED FOR MY HELP.
THEY UNDERSTAND THIS PLACE NEEDS SOME BIG CHANGES.

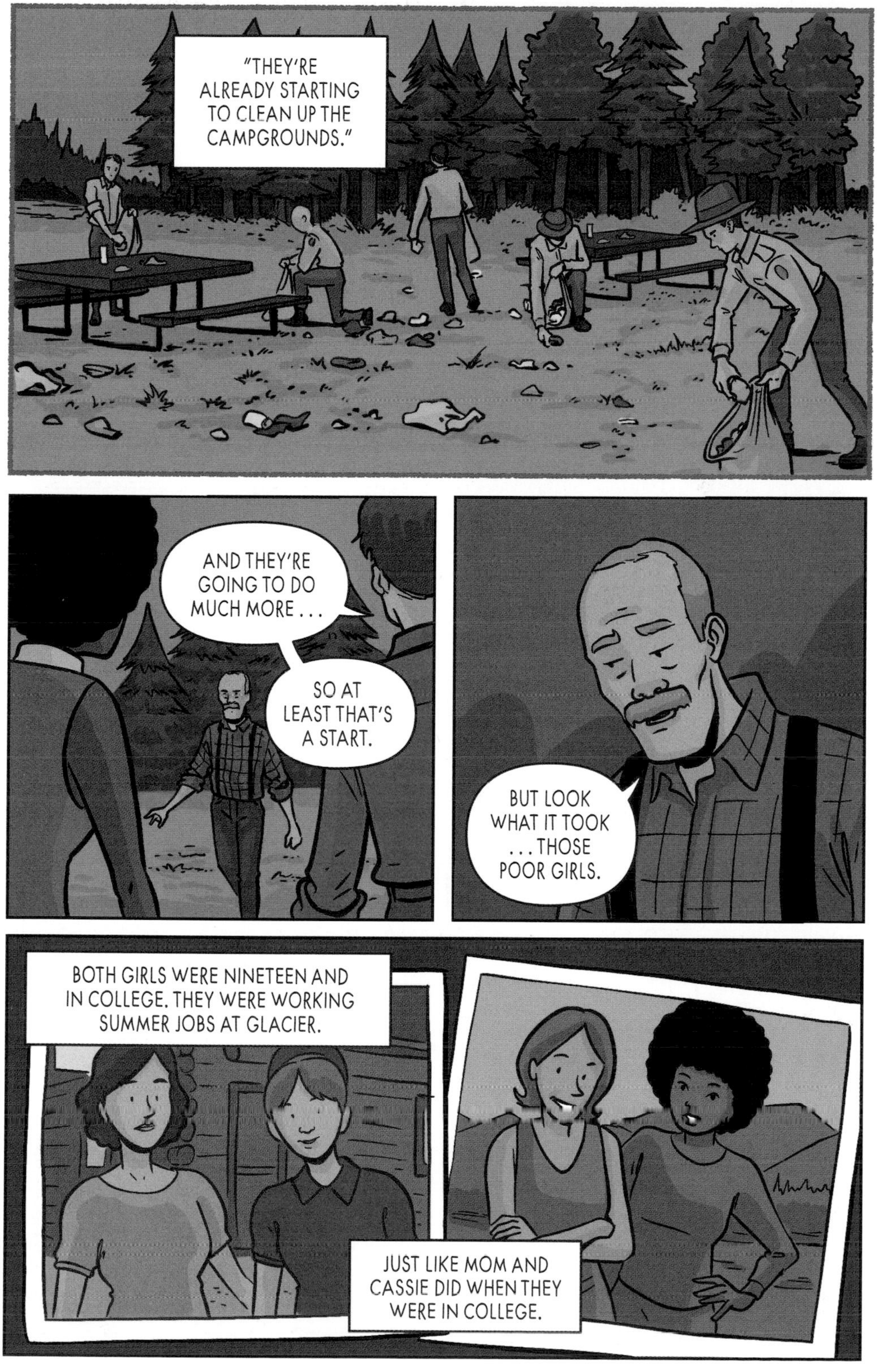
"THEY'RE ALREADY STARTING TO CLEAN UP THE CAMPGROUNDS."
AND THEY'RE GOING TO DO MUCH MORE . . .
SO AT LEAST THAT'S A START.
BUT LOOK WHAT IT TOOK . . . THOSE POOR GIRLS.
BOTH GIRLS WERE NINETEEN AND IN COLLEGE. THEY WERE WORKING SUMMER JOBS AT GLACIER.
JUST LIKE MOM AND CASSIE DID WHEN THEY WERE IN COLLEGE.

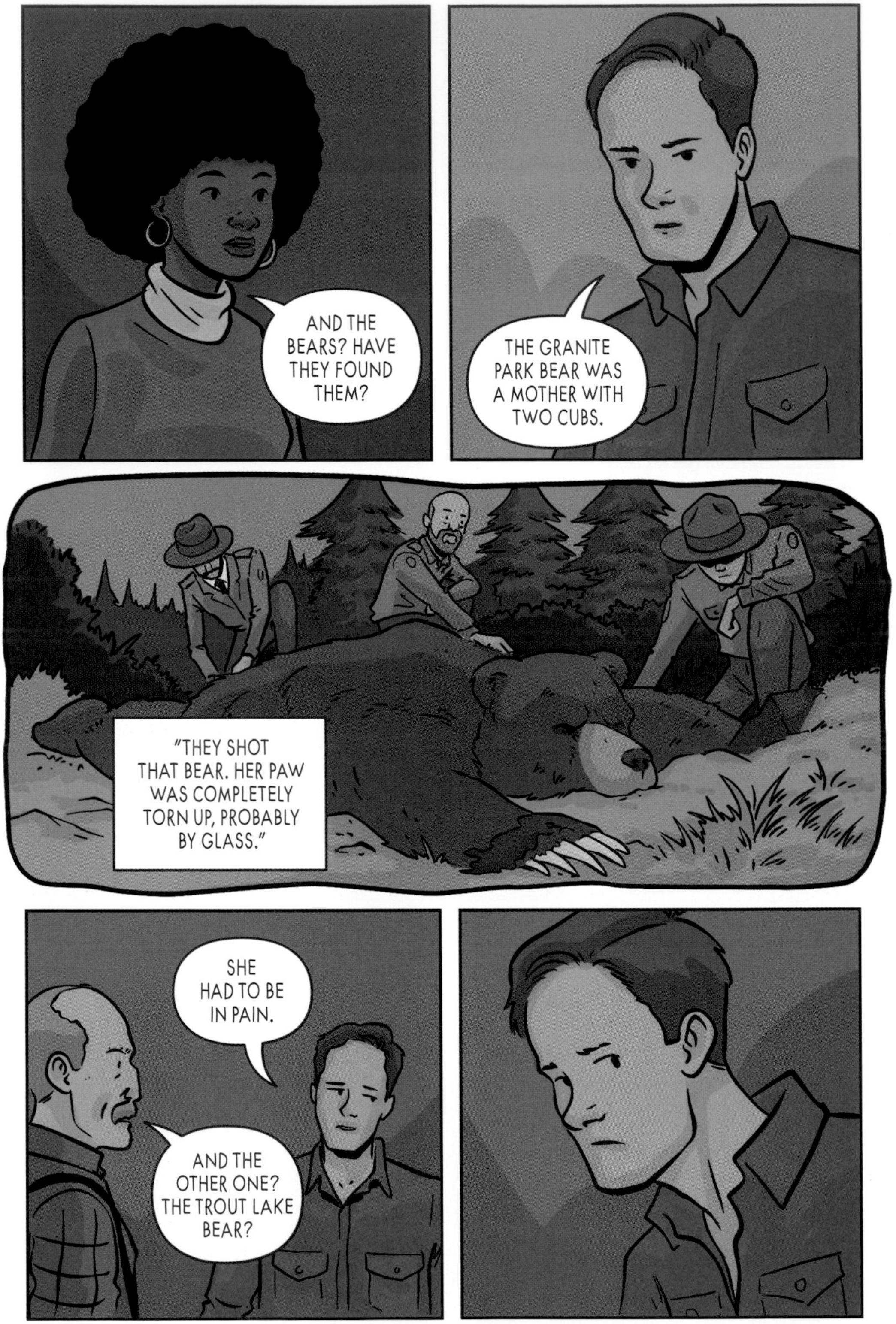
AND THE BEARS? HAVE THEY FOUND THEM?
THE GRANITE PARK BEAR WAS A MOTHER WITH TWO CUBS.
"THEY SHOT THAT BEAR. HER PAW WAS COMPLETELY TORN UP, PROBABLY BY GLASS."
SHE HAD TO BE IN PAIN.
AND THE OTHER ONE? THE TROUT LAKE BEAR?

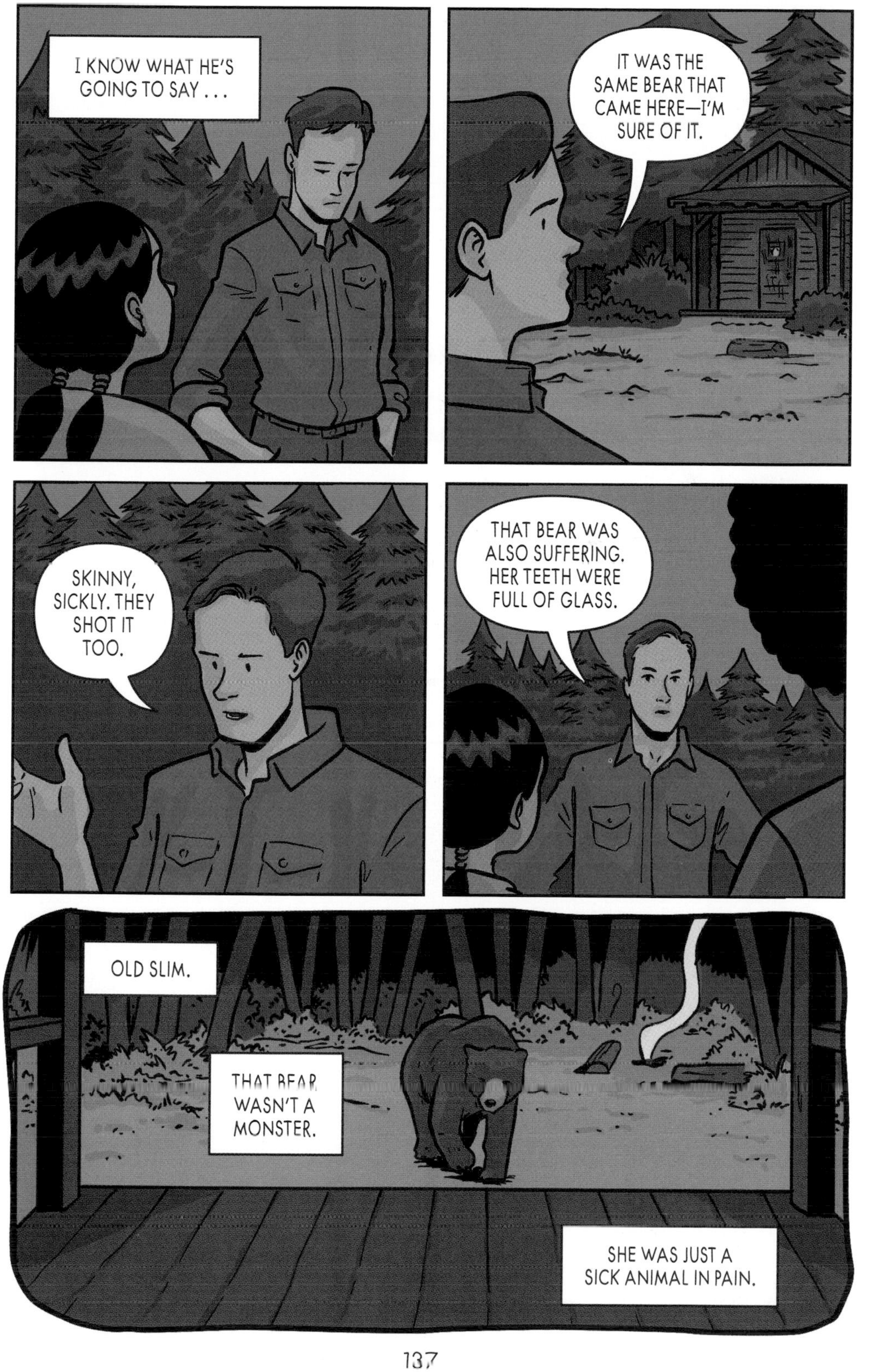
I KNOW WHAT HE'S GOING TO SAY . . .
IT WAS THE SAME BEAR THAT CAME HERE—I'M SURE OF IT.
SKINNY, SICKLY. THEY SHOT IT TOO.
THAT BEAR WAS ALSO SUFFERING. HER TEETH WERE FULL OF GLASS.
OLD SLIM.
THAT BEAR WASN'T A MONSTER.
SHE WAS JUST A SICK ANIMAL IN PAIN.

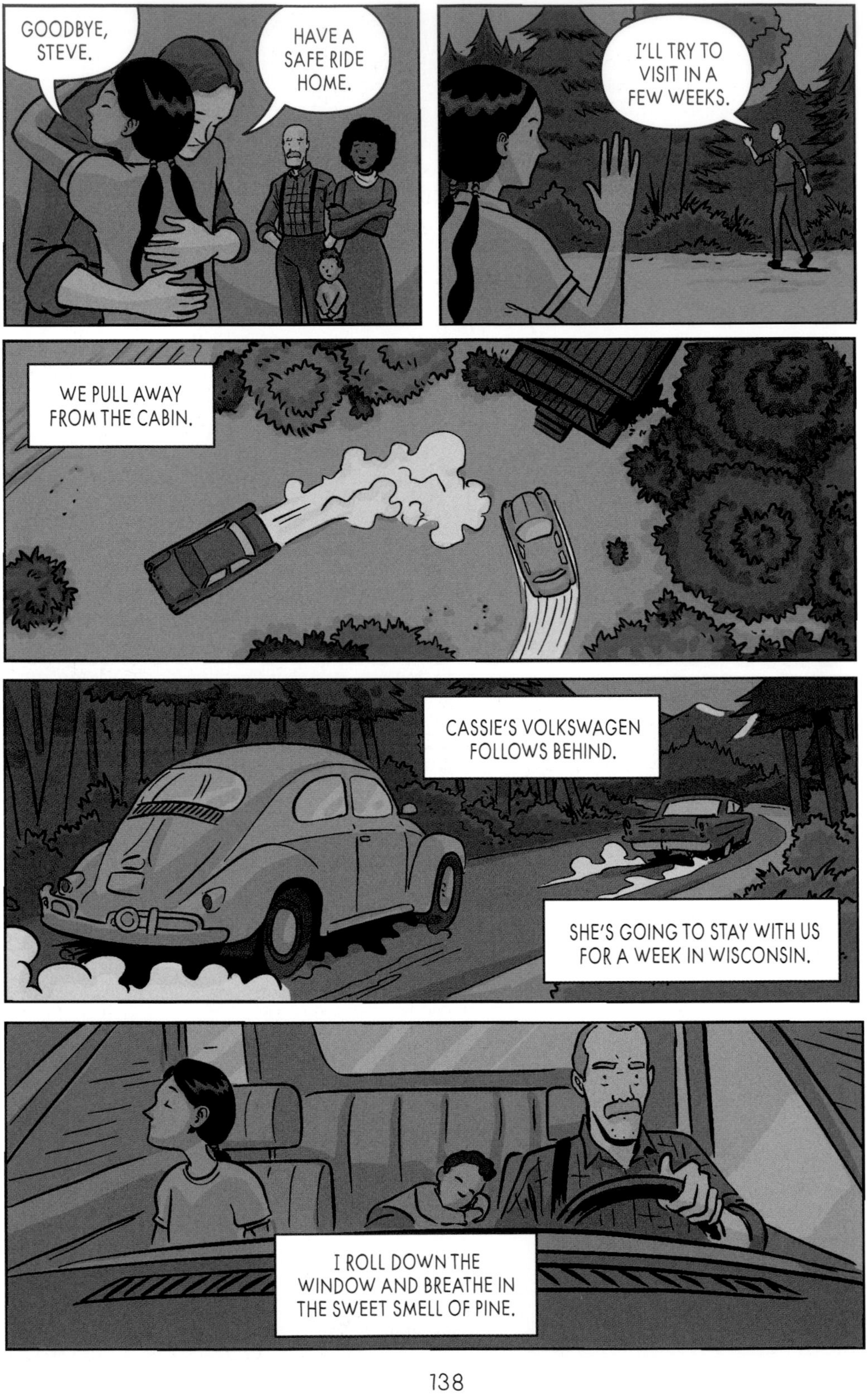
GOODBYE, STEVE.
HAVE A SAFE RIDE HOME.
I'LL TRY TO VISIT IN A FEW WEEKS.
WE PULL AWAY FROM THE CABIN.
CASSIE'S VOLKSWAGEN FOLLOWS BEHIND.
SHE'S GOING TO STAY WITH US FOR A WEEK IN WISCONSIN.
I ROLL DOWN THE WINDOW AND BREATHE IN THE SWEET SMELL OF PINE.

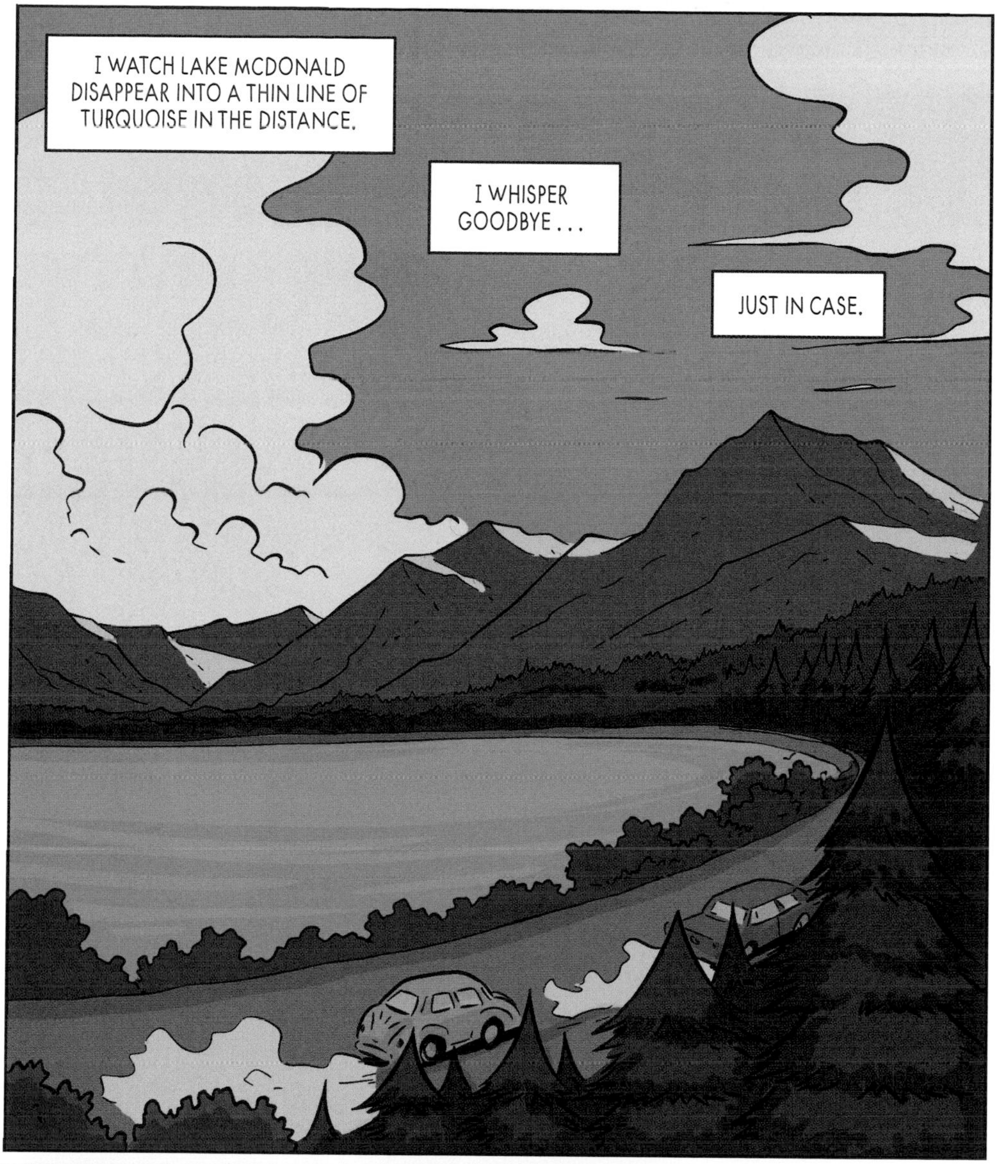
I WATCH LAKE MCDONALD DISAPPEAR INTO A THIN LINE OF TURQUOISE IN THE DISTANCE.
I WHISPER GOODBYE . . .
JUST IN CASE.

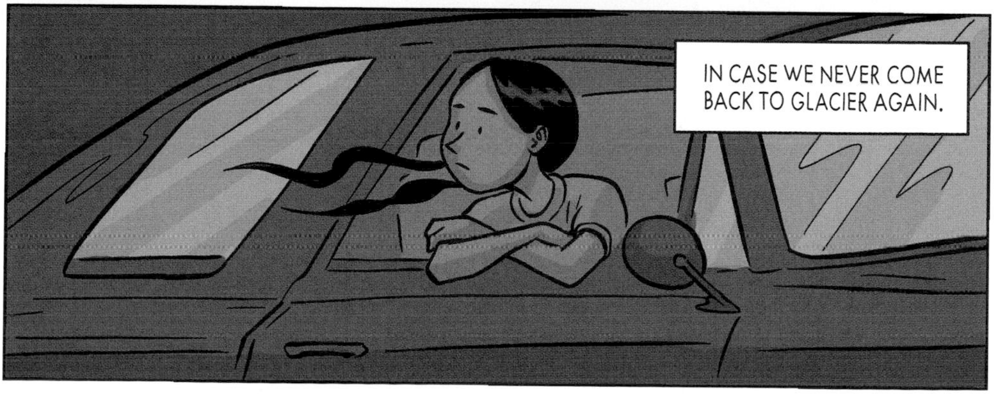
IN CASE WE NEVER COME BACK TO GLACIER AGAIN.

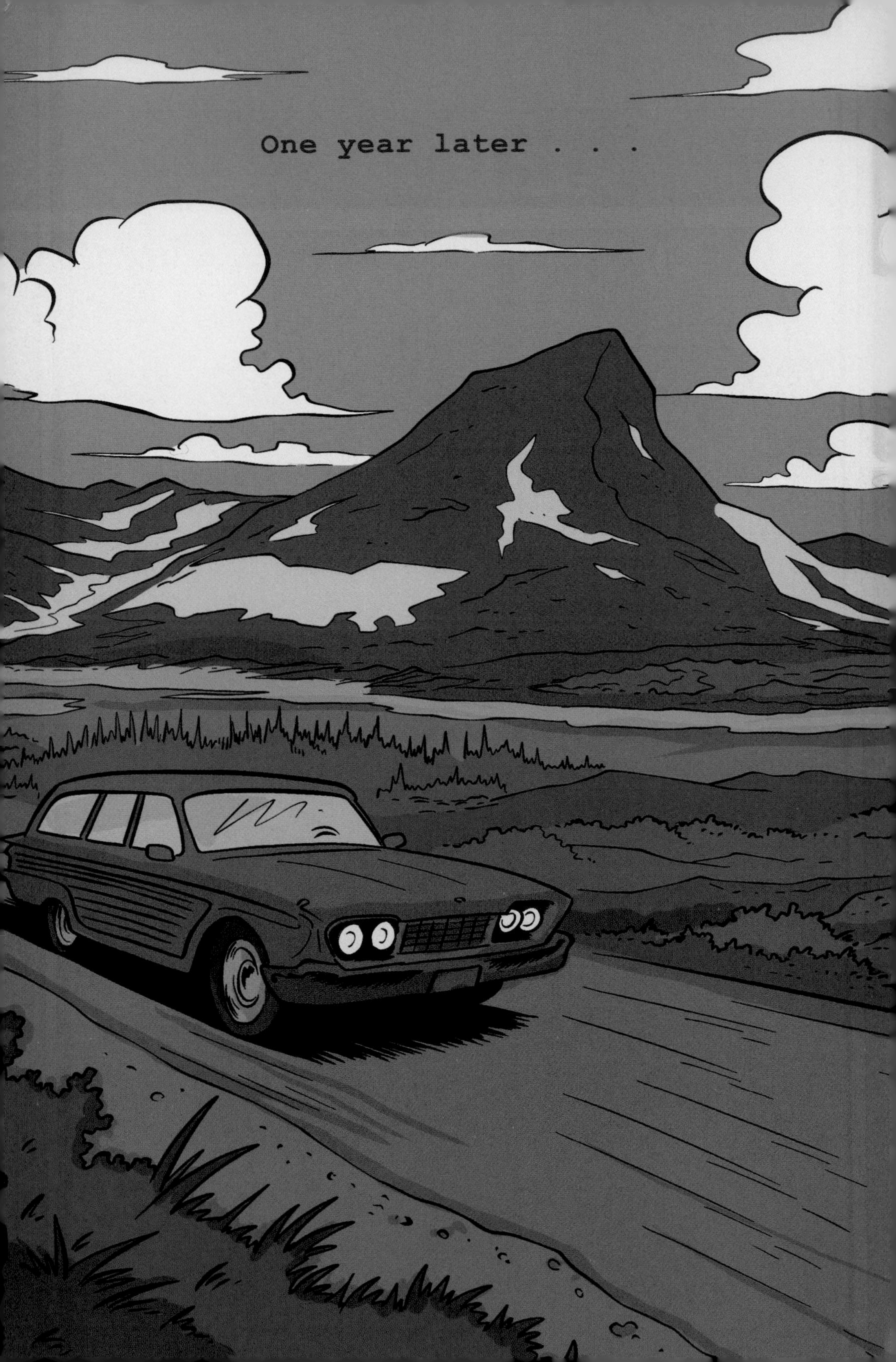
One year later . . .

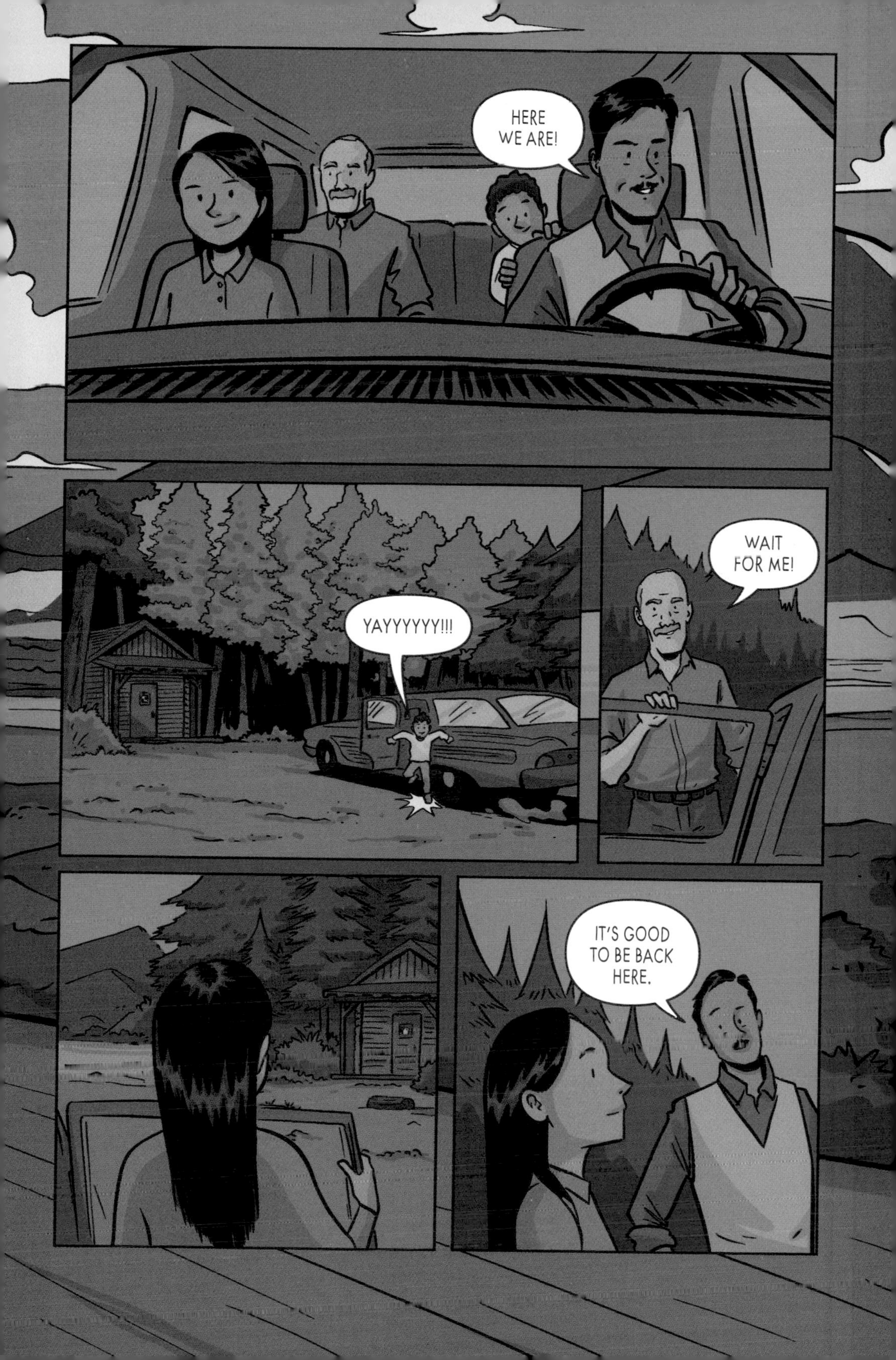
HERE WE ARE!
YAYYYYYY!!!
WAIT FOR ME!
IT'S GOOD TO BE BACK HERE.

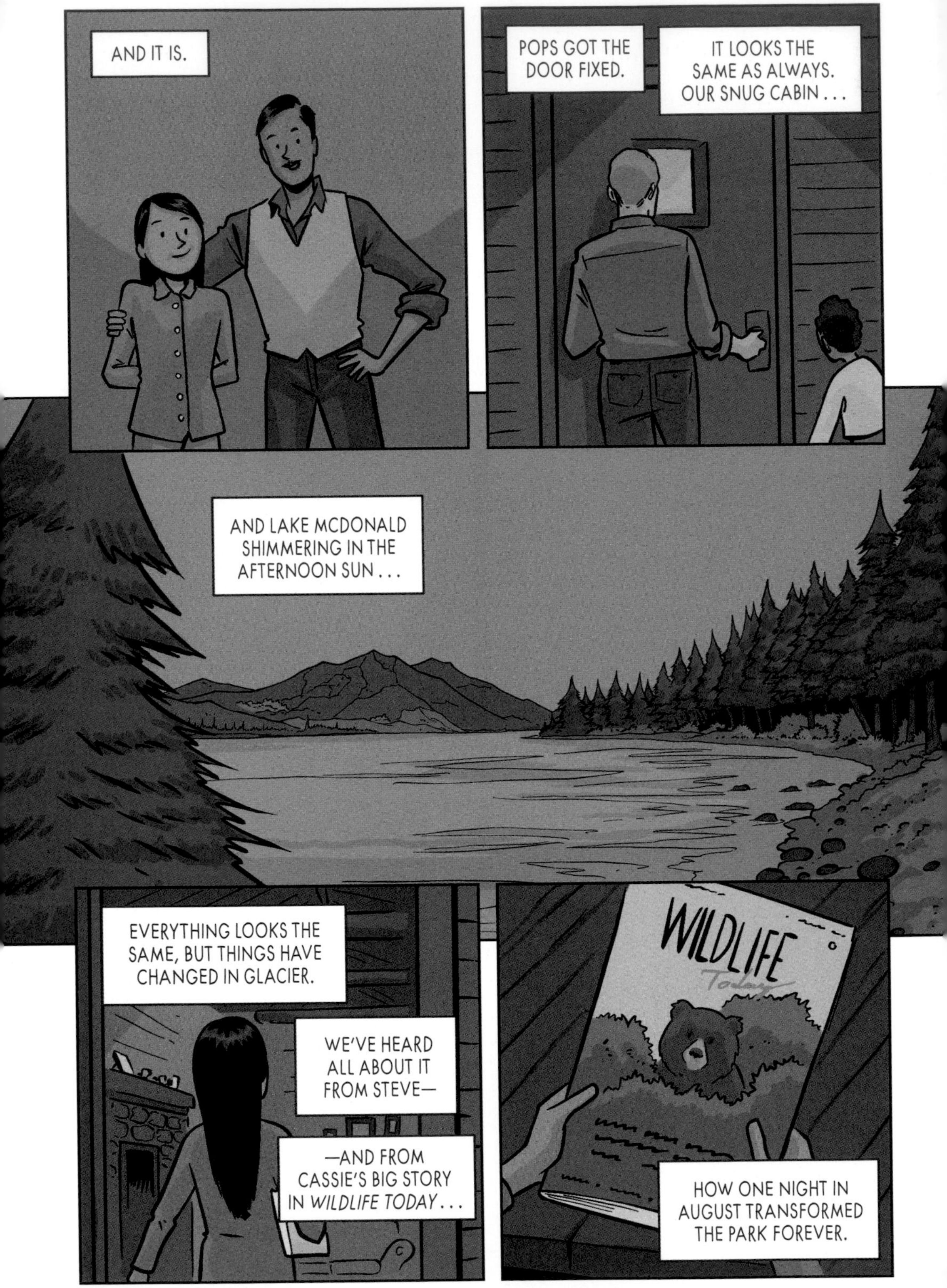
AND IT IS.
POPS GOT THE DOOR FIXED.
IT LOOKS THE SAME AS ALWAYS. OUR SNUG CABIN . . .
AND LAKE MCDONALD SHIMMERING IN THE AFTERNOON SUN . . .
EVERYTHING LOOKS THE SAME, BUT THINGS HAVE CHANGED IN GLACIER.
WE'VE HEARD ALL ABOUT IT FROM STEVE—
—AND FROM CASSIE'S BIG STORY IN *WILDLIFE TODAY* . . .
WILDLIFE
Today
HOW ONE NIGHT IN AUGUST TRANSFORMED THE PARK FOREVER.

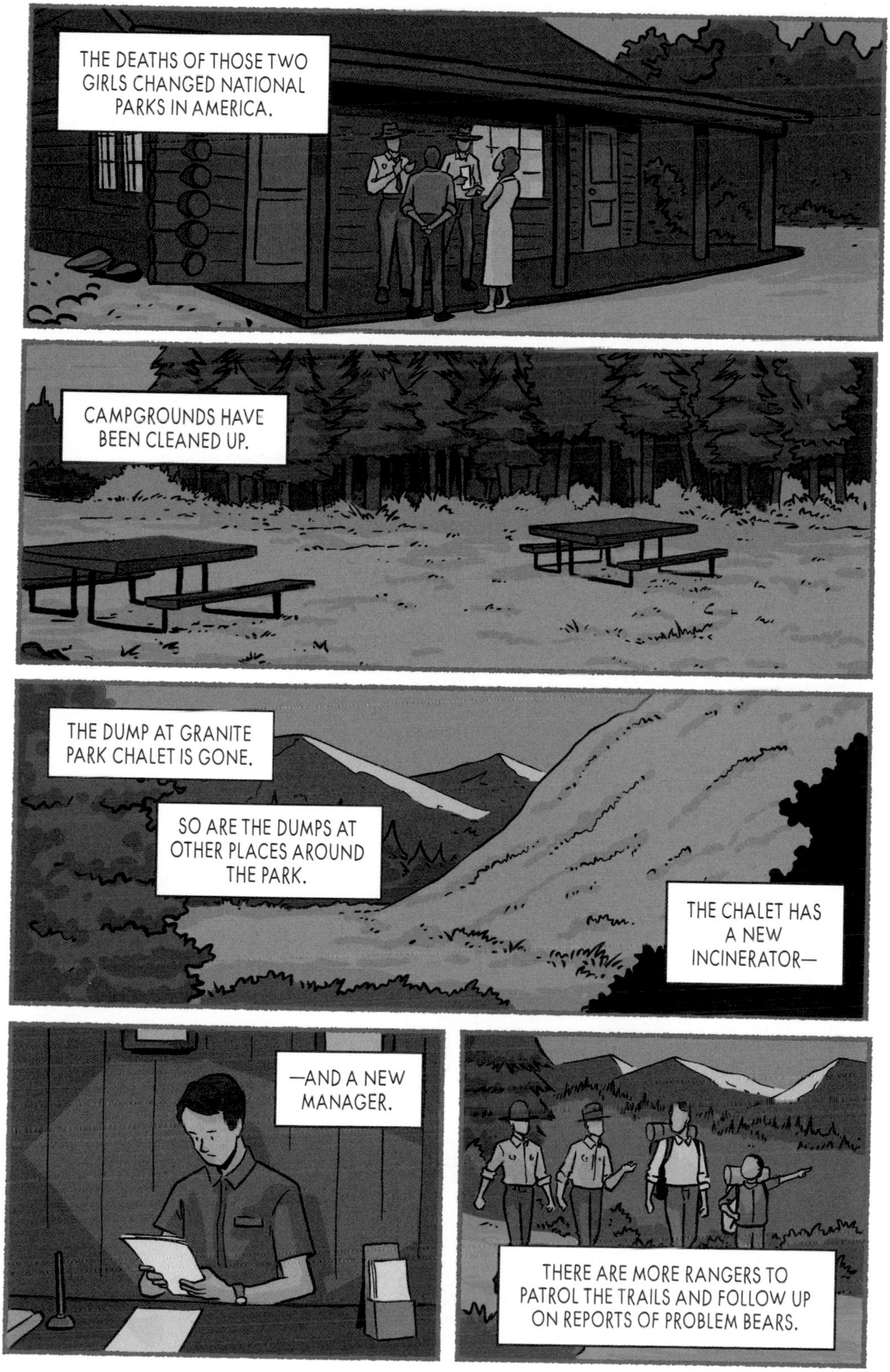
THE DEATHS OF THOSE TWO GIRLS CHANGED NATIONAL PARKS IN AMERICA.
CAMPGROUNDS HAVE BEEN CLEANED UP.
THE DUMP AT GRANITE PARK CHALET IS GONE.
SO ARE THE DUMPS AT OTHER PLACES AROUND THE PARK.
THE CHALET HAS A NEW INCINERATOR—
—AND A NEW MANAGER.
THERE ARE MORE RANGERS TO PATROL THE TRAILS AND FOLLOW UP ON REPORTS OF PROBLEM BEARS.

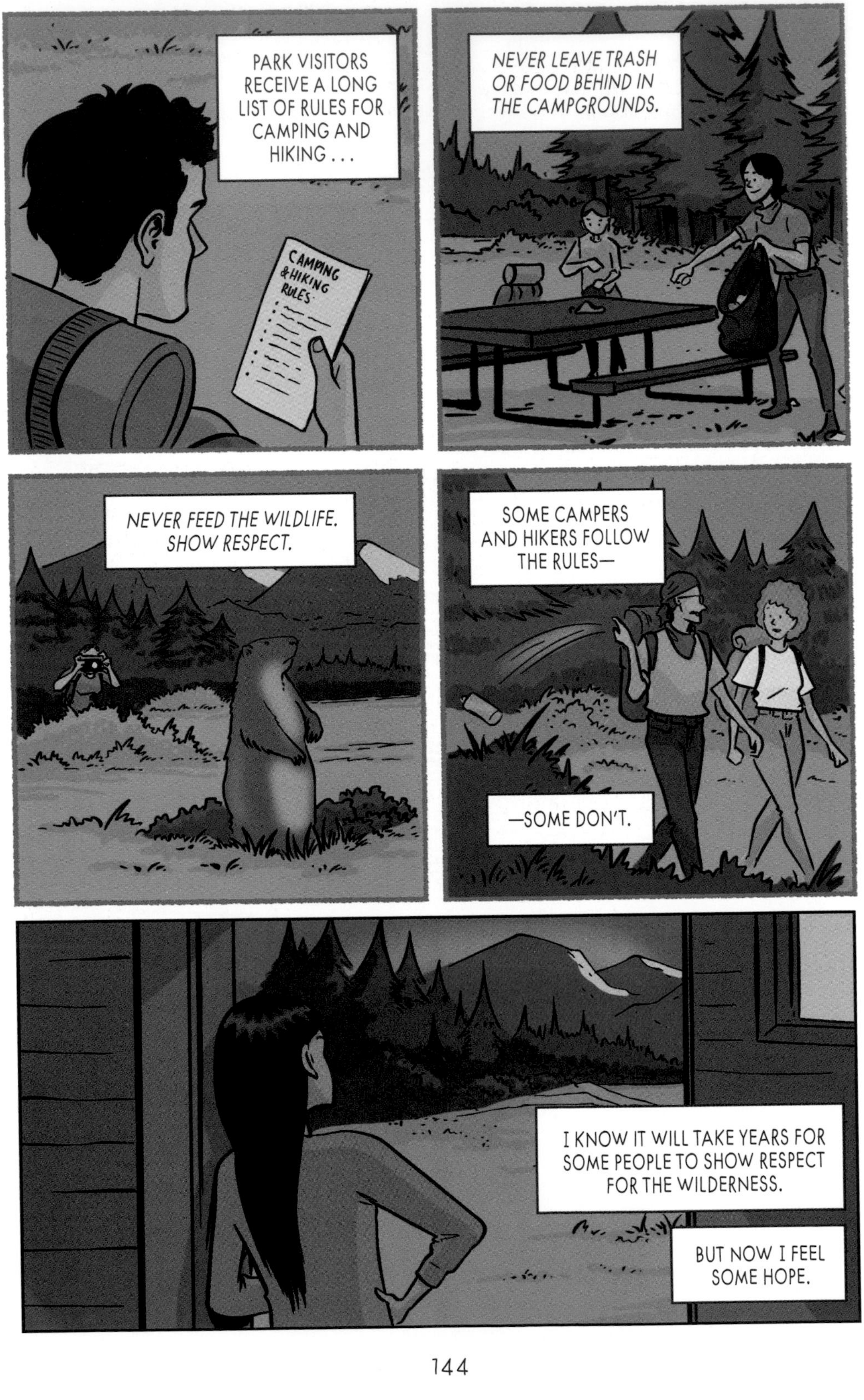
PARK VISITORS RECEIVE A LONG LIST OF RULES FOR CAMPING AND HIKING . . .
CAMPING & HIKING RULES:
NEVER LEAVE TRASH OR FOOD BEHIND IN THE CAMPGROUNDS.
NEVER FEED THE WILDLIFE. SHOW RESPECT.
SOME CAMPERS AND HIKERS FOLLOW THE RULES—
—SOME DON'T.
I KNOW IT WILL TAKE YEARS FOR SOME PEOPLE TO SHOW RESPECT FOR THE WILDERNESS.
BUT NOW I FEEL SOME HOPE.

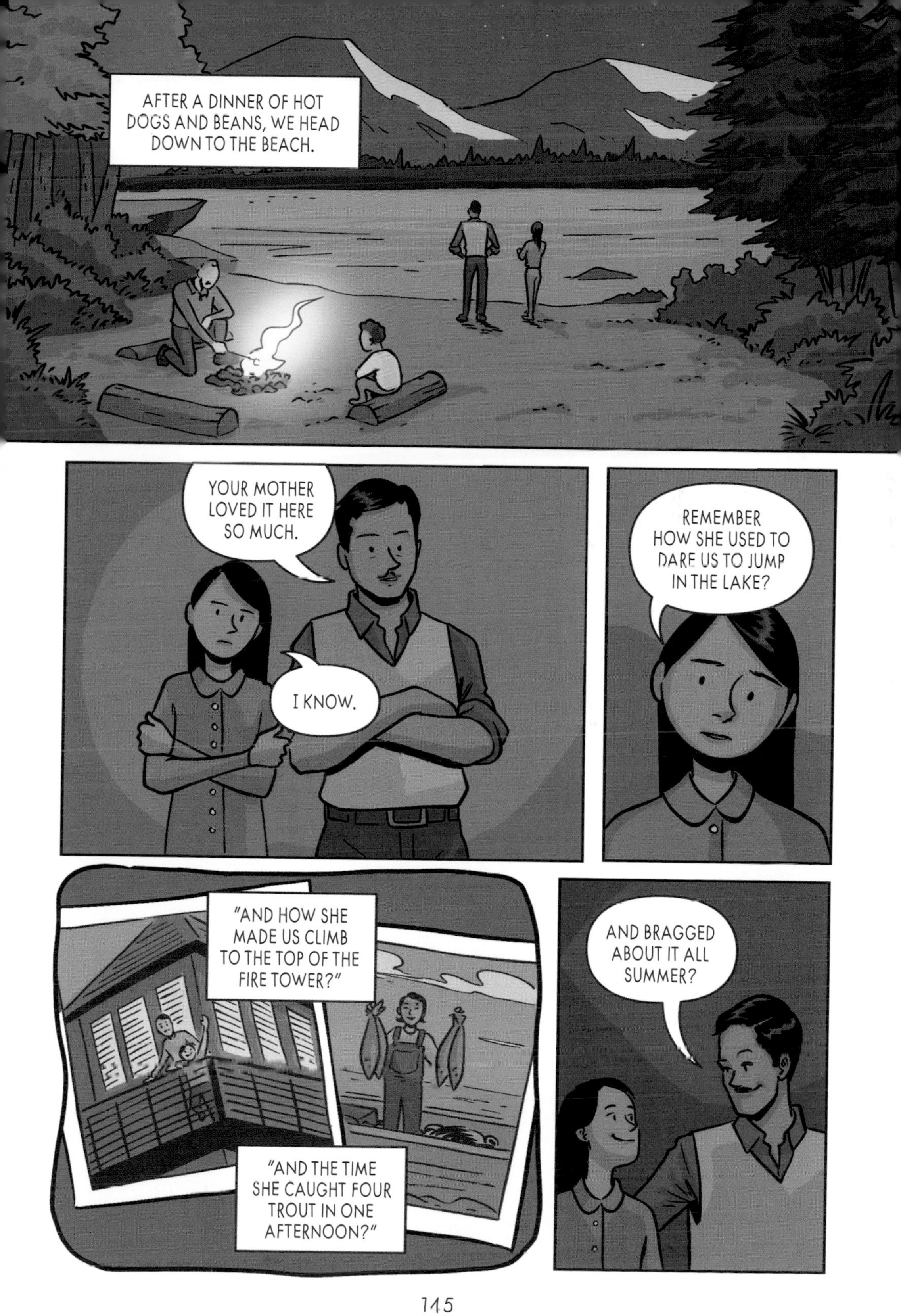
AFTER A DINNER OF HOT DOGS AND BEANS, WE HEAD DOWN TO THE BEACH.
YOUR MOTHER LOVED IT HERE SO MUCH.
I KNOW.
REMEMBER HOW SHE USED TO DARE US TO JUMP IN THE LAKE?
"AND HOW SHE MADE US CLIMB TO THE TOP OF THE FIRE TOWER?"
"AND THE TIME SHE CAUGHT FOUR TROUT IN ONE AFTERNOON?"
AND BRAGGED ABOUT IT ALL SUMMER?

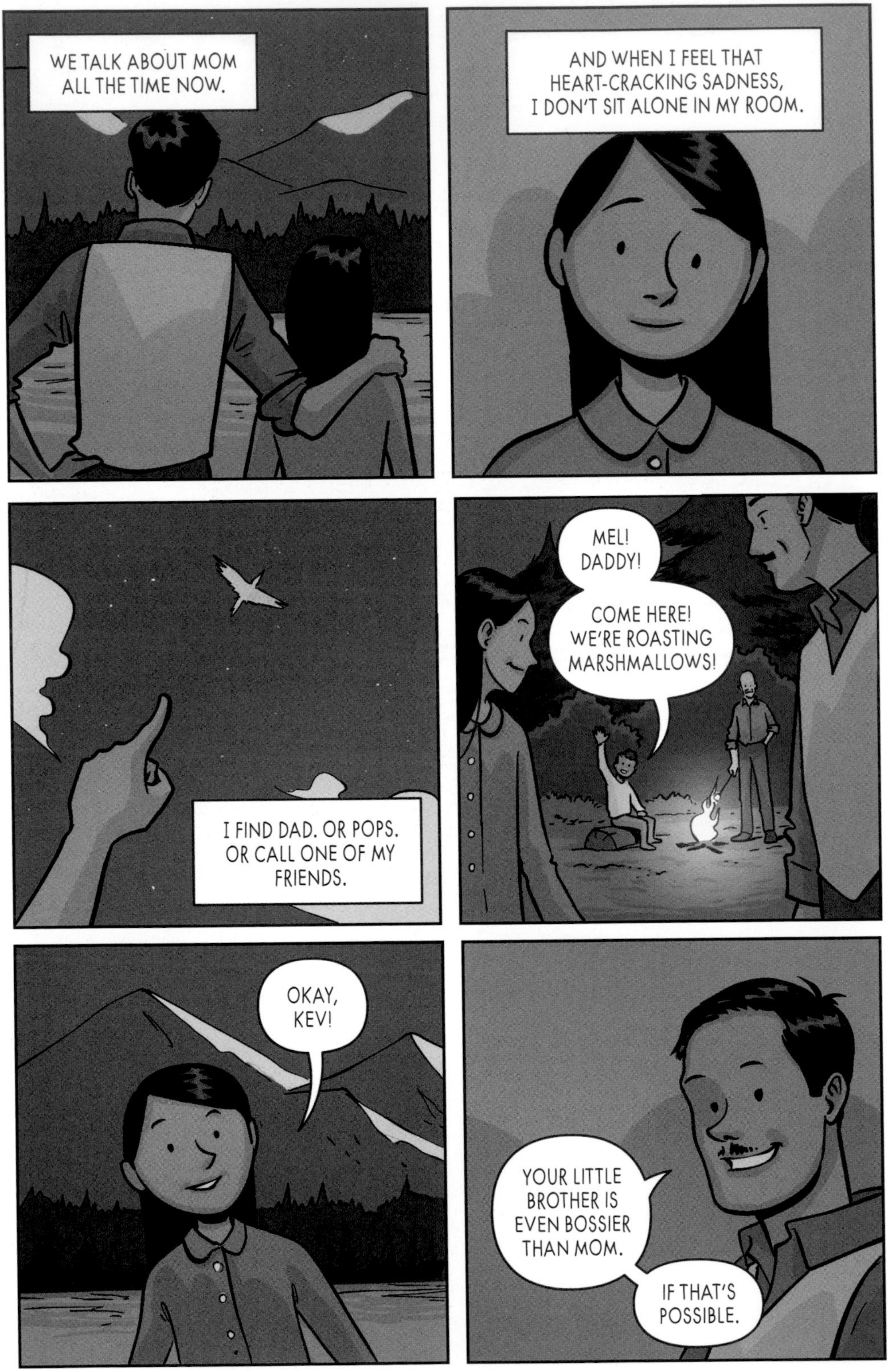
WE TALK ABOUT MOM ALL THE TIME NOW.
AND WHEN I FEEL THAT HEART-CRACKING SADNESS, I DON'T SIT ALONE IN MY ROOM.
I FIND DAD. OR POPS. OR CALL ONE OF MY FRIENDS.
MEL! DADDY!
COME HERE! WE'RE ROASTING MARSHMALLOWS!
OKAY, KEV!
YOUR LITTLE BROTHER IS EVEN BOSSIER THAN MOM.
IF THAT'S POSSIBLE.

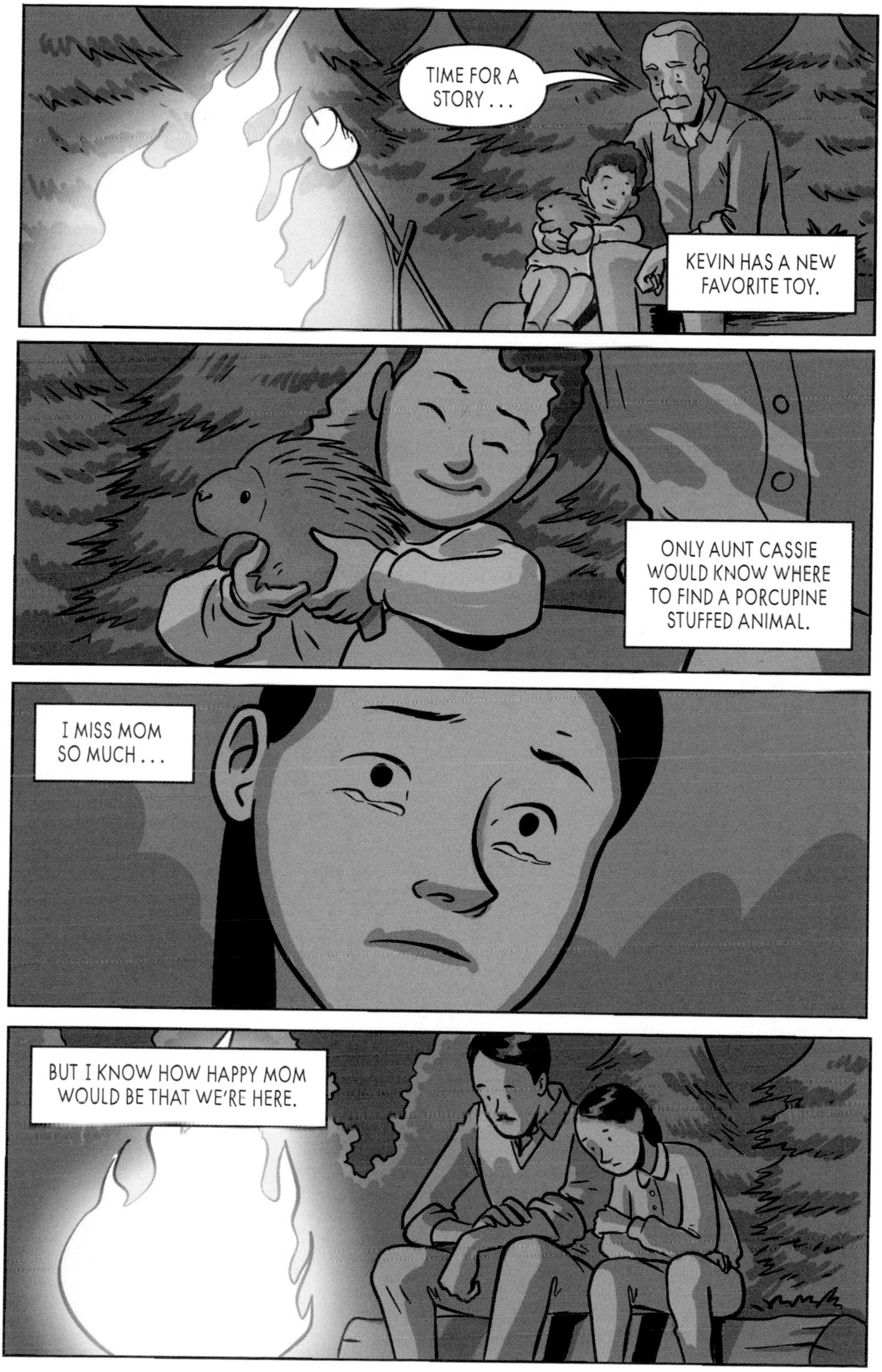
TIME FOR A STORY . . .
KEVIN HAS A NEW FAVORITE TOY.
ONLY AUNT CASSIE WOULD KNOW WHERE TO FIND A PORCUPINE STUFFED ANIMAL.
I MISS MOM SO MUCH . . .
BUT I KNOW HOW HAPPY MOM WOULD BE THAT WE'RE HERE.

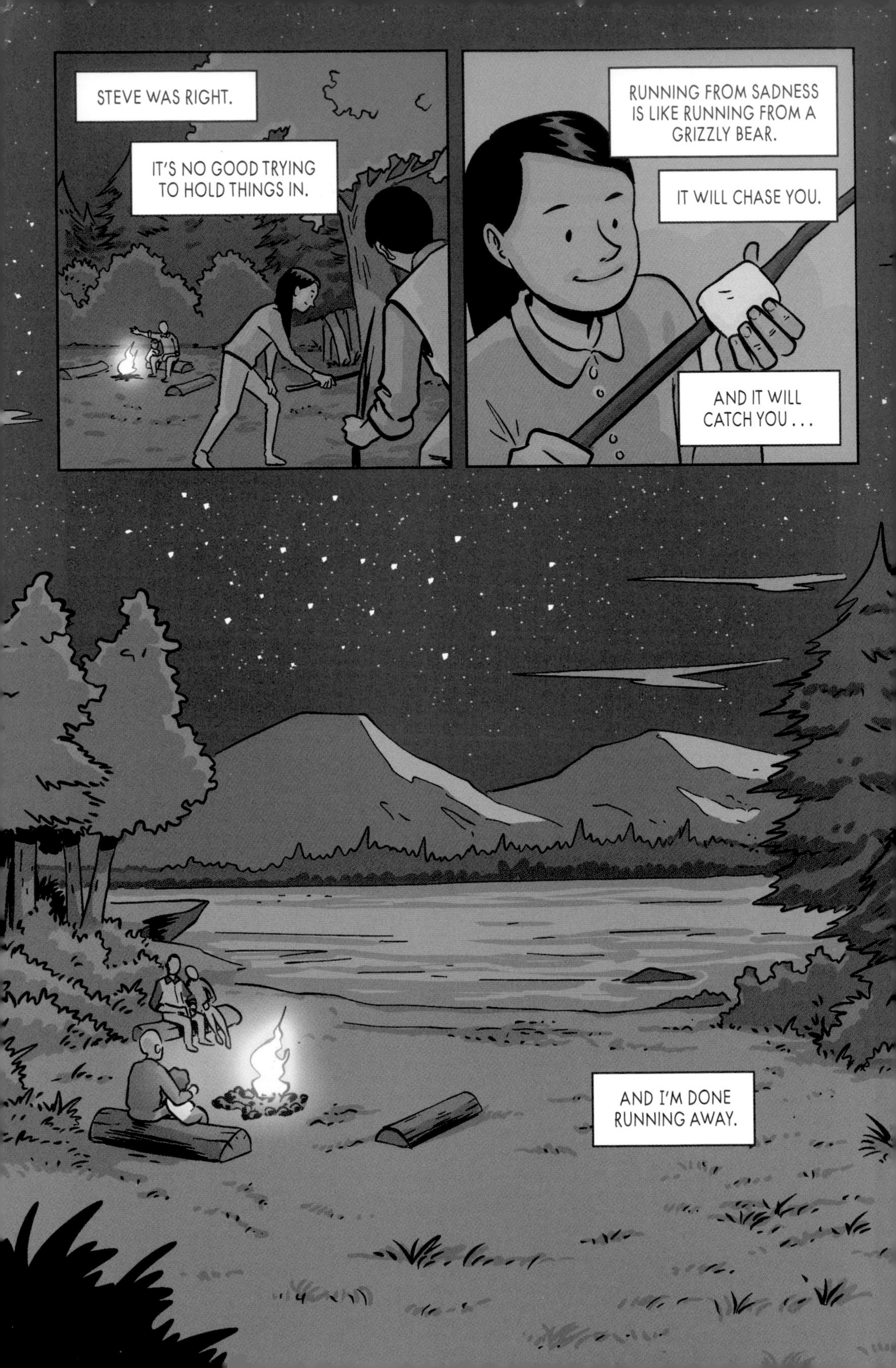
STEVE WAS RIGHT.
IT'S NO GOOD TRYING TO HOLD THINGS IN.
RUNNING FROM SADNESS IS LIKE RUNNING FROM A GRIZZLY BEAR.
IT WILL CHASE YOU.
AND IT WILL CATCH YOU . . .
AND I'M DONE RUNNING AWAY.

TURN THE PAGE
TO LEARN MORE ABOUT
THE REAL-LIFE EVENTS OF

THE ATTACK OF
THE GRIZZLIES

AND HOW YOU CAN HELP
HUMANS AND ANIMALS EXIST
TOGETHER IN THE WILD

Dear Readers,

You might think that after writing this book, I'm hiding under my desk with my poodle, Roy, nervously watching out the window for grizzlies. But no.

Working on this book taught me that grizzlies are not to be feared. They are magnificent animals whose habitats are under constant threat from humans. This book is not really about two terrifying animal attacks. It's about what happens when humans don't respect the wild.

I first learned about the bear attacks of 1967 a few years ago, when I was visiting Glacier National Park. I spotted a book called *Night of the Grizzlies* by Jack Olsen in the ranger station bookstore. Was it smart to read about grizzly attacks during a vacation in Glacier Park? Maybe not. But after reading just a few pages, I knew I had my next topic for the I Survived series.

As always, I did an enormous amount of research to create this story. I read books, watched videos, and studied the true stories of people who had been attacked by grizzlies. In most cases, the person had accidentally surprised a grizzly in the wild. Others had purposely approached a grizzly, hoping to get a photograph.

And that's what made the events of August 1967 so shocking. The young women who were tragically killed—Julie Helgeson and Michele Koons—had not surprised or threatened the grizzlies that attacked them. Both had been sleeping in campgrounds.

But as scientists agree, the grizzlies cannot be "blamed" for those attacks. Read on to learn more about how humans caused that terrifying summer in Glacier National Park and how you can help protect our wilderness and the animals that live there. Mel, Kevin, Pops, Steve, and Cassie are there to guide you.

And I do hope you get to visit Glacier National Park at some point in your life. It really is a magical place. It's doubtful you will see a grizzly. But if you do glimpse one—from a safe distance—consider yourself lucky!

Lauren Tarshis

SETTING THE SCENE FOR THE 1967 ATTACKS

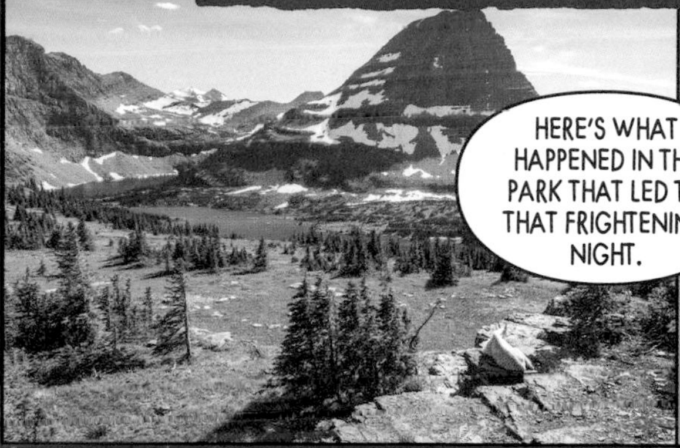

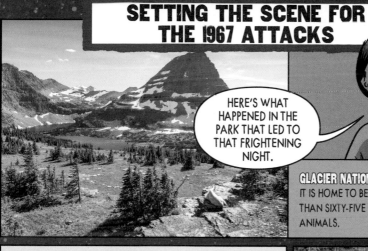

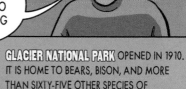

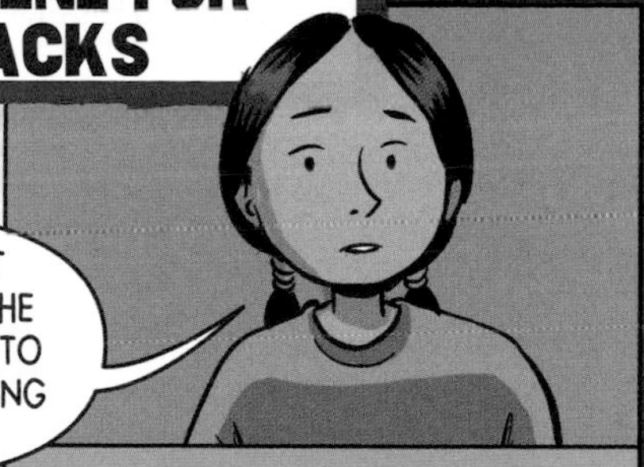
HERE'S WHAT HAPPENED IN THE PARK THAT LED TO THAT FRIGHTENING NIGHT.

GLACIER NATIONAL PARK OPENED IN 1910. IT IS HOME TO BEARS, BISON, AND MORE THAN SIXTY-FIVE OTHER SPECIES OF ANIMALS.

BY THE 1950s AND '60s, **CAMPING** IN NATIONAL PARKS WAS A POPULAR SUMMER ACTIVITY. IT WAS COMMON FOR PEOPLE TO FEED WILDLIFE.

PEOPLE WERE ALSO CARELESS WITH FOOD AND GARBAGE. BY THE LATE '60s, **LITTERING WAS COMMON**.

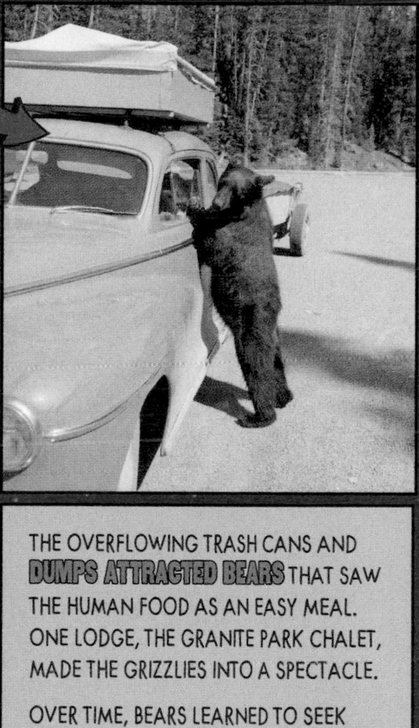

IT WASN'T JUST INDIVIDUALS, THOUGH. LODGES HAD INCINERATORS, BUT THEY COULDN'T BURN THE GARBAGE FAST ENOUGH. LODGES **DUMPED EXTRA GARBAGE** INTO THE PARK.

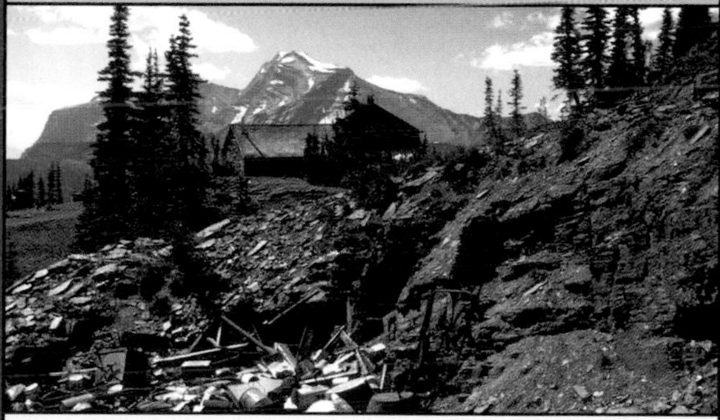

The dump behind the Granite Park Chalet.

THE OVERFLOWING TRASH CANS AND **DUMPS ATTRACTED BEARS** THAT SAW THE HUMAN FOOD AS AN EASY MEAL. ONE LODGE, THE GRANITE PARK CHALET, MADE THE GRIZZLIES INTO A SPECTACLE.

OVER TIME, BEARS LEARNED TO SEEK FOOD AROUND PEOPLE.

IN THE SUMMER OF 1967, **FOREST FIRES** DROVE BEARS FROM THEIR NATURAL HABITATS TO AREAS WITH MORE PEOPLE. BY AUGUST, GRIZZLY BEARS WERE A COMMON SIGHT AT CAMPGROUNDS. THERE WAS ONE BEAR, DESCRIBED AS THIN, THAT WAS OFTEN SEEN NEAR TROUT LAKE.

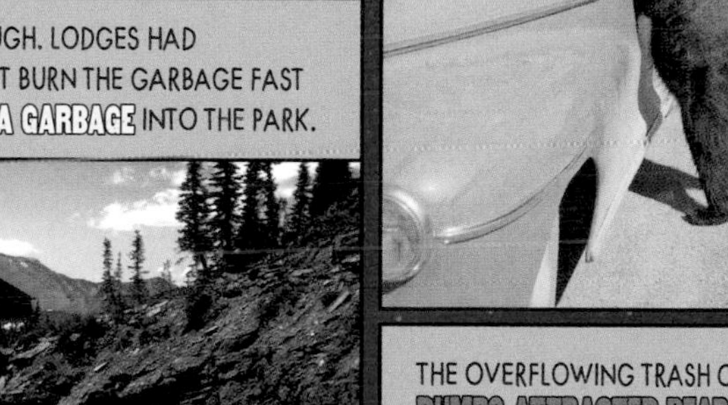

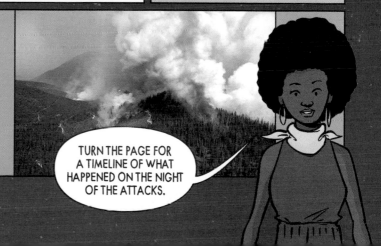

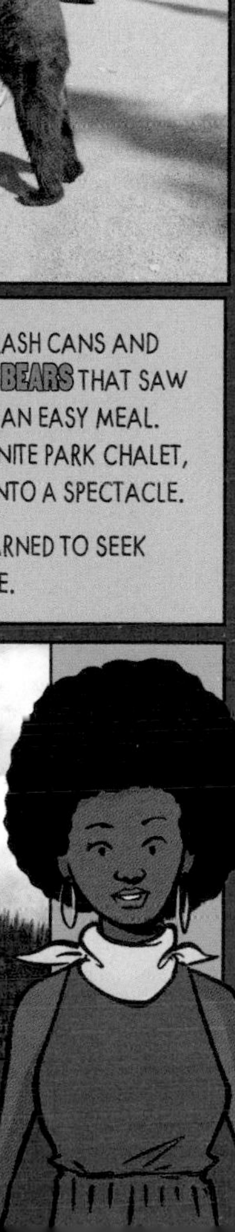
TURN THE PAGE FOR A TIMELINE OF WHAT HAPPENED ON THE NIGHT OF THE ATTACKS.

TIMELINE OF THE REAL-LIFE ATTACKS

SUMMER 1967:	JULIE HELGESON and MICHELE KOONS are both nineteen years old. They are working at lodges in the park while on summer break from college.
AUGUST 12:	Julie and Michele begin separate overnight camping trips. Julie and her friend Roy Ducat camp at the GRANITE PARK campground, down the hill from the Granite Park Chalet. Michele and her friends stay at the TROUT LAKE campground.
AROUND 8 P.M.:	A GRIZZLY crashes the Trout Lake campground. While the bear eats their food, Michele's group moves to the beach and builds a CAMPFIRE. They arrange their sleeping bags around it.
AUGUST 13 AROUND 12 A.M.:	JULIE AND ROY, who are asleep in their sleeping bags, are attacked by a grizzly. Julie is dragged away. Roy is injured but goes for help. A helicopter takes him to the hospital, where he later recovers.
AROUND 2:30 A.M.:	A search party heads out to look for JULIE.
BETWEEN 2 AND 3 A.M.:	A grizzly at the lake's edge awakens Michele's group. When it wanders away, the campers rebuild their fire. They try to STAY AWAKE but eventually fall asleep.

THIS WAS SMART— BEARS THINK TWICE BEFORE GOING NEAR FIRE.

Glacier Grizzlies Kill Two Girls, Maul Youth

The Missoulian

Missoula, Montana, Monday, August 14, 1967   SINGLE COPY 10¢

2,000 Fighting Region Fires

Captive rewmen

Michele Koons, Julie Helgeson, and Roy Ducat in a newspaper clipping.

GLACIER NATIONAL PARK

Granite Park Campground — *First attack*

Trout Lake

Logan Pass

Second attack

Area of detail

MONTANA

Lake McDonald

Going-to-the-Sun Road

0   2
MILES

A grizzly near the edge of a lake.

AROUND 3:45 A.M.:	The search party finds Julie badly injured. Two hikers who are doctors try to help, but **SHE DIES FROM HER INJURIES.**
AROUND 4:30 A.M.:	The **TROUT LAKE** grizzly reappears at Michele's camp. Michele's friends climb trees. Before Michele can join them, though, the grizzly drags her away. Once the bear leaves, her friends go for help.
AROUND 8:30 A.M.:	**PARK RANGERS** find Michele's body.
THE NEXT DAY, AUGUST 14:	In the days following the deaths, rangers **SHOOT FOUR GRIZZLIES,** including the Trout Lake bear that killed Michelle and the bear suspected of killing Julie.

A ranger examines the body of the Trout Lake bear.

Some Glacier Park rangers believe that these bears were also **TRAGIC VICTIMS** of problems at the park, that years of people littering and feeding bears had changed bear behavior. They begin cleaning up the park immediately.

SEVENTEEN BAGS OF TRASH ARE COLLECTED FROM THE TROUT LAKE CAMPGROUND ALONE.

Bear Country

Bears Enter This Campground
Store All Food In Vehicle
All Wildlife Is Dangerous
Do Not Approach Or Feed

A bear warning sign at Glacier National Park today.

In the following months, Glacier creates **NEW RULES** for food storage. Rangers ticket campers who feed bears. **BEAR-PROOF TRASH CANS** are installed. Areas with grizzly sightings are closed until the bears move away. By 1970, many other national parks have adopted similar policies.

Thank you for cleaning up.
A fed bear is a dead bear!
Help us keep our wildlife wild.

THE ATTACKS OF AUGUST 1967 REALLY DID CHANGE GLACIER AND ALL OF AMERICA'S NATIONAL PARKS. BUT THERE'S STILL WORK TO DO . . .

HOW YOU CAN HELP

TODAY, OUR WILDLIFE FACES NEW PROBLEMS, SUCH AS HUMANS WANTING TO GET CLOSE TO SNAP A PHOTO FOR **SOCIAL MEDIA**. AND POLLUTION CONTINUES TO THREATEN WILDLIFE.

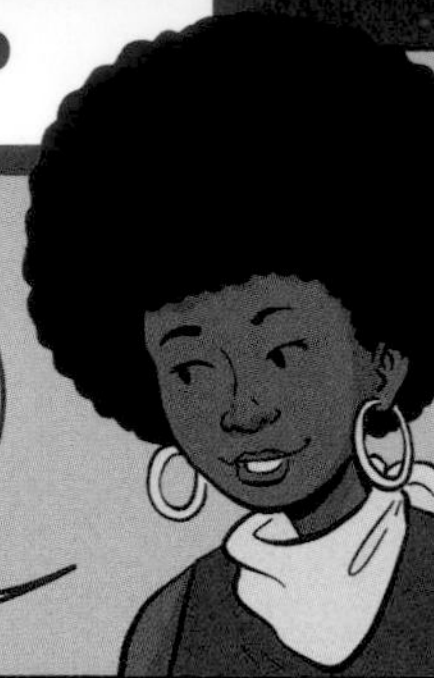
HERE ARE SOME WAYS YOU CAN HELP KEEP YOURSELF AND WILDLIFE AROUND THE WORLD SAFE.

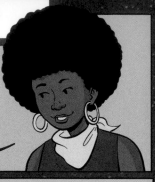

IN YOUR EVERYDAY LIFE . . .

- THERE'S A GOOD CHANCE ANY PLASTIC YOU USE WILL END UP IN NATURE, SO AVOID IT WHENEVER YOU CAN.
- DON'T BUY SINGLE-SIZED SERVINGS OF CHIPS AND COOKIES. THEY CREATE TOO MUCH WASTE.
- ENCOURAGE YOUR SCHOOL CAFETERIA NOT TO USE PLATES OR UTENSILS THAT GET THROWN AWAY.
- LEARN MORE ABOUT RECYCLING.

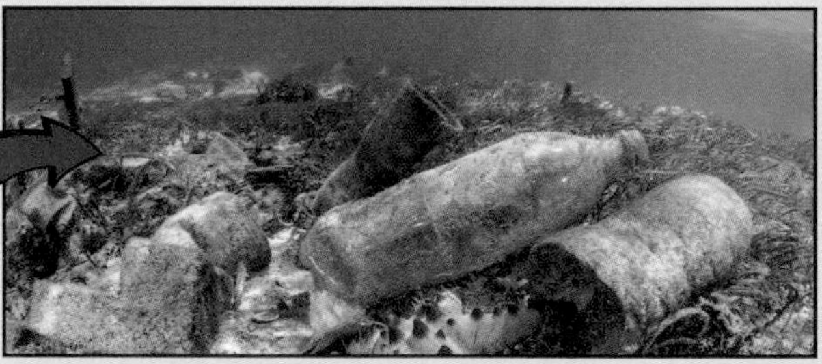

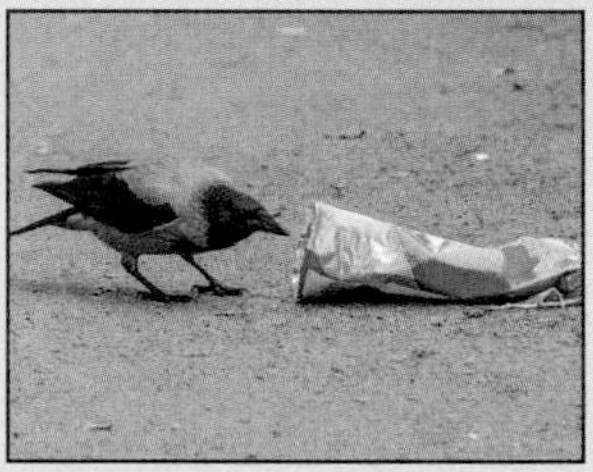

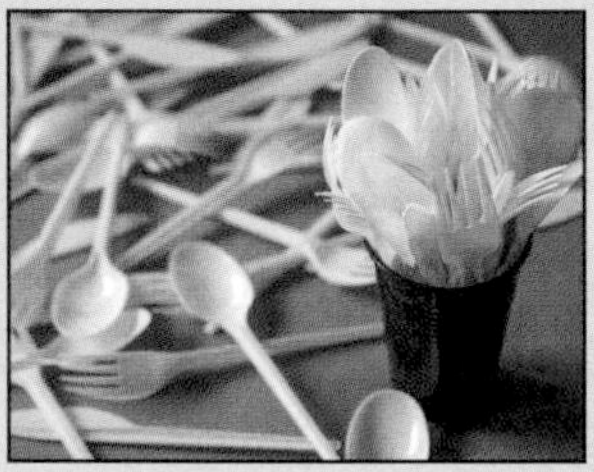

WHENEVER YOU'RE OUT IN NATURE . . .

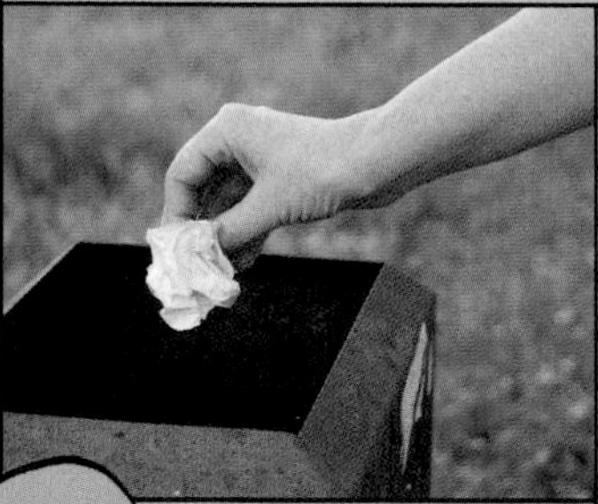

- TAKE YOUR TRASH WITH YOU OR USE THE PROVIDED TRASH CANS.
- STAY ON TRAILS—GIVE WILDLIFE THEIR SPACE.
- DO NOT EAT ON THE TRAILS—EAT ONLY IN DESIGNATED AREAS.
- KEEP YOUR DOG LEASHED.
- NEVER FEED OR LEAVE FOOD FOR ANIMALS.

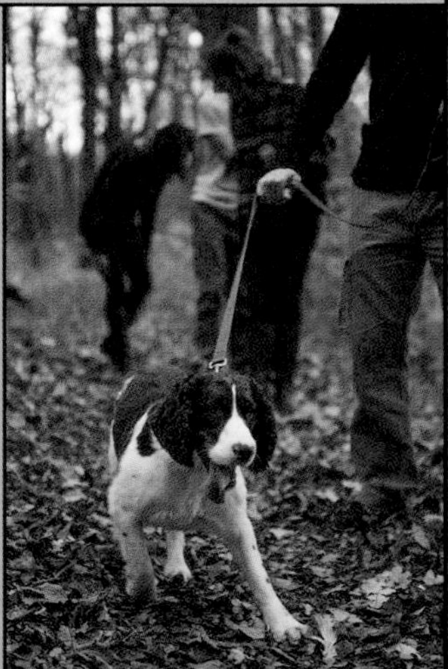

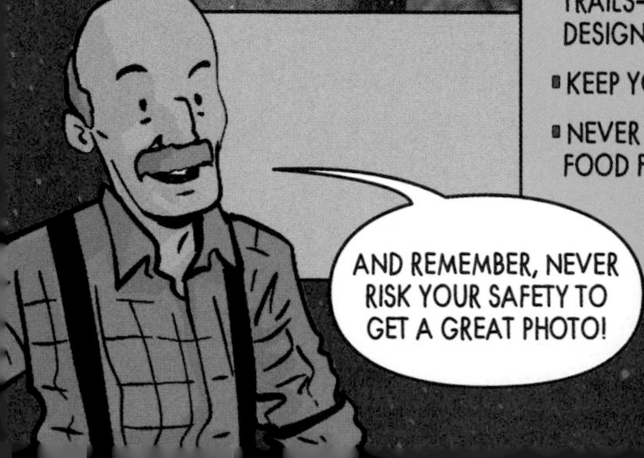
AND REMEMBER, NEVER RISK YOUR SAFETY TO GET A GREAT PHOTO!

BEAR SAFETY

IF YOU'RE IN BEAR COUNTRY, REMEMBER THESE SAFETY GUIDELINES:

- LEAVE YOUR DOG AT HOME.
- HIKE IN GROUPS OF THREE OR MORE.
- TELL OTHERS WHERE YOU'RE GOING AND WHEN YOU'LL BE BACK.
- WATCH FOR TRAILHEAD WARNINGS AND BEAR TRACKS AND SCAT.
- MAKE NOISE—CLAP, SING, OR TALK LOUDLY.
- PAY EXTRA ATTENTION WHEN YOU CAN'T SEE AROUND YOU, OR WHEN YOU'RE NEAR A BEAR FOOD SOURCE, LIKE BERRIES.
- HAVE YOUR FAMILY BRING BEAR SPRAY.

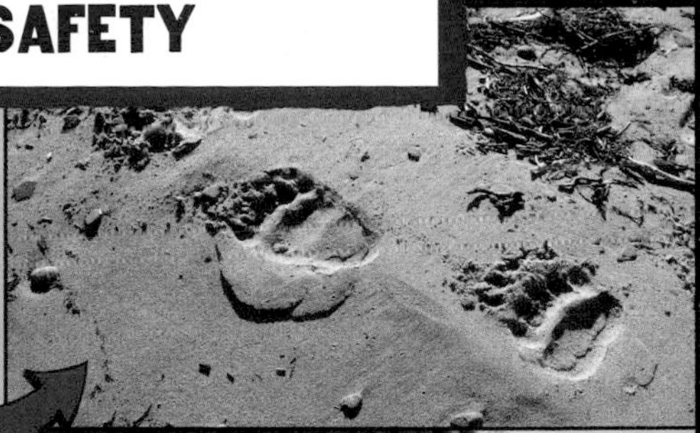

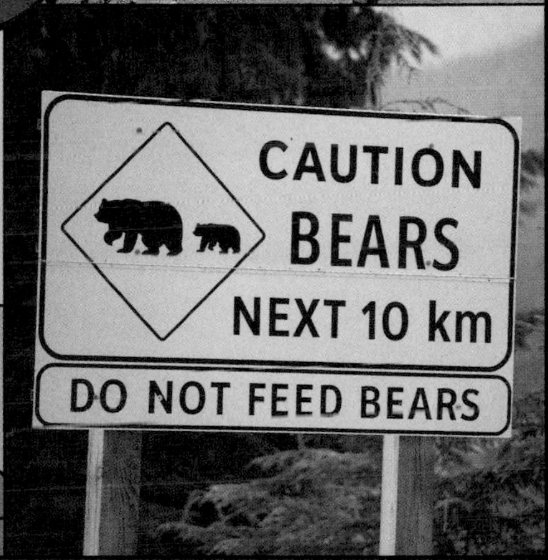
CAUTION
BEARS
NEXT 10 km
DO NOT FEED BEARS

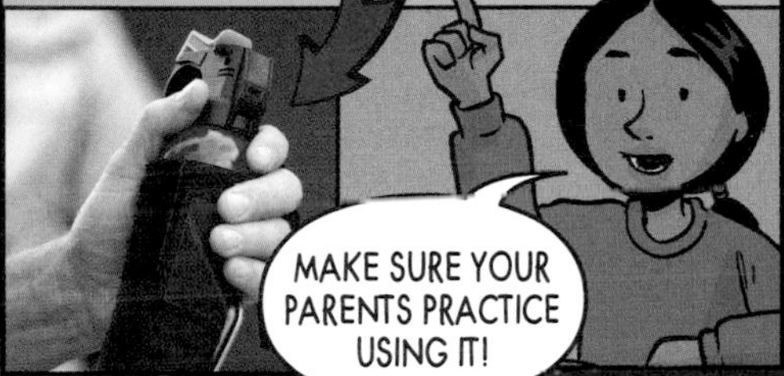
MAKE SURE YOUR PARENTS PRACTICE USING IT!

IF YOU ENCOUNTER A GRIZZLY

NO MATTER HOW CAREFUL YOU ARE, IT IS STILL POSSIBLE THAT YOU MIGHT **SEE A GRIZZLY** IN THE WILD. HERE'S WHAT TO DO:

- DO NOT RUN.
- KEEP YOUR EYE ON THE BEAR.
- SPEAK IN A LOW, CALM VOICE.
- FACING THE BEAR, WALK SLOWLY AWAY.

REMEMBER:

- A BEAR STANDING UP IS JUST CHECKING YOU OUT.
- SOMETIMES A BEAR WILL CHARGE TO SCARE YOU, BUT YOU SHOULDN'T RUN. MOST "BLUFF CHARGES" STOP BEFORE THE BEAR IS VERY CLOSE.
- CLIMBING A TREE IS NOT A DEFINITE ESCAPE—SOME GRIZZLIES CLIMB!
- MOST GRIZZLY ATTACKS TODAY ARE NOT LIKE THE 1967 ATTACKS, WHERE BEARS ATTACKED SLEEPING PEOPLE. THEY GENERALLY HAPPEN WHEN SOMEONE SURPRISES A BEAR—ESPECIALLY A MOTHER WITH CUBS.

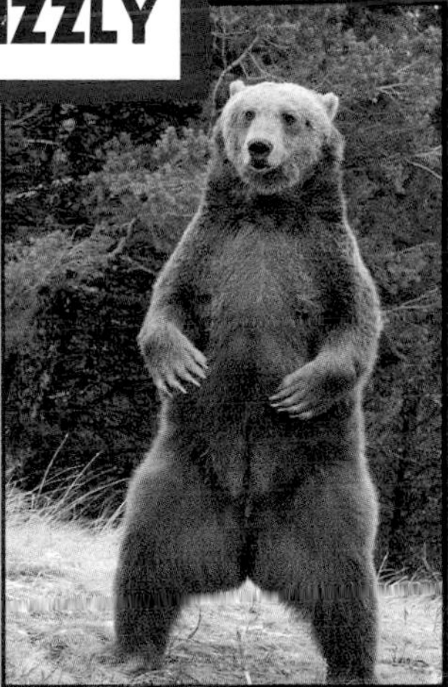

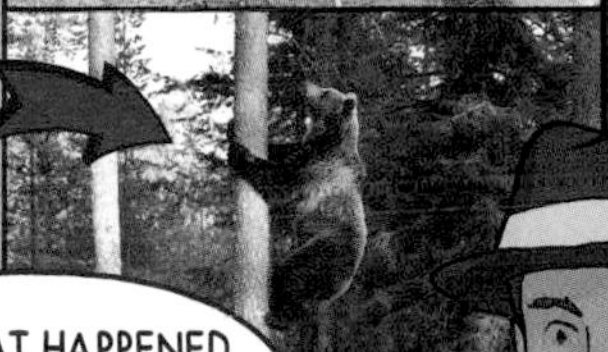

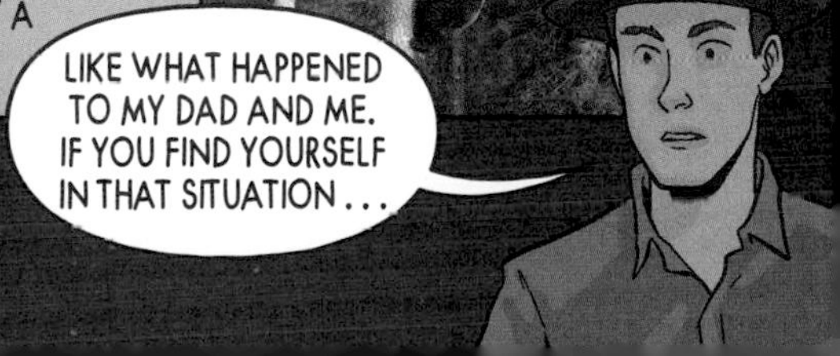
LIKE WHAT HAPPENED TO MY DAD AND ME. IF YOU FIND YOURSELF IN THAT SITUATION . . .

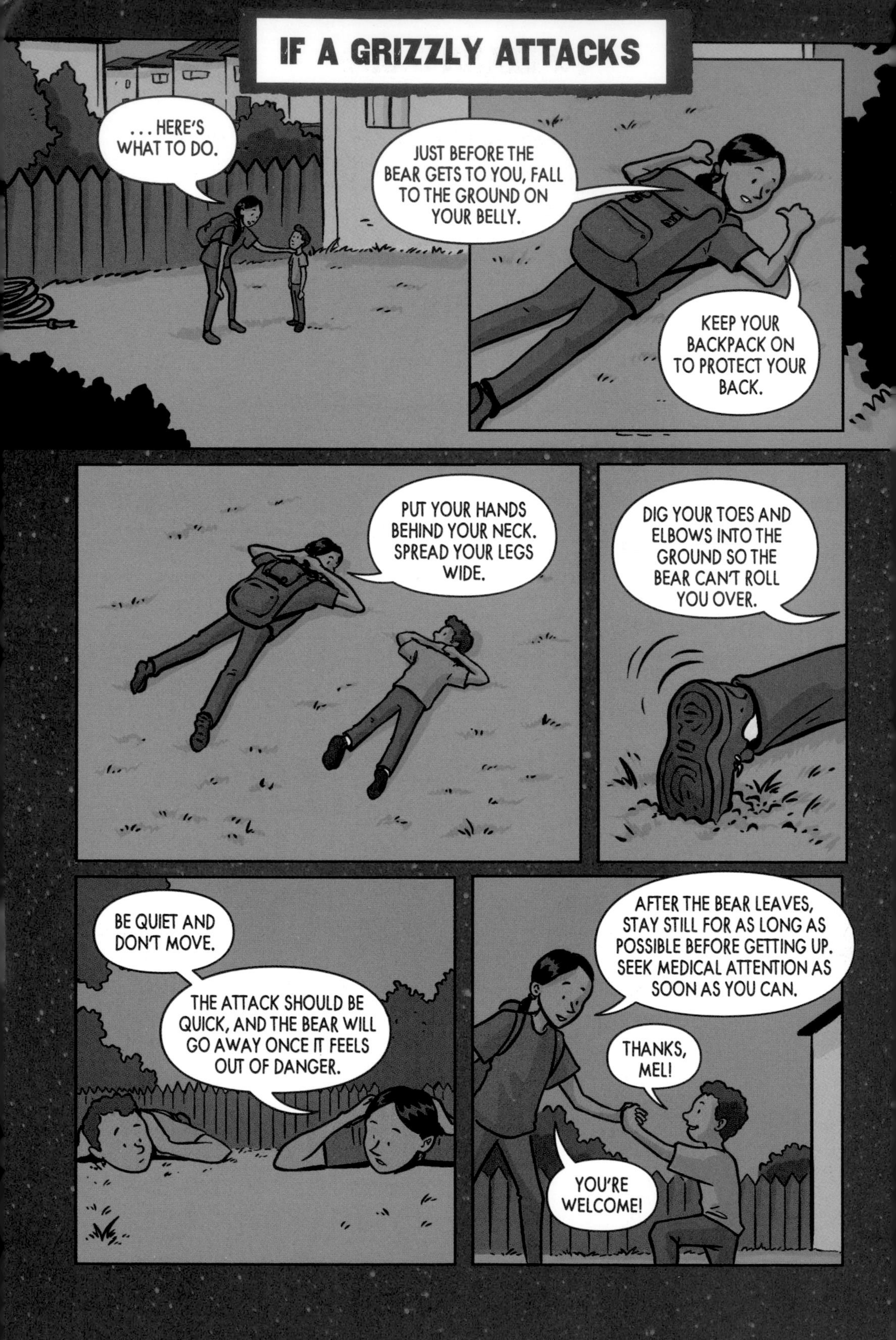
IF A GRIZZLY ATTACKS
. . . HERE'S WHAT TO DO.
JUST BEFORE THE BEAR GETS TO YOU, FALL TO THE GROUND ON YOUR BELLY.
KEEP YOUR BACKPACK ON TO PROTECT YOUR BACK.
PUT YOUR HANDS BEHIND YOUR NECK. SPREAD YOUR LEGS WIDE.
DIG YOUR TOES AND ELBOWS INTO THE GROUND SO THE BEAR CAN'T ROLL YOU OVER.
BE QUIET AND DON'T MOVE.
THE ATTACK SHOULD BE QUICK, AND THE BEAR WILL GO AWAY ONCE IT FEELS OUT OF DANGER.
AFTER THE BEAR LEAVES, STAY STILL FOR AS LONG AS POSSIBLE BEFORE GETTING UP. SEEK MEDICAL ATTENTION AS SOON AS YOU CAN.
THANKS, MEL!
YOU'RE WELCOME!